Praise for
ANNE O'BRIEN

'A cracking historical novel'
Good Housekeeping

'O'Brien cleverly intertwines the personal and
political in this enjoyable, gripping tale'
The Times

'O'Brien is a terrific storyteller'
Daily Telegraph

'A gripping story of love, heartache and political intrigue'
Woman & Home

'There are historical novels and then there are the
works of Anne O'Brien – and this is another hit'
The Sun

'The characters are larger than life…and
the author a compulsive storyteller'
Sunday Express

'This book has everything – royalty,
scandal, fascinating historical politics'
Cosmopolitan

'A gripping historical drama'
Bella

Queen
of the
North

ANNE
O'BRIEN

ONE PLACE. MANY STORIES

HQ
An imprint of HarperCollinsPublishers Ltd.
1 London Bridge Street
London SE1 9GF

This edition 2018

1

First published in Great Britain by
HQ, an imprint of HarperCollinsPublishers Ltd. 2018

Copyright © Anne O'Brien 2018

Anne O'Brien asserts the moral right to be
identified as the author of this work.
A catalogue record for this book is
available from the British Library.

ISBN:
Hardback: 978-0-00-822541-4
Trade Paperback: 978-0-00-822542-1

MIX
Paper from
responsible sources
FSC™ C007454

Printed and bound in Great Britain by
CPI Group (UK) Ltd, Croydon, CR0 4YY

For George, who almost lost his status as the only hero in my life to Harry Hotspur. George retains his supremacy, and always will.

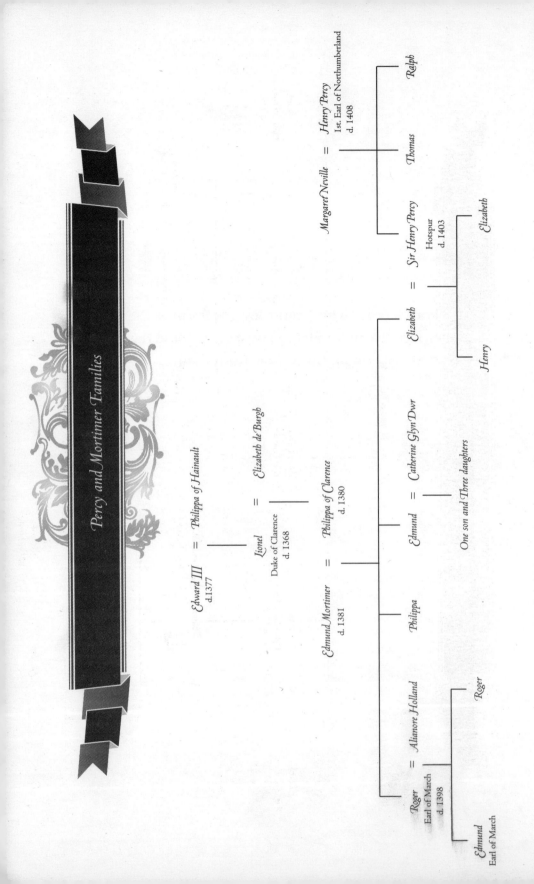

Percy and Mortimer Families

Edward III = Philippa of Hainault
d.1377

Lionel = Elizabeth de Burgh
Duke of Clarence
d. 1368

Edmund Mortimer = Philippa of Clarence
d. 1381   d. 1380

Margaret Neville = Henry Percy
1st. Earl of Northumberland
d. 1408

Philippa   Edmund = Catherine Glyn Dwr   Elizabeth = Sir Henry Percy   Thomas   Ralph
Hotspur
d. 1403

One son and Three daughters

Henry   Elizabeth

Roger = Alianore Holland
Earl of March
d. 1398

Roger

Edmund
Earl of March

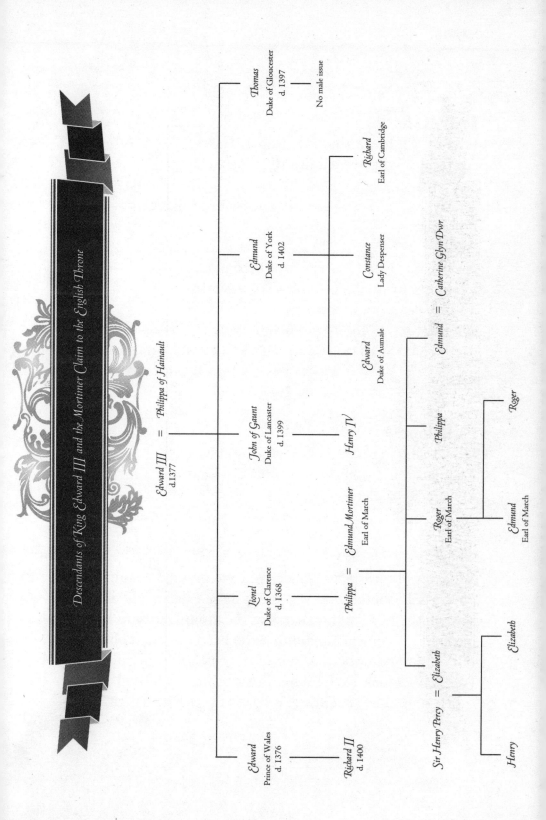

Descendants of King Edward III and the Mortimer Claim to the English Throne

Edward III = Philippa of Hainault
d.1377

Edward   Lionel   John of Gaunt   Edmund   Thomas
Prince of Wales Duke of Clarence   Duke of Lancaster   Duke of York   Duke of Gloucester
d. 1376   d. 1368   d. 1399   d. 1402   d. 1397

Richard II   Henry IV   No male issue
d. 1400

Philippa = Edmund Mortimer   Edward   Constance   Richard
           Earl of March   Duke of Aumale   Lady Despenser   Earl of Cambridge

Roger   Edmund = Catherine Glyn Dwr
Earl of March

Sir Henry Percy = Elizabeth   Philippa

                                   Edmund   Roger
                                   Earl of March

Henry   Elizabeth

Lady Kate:
In faith, I'll break thy little finger, Harry,
An if thou wilt not tell me all things true.

Hotspur:
Away,
Away, you trifler! Love! I love thee not,
I care not for thee, Kate: this is no world
To play with mammets and to tilt with lips:
We must have bloody noses and crack'd crowns . . .

WILLIAM SHAKESPEARE: HENRY IV PART I (ELIZABETH IS
SHAKESPEARE'S LADY KATE)

Lady Percy:
He was the mark and glass, copy and book,
That fashion'd others. And him, O wondrous him!
O miracle of men!

WILLIAM SHAKESPEARE: HENRY IV PART 2

Whereas of our special grace we have granted to our
cousin, Elizabeth, who was the wife of Henry de Percy,
knight, the head and quarters of the same Henry to be
buried. We command you that the head aforesaid placed by
our command upon the gate of the city (of York) aforesaid
you shall deliver to the same Elizabeth to be buried . . .

E. B. DE FONTBLANQUE: ANNALS OF THE HOUSE OF PERCY

Prologue

Alnwick Castle: Spring 1399

I lifted my daughter Bess high into my arms, so that she could see over the stone coping of the parapet.

'Don't wriggle,' I said. Without noticeable effect.

We were standing at the highest vantage point of the barbican, bold in its crenellations, our various hair and veils and enveloping cloaks straining against the constant breeze from the north-west. In my memory it was always autumn or winter at Alnwick, whatever the month decreed, and even now in my maturity it was a cold place. The sable lining of my cloak felt chill, like a cold cat, against my throat.

We had been ordered here to the barbican by the command of the Earl, a man as unbending as the wind that harried us. Three generations of the mighty Percy family hemmed me in, three generations of darkly red-haired power, now glowing mahogany under the noonday sun. Henry Percy, Earl of Northumberland, my father by law. Sir Henry Percy, his son and heir and my husband. Henry Percy, my son, aged five, more interested in the ants' nest beneath the stones than the spread of acres on all sides. All Henrys. All long-limbed with the musculature of a

I

soldier. All blessed, or cursed some would say, with a driving ambition for power. Even my son, growing in fine Percy style, was directing the ants in a path of his choosing with a strategic pile of pebbles.

The Earl's arm swept in an expansive gesture to match his gaze, taking in all to be seen. To the east, the wooded pastures in the direction of the sea and Warkworth, another Percy stronghold. South across the deep ravine towards the benign reaches of England. West where the March stretched to the further coast, far beyond our sight. And then north, across the great bailey and the formidable towers of our home, across the River Aln, to the threat of the darker hills of Scotland and a darker marauding Scottish power, for here in the northern March the Scots were our enemy.

'This is ours,' the Earl said, voice clear enough though beginning to crack with age and much bellowing across Scottish battlefields. Now it disturbed a pair of roosting jackdaws that lifted into the wind with their sharp repetitive cries. 'Every acre, every tree, every sod of earth. All fought over and won. We will hold it, and more, until the Day of Judgment, when all earthly things come to an end.'

'As long as the King of England allows it,' I said, my eye on my son who had abandoned the ants and begun to climb dangerously. Lowering Bess to her feet, I kept her hand clasped in mine; she was too young at four years for these excursions to the windswept heights to witness our greatness. True, these Percy lords were Wardens of the East and West March in the north, guarding England against Scottish incursions, but such office was dependent on the favour of the King of England. What was given with a generous hand could be taken away by one dripping with malice, or simply a desire to reward a different lord. Our King was known for his unpredictability.

'We have a right to it.' The Earl was unimpressed by any comment I might make on royal limitations on our northern supremacy.

'As long as Ralph Neville gains no more power at our expense.' Sir Henry leaned, elbows sharp against the wall, looking west in the direction of Raby Castle where Ralph Neville, Earl of Westmorland, sat and probably gloated over his growing power. 'Our King is inclined to favour him.'

'Our King is sometimes a royal fool.' The Earl turned his back on Raby, narrowing his eyes against the sun, thus summarily dismissing King Richard. He sniffed. 'There is change in the air.'

'For good or ill?' I asked, in no manner cowed by the previous rebuff.

'For good. Always for good.' His eyes rested on me, surprising me with their speculation, as if some thought had lodged in his mind to which I was not privy. There were always plots and stratagems in the Earl's mind to which I was not privy. 'There will be no challenge to our power, Elizabeth. Are we not Kings of the North?'

'We'll be frozen Kings of the North if we remain here much longer.' Sir Henry tucked our daughter under one arm and, with his free hand, led me down the narrow stair to the busy bailey in the wake of our son.

Kings of the North.

Indeed we were, for there was no real challenge to Percy hegemony. I was Elizabeth Mortimer, of royal descent; wife of Sir Henry Percy, heir to the Earl of Northumberland. Sir Henry Percy whom the Scots, in their wisdom, their admiration and their fear on the battlefield, called Hotspur. One day, when the Earl's earthly days came to an end and Sir Henry took ownership of the cushioned chair at the head of the Percy deliberations, I would be Queen over these northern acres.

Chapter One

Warkworth Castle: June 1399

I knew that he had come home. It was impossible not to know, given the assault on the ear of men and horses that filled the bailey beneath my south-facing window, the heavy rumble of wagons echoing off the stone walls. I paused, my hand on the door latch. Considering.

I could hitch my skirts above my ankles like a girl and run down the stairs to greet him, to share the same space, to breathe the same air as the man I loved more than the sum of all the Percy acres and Percy jewels. Or I could walk down, with all the dignity appropriate to the female head of the Percy household, mistress of Alnwick and Warkworth and many other castles from one end of the northern March to the other, since the Earl's second wife Maud had died of a deep melancholy the previous year. Or I could remain here in my withdrawing chamber above the great hall and wait.

I smiled, sat, picked up some stitchery which would occupy my fingers but not my mind. I would wait. I had grown wiser in my time here, my twenty years of marriage from the distant age of eight years. Now I had twenty-eight years' experience of life and Percy caprice, and knew how to use it well. He would come to me when he had done what needed to be done, until which time I would be a hindrance. Besides, the Earl was also in residence here at Warkworth, the castle much favoured above the stark environs of Alnwick. I did not willingly cross his path except through necessity, when we were both impeccably polite, until the Earl forgot to mind his manners. I never forgot to be discreet, but the Earl enjoyed his reputation for enforcing his will with brutal words. He would be in the courtyard, faster than I could sneeze, to welcome his son. I would wait where I was.

But in anticipation, I sent my women away, to gossip elsewhere.

The minutes passed, the hubbub in the bailey lessening, the tendrils of some fanciful plant growing rapidly under my needle, my thoughts with the man who should be climbing the spiral stair even now. My blood heated a little, my heart quickened its beat a little, but I knew there was no trace of it on my face.

At last.

Booted feet, leaping from one stair to the next. He rarely walked up any flight of stairs, as if speed and hurry had been sprinkled over him in a golden shower on the day that he was born thirty-five years ago. Now he had been absent for two months in his capacity as Warden of the East March, a position he had held for four years, a position that was as important to him as the much-prized sword at his side, but which demanded heavily on his time away from me. It did not surprise me that he ran.

The door was flung back so that it smacked against the wall. There he was, framed in the arch.

'Elizabeth.'

'You are right welcome, Harry.'

I was already standing, hands demurely folded, my stitchery

6

tidied away, a suitable decorum for a future Countess of Northumberland, curtseying to the future Earl. Tall and lean, his skin fair, the gift or blight of many who were blessed with his colouring, he was from head to toe a man of action, evidenced by an abrasion on his chin and along his jaw that he had acquired at some point in his journeying. Energy spiked around him as his hair caught fire in a burst of sun through the high window.

'You look well,' I observed, any longing to step closer and touch him in the flesh disguised, for I was overcome with a breath of reserve after so long an absence. It always surprised me that it should be so, but his presence in my chamber was overwhelming. 'In spite of riding over half of the northern reaches of this realm,' I added.

'As ever.'

He shrugged, careless of his health, as the door was shut with as much force as it had been pushed open. His eyes were bright, brighter than any jewel. Harry rarely wore jewels. As Warden of the East March, lurching from one affray to another, he rarely saw the need, unless he was summoned to the Royal Court when, grudgingly, he made the effort to play the great magnate.

'Did you find a suitable mount for Hal?' I asked. Our son was now of an age to be riding.

'I did. A sturdy roan with just a hint of mischief in her eye. Hal will enjoy her.'

'Good. No fighting in the March?'

He was stripping off gloves, letting them fall to the floor at his side along with the soft cloth that protected his throat, then unlatching and unbuckling his brigandine. Once it had been graced with a fine damask finish with even a hint of gold thread at neck and wrist; now the metal plates were bare

7

in places. He needed a new one. It too was abandoned on the tiles, hiding the boldly painted Percy lions that pranced beneath our feet, announcing the ownership of this fortress if any should be in doubt.

'None worth mentioning. The odd skirmish, to keep the border reivers in check.'

'So that's why your garments look as if they have been in the thick of a battle. How fast have you ridden?'

I knew of course without asking him. He beat some of the dust from the tight-fitting sleeves of the gypon. Unfashionable they might be, with not even a nod to the dagged fripperies so much in vogue at Richard's court, but Sir Henry had as little interest in fashion as in gems, whereas swords and horseflesh moved him to extravagant admiration.

'Fast.' His arms were spread wide. 'Well, my wife. Will you keep your distance? If you don't mind a muddy smear or two on your fine gown...'

'It's the fleas I take exception to.' I was already walking towards him, my demureness falling away step by step with my diffidence as he grinned and ruffled his hair into sweaty disarray. I would swear that he had the vigour to charm the rats from their nests in the stables. 'I'll tolerate a muddy smear on this gown – which is not fine if you looked carefully enough.'

'Old enough to be cut up for kitchen clouts,' he mocked for I was never ill-clad. 'So you were expecting me, in all my dust, and dressed for the occasion.' He arms were around me, his mouth seeking mine, to my delight. This was where I desired him to be.

But then we were not the only two people in the chamber. The door once more was opened, the voice that broke apart our reunion hoarse with unconcealed enthusiasm.

'He's done it. Did you hear?' The Earl of Northumberland.

'No,' Harry said, looking up. 'Who's done what? I've just ridden in from Berwick.'

His arms had already dropped away from their enveloping. Harry was as much in the dark as I. All my senses were goaded into life. Whatever it was that had been done, and by whom, had stirred the Earl to an unusual heat.

'He's here, at Ravenspur. With not enough men to make an impression on a dozen village elders, much less against a King with an army to hand.' Having announced this news, the Earl thumped the flat of his hand against Harry's shoulder blade. I, in my own solar, was ignored. 'Time for us to make a decision, Harry. And smartly.'

Not even flinching at the paternal blow, Harry's brows levelled. 'I thought we had already made it.'

'Making it and doing it are two different bites of the haunch of venison.' Impatience flickered over the Earl like summer lightning; it had no appreciable effect on my husband who merely stooped to scoop up the items of his discarded clothing, as if he might don them again immediately to answer some call to action necessitated by this arrival at Ravenspur.

'So we swallow the haunch whole,' he said, enforcing my impression. 'Raise the banners, call out the retainers. There, decision made, sir. We set out as soon as we have a force vast enough to make an impression on more than a dozen peasants.'

Which could, I thought, be within a handful of days. Grass did not grow under either of these Percy feet, but where I might have been irritated at my lack of participation in this planning, my interest was piqued. Here was something of import. Another Scottish incursion? But Ravenspur was south of where we were at Warkworth, on the east coast, far below Berwick. So not the Scots. And whoever had come to excite the Earl, had done so by sea. The Scots simply raided over the border.

'I've already given the orders,' the Earl growled. 'Just in case we decide to march.'

He knew that they would, even as he had asked his son for his opinion. The appearance of indecision was a mere distraction: the Earl had made up his mind to do it. Whatever it was. Harry simply lifted a shoulder, as awake to his father's mode of decision-making as was I.

'Where is he going? Do we know?' Harry asked, dropping his clothing again.

'Into his own country in Yorkshire and then south, to pick up what forces he can from his own lands, I'd say. He's come with precious few. Sixty, I hear. God's Blood! Of what value is that? He'll need all the help he can get.'

'So we'll take ours and join him.'

The Earl's smile, which spread over his countenance to remind his audience that once he had been a handsome man, was as thin as spring ice.

'And if he is sufficiently grateful for our support, who's to say what we'll gain from it?'

'Timing, sir, is everything.' Harry returned the smile. 'If we are the first to show our support, he'll be liberal in gratitude.'

Father and son clasped right hands.

Throughout all this I allowed the exchange to continue over my head. There was a difference here from the usual discussion of military intervention in local squabbles. Here was a sudden underlying tension, hot and sere, in this household that was famous for its tensions one way or another. And

I knew nothing about it. I might guess, but this planning had been conducted at some point in the past weeks without my being aware, presumably even before Harry went on his circuit of the March. Both father by law and husband had been as tight as Tyne mussels, which for them was unusual, when any prospect of military manoeuvring was heralded by horn from the battlements for all to hear. Nor had I received any information in my usual round of family communications. I found it unsettling to be so ignorant. A tight knot of anxiety surprised me as it grew in my belly.

Why I should be so disturbed, I was unable to determine. I had no gift of second sight, and was well used to being left to watch the Earl and Harry disappear in a glint of armour and armed men with the Percy lion displayed on every breast. But there was something here to wake what I could only think of as fear. Yet what should I fear? My son and daughter were safe in the nursery chambers in the western range of rooms. My husband was alive and luminous with health. The King, my cousin, was campaigning in Ireland but was in no danger that I was aware of.

But something…

I made my voice heard.

'Which one of you will consider furnishing me with an explanation of what you are planning? Since I am the only one of the three of us to be unhappily in ignorance.'

The Earl's pale eyes came to rest on my face.

'It's men's work, Elizabeth. Nothing to concern you. Go back to your stitching.'

Men's work? A curl of temper bloomed in my throat, hot words jostling for freedom, but I knew better than to voice them when it would only bring a further denial of a woman's place in this household. Instead I closed my lips and plotted.

There were ways of discovering what I wished to know; Harry would not dare to treat me with such casual disdain. Yet I was reluctant to give way so easily in this admittedly insignificant battle of wills, and indeed I thought that the Earl would be disappointed if I retired from the battlefield so easily.

I fixed my husband with a straight stare. 'Are you going to tell me to ply my needle too?'

But Harry was too caught up in unseen possibilities to take much heed of the fire in my eye. 'Do we inform him we are coming?' Harry was considering aloud. 'Or do we wait to see what transpires? Perhaps we do not commit ourselves too early, although it goes against the grain with me to resort to subterfuge.'

Subterfuge was a dangerous word. 'Commit yourselves to what?' I demanded.

'Thomas would advise discretion, of course,' the Earl said.

'Thomas would advise loyalty to the crown at all costs,' I said, snatching at this nugget of information.

Thomas Percy, Earl of Worcester, my father by law's impeccably diplomatic brother. The third in this Percy triumvirate of power. He was at present making use of his skills with King Richard in his military campaign in Ireland. No man was firmer in his fealty to King Richard than the Earl of Worcester.

'Thomas is not here,' my husband replied. 'So we'll ignore his advice.'

Upon which the Earl grunted a laugh. 'This is the plan. We go armed to meet our invader, but with a smiling visage and a sheathed sword. We'll not be turned away. Then we watch and wait and see what sport plays out.'

I disliked being ignored. 'And who is it that will be glad

to see a Percy force at his gate?' I asked. I sharpened the timbre of my voice a little to make my point. 'Should I not know before you ride out from here if you will return on horseback or on a bier?'

Which produced a response from the Earl. 'You are impertinent, madam.'

'If it is the latter, sir,' I continued, with even more impertinence, 'I would wish to make provision for your interment.'

A little shiver blew over my skin as if someone had opened the window, an unpleasant sensation that was instantly dispelled by the Earl's request, coldly trenchant, of his son.

'Would you like to take your wife in hand?'

'I would like to see him try,' I said.

'My wife does not need taking in hand.' But Harry did wind his fingers with mine to draw me towards the doorway where, the door still ajar as the Earl had left it, he pushed me gently out through the arch.

'Are you telling me to leave my own solar?'

'Yes.'

'Harry…!'

'Not now. I will come to you.'

'If you are to meet your doom, I deserve to know. I shall become a wealthy widow.'

'I did not know you were so mercenary.' He drew his knuckles down my cheek.

'But yes. I have to be prepared for an uncertain future. A Mortimer widow retains a third of her husband's possessions as her dower. I will be much sought after.'

He replied with a grin. 'You will be a Percy widow, not a Mortimer one, with barely a rag for your back, and so unsought. I'll try hard to save you from such an eventuality. Now go.'

I nodded my acquiescence, looking beyond him to where I caught the regard of the Earl. Something was afoot, something that was stirring the Earl's aspirations, probably the opportunity to enforce his hold on another swathe of territory. Then the Earl's eye slid from mine. Here, I acknowledged, was a deeper concern than the acquisition of more land, of more Percy prestige. And I still did not know who had made landfall at Ravenspur.

I would soon discover all. Would not Harry tell me? Without doubt he would. My skills at extracting news from a sometimes taciturn man had been honed to perfection. I would make him tell me by one means or another.

Who was I, Elizabeth Mortimer?

It was Harry's pleasure, when he was in a chancy mood, to say that I was the product of a long line of marcher brigands and the self-seeking, arrogant, wily Plantagenets who would snap up anyone's property, granted a fair wind. How, given that, would I be an easy wife to live with? Which was on the whole true. My father was Edmund Mortimer, Earl of March, one of the great marcher lords of the west with much land and many castles to his name. My mother was Philippa, daughter and only child of Lionel, Duke of Clarence, second son of King Edward the Third. Thus I was a desirable bride when the Earl of Northumberland had caught me in his marriage net for his eldest son. After all, was I not second cousin to the King himself, Richard the Second? The Earl had doubtless seen the value of my Plantagenet connections, as well as my Mortimer blood, from the very beginning.

For although my own family might own ambitions to extend their power, the Percy lords of the north were no less grasping. The Earl liked to appear as a rough and ready marcher lord who did not mince his words, one who was more ready to wield a sword than engage in well-bred niceties to hammer out an alliance or put an end to a dispute. What an astonishingly false image that was, for the Percys were as royally connected as I. The Earl's father, another Henry Percy, had wed Mary, descended through the Dukes of Lancaster from King Henry the Third and his wife Alianore, which gave my father by law more than a taint of royal blood.

The Earl had been educated to know appropriate demeanour in the royal household of King Edward the Third and that of the King's uncle Henry, Duke of Lancaster, with the result that the Earl, despite his occasional mummer's antics, was a man who could adopt a courtly costume, chivalric manners and diplomatic speech worthy of any European ambassador. The Earl could apply a knife to his meat at a royal banquet with more sophistication than most. Woe betide any man who thought him nothing but a rude and ill-bred lout, even though it was on occasion easy to do so. This man who had dominated my solar with no apology was rarely questioned or thwarted; the years might be silvering his hair and beard but they had still to drain either his resources or his arrogance.

Nor was Harry, with whom I could claim a distant cousinship as well as a more intimate relationship, no more than a border brigand in dusty garb or well-worn armour, driven to exchange blows with any man who would entertain him. Harry was…

I considered it as he closed the solar door softly at my back.

Well, Harry was Harry, a man of some talent and much attraction.

I did not need Harry to inform me of the identity of the man who had landed in England. It took no time at all for me to deduce whose arrival had caused such a stir: there was only one deduction possible. Who else would make landing at Ravenspur, and in doing so fill the Earl's eyes with bright speculation? It was Henry Bolingbroke, Earl of Hereford, and it had been a return much anticipated in some quarters and feared in others. His father, John of Gaunt, the old Duke of Lancaster, my grandfather's brother, had been dead since February. Henry would surely return to reclaim his inheritance.

But it would not be an easy return.

When Richard had waged a vicious campaign against those who had had the temerity to shackle his power earlier in his reign, he had connived at the death of some, while banishing his cousin Henry Bolingbroke from English shores for six years as a foresworn traitor. On Lancaster's death Richard had seen the opportunity to be permanently rid of an enemy. The terms of the banishment had been changed to lifelong exile, and the whole of the Lancaster inheritance had fallen into Richard's hands for the use of the crown. Cousin Henry had been effectively exiled and disinherited.

And now he was back. I pursed my lips as I considered the repercussions.

All would depend on cousin Henry's demeanour when he met with the hostile King. The problem of the inheritance and exile could be solved if Richard was prepared to be gracious and forgiving. Or a raging fire could be lit to ravage the country. The thought disturbed me, but not unmercifully. Family disputes had a habit of being settled, if not equably, at least to the satisfaction of both sides, when there was really no alternative but to come to a settlement. Would not the alternative in this case be war?

Harry found me without difficulty, where we always met to enjoy moments of privacy, even in this great castle with its vast array of infrequently used rooms. There would be no eavesdroppers here in the chamber in the Lion Tower, far from the Earl's private space in the great chamber, with its excellent view of the castle environs and the River Coquet that encircled us in its gentle flow. Yet still Harry took care to hover, head bent, to listen at the door after he closed it, before turning to me, drawing his palms down his cheeks, wincing as they came in contact with the abrasion. In the intervening time, someone had tipped a ewer of water over his head, probably at his own bequest, so that his hair was damply clinging to his neck.

Our reunion, redolent of restored intimacy that had been destroyed in my solar, could not yet be resurrected. I regretted it, but there was an issue which must be addressed.

'I'll not apologise for the Earl.' Harry was invariably honest.

'There's no need. He does not rank women highly.'

'Apart from my mother, whose name remains engraved in gold in his memory.'

'I will say nothing against her. She must have been a saint.'

Margaret Neville, older than the Earl at the time of their marriage and already a widow. He had not attained his earldom when he had wed Margaret and had valued a well-connected bride. She had carried five children and had been much mourned on her death when I was little more than a babe in arms. I suspected that Margaret held more importance for the Earl than the Blessed Virgin.

'Never a saint, but a woman of steel-like will.' Harry smiled briefly.

'I'm sorry that I never knew her. But that's not important.'

'No.' He studied me from under his emphatic brows, so like his father's. 'You know what it is. I think we've all been anticipating this day for the last six months.'

'Of course I know,' I admitted. 'It is Bolingbroke.'

'Yes. Or Lancaster as we must now remember to address him since the title came to him by legitimate right on Gaunt's death, however much the King might dislike it.'

'And he has not brought an army with him?' I mused as I recalled the Earl's derisory comment.

'No.'

Harry was watching me. After all, Henry Bolingbroke, the Lancaster heir, being first cousin of my mother, was also claimed in as close a cousinship with me as was King Richard. It might be that family loyalties were about to become uncommonly stretched. Broken even. Glancing up, I knew exactly the content of Harry's gaze, heavy on mine, the question openly being asked. Where would my own loyalties lie if a breaking did occur? I was too close to both to be objective in my cousinly appraisal. I knew them both. I held an affection for and a family duty to both. Glory of kingship would keep me loyal to Richard, the demands of justice would win my compassion for Henry. I hoped that I would never have to choose between one and the other. It could make for an agonising choosing.

And if a choice had to be made, where would the Percys stand?

I did not enjoy the breath of concern that stirred my thoughts.

'What will Henry Bolingbroke do?' I asked, rejecting

Harry's unspoken query, seeing his grimace as he acknowledged that I would, for a little while, keep my own counsel. 'It can't be a coincidence that he has chosen the perfect moment to break the terms of his banishment, when Richard is away in Ireland and so in no position to take action against him.'

'No coincidence at all.'

Harry was now perched sideways on a window ledge, ruminating, digging his fingers into his scalp as if it would aid clarification.

'Blessed Virgin, Harry! Are you going to tell me anything about Percy plotting?'

'How can I tell you what I don't know? I know what you will say,' he replied shortly. 'If we don't know what he wants, is it wise to ride to Lancaster's side? It all depends what his intentions are. And we won't know until he tells us. And we won't know that until we meet up with him.'

'Whatever he tells you, is it wise to pin your banner to his? After all, Richard sent my cousin Henry into exile for life.'

And so he had, all because of the rebellious affair of the Lords Appellant when Richard's infatuation with the charms of Robert de Vere had reached its apex, Richard endowing his favourite courtier with patronage, unable or unwilling to see the consequences. Resentment was stirred amongst five great magnates, my cousin Henry, the youngest of them, joining forces with Gloucester, Arundel, Nottingham and Warwick.

Harry was now staring out of the window. Where his attention was, I could not guess.

'Are you listening to me?' I asked.

'I always listen to you, my purveyor of excellent advice.'

I would not respond to his innocent smile as he turned once

more to face me, arms folded across his chest in a deceptive attitude of concentration.

'Would that Richard had listened to excellent advice in his choice of friends,' I added.

But he had not. The five Lords Appellant were driven to challenge royal power, resulting in a battle at Radcot Bridge, where they defeated the ill-starred de Vere, driving him into exile and forcing Richard into a bared-teeth compliance. The lords had emerged triumphant with their curb on the young King's powers, but Richard had never forgiven them. As soon as he considered himself powerful enough, he set his sights on these lords, with devastating results. Gloucester was murdered in his bed in Calais; Arundel, my sister's husband, executed; Warwick imprisoned; while Nottingham and my cousin Henry were banished from England. A notable coup over which Richard had preened. He would assuredly resist any attempt to overset it.

'If my cousin Henry returns without royal sanction,' I observed, holding Harry's regard, 'then that precious life of his will be forfeit. Richard already has you on his list of those with dubious loyalties after your recent outburst. When he returns from Ireland he will not let you go unpunished. He can be vicious when roused. His revenge on the Lords Appellant, as my poor sister is all too aware, was grim. Her husband's death on Tower Hill was bloody and unnecessary. So if you are in collusion with Lancaster...'

'If we are in collusion as traitors, then we are all under the shadow of the axe. We already are, for our sins.'

'It was your own fault, Harry.'

'It needed to be said. Richard has been too quick to trample on Percy authority. What's more, I'd say it again tomorrow.'

'And probably just as badly.'

Harry had found the need to express, in vivid and crude terms, his disapproval of King Richard's flexing of royal muscles in the north, to the King's displeasure. Meanwhile Harry's expression had closed, leaving me in no doubt that he would not discuss the clash of opinion with King Richard that had left a lurking shadow over our family, so I abandoned it for a meatier subject that would draw Harry back to the matter in hand.

'What do *you* think Lancaster will do?'

'I think he will say that he has returned to take back the Lancaster inheritance and his title.'

I took note of the careful wording. 'I'd be surprised if that's all, whatever he *says*.' I knew my cousin Henry better than that. He would never tolerate injustice. If he was the victim of such injustice, cousin Henry would be driven into action to right the wrong. Stepping behind him, I dug my fingers into Harry's shoulder, making him flinch as I discovered a knot of taut muscle. Peeling back the cloth I discovered a newly scabbed-over cut. It had been a deep one. Another scar to add to the collection.

'Knife?' I asked conversationally to negate the familiar brush of fear that his life was so often in danger of being snuffed out.

'Sword,' he replied. 'Before I took the weapon from its owner. He'll not be needing it. And it was a poor weapon.'

Since there was nothing more for me to say, and it was healing cleanly, I returned to the simple, or not so simple, matter of treason.

'Do you think my cousin Henry will claim the throne?' I asked, deliberately ingenuous.

It was as if I had dropped an iron pan onto a hearthstone with an echoing clang to draw every eye. Harry's shoulder acquired a rigidity under my hand.

'Now there's a dangerous question. What makes you ask that?'

'Merely a thought.'

'You never merely have thoughts. All I can say is that Lancaster will not be well disposed to Richard. Nor will he trust him.' He grunted. 'By the Rood, Elizabeth, have mercy. I swear the Scots could learn a thing or two from you about torturing prisoners.'

As I continued to knead, but more gently, I caught the slide of Harry's eye to where he had left his sword propped beside the door, an elegant Italian weapon with a chased blade at odds with the soldierly hilt. Harry had brought it back from a tournament somewhere in his early travels, since when it had become his pride and joy, rarely leaving his sight except when exhaustion took him to his bed.

'So tell me what is in your mind,' I said, my fingers stilled at last, my thoughts waywardly turning into those dangerous channels.

'Not a thing.'

'You looked positively shifty.'

'I am never shifty. My thought processes are as clear as a millpond. I was thinking what you are thinking. That Lancaster's not the only one with a claim to the throne. I don't recall Richard, childless as he is, and will be for some years, ever naming Lancaster as his heir.'

'No, he would not. There's too much antipathy between them. Wasn't it Edward of Aumale whom he named, at the last count?'

Edward of Aumale was another distant cousin of mine, son and heir of Edmund, Duke of York. I had more than enough cousins to rustle the leaves of England's royal tree.

'Yes, Aumale has been given that honour, but before that,

as I recall, until his unfortunate death in Ireland, the heir was recognised as your brother Roger, Earl of March.'

So we had reached that scenario at last, as I knew we would. The Mortimer claim to England's crown. It might have been rejected by a fair-weather Richard in favour of Aumale who had become the recent recipient of Richard's affections, but the Mortimer royal blood was still there, looming over the future succession of a childless King, as immutable as ever it had been. In the opinion of a goodly number, and in mine, my brother Roger had had a stronger claim to the throne than ever Henry of Lancaster did. A claim inherited by his son Edmund, my nephew. It was temptingly close, terrifyingly close. If Richard were to die without a son, the new King should be Mortimer. If Richard were no longer King by whatever means, the new King should be Mortimer.

Harry's gaze, looking up and over his shoulder, held mine, daring me to make the Mortimer claim out loud. But I would not. Richard was King, and there was no question of his right to be so.

'Except that Richard then promptly unrecognised Roger when he fell out of favour,' I said lightly, 'to replace him with Aumale.'

'That's what happens when your brother and your uncle were hand-in-glove with the Lords Appellant.'

'Roger was not, as you well know. Roger was loyal to Richard all his life.'

In a travesty of justice, Roger had gained Richard's enmity by refusing to arrest our uncle Sir Thomas Mortimer for his admittedly too-close connections with the Lords Appellant who had forced the King to bow to their demands for good government.

Harry was not to be deflected. 'Yet there is still that strong, and dangerous, dose of Plantagenet blood running through the Mortimers. And your sadly deceased brother Roger has a son to take on that Mortimer mantle.' He paused, removing a knife from his belt, testing its sharpness against his thumb as he escaped my ministrations and ranged the length of the chamber and back.

'What are you saying?' I asked as he returned to stand before me, frowning down at the weapon.

'I am saying this. Lancaster is back, that we know. Would we be naive, Elizabeth, to believe that he would risk a return to England, to an even more serious charge of treason from a furious King, for the sole purpose of supporting the Mortimer claim to England's crown before his own?'

'Yes. We would be naive.' Suddenly, as if a candle sconce had been lit, I had no doubt of cousin Henry's ambitions. If it became a struggle for power between Lancaster and Richard, Henry would not have Mortimer interests uppermost in his mind.

'Yet I would hear his own words on the matter,' Harry said. 'Lancaster is not, I think, a man without honour.'

'So you might be willing to give him your support and the use of your retainers.'

'I might.'

An image insinuated itself into my mind, which I forced myself to consider: of King Richard returning with an army from Ireland to discover a considerable Lancaster force awaiting him, prepared to engage in battle. We were used to war and skirmish year on year in this northern March, where the Scots encroached at every opportunity and the Percys pushed just as wholeheartedly back, but this new power being set up might mean something of a far greater magnitude. I wondered if I should be fearful. And decided that I should.

'It sounds like war, Harry.'

He nodded. 'If it is in Percy interests, I will consider it.' The knife sliced through the skin, his blood red along the edge of his thumb, which he wiped on his sleeve. 'I'll fight to the death to preserve what we have and what we can get. We need a King who will see the value of our control of the north and allow us free rein to exert it. If we have such a King, then my loyalty is ensured. But any man who threatens our hegemony here in the north is an enemy, and I'll act accordingly.'

There it was, engraved in the line between his brows and the stain of his blood, the words that would be engraved on Harry's tomb. Ambition. Power. Suzerainty over the lands of the northern March.

I raised a smile in an attempt to dispel the thought, dragging my eye from the blood on his sleeve. 'It seems to me that you have three choices,' I said.

'Only three?'

The knife tossed from right hand to left, Harry had snatched at my fingers and raised them to his lips. By the simple expedient of latching my fingers with his, I kept him beside me.

'Three. Richard. Henry of Lancaster. My dead brother's son Edmund Mortimer, Earl of March.'

Harry tilted his chin. 'Go on.'

'If Lancaster was of a mind to remove Richard... If he was of a mind to support the Mortimer claim as more important than his own and make my nephew King, albeit a very young one, where would your loyalties then lie?' I paused momentarily to marshal my thoughts. 'Not that I think there is any chance that Lancaster would do so. Why hold a golden crown in your hand in one breath and give it away in the next? If Lancaster ever seizes the crown from Richard's head, he'll hug it to his chest for ever. But if he did consider a Mortimer King, would you remain loyal to Richard, to the man to whom you vowed allegiance at his coronation? Or would you see opportunities elsewhere?'

Harry had become very still.

'What are you suggesting, my wife?'

I considered whether I should speak what was in my mind, and decided to do so.

'I am suggesting to you the advantages of having a Mortimer King. To have a Mortimer King of England, and one who is of no age to rule, might seem to some of our great magnates a desirable circumstance to embrace. To have a wife of Mortimer blood, as you have, would place you suddenly very close to the crown. A crown that would demand a regency and an influential council for the coming years. Such a powerful position is not one to be carelessly swept aside when you would be uncle by marriage to the young King. I suppose you have thought of all that.'

'No. It has not crossed my mind.'

His face was supremely enigmatic. Harry was not without his talents, on or off a battlefield. Occasionally, when it suited him, dissembling was one of them.

'And I suppose it did not cross the mind of the Earl, years ago, when he was negotiating marriage alliances for you?'

'My father's mind has a depth that I am often unable to plumb.'

'And was my value as a Mortimer bride in your mind when you married me?'

'Of course not.'

'But it might well have been in your father's!'

'Well, it wasn't in mine. You were eight years old.'

'And you were fifteen and precocious.' But I had long ago abandoned any bitterness, even if it had ever existed, that my marriage had been negotiated merely to make a worthy alliance between Mortimer and Percy. My lot had been no different from that of any royal daughter. Now it was just an effective weapon with which to needle Harry. 'I swear it would be in your father's mind, that at some point in the future it might be an asset to have a Mortimer wife for you, with royal Lionel's blood directly in her veins. Your father snapped me up as a beggar would snatch at a gold coin he spied in the gutter. What an appealing alliance. What an opportunity for the future to catch a wife of royal blood, descended from the old King's second son. I swear you were aware of it too.'

'Of course I was,' he capitulated at last, 'and of course I have considered the possibility of a Mortimer King.' He leaned swiftly to kiss the edge of my jaw before I could evade him. 'Quite a catch indeed. All I wanted was the Plantagenet blood in my bed, when you were old enough for me to get you there.' He became serious. 'But in all honesty, Elizabeth, none of us could have seen this eventuality. There was no thought that we would have been left with Richard, unpredictable at best, dangerously capricious at worst, and no direct heir on the horizon after him. The child wife he has taken will be no good to him for many years.'

Which rough summing-up of the situation worried me even more. 'Your father sees all eventualities that can bring him power. And it was certainly in his mind. I was a gift from heaven. Look where my royal connections could now lead us.'

Harry understood perfectly. 'I am looking. But to what purpose? All will hang on where Lancaster sees his future.'

Indeed all hung in the balance. All rested with Lancaster himself. If he had returned merely to claim his dukedom and his estates, then what cause to worry? Richard would remain gloriously King of England with Lancaster his cousinly counsellor. But if Lancaster had greater ambitions, what then? If the succession was in any manner disturbed, the royal blood of my Mortimer nephew must be thrown into the mix. And what would Lancaster do about that? If he proved not to be willing to bow the knee before Richard, would he be prepared to recognise a Mortimer claim before his own? But had I not rejected such a possibility? There was suddenly, out of nowhere, an air of menace in the room, of battle and bloodshed. I feared it but there was no means of dispelling it. As Harry said. All rested with Lancaster.

It was Harry's voice that dragged me from my thoughts.

'We have some unfinished business.' Knife at last discarded, he pulled on my hand, so that I was in his arms, that brief earlier moment of intimacy restored to our pleasure. This room had a curtain-shrouded bed in it. 'Dear Elizabeth. Do you recall our wedding?'

'Yes. You patted my head, gave me a pair of gloves and a hawk, probably because someone instructed you to do so, then abandoned me to join in the jousting.'

'And you returned to live with your parents.'

'And when I came back, within two years my parents were dead, so was the hawk.'

'I gave you another.'

'So you did.' I smiled at the memories of my growing up at Alnwick. 'You were always kind, even before you decided that you loved me.' And while he was distracted, pressing his mouth against my throat: 'If you go to meet Lancaster – when you go – I will go with you, dear Harry.'

He was not distracted at all. 'No, you will not. As the Earl would say, it's no place for a woman.'

Was it not? I turned my face so that my lips met his, murmuring: 'Now that we have that little domestic issue out of the way, let us take up where we left off.'

'There is a bed.'

'And you still reek of horse and sweat and leather and…' I sniffed.

'You are too fastidious.'

'I am not fastidious enough.' I made him laugh as I unlaced his shirt. 'If you wish me to be quicker I can use that knife.' It lay on the floor beside us.

'I don't need a knife. I can be very fast. Are you going to be a submissive wife?'

'Mortimer wives are never submissive.'

'Which I am of a mind to disprove.'

Disrobed in no time at all, our reunion was sweet and thorough, with no more forays into family loyalties until Harry was lacing himself into a damask robe of vibrant colour that even dulled his russet hair.

'We will be leaving before the end of the week.'

'I know.'

'I will deliver your cousinly good wishes to Lancaster.'

'Thank you.' And then, because I could not completely dispel my worries: 'I have a bad feeling about this, Harry. Make sure that you know what Lancaster wants from you.'

Harry belted the garment loosely around his hips.

'Oh, we will. And we will make sure that he knows what we want from him.'

And I would know too. I had no intention of being left at

Alnwick when contentious issues were raised with my cousin of Lancaster, but better not to reveal my plans. Better to allow Harry to believe that he had persuaded me to be compliant. How had we been wed for so many years and he not realise that when he marched south, I would be with him? For the moment I would make my preparations, without fuss, as he made his.

Chapter Two

The Percy household spent the following days exclusively in making preparation for the march south to meet up with Lancaster, the Percy retainers arriving in number to camp both inside and outside our walls when space became an issue. Meanwhile two letters arrived for me, brought in a package of correspondence for the Earl. With a sister, a sister by law, as well as a slew of royal cousins, I was rarely without sources of information. Knowledge was power, knowledge tucked away within the lines of female and family gossip, which was in short supply for me in the northern March.

Seated in solitude in my chamber, selecting my sister's note first, I could imagine the venom with which it was written before I saw the familiar hurried scrawl. Four years younger than I, Philippa had acquired a forthright turn of phrase, and why would she not? Her second husband, Richard FitzAlan, Earl of Arundel, had met his death in the horrifying fashion of that doled out to a traitor, at Richard's hands on Tower Hill for his part in the uprising to force Richard into seemly behaviour. Although she was now married again to Sir Thomas Poynings, revenge against Richard was never far from Philippa's heart. And so it proved to be.

To my dearest Elizabeth,

I do not know where this will find you, since I imagine your Percy lords will not be slow in declaring their intent with this recent invasion, if that is what it turns out to be. It is my hope that they will declare for Lancaster. I will never forgive Richard for the blood on his hands. If you have any influence, use it in the memory of the agony our royal cousin brought to me. My lord of Arundel did not deserve death, nor the manner of it. I know that to act against the King could be damned as treason, but it was with the best of intentions, and for Richard to have my lord's head hacked from his body in so foul a manner is beyond forgiveness.

Nothing here that I would not expect. But this next surprised me, that Philippa was so well informed.

If Henry of Lancaster is determined to recover his inheritance, I do not see him stopping there. He was always a boy driven by principle, even if it was only to put Richard in the dust when they had nothing more than wooden swords. I would welcome any choice he makes to take the crown for himself. In fact I would support him wholeheartedly, although I suspect that our nephew Edmund of March is in your mind. I cannot give such a claim my blessing, Elizabeth. If he were older then I might. As it is, his youth would lay England open to those who are power hungry and would use him to their own ends. Henry of Lancaster will be his own man.

Perhaps we will see each other at his coronation, sister. It would be sweet retribution against Richard, to have his power so bespoiled. I never thought that I was a vengeful woman but Arundel's death changed all that.

What will Northumberland do, Elizabeth? If you have your husband's ear, then use your wifely charms. Northumberland's power behind Lancaster could tip the balance. My lord, Sir Thomas, is of a mind to remain loyal to Richard, so I do not talk about my desires here at home.

I folded the letter tightly, scoring the folds with my thumb-nail. Treasonous talk here. So Philippa's heart was set on the Lancaster cause, the Mortimer claim rejected for purely practical reasons. Philippa was drenched in vengeance, and who better to achieve it than Lancaster? I was disappointed. Our Mortimer claim had been rejected, so it seemed to me, on purely selfish grounds, and yet, as ever, Philippa had stirred my thoughts. A young King, in need of a regent or a council to advise, could be open to gross manipulation. I wondered what Harry thought about that.

I picked up the second letter, knowing that the tone would be very different in this package. The writing was careful, well formed, almost fragile, but Alianore was never fragile. She had a will of iron, as had her grandmother Joan, Countess of Kent. Alianore Holland had been wed to my brother Roger, Earl of March. Left with two sons and two daughters, Alianore was now wed to a Welsh marcher lord, Edward de Charleton of Powys, so I enjoyed her letters of the region where I was born and recalled my earliest memories spent at Wigmore and Ludlow.

Elizabeth.

No polite usage here. Alianore was in a state of agitation, all driven by family honour.

What are we to do? I fear for my children, for my sons, for we know the strength of the Plantagenet claim to the throne is strong in their inheritance. If Richard is not King, then we both know it should be my son Edmund. The boys are royal wards since Roger's death. If Lancaster ousts Richard and takes on their wardship in his own name, becoming their governor, can I be certain that Edmund will live to attain his majority and the right to rule in his own name as Earl of March? Should he not be King of England?

I live with a great foreboding hanging over me that robs me of sleep. Will Northumberland support Lancaster, or will he raise his banners in the name of Mortimer? My son's claim through a female line should not be allowed to divert rightful inheritance. I beg your support and any influence you have to protect my sons. I know that the pre-eminence of the Mortimer family is as important to you as it is to me.

I am certain that Harry will listen to you.

Alianore had signed without any query after my own health. So much dependence on my influence, when, in truth, with Northumberland I had none, and it was the Earl's voice that was still loudest in this household.

I folded Alianore's letter and placed it in my coffer with the first. Both as treasonous as each other, but with diverse inclinations. What were my own thoughts? Lancaster or Mortimer? It was unfortunate that the Earl of March was so very young. Besides, there was as yet no evidence that Lancaster had any intention of removing Richard's crown and wearing it himself. Perhaps all hostility between the two of them would be smoothed over, as calm and innocuous as the surface of a newly made *Blomanger of Fysch*, and Richard remain King with Lancaster, his titles and lands restored, at Richard's side as his most loyal subject.

Perhaps.

I was still staring at the pages where I had placed them when Harry entered, in a hurry.

'News from the family?'

'Yes. Philippa and Alianore. My brother Edmund never writes. Not news so much as fear and vengeance and demands for support.'

'I have misplaced a small leather-bound coffer. Have you seen it? There it is. What is it doing in here?' He discovered it lurking beneath a pile of discarded rent rolls which should have been demanding his interest, and scooped it up. 'What do they want?'

'Philippa to support Lancaster and remove Richard, punishing him for Arundel's death. Alianore to keep an eye on her two sons and their throne. Keeping both out of Lancaster's hands and getting the crown for her son.'

'Ambitious. And what does sister Elizabeth think?'

'Since Lancaster's intentions are deliberately opaque, sister Elizabeth is torn between loyalties.'

'Let me know when you have decided.' Then, in passing, he placed his hand on mine, his fingers firm, the planes and angles of his vivid features softening. 'If those letters are as treacherous as you seem to be suggesting, it might be best if you burned them. Who knows? This may turn out to be nothing more than a ripple caused by a wasp dropping into a goblet of ale. Next month we might all be bowing in utmost respect before King Richard again with this whole Lancaster episode forgotten, and Lancaster restored to the royal bosom. Let us then be circumspect in what we say and what we do. I advise you not to reply to either.'

I did not question his judgement. Yes, it was treason to discuss the removal of the crowned and anointed rightful King, to replace him with another, whether he be Lancaster or Mortimer. All was so ephemeral, like stars in a night sky when a spring mist descended to blot them out, one by one so that the constellations could no longer be recognised. All was so uncertain.

When he had left the room I consigned the pages to the flames, but the fire could not obliterate the conflicting concerns of my sisters. They remained firmly embedded in my own mind, one struggling for pre-eminence over the other.

If anything surprised me, it was Harry's circumspection. It was unusual for him to be so wary. Which awakened me even more to the hazards about to land on our doorstep with cousin Henry returned from exile.

The whole country would be holding its breath.

And the one pertinent fact that I had signally failed to discover: were the Percys breathing easily?

It was a sight to smite at the senses. The noise, the vivid colour, the snap of energy. Here was an array to grasp the imagination, to awaken every emotion, the whole overlaid by sheer arrogance, as I sat my mount in the shadow of the walls of Warkworth. Here was the Percy retained army, archers, foot soldiers and mounted men, slick and gleaming as they were at the beginning of every campaign. But this, in some subtle manner, was different. Every weapon shone, but no more so than the horseflesh, burnished to glow in the morning sun. On every breast, every pennon, every banner, reared the red-clawed lion of the Percys, rampant in azure on its golden field. They waited to move off in well-ordered ranks, so different from the usual noisy melee. This was a meticulously created power, prepared to face any opposition, with force of arms if necessary, or to cow into surrender by the impressive display of the might of the Earl of Northumberland.

The Percy retinues were marching south and I, despite Harry's belief to the contrary, was marching with them.

I could not fail to be drawn in, to become part of this enterprise. I could not recall ever seeing so large a force. If the Earl intended to present Lancaster with a tally for his use of these Percy men, it would be a goodly sum indeed.

The discussions about the number of retainers and the manner of our meeting with the returning exile had been long and heated but here was the glorious culmination of it all. I thought that there had been no doubt about this outcome from the very beginning. It was simply that the men of this household liked the sound of their own voices in hot argument. But were we not in truth contemplating bloody treason, choosing to raise a body of troops in England that was not to be used for the explicit policies of our King?

Even more stirring, the numbers were augmented by the red livery with its silver saltire, the retained men of the Earl of Westmorland who had thrown in his lot, whatever it might be, with us. A hazardous alliance, since Westmorland was one of those men considered a threat to Percy sovereignty in the north, and thus a potential enemy, but the Neville Earl was wed to Lancaster's half-sister Joan Beaufort. He too would have an interest in hearing what the new arrival had to say for himself.

And yet I was forced to acknowledge that Richard was our rightful King through true descent, with oaths of fealty laid at his feet. What we did on that day in July of 1399 could be called subversion, unless we retired home again without lifting a sword, without Richard being any the wiser when he returned from his campaign in Ireland. An unlikely outcome.

What we did here today was assuredly treasonable. Here was rebellion in the making.

So the Earl ordered his men to march south, and I, as the ranks of retainers drew away from the curtain wall and gatehouse of Warkworth, drew my most stalwart horse up level with Harry's. Momentarily he frowned, as I had anticipated he would, but gave no indication that my appearance offered him any cause for consternation, or even surprise.

'What are you doing?' he asked, bending a flat stare.

'Coming with you.' Meeting it, I preserved the blandest of expressions, masking the tight fist of emotion that had nothing to do with my defiance of a husband's clearly expressed will and everything to do with a sudden anxiety at where this expedition would end.

'I thought we had agreed,' Harry stated.

'No, we did not agree. You denied me. I simply retreated from what would have been a useless exchange of opinion, and here I am, as I said I would be.'

I had said nothing when we had parted company after breaking our fast on that morning. If Harry had not realised I was dressed for travel, his mind caught up in the urgency of moving men and equipment as we had exchanged a perfunctory embrace, that was to my advantage. Besides, what could he do? It was not a matter of my asking permission from my Percy lord. He could of course have locked me behind the walls of Warkworth but why would he? My arguments for my accompanying this expedition, if he had chosen to listen and if I had chosen to make them, were superb and Harry had none to offset them, other than that I would be in the way. Of which I took no heed.

'You will be in the way,' he said.

'I knew you would say that. And I will not. I will even polish your armour if you ask nicely so that you make a good impression on cousin Henry.'

I was rewarded with a gleam of appreciation and a grin from his squire. The Earl, riding up at speed, majestic in an azure tunic and chaperon, with Westmorland in tow, was another matter. There was no appreciation.

'You will not accompany us, madam.'

Since here was neither courtesy nor room for discussion, I gave no argument, instead gesturing to the sumpter horses that carried my travelling coffers, to the two women, efficiently mounted and wrapped in layers against the chill wind, who accompanied me. We were well used to hard travel after a lifetime of living in the March.

'This could be war, woman.'

'Could it? I thought we were going to offer Henry welcome and support. Do you foresee a passage of arms?' And then smiling beyond him: 'Good day, my Lord of Westmorland.'

'Good day, Lady Percy.' Westmorland bowed his head with a quirk to one brow. Another relative by marriage, if an even more distant one.

'It is good to have your company,' I said.

The Earl of Northumberland waved any further niceties aside, swooping on my original query like a hawk on a vole, quick to deny any deliberate aggression.

'I foresee nothing as yet.'

'That is good. Then I accompany you. If there is a battle, I take refuge in the nearest fortress.'

The Northumberland brow became heavier.

'This is to be a matter of heavy negotiation, madam, not a social visit.'

'This is family, sir.'

'Family! We are all family!'

The Earl looked as if he would happily dispense with some of them. But was it not true? Did it not cause the worst of heartbreak when loyalties were strained to the limit by demands of cousinship, either close or distant? Whatever the outcome in this coming contest, it would not be without its sorrows and pain, for all of us. Even the Earl, through his royal forebears, could not pretend that the victor held no personal interest for him.

'I am going to meet my cousin and welcome him home,' I continued with seemingly naive pleasure. 'I see no reason why I should not be here as a representative of the Mortimer branch of the family since neither my brother nor sister will make the journey.'

Which gave him momentary food for thought, as I knew it would. His eye held mine as if weighing up how much I knew of the developing situation. Did he really think that his son and I conversed about nothing but the health of our children? When I did not look away, he turned his eye, still choleric, on his son and heir.

'I suppose you see no reason why she should not be here?'

'None.'

Harry was comfortingly loyal.

With no more than a grunt, for he had lost the skirmish, the Earl spurred his horse into a smart canter towards the head of the column where his banners were unfurled, their colours advertising that Percy was on the move.

'How gratifying,' I acknowledged Harry with a slide of eye.

'I don't see that you needed my help. You were doing quite well on your own.'

Upon which exchange, Harry fell into easy conversation

with Westmorland, leaving me to enjoy the familiar scenery and ponder. Yes, it was a matter of family. But what predicament would these complicated family ties drag us all into? This family that had sworn fealty to Richard now seemed prepared to discard those oaths as so much dross. But there was no true bafflement for me there. It was not difficult for me to see that severe dissatisfaction had been looming on our northern horizon for some months. Now, for my own satisfaction, I slotted the problems together into a snug-fitting mosaic.

It had to be said that the Earl of Northumberland, bending the ear of his standard-bearer, had become increasingly restless with Richard's interference in what he saw as his own preserve, even though he and Harry between them held the positions of Warden of the West and East March and thus in effect, in the King's name, controlled the north. The Earl had much to thank Richard for. At the banquet to mark the coronation of the child King back in 1377 Henry, then Lord Percy, Marshal of England, had been created Earl of Northumberland. In the previous year, Harry and his two brothers had all been knighted by the old King Edward the Third. Thus all would seem set for Percy prosperity and influence as royal counsellors and controllers of the border region, notorious for insurrection.

But all was not well, either in London or in the northern March. Here on our own doorstep Richard, in his wisdom, was intent on negotiating with the Scots to achieve a permanent peace. Not a situation that would endear itself to a warlike family that looked for every opportunity to increase its territory and wealth in its raids against its neighbour. No room here in Richard's planning for Percy territorial ambitions, interests or traditions. Peace with the Scots was not smiled upon over a dish of Percy pottage. Disillusionment coated the venison with a slick glaze. Richard's policies were, within the fastness of our own walls, heartily condemned.

Nor was this all. I cast a glance across at the Neville Earl of Westmorland, busy discussing with Harry the punishment of a band of enterprising brigands from over the border, with no evidence of bad blood between them. But there was more than a hint of wariness on both sides. The Neville family had appeared within our environs when this Ralph Neville was created Earl of Westmorland by a silkily smiling Richard, along with the gift of the border town of Penrith and other lands in Cumberland. Westmorland's intentions became an item of suspicion in Percy discussions. No Percy enjoyed a competitor for the length and breadth of their authority in these lands. Northumberland's vision of the north held no role for Westmorland.

But so much power invested in the Percy lord could be deemed dangerous. Richard had known perfectly well what he was doing in promoting the power of the Nevilles in our midst. Promote a Neville, curb a Percy. Which placed Richard firmly in the role of enemy to Percy ambitions.

But would this mild dissatisfaction encourage my family by marriage to rebel against the King? I did not think so. Would our power not be enhanced through bolstering Richard rather than undermining him? Royal gratitude could pave our path in gold.

'I'm Warden of the East March, appointed for ten years.' Harry's dogmatic statement in reply to some Neville query reached me as if in response to my line of thought. 'We wield the power Richard has given us and hold on to what we have. We'll not question Richard's right to rule.'

No disloyalty. No frisson of treason here. But here we

were, riding south to meet up with my cousin of Lancaster who had just branded himself the greatest traitor of them all.

'That's not the talk of the March, as I hear it,' Westmorland suggested.

'Never believe the talk of the March.' Harry's shoulders, neatly encased in a new brigandine for the occasion, complete with gold stitching, lifted in a shrug of sorts. I could not see his expression for the fall of his hair beneath his brimmed beaver hat.

'What do you say, my lady?' Westmorland leaned forward to catch my eye.

If I was flattered to be asked, I showed none of my pleasure. 'I'd say that Harry has still not learned to keep his mouth shut when pricked by outrageous irritation.'

'Well, it was outrageous,' Harry responded. 'And I spoke as I thought.'

'There you are. Guilty as charged.'

A guffaw from Westmorland indicated that he knew full well the source of this irritant that had caused Harry's challenge to royal power. No one with ears in the locality could have missed it when Richard had begun to draw power more securely into his own fist, starting with the demand for vast payments of money from nobles who caught our suspicious King's attention.

Most noble families kept their dissent between themselves and paid up. Harry, of course, had to be the one to voice his disfavour, which some mischief-maker was quick to report to our King in all its unsavoury language.

Richard had subsequently muttered about banishment from England, a favourite ploy to rid himself of those who stepped on the toes of his elegant shoes. There were also threats of forfeiture and death, before Richard postponed all his punishing of recalcitrant magnates until his return from his campaign in Ireland.

'No,' Harry was in the process of agreeing, 'it was not wise, but temper, and a cup and more of inferior wine with a pompously wordy royal courier, got the better of me. Now we await Richard's return to see whether he smiles on us or wields his power to batter us into submission. I don't fear banishment. We are too useful to him, and Richard will have had time to reconsider.' His smile was cynical. 'Our King was as hasty as I.'

'He might not be in the most friendly of moods,' Westmorland warned. 'The Irish expedition has gone badly.'

'We'll meet that when Richard comes home.'

Which left me wondering if Harry was as phlegmatic as he appeared. He might have need to be afraid of Richard who used banishment with high-handed authority. I had a sudden vision of packing my clothes to accompany Harry on a long sojourn in France.

'Another question for you,' Westmorland offered.

Harry raised his brows.

'If your uncle of Worcester were in England, would he be here with us today?'

I sensed Harry stiffen, infinitesimally, at my side, his horse shaking its head as the reins tightened.

'Why would he not?'

'Loyalty is bred into your uncle of Worcester as savagery is into a wild boar.'

'True.'

I glanced again at Harry.

'He is, at the present moment,' Westmorland continued, 'most loyally disposed at Richard's service with men at arms and a hundred archers, in Ireland. Is he as prone to rebellion as you?'

Again the breath of a shrug. 'Get one Percy in your camp, and you get the rest.' And then: 'Who's calling this a rebellion?'

'If Richard gets wind of this venture,' Westmorland's hand closed hard on his sword hilt, 'the penalty of failure could be death for all of us.'

'So we are merely riding to ensure the peace of the March. We will return home after a few weeks, as good loyal subjects.'

Harry was deliberately avoiding my eye.

'I don't see it.' Nor was Westmorland persuaded. 'And what is your opinion, Madam Elizabeth?'

I smiled my thanks for his generosity, but was careful in my reply, for this was a more serious question than Harry delving into my thoughts on my sisters' possible treason. I leaned towards extreme circumspection.

'The Earl my father by law considers opinions to be above the minds of females in his household. Thus I have no opinion.'

'And if you believe that,' Harry added since Westmorland could find no immediate response, 'you will believe that Richard will welcome Henry of Lancaster home with forgiveness and celebration and the handing back of his traditional acres!'

We rode on, Harry eventually abandoning me to a companionable conversation with Westmorland about his numerous offspring. The breeze dropped, the sun was warm against my face and shoulders so that I shrugged off the cloak. The land was at peace as we passed, signs of harvest and plenty on all sides in the fields and on the fruit trees. No signs or portents of dangerous prediction. No storm crows to call their warning.

The hard knot of concern in my breast almost melted away. We were not traitors, merely families of some power, concerned for the rightness of things.

Chapter Three

We rode through the array of tents on the banks of the River Don where it wound round the small town of Doncaster. The temporary encampment stretched around us as far as the eye could see, groups of emblazoned retainers sitting at their ease, their weapons stacked to hand, their horses being groomed and readied for action when the call was given.

'I thought the Earl said he had returned with only a smattering of followers.' I was both impressed and disturbed by what I saw.

'So he did. Our cousin of Lancaster has been energetic,' Harry replied softly in my ear.

However small the group that had accompanied him, returning from his exile, Lancaster's followers now numbered into the hundreds. The heraldic achievements of noble families I knew well were adorning pennons, jackets and tents on all sides; the flower of the Yorkshire magnates and gentry, keen to be seen in support of their returned lord. Lancaster was not without friends it seemed.

Lancaster was waiting for us outside his tent, hand raised to shield his eyes from the sun. It was to me that he looked. Whereas he might have addressed the Earls first, it was to me that he strode, catching my mount's bridle and offering a hand to help me dismount. It pleased me. Blood mattered after all.

'Elizabeth.' Effortlessly he lifted me and placed me on my feet. 'I did not expect to see you here.' There was a smile in his eyes although his mouth remained stern enough, as if unused to smiling of late. 'Did you have to fight to achieve it?'

'Certainly not. I have come to greet you on your return, as any cousin should.'

'It's good to see family who are not breathing fire and destruction in my direction.'

Which raised a smile from both of us. I knew his reference. Richard had left the power to repel Henry's invasion in the incapable hands of Edmund of Langley, the Duke of York, his ineffectual uncle.

'And where is our uncle of York?' I asked.

He was not a figure to instil fear into any man.

'Still in London I hope, sending out orders to garrison the northern castles against me.' Lancaster was drawing me out of the throng of horses and busy pages. 'Or even, if luck is on my side, heading west rather than north. At least he is not here.' He nodded over to where the distant walls of Conisbrough could be seen, a castle much loved by York. 'I expect he is changing his mind as oft as he changes his hose. He never could make up his mind, even to take cover in a thunderstorm. But I don't expect to be staying long in the north,' he added with grim decision as I was enveloped into an embrace, my cheeks kissed.

Set aside as he addressed himself to greeting the Percys and Nevilles, I was left to accept a cup of wine from an attendant page and watch the proceedings, and particularly to take stock of Henry of Lancaster as he embraced Harry, renewing an old friendship. Our future might hang with the success or failure of this man who was exchanging some military reminiscence with Harry, which reduced both of them to laughter. There

48

was a closeness here that I had not expected, but perhaps I should have. Shared experiences on the tournament field created strong bonds between men of valour.

A new thought crept from nowhere into my mind.

Your happiness might hang in the balance too.

I resented its intrusion. By what reasoning was my peace of mind threatened? Harry and I were at one. Nothing would destroy that.

I turned my attention back to my cousin, the new Duke of Lancaster since stepping into his father's shoes. He had been in exile for a year but seemed to have changed very little unless it was to be seen in the fine web of lines that marked his brow. He had had much to trouble him but he was still a well-set, agile figure, a man who excelled on the jousting field as well as in battle, a man to take the eye from his close-cropped hair to his capable hands with their fine array of jewels despite the overwhelmingly military climate of his camp. And there was the Lancaster arrogance in the tilt of his chin, the direct stare. It was a tilt that I recognised, for Harry possessed it in full measure.

Harry came to stand beside me now that the preliminaries were over, leaving the field of hand-clasping to the two Earls.

'What is he saying?'

'Nothing in public. We are to meet privately later.'

So here was the new Duke, come home to claim what was rightfully his. The problem was, for everyone concerned, what did he have in mind? What exactly did he see as right-fully his – the Lancaster inheritance, or was there more? That was why we were here. It was an uncomfortable number of troops just to take back an inheritance, even if it was the vast tracts of the Lancaster lands. Henry was indeed a man of honour, of piety, but even so…

'What would you do,' I asked the man at my side, 'if the whole of your inheritance was snatched from you by Richard?'

'I would raise an army and snatch it back.'

There was no hesitation in him.

'And would you retreat to your lands, once you had forced Richard into compliance?'

'It would depend on whether I trusted Richard to live by his promises to return the land to me and to my heirs.'

'And would you trust him?'

Harry's eyes, fixed on Lancaster who was deep in conversation with Westmorland, were surprisingly distant and formal.

'That would remain to be seen, my love.'

'So will you be willing to trust Henry of Lancaster to keep any promises he might make?'

Harry's eyes swung to mine, now bright with those memories that this meeting had resurrected. 'I fought with him and against him in the tournaments at St Inglevert eight years ago. They were good times. He is a worthy opponent and a bold ally to have at your back with a mighty sword-arm. He has saved me from a sore skull more than once, as I have saved him, and he has a hard head for celebrating when the ale is strong. He proved to be a good friend. I have no reason not to trust him. Do you?'

I wrinkled my nose, strangely uncertain. 'I don't know.'

Harry tucked my hand into the crook of his arm. 'Then let us go and see what the man himself has to say.'

At Henry's invitation, although Westmorland made his excuses to absent himself and seek out old friends, we withdrew into his pavilion where stools were brought while Henry sat on the edge of his campaigning bed. It made me remember that all this would not be new to him after a lifetime of journeying, crusading and competing in the tournaments of Europe. It was as comfortably furnished with hangings and cushions as any lady's bower, unless you spied the open coffer containing extraneous pieces of armour, a pair of well-worn gauntlets, a battered cuirass. Against the canvas wall was propped a sword and a helm, both shining with care from the efforts of the diligent page who had poured my wine. In the corner were piled the accoutrements and trappings of his warhorse.

This was a man well used to the tournament world, where he had earned considerable renown. He could equally be a man of war.

We sat. We raised our cups in a toast to the returned warrior of renown.

'And now to business. I am more than pleased to see you ride in from the north. My support here is strong, in my own lands, but I need to know what the north will do.' And then: 'Can I rely on your support? I presume I can, or why else bring your retainers in such numbers?'

As forthright as I recalled, he would push for a reply, an admission of intent.

'That might all depend.' The Earl, his mind still as keen as Lancaster's newly honed sword.

Lancaster waited, brows lifted in mildly eloquent enquiry, aware of the power of silence in matters of negotiation. There was nothing mild about him. Nor was there in Sir Henry, who shifted restlessly at my side.

'It might depend on what it is that you hope to achieve,' the Earl added.

'Does it need saying? A restoration of what is mine.'

'As we would agree. And we would support you in that. The great lords of this realm must protect themselves from...'

The Earl smiled thinly. 'From royal encroachments.' The Earl raised his cup and drank, all self-deprecation again. 'But our own position is ambiguous. Our wardenship of the March is dependent on the gift of the King. We already have old treasons breathing down our necks thanks to my son. Westmorland's power is on the increase, thanks to the King. I would do nothing to put our authority in the north in further jeopardy, which I assuredly would if I supported you in an insurrection that collapsed at the first hurdle.'

'As I appreciate.' Henry of Lancaster stood to go to the tent door, to look out over the ranks of his newly come supporters, raising a hand to acknowledge the arrival of another old friend, Sir Robert Waterton. 'Although I anticipate no failure in my planning.' He looked back over his shoulder. 'My position is as clear in my own mind as is Richard's perfidy. Who would argue against it? On my father's death I inherited the title and the Duchy of Lancaster, waiting on the end of the six years for which I was banished for a treason I never committed. Not an ideal situation but I could have accepted it. There were places I would be welcomed. I might go to my sister Philippa in Portugal. Or join another crusade. I could accept the need, even though I might not like it.'

He drank again before running the pad of his finger around the rim of his cup.

'Until Richard changed my banishment to life. As your brother Worcester will have informed you in detail, Richard forbade the legal settlement of my estates on me, and took them all for his own. There is no ambiguity whatsoever for me. The lands are mine and I have come to take them back.' He surveyed us with an all-encompassing gaze. 'I would hope that your presence here would show your support for me in that enterprise. And I expect Worcester, as my attorney, to join forces with me too. To put right a momentous wrong. My father will never rest in his grave until it is done.'

The Earl's reply was an essay in moderation. 'I'll be honest with you, Lancaster. Richard's truce with Scotland does not play into our hands. We resent interference in what has been ours for generations. Not least we oppose the appointment of royal officials who have no foothold in our region other than what Richard is foolish enough to give them.'

'Such as Ralph Neville.'

'Worse than Neville, who at least has a power base there, however much I might despise it. Edward of Aumale is quite another matter, an ambitious interloper who sees his own aggrandisement at my expense.'

'So what are you saying?'

The Earl glanced towards his son. 'I am saying that we will support you in an attempt to bring Richard to heel, to wring from him a promise of justice and fair government. A promise to uphold the laws and all tradition.'

Henry had walked back to sit once more on the edge of his bed, elbows propped on his knees, his now-empty cup held lightly between his palms. 'Then we are at one. With a show of force we will persuade Richard of the need for justice. I claim my inheritance and my banishment is cancelled.' He paused, head tilted. 'Your authority as Warden of the March will be recognised by Richard in perpetuity. The Earl of Westmorland you will deal with in your own manner.' My cousin smiled although there was little warmth in it. 'Will you take my hand on this? To have the Percy fist with all its might behind me is of greater value than all the lords and knights that you see camped outside this tent, as we both know, and I will show my gratitude when I come into my own. I will not step on your toes in the north, even though my father was wont to do so. I will honour your allegiance to my cause in any way I can. I will make your support of me an undertaking on your part which you will never regret.'

It was a speech worthy of any ambassador well versed in the demands of diplomacy. At last Lancaster's smile became one of genuine pleasure, lighting his face, yet I saw his cleverness in offering this prime piece of meat to the raptor, to entice it to come to hand. Permanent wardenship of the March was of inestimable value to any Percy lord. As for my cousin's soft hand of flattery, it was monumental.

'I know that I need your support,' he repeated. 'I cannot take back my inheritance without it.'

'But would you be willing to accept my price?' The Earl did not hesitate.

'What is your price?'

'Nothing beyond your power – as Duke of Lancaster – to pay.'

Which took my interest. I glanced at the Earl, whose face was inscrutable. Had not Lancaster already been generous in his promises? Was this another layer of negotiation which had passed me by? It should not surprise me that the Earl was demanding every drop of blood from this alliance.

Lancaster was unperturbed. 'Then I will pay it, for your alliance in person and in military might is beyond price.'

Flattering indeed, and presumably I had been mistaken for the Earl nodded slowly in easy agreement. He moved as if he would take Lancaster's hand, both now standing and facing each other. So it was all to be settled with Harry and I as mere spectators, watching the manoeuvring of these two powerful men.

And yet it astonished me that Harry had remained silent for so long. I could feel the tension in him as he allowed the Percy future to be decided, as if he were carried along by the ambitions of others, while I had the sense to bide my time. I neither could nor would add anything to this heavy debate in which my opinions would hold little weight, but how long would Harry remain a bystander? His compliance would be crucial to the whole venture.

'God's Blood!'

There it had come at last. The thrust of Harry's muscles as he sprang to his feet, stretching out his hand in denial.

'This is too precipitate. There is another matter that concerns us, that has not been addressed.'

'Has he not answered everything to our pleasure?' the Earl growled, his hand falling to his side.

'As far as it goes, I'll not argue against it. But there is one question that no one has asked or answered. There is the question of the crown itself. Who will be wearing it by the end of the year?'

Lancaster waited, and I saw the dark gleam in his eyes, as if he had been waiting for this all along, as indeed he must. Then: 'Who do you think, Hotspur?'

'I think it is all cast in shadows. I think you should state your ultimate goal here, Lancaster, before there is any clasping of hands.' It was a demand that blazed forth in the confines of the canvas walls as Harry rejected the intimacy of the name Lancaster had bestowed on him. 'You now have a powerful force at your disposal. You have much sympathy for your disinheritance. But if Richard does not comply with your demands, what then?'

'What are you asking?'

And since it could affect my own family so closely, I decided to participate. I moved to stand beside Harry, presenting, I hoped, a formidable front. If no one else was prepared to commit himself to speaking the unspeakable words, then I would do it.

'He is asking – we are asking – if you would consider taking the crown of England for yourself.'

The Earl scowled but Lancaster's gaze rested softly enough on me.

'So that's what you think. But that would be treason, Elizabeth.'

'It would indeed. You see our position if we throw in our lot with you. You are not Richard's heir.'

'No, I am not.' It was admitted lightly enough, but he was watchful. 'The last I heard Richard had recognised my cousin of Aumale, who by my reckoning has no right whatsoever to the crown. His father was King Edward's fourth son. My father was the third.'

'No, Aumale has no right by blood to wear the crown. There are others with better.' I paused but only for the length of a breath. 'But the Mortimers do have a claim. A claim that comes before your own.'

'Ah.' Tossing the empty cup onto the bed, Lancaster laced his fingers. He had expected this, and confirmed it. 'I should have known that's why you had come on this expedition.'

'Richard recognised my brother Roger as his heir,' I said.

'Then promptly disinherited him when he considered him guilty of treason. If the Earl of March had not died in Ireland, your brother could well have joined Arundel and Gloucester, dead by some foul means or another. His role in Ireland was already terminated.' Lancaster's regard was open and honest. 'It would be hard for you to make your claim for his son, your nephew Edmund Mortimer. What is he? Eight years old, I think. I understand your family loyalties but I doubt there are many who would support another child King.'

I shook my head, refusing to give way. The Mortimer family had much experience of minorities whose interests had to be nurtured. 'So he is still a child. But there are many who would say that my nephew's claim is stronger than your own, through the line of Lionel, the old King's second son.'

'Through the blood of your mother. A female line. It is not to everyone's taste.'

It was stated unequivocally.

'But has not the young Earl of March's claim as Richard's heir already been supported by parliament?' Harry queried. 'It is a delicate point, I accept, but one that brings us back full circle. What are your intentions, Lancaster? Who will wear the crown if it is not Richard? And you in possession of a powerful weapon in those men camped out there, under your aegis.'

'We could not support any action that undermined my nephew's claim,' I said.

'You see an undermining that does not exist.'

Harry, fast losing patience, was far more brutal in his choice of words. 'If Richard dies without an heir I would not like to see you robbing my nephew of his rights. You know all about being robbed of legal rights.'

'So I do.'

'Are we participating in a usurpation here?'

The tightening of my cousin Henry's lips seemed to threaten a squall of temper but his control was stronger than Harry's and his reply equable. 'I have not said that.'

'Some would say it was a usurpation for you to land and collect an armed force. It questions the King's supremacy.' Harry pushed harder. 'Do you intend to destroy it?'

'Not if the restoration of my inheritance can be achieved any other way.'

Which I considered a supremely enigmatic statement. So much polite wording. So much circling. So much left uncertain.

'Is it in your planning to remove Richard and take the crown of England for yourself?' I persisted in plain words.

Now the Earl sighed loudly, moving from one foot to the other. Lancaster's glance at me was brief and dismissive, before he addressed Harry. 'Here it is. If I can convince you that my intentions are naught but good, will you give me your hand, Harry Percy? Your father will, but I need you too. You are well named, Hotspur, and there is no one I would rather have riding beside me as we face the unknown.'

'If you can convince me, I'll give you leave to call me Hotspur again. You see my concern. You have a following strong enough to play whatever hand you wish.'

'So I have, but I also have integrity. I know a way to convince you all, I think.' His glance slid in my direction again. 'Even you, Elizabeth, with all your Mortimer loyalties.'

His smile held a quality that was hard to withstand, but I would wait and see if he could convince me. Family loyalties were one thing; family assassination was quite another. If Richard had no heir of his own body, my little nephew should be the next King of England.

'You wish to know my intentions. Then you shall.'

Without more ado we mounted and reconvened at the House of the White Friars on the outskirts of the town of Doncaster; there we were received by the Abbot in full regalia who, without question, ushered us into the chapel. We were expected. Which reminded me never to underestimate my cousin of Lancaster. Foreseeing the doubts that would be raised, with masterful cunning he had made contingency plans to answer them. Expectation and holy awe rippled through my blood. What would be our participation in this sacred place? The saints regarded us with a flat judgement in their painted eyes, making me shiver.

'I think we have been outplayed and outfoxed,' Harry said as we knelt in the silent grace, the chapel filling up behind us with Lancaster's followers, the Abbot offering up prayers for the efficacy of this meeting. Westmorland was here, a sprinkling of other heraldic badges, all of us disarmed in the sacred atmosphere, all eyes fixed on a jewelled coffer which rested on the altar. Lancaster had come here to the White Friars more than prepared. Here, unless I was mistaken, were relics of some importance.

With God's blessing residing with us, thick as the incense that filled our lungs, Lancaster stood while the Abbot opened the coffer, lifting out a number of gold-girt bones to place them on the altar. Then, both bowing in heavy reverence, Lancaster took from the Abbot and held aloft the jewel-embossed Gospel, raising it to his lips while we looked on, consumed with as much curiosity as piety. What would Lancaster say? This would be as binding an oath as it was possible to make. How binding for the future was Lancaster prepared to be? To my right, the Earl was looking straight ahead as if the proceedings were of no account. On my left, Harry's fists were clenched against his thighs. I went back to staring at my cousin's averted face, his head bent in utter respect.

His voice when he spoke was clear, carrying to every man here present, but not loud. It was, I decided, as if he communed with God Himself.

'I stand here as Henry, Duke of Lancaster, robbed of my inheritance by an ill-counselled King. I have returned to

England to reclaim what is rightfully mine, and that is the title and lands of the Duchy of Lancaster. I swear, before all present and in the sight of God and His Holy Spirit, on these Holy Gospels of St John of Bridlington and on his sacred bones, that I will take no more than those things that are mine by law and tradition. I am here to right a wrong.'

Lifting his head so that he might survey the congregation, he took a breath, impressive in his solemn dedication.

'I swear that I am not come to seize the throne of England. If there is any question of the unfitness of Richard to rule, then I will not be the one to make the accusation. If there is any man in this realm more worthy of the crown than I, then I will willingly stand aside for him. I will not be guilty of taking the throne by force.'

A pause as I marvelled at his willingness to be judged.

'If it becomes necessary for me to raise money for this venture, I will levy no taxes on the people of this realm without due consent of parliament.'

Which made me catch my breath. This was a forswearing of royal power.

'I swear this on these holy relics of John of Bridlington. God so judge me in my keeping of this oath.'

Once more he kissed the Holy Gospels, and knelt to receive the final blessing from the bejewelled hands of the Abbot.

'Amen.'

Which we all repeated with sacramental fervour in a sigh of reverence.

All very seemly, except that Lancaster might have removed his sword, but he was still clad in armour, burnished for battle, which gleamed in the candlelight. A soldier dedicating his future to God.

The Earl, Harry and I were left alone in the White Friars' chapel to consider what we had just heard.

'Which makes it all clear enough,' the Earl huffed. 'Does it not?'

Harry made no response, more concerned with collecting his sword from the antechamber, clasping his belt around his waist as if he were unclad without it.

Was I the only one to have doubts of Lancaster's veracity? I opened my mouth to say that nothing was clear to me, but decided against it. It was like staring across a thick winter mist with figures looming. Despite the terrible sanctity of the oath, nothing was clear, nothing decided. Not that I would necessarily believe Lancaster to be capable of deception, no more than any other man of ambition; no more than the Earl whose principles were compromised as soon as his authority came under threat. Sometimes it was necessary to tread warily when the future was not clear-cut. And yet my cousin had sworn an oath on his soul, on those holiest of relics.

I regarded Harry who was still occupied with the stiffness of the buckle. I could not read him as well as I would like. A light-fingered hand gripped my heart and squeezed a little, a forewarning.

Then Harry looked up, buckle forgotten.

'Do you believe him?' His demand, addressed to the Earl, cracked the stillness of the now-empty chapel, the precious relics returned to their domed coffer. 'That he will only take what is his? Are we suitably overawed by this show of magnificent reverence and ceremonial?'

'What do you still fear? That he will still have designs on the throne?' The Earl seemed to me strangely complacent as if it mattered not at all.

'With an army this size at his beck and call? Why not? And he is talking about raising taxes.'

'Which is sovereign power,' I added, seeing the direction of Harry's thoughts. 'Dealing with parliament to raise taxes, with or without consent, is royal power.'

The Earl rewarded me with a glance, utterly disparaging, below his brows. 'Lancaster swore that he would not seize the crown. He would stand aside for any man more worthy.'

'Depends what he means by worthy,' Harry grimaced.

I glanced from one to the other. 'What are you saying? Or not saying? That it would be unwise to explore the term worthy? But he swore on the relics.'

How conflicted my loyalties, and Lancaster had barely set foot on English soil.

Harry was still in explosive mood. 'Oaths can be broken.'

'Lancaster has a reputation for piety,' the Earl acknowledged.

'The Lancasters have a reputation for hard-headed ambition.'

'There is no outward treason here.' The Earl gripped his son's arm. 'It is my advice that we go with him and ensure that he keeps the oath. If we wish to retain our power in the north, it would be unwise to stand against him at this juncture. Let us assess the lie of the land when Richard returns from Ireland. A decision made now can be undecided. If we think Lancaster's scheming is not to our taste, then we withdraw. We have committed nothing but our presence and can take it day by day. It may be that it will all fall out to our advantage.'

For the Earl it was quite a speech. I felt that he saw a need to persuade his son, and for a long minute Harry considered, studying the sword callous on his palm, as if of a mind that a decision made here today would result in more sword galls to come. Then he nodded, looking up, eyes catching briefly in the few candle flames that had yet to be doused.

'I say that we go with him, but we remain awake to what particular dish might be cooking in his pot.'

'We remain awake,' the Earl repeated.

They clasped hands in Percy unity; for better or worse we had thrown in our lot with Lancaster. The divergent paths worried me. Better? Settle the irregularities, bring Richard to book and restore good government. Secure Percy power. Worse? The penalty for treason was death.

Instead of following Harry I chose to remain in the chapel, walking slowly to the altar where I bowed my head as I placed my palms on the dome of the little coffer. The jewels gleamed and glinted as the candles finally guttered and died. I thought to offer up my own prayer to St John of Bridlington whose bones were renowned for working miracles, but for whom or for what should I pray? In the end I lifted my hands, covered my face with them and offered up a plea to the Blessed Virgin, for all of us.

In this valley, restless, grievous and changeable,
Turn to us, O Maiden amiable, our Mediator and Advocate, your eyes,
Full of the joy of paradise.
That we may gain eternal joy and pleasure.

It was a prayer that soothed, but my previous conflict refused to be overborne: who would have the power to stop Lancaster from doing exactly what he wished?

All as complex and mischievous as kittens in a box.

I could not imagine for one moment that Harry had not allowed this consideration to occupy a significant moment of his thoughts. But was I guilty of an unwarrantable cynicism in my suspicions that Lancaster might be more than willing to break so solemn an oath, sworn on such powerful relics? The scene so recently enacted in this chapel remained vivid in my mind, the holy words, the sacred incense-filled atmosphere that still dried my throat, the stern voice of absolute assurance from the royal vow-taker. A man could be damned for breaking so reverential a vow. Was not my cousin a man of proven honour and integrity?

'Blessed Virgin, keep me safe from all mean doubting,' I murmured in a final heartfelt plea. 'And preserve Henry of Lancaster in the vow to which he has committed his soul.'

How could I not accept such dedication? Lancaster would do what was right and just.

I said my farewells to Harry. Lancaster's army was marching south, supported by Percy forces, to the Lancaster fortress at Leicester where more troops would join with them, but I would not be there. With a fast-riding escort in Percy livery to deter any well-wishers, I had decided to make my way to London where I would claim accommodation at Westminster and glean as much as could be gleaned from friends and family. Better to be there when Richard returned from Ireland to face his nemesis than isolated in the north, for London was where the future would be decided.

I was sitting on the bed in Harry's campaign tent while Harry strode around me, stuffing items of clothing into a coffer. A squire was waiting for it outside the canvas door-flap.

'Keep safe,' he said in passing. 'Go straight to London. I doubt you'll meet up with His Grace of York. We hear he's in the west after all, searching for invisible rebels.'

'And you keep safe too.' I turned my head to watch him in

his perambulations. 'Will there be fighting? When Richard lands from Ireland?'

'I doubt Richard will have the stomach to take us on. York even less.' He paused, the groove between his brows becoming a fully fledged frown as he looked out to where the Earl was issuing orders. 'But there may be,' he admitted.

'Are you sure of all this, Harry?'

Harry threw a quick glance over his shoulder to ensure that the squire was out of earshot. 'He took the oath. You heard him.'

'So you expect Richard to return to London, where he will be feted as King, and with Lancaster following behind as his loyal subject?'

'I don't know. Lancaster seems well intentioned.'

'Lancaster seems well organised and single-minded to me. That oath no more than a clever ploy.'

'The Earl believes him.'

'Does he?'

A pause in which Harry pushed another under-tunic into the coffer that was more than full.

'Harry.'

'Yes?'

'Who is the more worthy ruler after Richard?'

Which brought a halt to his housewifery. He lowered his voice. 'We both know the answer to that. We have talked of it oft enough.'

Suddenly it was vital that I knew what was in his mind. 'Are we in agreement on this?' I asked.

'I think we are.' Giving up on the coffer, he sat on it as he fastened the lid. 'I have not entirely changed my mind about the possibility of a Mortimer King. If, that is, the crown falls by whatever means from Richard's head.' His frown deepened again. 'I think I would rather you returned to Alnwick, out of harm's way.'

'Or where I will not be able to voice an opinion which will stir lambent ashes into a conflagration? Much as you might do.'

With a sudden lightening of the atmosphere in the tent, Harry grinned, showing his teeth. 'Something like that.'

'I am in no danger.' I went to him and, taking the final tunic from him, folding it neatly, I put my arms around him. 'I will say nothing untoward.' I kissed him. 'I promise.' Any obvious fears that Lancaster would fail and Richard return to London, burning with ire, to punish all who had dared to support Lancaster, were not to be dwelled upon. Nor would I burden Harry with them. Besides, Harry would see no possibility of failure in this enterprise, as I could not envisage my own death at the hands of King Richard. I doubted that he would make war on a woman.

'I will see you in London,' I said.

'Whoever is King.'

I sighed a little. 'Whoever is King.' I thrust aside the tangle of conflicting loyalties because to become enmeshed would do no good at all. 'Before God, Hotspur, I love you.'

And he replied, his mouth on mine sealing the promise. 'Heart of my heart, look for me in a month. Then all will be made plain.'

My journey to London gave me much opportunity for thought. I may have promised to take care with what I said aloud, but the workings of my mind were my own, and entirely predictable, as I recalled Lancaster's carefully worded oath. So Lancaster would look for a more worthy claimant, would he? What a clever word was 'worthy'. It was all very unsettling, yet Harry's farewell embrace had gone a way to reconciling me. We would work together for the future. What was it he had said?

We go with him, but we remain awake to what particular dish might be cooking in his pot.

It was all we could do.

And yet, the Earl had been quick to ask if Lancaster would be willing to accept his price, that it would not be beyond Lancaster's power to pay. It may be that my fleeting suspicions of the Earl's calm questioning were more than justifiable. Once again I found myself wondering what that price might be.

Chapter Four

Eltham Palace, London: August 1399

Isabelle, Queen of England, requests the company of Lady Henry Percy at Eltham Palace at the earliest opportunity.

Thus my sojourn at Westminster, where I was welcomed and accommodated as Philippa's daughter, was invested with an element of unwelcome drama when I was summoned to the palace of Eltham, across the Thames. A politely worded invitation indeed, although I accepted that within its carefulness there lurked more than a simple request. The little Queen, Isabelle, living in forlorn loneliness, wished to speak with me, but to what purpose was beyond my fathoming.

I made that journey to Eltham, disquiet a close companion. Whatever she asked of me, I had nothing to tell Isabelle about Richard or the conflict of interest with Henry of Lancaster that would bring her comfort. In habitual campaign mood, Harry was too engrossed to communicate with me. All I knew, from lack of pertinent news, was that there had been no bloody meeting on a battlefield. It had soothed some of my fears, but I doubted that it would satisfy the Queen.

I was bowed into her presence in the large audience chamber at Eltham where Isabelle sat, this young girl who had been sent to England to be Queen purely because a French alliance would gild Richard's reputation in Europe; this child bride now surrounded by all the royal glamour lavished on her by Richard who was never loath to make a show of his power. I curtsied, eyes lowered to the gilded shoes that peeped beneath her embroidered and furred skirts. Her ladies-in-waiting hemmed her in.

'Come and sit with me.'

Isabelle de Valois beckoned, charmingly imperious, with a jewel-heavy hand. Her voice had lost nothing of its accent in the few years of her domicile in England.

How very young she was with her light voice, her unformed features, her hair severely curtailed within a lace-edged coif. I had forgotten. She would be barely ten years, little older than when I wed Harry. I swore that I had more awareness than she of what a marriage would mean; Isabelle, despite three years of marriage and all the Valois dignity bred into her frail body, looked a mere child in rich folds of damask and fur and encrusted embroidery, so that I presumed that she had dressed for this occasion. My eye was taken by the glitter of her figure, for she was festooned with jewels that had been part of her dowry. Chaplets and collars, brooches and jewelled clasps were pinned to and draped over every surface. On the coffer beside her there were gilded drinking vessels and a ewer set with gems. Richard had instilled into his wife the need to make an impression on her subjects.

'I trust it was not inconvenient, my summoning you here, Lady Percy.'

Her lips curved in a smile, and I found her worthy of my pity. She was like my own daughter, caught dressing in cloaks and costumes from the Twelfth Night coffers. Moreover I thought that there was fear in her pale grey eyes. Her dolls, brought to England along with their miniature silver furnishings, I suspected had been packed away. In the present unrest she could be allowed to be a child no longer.

I took as indicated a low stool below the little dais where she sat, smoothing my skirts, pleased that I had made an effort with my own raiment despite arriving at the palace on horseback, waiting on the Queen who said nothing but waved her damsels to a little distance. She took a visible breath. 'I wish to know, Lady Percy, what happens in the country. I think that my damsels keep dangerous news from me.' She leaned towards me, lowering her voice. 'I think my husband has returned from Ireland,' she said.

'Yes, my lady.' That was common knowledge. 'He landed at Milford Haven in Wales. In the final days of July.'

'But July is so long ago and he has not come to me. I understand that our uncle of York has taken forces to lend my lord the King aid against the…' She thought for a moment, as if to choose her words with care, before abandoning all discretion. 'Against the rebels who commit treason against him.'

It was as if she had learned the lines, to repeat when necessary.

'So I understand. Although my Lord of Lancaster would deny that he has treason in mind. All will be resolved when they meet.' And then when she burrowed her neat little teeth into her lower lip: 'Why have you sent for me, my lady?'

Isabelle became suddenly more than direct, her eyes alight with knowledge. 'Because your family, Lady Percy, are the rebels. They are marching with Lancaster to force my lord the King into compliance.'

I felt a heat at my temples and I smoothed my palms against my skirts. I had not expected this accusation.

'They mean you no harm, my lady,' I replied smoothly to reassure, for behind the outward composure, she was not calm. 'Nor will they harm King Richard. The Earl of Worcester, my lord Percy's uncle, is still in service with the King. They will talk with him and come to an agreement acceptable to all. The King and his cousin of Lancaster will clasp hands once more in friendship.'

'Do I believe you?' Isabelle lifted her chin, allowing me to see the Queen that she might one day become, in authority as well as in name, if fate allowed it. Now there was fire in her eye and colour in her cheeks. 'I hear that your father by law, the Earl of Northumberland, has been sent to Conwy to take my lord the King prisoner. I hear that your husband has taken control of Chester, to persuade the loyal citizens to support the usurper Lancaster. I hear that your husband has been defeating loyal men in Cheshire who would support my husband. I hear that the Earl of Worcester, my lord's steward, has broken his rod of office and joined forces with the rest of the Percy traitors. The despicable Lancaster is pulling the Percy strings. What do you know of this, Lady Percy? Are you seeking to take the sacred crown from the King my husband because Lancaster commands you to do so?'

I was taken aback at both the extent of her knowledge and the venom in her attack. Moreover I liked not the presumption that we were mere puppets of Lancaster. We did not dance to his piping but to our own convictions. Anger rose fast and hot in my throat, words forming to deny our complicity in taking Richard's crown. Until good sense snuffed out my outrage. This was neither the time nor the place for rancour.

Instead, in measured tones I said: 'You are better informed than I, my lady.' She obviously had her sources. I had not realised that the threatening conflict had progressed so far. 'At least it seems that there has been no battle, no bloodshed.'

'Is that good news?' Her eyes bored into mine. 'What I do not know is what has happened to my lord the King. Is he still free? What will happen to him if he is taken prisoner?' She clasped and unclasped her hands, her rings reflecting the light again and again. 'I fear for his safety.'

'There is no need. My lord of Lancaster took a sacred oath that he wanted only what is his by inheritance. He intends no harm to his cousin.'

Which Isabelle ignored, her fingers now toying with some glittering fairing tucked into her sleeve. The venom had dissipated as fast as it had appeared. Again she was merely a woeful child, which engaged my compassion. 'What do I do if my lord is no longer King?'

'Hush, my lady.' I tried to dispel the panic that sat on her shoulder like some chattering creature. 'We do not know that he is no longer King. My lord of Lancaster has assured me that…'

The panic swelled, her voice rising. 'What do I do if he is dead?'

'He is not dead. You must not fear that, my lady.'

She lifted a square of linen to her eyes, to her nose; she sniffed like the child she was, but when she spoke again her voice was clear.

'My lord gave me this.' From her sleeve she drew the fairing which showed itself to be a jewel-encrusted whistle. 'It was a gift to him from the Bishop of Durham. He said that if I were ever in danger I should blow on this whistle.' She gave a sharp toot that caused the finches in the cage at her side to hop in matching panic from side to side. 'He would hear it and come to rescue me, he promised. But I fear that he never will.'

Poor Isabelle. Standing, stepping up onto the dais, I encroached on her royal dignity to clasp her hand around the whistle, even though she stiffened at the contact. She feared Richard's death, and it would be impossibly foolish to say that it had never crossed my mind. While I considered some suitable words of comfort, Isabella, looking up into my face said: 'If our marriage is unconsummated, I must return home to France. It is my father's wish. My dowry and jewels must return with me. I expect that I will marry again.'

'You must not ill-wish the future, my lady.' I released her hands as if they burned.

'I do not know what to do. What would you do?'

'If I were you, I would live in hope that all can be resolved.'

'How can I?' Abruptly she rose to her feet so that I perforce must retreat. 'How can I? I am in despair.'

When I saw tears on her cheeks, forgetting that she was Queen, I took her into my arms as I would have embraced my daughter in a moment of her distress, so that she rested there, her jewels a hard carapace, her cheek against my breast.

'You must be brave,' I murmured.

'I think my heart will break,' she replied. Then, pushing against me: 'You must release me now.'

Isabelle walked away, collecting her damsels, leaving me to curtsey to an empty room, to mull over the dangers that had erupted to threaten her marriage and her existence as Queen of England.

What do I do if he is dead?

Isabelle's fear suddenly found an answering chime within me. Harry led a charmed existence, returning from battle and skirmish without undue harm. Even when he had been taken prisoner at Otterburn, he had been ransomed and released, healthy and unharmed, after a year of captivity.

What would I do if he was dead? My mind could not encompass it.

Broken hearts suddenly became a real fear. But for whom? All I knew in my own heart was that the resolution of these events would never be to Isabelle's contentment.

I waited, carved emblems of royal power pressing down upon me in case I should forget who was King of England. Would he be in shackles? I thought it not appropriate that he should be.

Even at this moment of high anxiety, the Great Hall at Westminster, newly furnished and embellished, heralded the power of King Richard the Second. His personal emblem, the white hart, collared in gold, was repeated again and again, with a throng of heavenly angels carved at the end of each beam in the great hammer-beam roof. Each angel carried a shield, the majesty of the fleur-de-lys of France quartered with the three leopards of England. Richard's heraldic symbol. This was Richard's hall, built by him, with a new throne that he had had carved, complete with a gilded cushion, positioned on the dais for all to see.

I was here because I had been told that Richard was coming. I was here because I thought it my duty to be here to witness the return of my cousin.

Without warning the great doors were dragged back; in marched an armed guard, and there at the centre of their protection, or perhaps their containment, walked King Richard.

The guard came to a halt and so did the King.

I could not take my eyes from his face.

Never had I seen Richard so unkingly, whether in demeanour or in apparel. Pale, dishevelled, his soft lips pressed hard together, he stared around him as if he had still to accept where he was and why he was here, hemmed in by soldiers not in his livery. Without thought, so it seemed to me, he was plucking at the hem of his tunic, a garment that he might have been wearing for the whole of the journey from Wales, so travel-worn and stained as it was. His boots were covered in dust, and his hose to the knee. His eyes looked wild and uncomprehending as if he had been pushed beyond his bearing. Strained, even hollow-cheeked, he might not have eaten a good meal since he had fallen into Lancaster's hands.

At last Richard's vacant gaze fell on me, so that I stepped forward, and from a lifetime of custom and loyalty I curtsied. The King made no sign of recognition. At close quarters, his eyes were glassy as if unknowing of what was expected of him. Perhaps that was the problem, I thought, watching the febrile glance he cast this way and that. For the first time in his adult life nothing was expected of him. He was not in control of who must do what at his royal command. And I realised the enormity of what had happened. What Lancaster had done. What we had done. Whatever my ambitions for my Mortimer family, Richard was the true heir. No one could promote a legitimate case for his not wearing the crown. His blood was true in descent from King Edward the Third, eldest son to eldest son. Yet what hope was there for him now?

Compassion touched my mind, as it had for Isabelle.

As he was led away, his shoulders bowed, I knew that Richard would never again take his seat on the throne beneath the angelic throng.

Fleetingly, I wondered if Isabelle would be allowed to see him.

More critically, as I watched Richard being escorted to some place of confinement, I wondered if Lancaster was still intent on keeping his oath, that he would not disturb the true inheritance. A warm fear rose to fill every space in my mind, in my heart. What we had done, whatever it might be, was irrevocable. I could not yet see with any clarity the road that I would be forced to tread. And beneath the fear, struggling to be born, was just the faintest breath of guilt.

Chapter Five

Westminster: 13 October 1399

Cold and cramped, I stood in my chamber in the rambling palace of Westminster, clad in robes that were not of my choosing although the fit was remarkably good, aided with a pin and a stitch here and there. Opposite me stood Harry, even more resplendent, hands fisted on his hips. Harry looked uneasy as if he would rather be in hunting leathers or readied for some Scottish skirmish, but there was a determination in the rigidity of his jaw as he carried the finery of a full-skirted, ankle-length houppelande well, with its dagged sleeves and ermine edges. The draped folds of the chaperon, set squarely on his head as if some furred animal, all fringed with gold, was of a similar hue. Unfortunately Henry of Lancaster had not considered Harry's red hair in the choice of garments.

'Well?' he asked, under my critical gaze.

I was in no mood for doling out admiration.

'I am not in agreement with this,' I announced.

'As you have made more than clear for the past se'nnight. But you will do it because I ask it of you,' was all the reply I got.

'Or because you order me to do it and I will concur, as a good wife should obey her husband.'

'If you wish. This is not the time for soul-searching, Elizabeth. We are here. We have walked at Lancaster's side every day, acknowledging all he has done. This is the culmination of all the weeks since we met with him at Doncaster.'

'Weeks in which the Earl your father broke as many oaths as did Lancaster. When Lancaster swore to bow before those with a superior claim to the throne.' I gave Harry no quarter. 'Of which there are two. Our erstwhile King Richard, now a prisoner, and then Edmund Mortimer, Earl of March. What happened to all the fine words at Doncaster? Trampled, it seems to me, under the joint mail-shod feet of Lancaster and Northumberland.'

These were weeks in which the Earl of Northumberland had played a significant, some would say an inglorious, role to ensure Lancaster's ultimate victory, plotting with habitual cunning to take control of Richard who had sought refuge in Conwy Castle on his return from Ireland. The Earl swore that Lancaster did not desire the throne, swore his own firm allegiance to King Richard, before taking him into custody and dropping him into the waiting hands of Lancaster at Flint Castle. Richard's friends and erstwhile counsellors had promptly made themselves scarce or sided with the Earl of Northumberland who promised them safe passage in his retinue.

'Lancaster did not get where he is today merely by force of arms.' Harry was glaring at my intransigence. He was in no mood to admire my own appearance either. The deep red of velvet and damask complemented my own dark colouring.

'No. He was led to the throne by self-serving magnates like the Duke of York, who conveniently changed sides when Richard capitulated to your father at Conwy and they saw which way the wind was blowing. But Percy arms played the major part in this travesty. Lancaster is not the heir. This is wrong, Harry!'

'Wrong it may be, but this is what will happen.'

'And your voice will not be raised against it?'

He stalked to where a flagon of ale and cups had been left for us, poured, emptied one in a gulp and gave another to me as he replaced his on the board with a smart thump.

'Of what value would that be, to raise one voice in the midst of thousands? Lancaster has been acclaimed by the rabble in the streets and by the lords and clerics at Westminster. One voice will not be heard amongst the rest.' He scowled down at his feet clad in softest unscuffed leather. 'Nor am I sure that I wish it to be.' He looked up at me under his brows. 'There is so much validity in Lancaster's claim. The Earl of March is too young, too untried, and the female line of his royal descent disliked by so many. The old King, your great-grandfather, saw the weakness of it when he issued a decree that after his death only males would inherit. Which neatly obliterated your mother's claim in spite of her Plantagenet blood. Yes, I know what you will say…' when I opened my mouth to argue, 'but it's a matter of right of inheritance against the demands of political expediency. I've thought much of this and…'

'You have changed your mind, haven't you? You will give your wholehearted allegiance to this man who fooled us with his mummer's oath-taking.'

I was baffled, horrified, that he had done so after our hearts and minds had seemed so closely in tune. Here was my husband, comfortably in political alliance with Henry of Lancaster. Disappointment was sour in my belly, churning with the acknowledgement that it would be beyond my powers to change Hotspur's mind, once it was fixed on the vision before him, whether it be the enemy across the battle-field or the usurper who already had the crown in his hand.

'Yes, for the most obvious of reasons. Young Edmund should be King, I'll not deny it, but it may be that our own power in the north will be more secure with a friendly Lancaster than a young boy who cannot hold the reins of power.'

'Unless Lancaster becomes unfriendly and decides to strip it from you!'

'He owes us too much to do that. There is no real support for Mortimer, and as you see, it is overwhelming for Lancaster. So I think in the circumstances to support the Earl of March would not be politic.'

'Does that make his claim an empty one?' I would propound every argument at my disposal to change his mind, quick anger surprising me, glossing my words with fiery eloquence. 'You know that it does not. It is no empty claim. Richard was crowned King as a child, little older than Edmund Mortimer. With a strong council England suffered no hardship. A child King did not cast England into revolt or attack from abroad. My nephew is the legitimate heir, and if the crown does not sit legitimately, what stability will it give this kingdom? The power will be on offer to every magnate who has ambition to seize it for himself. It should undeniably be Mortimer, not Lancaster.'

'I accept all that you say, but you can't argue legitimacy, Elizabeth. We unseated Richard fast enough when it suited us.'

'That was not Lancaster's sworn intention when he made that thrice-damned oath. We were all fooled. But if Richard is not King, it should be Edmund Mortimer by the right of his mother's blood and his father being King Edward's second son. You know that is the truth of it, but have clearly rejected it for the sake of your own power. Because it is *politic*.' I drew breath. 'And when were you going to tell me?' My anger was now hot beneath my sleek fur. 'I doubt your father gives any credence to the Mortimer claim either.'

'I doubt it too.' Harry found the need for another cup of ale. 'Whatever the rights and wrongs of it, here we are, trussed up like Christmas geese, and today Henry of Lancaster will be crowned King. Are you ready?'

I spread my arms. 'Do I look ready? Lancaster has paid for the clothes on my back!'

'You look magnificent.'

'So do you look magnificent, but to what purpose?' Even in my anger, he was beautiful. 'There's no need to be concerned. I will do you proud.' My jaw was as tense as his.

'Are you going to drink that?' I still held the untouched cup in one hand. 'I suggest you do. It will give you a mellow edge. And try to be polite. At least there will be no possibility of your conversing with your regal cousin until after the event, when he will be your King. It might put a curb on your tongue.'

I bared my teeth, and drank. For Harry's sake, and because I foresaw no good in creating dissention at this late point in the proceedings. I resolved, for this day at least, to be the perfect subject.

'I will curb my tongue today. But don't hazard your Percy acres on my being mellow tomorrow.'

Despite the desultory rain, the coronation of Henry, Duke of Lancaster, was an affair to be remembered in later years, when men gathered in alehouses or in their lordly castles, reminiscing over small beer and Bordeaux wine. As Harry had announced, my cousin Henry had been acclaimed King by the lords and commons, led to the vacant throne in Westminster Hall by his royal uncle the Duke of York and the Archbishop of York, thus awarding him the highest of commendations from church and state. This sacred crowning was merely the culmination in Westminster Abbey, ratifying the choice of the people of England in the sight of God. He had not taken the crown by force, although the rightness of Richard's imprisonment and the purloining of his crown was open to question. Lancaster had been invited to be King. Both Harry and the Earl had joined the lords to acclaim Lancaster King of England.

I considered him an oath-breaker.

Now, bareheaded but clad in cloth of gold, with nine water fountains teeming with red wine to win over the populace in Cheapside, Lancaster became King Henry the Fourth of that name.

Anger seethed afresh, despite my promise to guard my demeanour, as the ceremony unfolded. I nudged Harry, angling my chin toward the procession where the great swords of state were being carried in before the usurper monarch. Four of them rather than the traditional three. The two swords of justice bound in red and gold were carried by the Earls of Somerset and Warwick. Curtana, the blunt sword of mercy, was held aloft by Lancaster's eldest son who would now be designated Prince Henry. And processing before them all?

'Did you know about this?' I asked.

There leading the procession was the mighty Earl of Northumberland, swathed in red and ermine, carrying the great Lancaster Sword. A true sign of Northumberland's dedication. There was no element of age in his rigid spine, his braced shoulders as he bore the weight along the length of the nave up to the high altar. The pride in his face was as great as that of the new King himself.

'Did you know?' I repeated, when Harry merely watched his father's stately progress. I thought I read pride in him too.

'Yes.'

'So you are truly tied and bound to this King.'

'Tied and bound with iron chains,' Harry hissed. 'And before you meet with him again, my father has been given the highest accolade. He is now Constable of England for his services to the King.'

'Before God, he is not!'

So there was the reason for the Percy acknowledgement of this destruction of the true pattern of inheritance. The all-devious Earl of Northumberland now lay claim to being the chief official in the royal household, a position of much power and influence in deciding who should and should not have the ear of the King. It was a magnificent coup.

'Before God, he is. You can see the Earl's chain of office. It shines like a beacon on the northern hills.' I thought Harry sounded cynical, but his expression was bland enough. 'Perhaps this is not the occasion to use immoderate language, Elizabeth.'

I closed my mouth.

And so it was done, with consecrated oil, hallowed phrases and the holy objects of kingship. Lancaster was duly crowned King of England.

'Now all we have to do is smile, bow, and celebrate at the feast,' I said.

There was nothing else we could do, but it gnawed at me, tainted my acceptance of a life that pleased me mightily; a grub in the succulent flesh of a plum. Harry had been in agreement with me, I had thought, but how quickly he had abandoned this brave stance. Now he was all for Lancaster. As for the Earl of Northumberland, he had sold his soul for the office and chain of Constable of England. I was furious with them both. Nor was it a problem that I could imagine would disappear. Lancaster was King and we were his subjects and most valuable of counsellors.

I did not feel like celebrating.

Yet all was not lost in a seething cloud of disapproval, for here was the opportunity for family reunion; three sisters, meeting between the weight and solemnity of the crowning and the raucous feasting and drinking of the festivity to follow. Philippa, Alianore and myself.

'We look like three cunning women,' Philippa observed as we withdrew into a sisterly group, into a corner where we would not be buffeted by the milling lords, citizens and their hangers-on. 'Plotting our future.'

'Perhaps we are,' I said, kissing her cheek.

'We may have need to be,' Alianore offered, beaming at us both, but behind the smile I saw raw concern. 'Good to see that you stand high in Lancaster's regard, Elizabeth. Red becomes you more than it does Harry.' She fingered the opulent, gold-worked over-sleeve of my houppelande with what could have been distaste, before submitting to a sisterly hug. 'Even Harry looks presentable. For once he doesn't look as if he has just ridden in after a month of besieging a Scottish peel tower.'

'You are hardly clad as a beggar, Alianore. But we Percys are royally grand, are we not, down to the collar and cor-onet?' I touched my fingers to the intricate chain around my neck. 'And why not? We have been bought,' spreading my arms to set the damask with its sable trim rippling as if a living thing. 'A crown in return for a damask robe. Have you seen my gilded shoes?' I lifted my skirts a fraction. 'These were in payment for Northumberland carrying the Lancaster sword. Which is the greatest symbol of power, do you suppose? Gilded shoes or an edged weapon? Richard would have said shoes,' I added, admitting to a touch of guilt at his present incarceration in the Tower, recalling his love of extravagant footwear.

'Richard has forfeited his throne, shoes or no shoes.' Philippa's voice had a tendency to carry, until I nudged her. 'I'd wager on the power of the sword.'

'Best not to say that too loud, on this fine auspicious occasion,' I suggested, seeing heads turned in our direction.

'What will happen to Richard?' Philippa asked, dutifully lowering her voice. 'Can our new King afford to let him live?'

My sister did not seem overly concerned. We were all well versed in political necessity. How would we not be, brought up as we had been at the centre of political events? The first Mortimer Earl of March had met his death by execution after a remarkable history of treason, hand in glove with the Queen against the rightful King Edward the Second.

'I'll not be sorry if he dies a quiet death.' Philippa paused. 'Or even a violent one. I'll never forgive him for taking Arundel's head. It was disgraceful that Richard should be free to take such monstrous revenge.'

To bring a halt to this well-worn theme, I clasped her hand, thinking that she looked strained, more than was demanded by the weariness of the long ceremony. Perhaps it was true grief that ate at her stamina, despite the vast age difference between her and her late FitzAlan husband. 'I know. I am sorry that the loss afflicts you.'

'It was the manner of the loss,' she said. 'Richard does not deserve my pity.'

It had been a driving force within her, destroying any comfort that the passing of months and a new, kindly husband might have brought. Philippa had not had an easy life, considering the deaths of her two former husbands. An accidental lance to the groin for one, an axe to the neck for the other. It had destroyed any trace of the soft humour my sister had had when we were girls, nor had she a nursery full of children for her comfort.

'Where are your sons, Alianore?' I asked to deflect a further outburst of venom.

'Safely in the Welsh March. I sent them to stay with your brother Edmund at Ludlow, although I think he's taken them on to Wigmore. I'd not bring them here. I'll never bring them here.'

It had not been the happiest of deflections. Alianore and I regarded each other with a depth of understanding.

'We are committed to this new rule, Alianore,' I said. 'Our lords were all prominent during the bowing, oath-taking and anointing.'

'Except brother Edmund who is not here.' Alianore pointed out what we had all already acknowledged.

'Edmund is a law unto himself, pleasing unto himself. It is no surprise.' Philippa's bitterness continued to pervade every word she uttered.

'We are committed,' I repeated. 'We have to be so.' Bitterly, disbelievingly, I realised that I was echoing Harry's own words, when, less than an hour ago, I had been berating him for his betrayal. I felt no commitment.

'But are we content? I will never be content.' Philippa again.

'Nor I.' Alianore.

'Lancaster promised to support the most suitable claimant,' I said, studying the rings on my hands, trying for balance where there was no balance. I was as unsettled as my sisters.

'Suitable? What does that mean?' Alianore's voice climbed. 'What about God-given right? My son Edmund is suitable. He has the right.'

'But Edmund is so young.'

'He will grow. All he needs is a regent and a group of trusted counsellors. It has been done before, it could be done again. Richard had a council, and his lady mother, Princess Joan, until he reached his majority.'

I tried to be realistic, and loyal to Harry, when I had no wish to be so. My thoughts matched Alianore's. Princess Joan, Alianore's grandmother, had been a match for anyone in guiding a youthful King. But in my mind I heard Harry's warning echo and re-echo.

'No one will stand for a child, if Lancaster is here with an army and the support of the lords. No one would willingly choose a regency. Besides, it is done now. The lords have made their decision.'

'Any man of principle would be quick to choose the rightful bloodline,' Alianore said. 'Decisions can be unmade. Kings can be un-kinged. Have we not just proved it? It is a dangerous precedent, but it can be used to our advantage.'

'As Lancaster knows.' Playing devil's advocate was proving exhausting. 'He will be on his guard against any threats to his new power.'

Another unfortunate gambit. Alianore leaned to whisper in my ear: 'What do I do if he sends for the boys? They were royal wards under Richard. They will continue to be so. They are the only challenge to his power.' Her whisper became a sibilant hiss. 'What do I do if Lancaster sends for them? Can I refuse?'

'Let them come,' Philippa advised, our heads close. 'I don't believe Lancaster will do what is unjust. They will not meet a hasty death.'

'Is there ice in your veins, Philippa?' Alianore demanded.

'No. I am merely practical. Besides, what can you do? Short of hiding them in the Welsh March or sending them into the fastness of Wales, you can do nothing but obey. I think that we should smile on our new King. Unlike Richard, he has no blood on his hands.'

'Not yet. What do you say, Elizabeth?'

'I say I don't like the thought of them being here under Henry's dominion but I agree with Philippa. I don't see that you have a choice. Nor do I see King Henry being guilty of murder.'

Alianore proved intransigent. 'I thought we had agreed that he might very well arrange for Richard's demise in some distant castle. Why not my sons too? Then all opposition is destroyed, and King Henry can toast the untrammelled inheritance for his own four sons.'

'I know.' I sighed, acknowledging that I would not wish to send my own children into Lancaster's keeping. Not that I feared him, but I would not wish them out of my sight. 'There is no easy path, is there?'

Such disloyalty, such treachery, in such seemingly innocuous conversation when all around us were celebrating. The interruption, which effectively silenced us when it came, was smoothly inviting.

'You look to be in serious confidences together, cousins. Does the new reign already see the stirring of a plot?'

We turned as one to regard the newcomer, recognising the voice, the light timbre, the teasing note.

Constance of York, daughter of the ineffectual and allegiance-swapping Duke of York and his Castilian wife. Now Lady Despenser, Countess of Gloucester, Constance was fair-haired and fair-skinned amongst the Mortimer sallow complexions and dark hair, a goldfinch in the midst of sparrows – although today her hair was invisible, neatly coifed in a jewelled net. She was quite beautiful, and artful in presenting her beauty; in comparison her tongue could be uncomfortably sharp. Sometimes cousinship presented us with a high price, but on this occasion she seemed to be all gentle compliance. It pleased me that Alianore, who had inherited much of her grandmother's glorious golden beauty as the Fair Maid of Kent, was inclined to cast Constance into the shade.

Beside me I sensed Philippa and Alianore stiffening, but Constance was smiling. Perhaps for once she was not looking down her arrogant nose. Arrogance too was a family trait.

'You should know that we are never serious, Constance,' I said, summoning an engaging smile. 'We were discussing the metal contraption that our aunt of Gloucester is wearing to cage her hair. Is this to be the fashion? It is not flattering.'

My sisters, without a blink, added their comments about fur and veiling.

Until Constance lost patience.

'So are you – all three of you – not suffused with victory, as is the rest of this throng?'

I raised my brows; I would make her spell it out. Again, Philippa and Alianore took their silent lead from me.

'Will you be raising your cups in heartfelt appreciation of the new wearer of the crown?' Constance asked.

'Why would we not be?'

'Where the name Mortimer abounds – all three of you indeed – there will always be room for suspicion of other loyalties.'

Alianore seemed to be searching the crowd for someone who might rescue her. Philippa disentangled a gold chain from the fur at her neck with great concentration. I took up the challenge.

'No disloyalty here, Constance. We Mortimers know where to put our allegiance, but your own family could be prime meat for any muck-raking gossip. Your father was quick to lead an armed force in Richard's name, to prevent Lancaster's success, yet here we have seen him building essential bridges by leading cousin Henry to the empty throne. And how does your husband Lord Thomas stand in loyalty to King Henry? It was Richard who conferred the title of Earl of Gloucester on him. Would your husband not feel some allegiance to his royal benefactor?'

Constance continued, effortlessly, to smile. 'My father and husband have seen good sense in cutting their garments to suit the present cloth. We are now all true subjects of King Henry.'

'As have we Mortimers. Our garments are of King Henry's own making.' I returned the smile. 'Are you acting as King Henry's spy, Constance, to discover the opposition?' I spoke the lie seamlessly: 'My loyalties to the new King are beyond question.'

'I would not. How can you think it?' Her jewelled veils shivered brilliantly as she laughed. 'Our lords have all bowed the knee. Poor Richard is condemned to a life of obscurity. Expediency is paramount, for all of us. Even those with Mortimer sons.'

She touched Alianore's arm in sympathy. Alianore did well not to flinch.

I was relieved when Harry loomed at my elbow to draw me away with a masterful hand beneath my arm and a bow for Constance. I smiled at her, promising to continue our conversation after the feast. I would not tell Constance my innermost secrets, nor would I trust her two brothers with my life. Her demeanour might be perfect but there was a thread of self-interest running through them all.

Is there not through all of us?

It was a question I preferred not to answer.

I never made it to the feasting, raucous or otherwise, or to continuing an exchange of views with Constance. Harry kept a grip on my arm and drew me at a fast pace out of the crowd. From there he hurried me through courtyards, skirting screens, up staircases, all without explanation, weaving through knots of servants bearing platters of meat and flagons of wine.

We hurried on. Back to our chambers, it transpired, where he shut the door on my women, presenting me with the opportunity to expand on my distaste for the whole of the proceedings. I made no attempt to moderate my tone, despite its uncommonly shrill echo in my ears.

'Well, wasn't that a superb show of aggrandisement? My cousin Henry is now slick with holy oil and encased in royal gems. Not to mention four swords instead of three. Most apposite.' I sat on the bed with relief. It had been a long time, standing in the Abbey. 'I cannot believe that we stood there and accepted what happened. That travesty of justice.' Harry was stripping off his houppelande, which caught my attention, deflecting my vexation. 'What are you doing?'

'Trying not to listen to you.'

My vexation returned, twofold. 'I'll not keep up a pretence of satisfaction, Harry, just to save your ears. I've spent the past hour with magnificent hypocrisy, trying to keep a balance between Philippa and Alianore. If I speak of my loyalty to my cousin Henry once more my tongue will sear under the weight of falsehood. I despise what we have done. I despise even more that we are caught like an adder in a cleft stick and can do nothing but accept Lancaster's hands tight around our necks. You must have suspected this outcome all along.'

'Yes, I did. Now stop talking and collect your belongings.'

'Why?'

'We're leaving.'

I looked at him aghast. 'What about the feast? Do we not celebrate? If there is to be tilting and swordplay, how can you resist? King Henry will be delighted to defeat you and all comers. Will you not allow him that further victory against the Percy name?'

'I'll resist the temptation.' He sat next to me to pull off the extravagant shoes. 'There are only so many times I can bow before him on one day. Look, Elizabeth, it's done and we must accept it. For now at least. But I'll not sit through a ceremonial banquet with my father standing throughout, lofting the Lancaster sword as a symbol of what we have just done. I do not wish to see Westmorland holding the royal rod of office. Nor will I exchange lances or sword blows on the tournament field with the King. Enough is enough. It all leaves a sour taste in my throat.'

'What will King Henry say?' I took one shoe from him, then the other, smoothing the leather between my palms while he pulled on his boots.

'I'll not tell him.' My brows flew. I dropped the shoes.

'I'll send a message. I'll make some excuse of insurrection in Richard's name in the north that needs to be put down by the Warden himself. He'll happily send me off with his blessing *in absentia*.'

I was already on my feet, opening coffers and removing the jewels I had been wearing.

'What will your father say?'

Muffled in the folds of the plain wool under-tunic that he was pulling over his head, Harry's words were clear enough. 'He'll cry foul but we'll be gone.'

'So you'll not tell him either.'

Harry, emerging, grinned as I recalled him grinning when he was much younger.

'Be honest with me,' I said, helping him to pull on a thigh-length, more serviceable tunic, running my fingers through his hair to restore the semblance of order. 'I feel a need for honesty on this day. We seem to have been surrounded by trickery and false promises for too long.'

'There has been no trickery, Elizabeth. We are loyal subjects, we support Henry's authority, we make the most of opportunities in the north or wherever he demands our participation, and we will ensure that he pays us for the loan of our armed retainers. It will all be to our advantage.'

'But what about...'

'I know.' His fingers on my lips stopped the word 'Mortimer' before it could be uttered. 'Perhaps one day. Not now, not yet. And there is no point in blaming me.' He kissed me in passing, which went no way to soothing my heart, my sense of failure. 'We will rule the north in Henry's name.'

'Percy deceit and double-dealing.'

'No. Percy pragmatism. Can you accept that? I would

rather we were not at odds for the whole of the journey back to Alnwick.'

'Very well.' But I had not quite forgiven him. Or the Earl. Still, I tried for a lighter note between us. 'I know what it is,' I said. 'You can't bring yourself to sit silent through Sir Thomas Dymoke's challenge at the feast.'

Sir Thomas, King's Champion and full of conceit, would challenge to a duel any man who questioned the King's right to the throne. He would enjoy every minute of the ceremonial.

'No, I cannot.' Harry was grimacing. 'He's nothing but a pompous bagpipe, and I might be tempted to take him up on the offer. Now, are we ready to go?'

At last we had both set aside our finery. 'What do we do with these?' I asked.

Harry regarded them, symbols of Lancaster hegemony. 'Fold them neatly, I suppose.'

'You have never folded your garments neatly in your life...'

'And we will return them with thanks. Until the next time.'

'Harry...'

I waited until he turned to me. But then a rap on the door forestalled any further conversation, particularly as the door was opened without any invitation from within. The Earl stood on the threshold, casting an eye around the room as his presence filled it, equally garbed in red damask, three strips of gold braid on his right breast defining his rank. A crimson chaperon, decorated with a cloud of white fur, enhanced the impression of status and power.

His smile faded.

'What in God's name are you doing?'

'Going home.'

'Are you a fool, man?'

'I've done all that is necessary. I've acclaimed. I've witnessed. I've taken an oath that is binding unto death. I do not have to eat and drink and joust.'

'What's ruffled your fur?' He turned on me. 'Is this your doing? The claim of the Mortimer child is not worth mentioning. Why give it time and space?'

Accusations proceeded to fly between them, needing no intervention from me.

'You knew this was to be the outcome,' Harry accused.

'So did you if you will confess it.'

'Yes, but I don't have to like it.'

'You'll like the rewards well enough. Even your uncle of Worcester can come to terms with necessity.'

'As I have done.' Harry's temper, kept in hand in dispute with me, now flamed as bright as his hair. 'But I'll not sit at his table and raise a cup of his best spiced wine to seal what is a chancy alliance at best. I think we have been used as magnificent puppets, my lord father, won over by oaths and fair words. And gold chains.' He gestured to the sparkling gems on the Earl's breast. 'Are Percy jewels suddenly not good enough for you? Make sure King Henry pays you well for all our services. Without us he would never have been wearing that crown. Our prestige and our troops made all the difference. We were the first to support him with soldiery in any number capable of giving battle.'

'Without doubt, nephew.' The Earl of Worcester, similarly opulent in silk and fur and gold braid, had arrived in the wake of his brother. Shorter, less robust, but unmistakably Percy, he held himself with quiet confidence. 'We have become kingmakers indeed.' He smiled at me. 'I was about to say that you look superb, Elizabeth, but there seem to have been some rapid changes since I saw you at the crowning.'

He embraced me.

'A rapid change of plan,' I said.

Meanwhile Harry's stare remained severe. 'Have you too come to terms with your conscience, Uncle?'

'I have. It was necessary.'

'And yet you were at Richard's side in Ireland and when he landed.'

'And now I am here.'

'Well, Elizabeth and I will be in Alnwick by the time you have both finished roistering, and when you have returned Lancaster Sword to its owner, my Lord Constable.'

Worcester looked from Harry to me, as if he had known the tenor of the conversation before he arrived. Perhaps he had. 'There's no chance for young Mortimer, you know.'

Thomas Percy, Earl of Worcester. Younger than his brother, slighter in build, his features not so hawkish, Worcester had an air of gentle elegance about him and a gift of drawing advantages out of the most unfavourable of circumstances. Unwed, with no family of his own, he had dedicated his life to service to the King. He had a name for diplomacy and cool speaking that could smooth the clash of magnate ambitions. Erudite, educated, charming – I liked him. I could not quite understand how he had given his name to this change in circumstance, except that he had always been attorney to the Lancasters. Perhaps that had been the persuading element in his dramatic change of loyalty since no one would know better than he the crime committed when Richard had seized the Lancaster estates.

Harry, now in possession of cloak and gloves, replied to his uncle's soft criticism. 'No, there is no chance. But that does not mean that I have to like what has been done. We crowned the wrong man here today. The Earl of March has the right.'

'Right has nothing to do with it.' The Earl was already halfway through the door, taking his brother with him. 'Then go. But as you ride north, you should contemplate the benefits to us of having King Henry's gratitude showering down on us.'

'What did he mean?' I asked when the Percy feet had clattered down the stairs.

'Nothing more than I have already said. There will be rewards. Our King will assuredly pay his dues. But we'll not count our chickens before King Henry has hatched them.'

I thought he was being evasive. As we left London, looking back to the Tower, a memory alighted in my mind, and not a happy one.

'Do you think Isabelle will ever see Richard again?' I asked.

Harry growled. 'As you would say, I'd be a fool to wager my Percy acres, or even the shoes on my feet, on it.'

I could think of no response, realising as we headed north that I had exchanged not one word with my cousin Henry on the occasion of his coronation. To me he was a breaker of sacred oaths. Taken of his own volition on the relics of St John of Bridlington, yet he had denied them at the first opportunity. To those around me I would be a loyal subject, acknowledging this new line of kings through Lancaster to his own sons. In my heart I was a traitor. Henry had broken his sacred vow. He had always wanted the throne. The vow had been a piece of carefully planned and performed mischief to win over those who might be uncertain.

'Would you condemn him as an oath-breaker?' I asked

Harry as we rested briefly during our journey in the comfortable grandeur of Spofforth, the Yorkshire castle which was secure enough not to need dark crenellations and where Harry had spent some of his earliest years.

'I'll leave that to God on the day of Lancaster's death.' Harry lounged at his ease, apparently unaffected by our long journey conducted at his usual breakneck speed. 'We brought him to the throne. Now we accept it and concentrate on events in the north, where we'll ensure that Henry as King will not be to our disadvantage.'

Which encouraged me, in affronted silence that Harry had slid so effortlessly from Mortimer justice to Percy dominance, to retire to my chamber, unable to decide whether I should be guided by my head or my heart. And worst of all, I knew that Harry would enjoy wielding every inch of the authority that King Henry was about to cast into his lap.

My Mortimer dreams, I feared, were about to fade into insignificance within the scope of Percy plans for the future.

Chapter Six

Alnwick Castle: Early November 1399

King Henry's chickens were hatched smartly enough. Before the first frosts of November, the two great Percy magnates, Northumberland and Worcester, arrived at Alnwick with what could only be described as an air of smug achievement. They were soon closeted with Harry in the Earl's private chamber, dispatching servants for ale and food.

I considered listening at the door but decided that it was beneath my dignity either to eavesdrop or to demand admittance. I would discover all in due time.

So what had been our reward for helping Lancaster to his throne? I imagined it was generous, hearing the Earl's bark of laughter, Worcester's smooth rumble, the sharp query from Harry as I passed the still-closed door an hour later.

A further hour and the exchange of opinion continued, with more ale sent for, and I could wait no longer. Thus I arrived with the ale, waylaying the servant and taking the flagon from him. There they were, the three Percy lords deep in admiration of their ill-gotten gains and no doubt planning a raid along the Scottish border on the strength of their new powers, driving me to make, in a spirit of spiced malice, a suitably deferential obeisance in the presence of such overwhelming magnate supremacy. With the deftness of any serving wench, I refilled the cups, then laid a hand on Harry's shoulder, remaining behind him when he placed his hand to cover mine. Whether in warning or acknowledgement I was unsure. Worcester predictably rose to his feet with words of welcome. The Earl, equally predictably, keeping his seat, granted me a brusque nod of his head.

'So tell me the good news, my lords. Has our payment for services rendered been acceptable?'

King Henry's more-than-smooth accession still rubbed against my skin.

I took in the evidence at a quick glance. There were documents in the coffer on the table between them, some spilling out where they had been read and abandoned. Royal seals were evident, the figure easily recognisable as the King seated between two lions. How generous had King Henry been? I thought of perusing them for myself but that would spoil the Percy liking for pride and self-promotion. Harry was smiling at me as he took my arm, bringing me closer into the Percy council so that I perched on the arm of his chair. He pushed his own cup of ale into my hand.

'Come and drink to our achievements.' He rescued one of the documents, unrolling it for me to see. 'I am confirmed as Warden of the East March and Governor of the castles at both Berwick and Roxburgh. I have also the castle of Bamburgh to hold for life.' As he allowed the document to re-roll, I could not mistake the glow of satisfaction. 'My father holds the West March as we would expect, and the town of Carlisle. Between us we will dominate the north in the name of King and Percy. We could not ask for more.'

'My congratulations.' Raising the cup in a smart little salute, I drank, as I must; it would be churlish not to do so, for it was a substantial reward indeed, to put a seal on Percy ambitions. All that Richard had allowed us had been confirmed by Lancaster as King, and more. Between them the Earl and Harry held the military and civilian power in the north in their combined fists. As well as the Earl being Constable of England.

The Earl was not moved to be too complacent. 'It is regretful about Ralph Neville.'

From which I presumed that King Henry had not been backward in recognising the debt he owed to his brother by marriage. I waited. When the Earl merely grunted his displeasure through a mouthful of ale, it was Worcester who explained it for me, settling easily into his habitual laconic manner.

'Neville has been made Marshal of England and given the lordship of Richmond for life. We would rather he had not – Richmond is a strategic castle – but it is a drop in the ocean. He'll be no threat to us.'

So Henry was placing Neville as a tame hawk in the centre of the Percy raptors. Even though the office of Earl Marshal was a prestigious one, at the head of the King's forces, as my lord of Worcester admitted, it was no real threat to us. Yet it was a resourceful move on the King's part to keep a watchful eye on which prey the Percys might consider gobbling up.

'And you, my lord?' I asked Worcester. 'What is your reward? Your repudiation of Richard was formidable, and your work for Henry as his attorney must be recognised. Are you content?'

'The King has been generous. With five hundred marks to line my coffers every year for life, I am made Steward of Henry's household.'

'As well as Admiral of England, Treasurer and Keeper of

the Privy Seal,' Harry added. 'You won't have a moment's time to spend your five hundred marks. Our King will keep you hopping.'

'True.' Worcester's acceptance was calm, but I could see the sleek gratification writ large as he proceeded to re-roll the documents, neat as any legal man. 'Our King has ambitions too, to make his mark on the country. He looks to secure his borders against intransigent Scots, and the Welsh, thus to bring in a period of golden peace and fair government. If that does not strengthen his support throughout the country, nothing will.' His light smile might have held a touch of cynicism. 'I will do my best to smooth his path.'

'A fine achievement,' I agreed, as indeed it was. All was much as I had expected, and I could not deny the Percy triumph. 'Where is Richard in all this?' I asked. 'Will he be allowed to retire and live privately?'

Idly, picking up one of the rolls that had escaped Worcester's attention, unfurling it, I read it in a cursory fashion, taking Harry's seat when he rose to refill the cups, discovering a new one for himself. From the date it was one of the documents of intent, issued by Henry as King shortly after his coronation, with his signature and seal.

I allowed my eye to travel down the clerkly script.

'King Henry intended to transfer Richard from the Tower to his own fortress at Pontefract Castle,' Worcester was explaining from his position as head of the royal household. 'I expect he's there by now.' He caught my glance. 'He is in no danger. He'll be well looked after.'

But I was no longer listening. It was not Richard that concerned me, for my eye had caught on a date, a date that surprised me. I spread the roll more firmly, flattening it with both hands, and read again.

'Is this correct?' I asked, my mind racing.

'Yes.' The Earl answered since it was pertinent to his promotions. 'It confirms my supremacy in the West March and at Carlisle.' His mouth twisted. 'In case there is any who will question it. It is stated clear enough.'

'Yes. It does confirm it. It is very clear. It is the date that gives me food for some uncomfortable thought.'

'There's naught to concern you. The last day of October. A week ago.'

'As I see.' I looked up at the authoritative visage. 'But this is confirmation of an earlier agreement.' I looked at Harry. 'Did you know about this?'

'What is there to know?'

Harry shrugged his ignorance. Worcester was unimpressed; Northumberland blandly dismissive as he held out his hand for the document. It was a direction to parliament much to the Earl's benefit, and the date to me was most pertinent. Retaining it, I read aloud:

Henry by the Grace of God, King of England and of France.
    Since our very dear and faithful cousin Henry Percy, Earl of Northumberland, by force of our commission made unto him under our seal of the Duchy of Lancaster has had the custody of our castle and town of Carlisle and of the West March from the second day of August last past, we order you that to our same cousin you should cause to be paid from our treasure for the duration of the said time…

I skipped down the detail of payments.

Given under our privy seal at Westminster on the 31st day of October the first year of our reign.

'I see, my lord,' I addressed the Earl, 'that my cousin Henry made you Warden of the West March and handed over Carlisle to you in August, under his seal of the Duke of Lancaster. Before he was crowned King. Could he do that, as Duke of Lancaster, when the crown and the disposition of the March still belonged to Richard?'

The Earl had no hesitation in his reply. 'Clearly he decided that he could.'

So Lancaster was already usurping sovereign power. Such a grant was assuredly disempowering Richard long before his crown was taken from him. Harry placed a warning hand on my arm as he felt me shift beside him, but I shook it off. I might accept the Earl's becoming Constable of England. He was well fitted to be so. But this. This incriminating date thickened the atmosphere in the chamber.

'He bought you, didn't he?' I accused. 'He bought you twice over. Once with the position of Constable, but long before that when he did not have the power to make this promise, when it was not within the scope of his authority. You knew what Lancaster intended from the very begin-ning, even as he took the oath at Doncaster. He never intended to keep it, to stand aside for any man with a better claim to be King, as you knew full well. And you made Percy support conditional. Of course you did. You accepted Lancaster's grant and condoned the audacious assumption of royal prerogative, to protect your family interests against the Nevilles and tighten your grip on the March. It was all signed and sealed long before Richard even returned from Ireland.'

The Earl was suavely confident in his response. 'I'll make no apology. I took what was on offer.'

'You knew that he would break that foolery of an oath!'

'And you were unaware of what Lancaster intended? You are not so naive, Elizabeth.'

'Is it naivety to believe that he should not be King? No wonder you were at the forefront in helping to get Richard securely into Henry's hands at Conwy Castle. I knew you were self-serving, my lord, but to be tight-knit with him from the beginning when you knew he had not the right... You told him you had a price at Doncaster. By God he paid it, and your hands are smeared with filth.'

'Enough, Elizabeth.'

'It is not nearly enough. It was all deceit and double-dealing, all empty, broken promises, which you condoned. And you expect me to accept it, because it has worked out so well for Percy supremacy.'

I was on my feet, finding it impossible to sit, when the Earl leaned across the rolls, all but spitting out the words.

'You will be quick enough to accept when you benefit from our power. When Harry steps into my shoes, you will be indeed Queen of the North, with no one to challenge it.'

He knew well the road to take to appeal to my ambitions, for myself as a Percy wife, and for my Mortimer connections, but I would not be distracted.

'Your son is as deceitful as his father,' I retaliated. Perhaps Harry's possible perfidy hurt more than all else.

Oh, I had accepted that there had been true justification for Lancaster's return to England, but the promises he had made on oath that day had been as ephemeral as cobwebs, dispersed in a gale. There never would be a worthier King in his mind. Lancaster had intended to seize the throne from the very beginning; the Earl had taken the payment for his allegiance long before Lancaster was King. All this incriminating document did was ratify our involvement after the event. And Harry? Had he known? Had his talk of a Mortimer King been as empty as his father's?

As if reading my mind, Worcester said gently: 'There never was any thought of the Earl of March taking Richard's crown, Elizabeth. Who would have supported him? Lancaster had the power and the opportunity, as well as the will of the great magnates of the land behind him. The barrenness of Lancaster's oath is irrelevant. It served its purpose in winning men to his side. The crown marked his victory, and we are beneficiaries.'

The smooth argument of a man of law. Without an excuse I left them, distancing myself as far as possible, climbing the steps to the wall-walk on the barbican where we had once stood to look out over the extent of the March. I turned full circle. Our power over these lands, as far as the eye could see and beyond, was so much stronger but the Mortimers had been betrayed.

I had no wish to talk to Harry.

Except that he followed me. I heard his footsteps, saw the swirl of his hair emerging above the stonework.

'Did you know?' I demanded even before he had climbed to be on a level with me.

'Of the agreement, no. That was between my father and Lancaster.' He had the sense to keep his distance from me, instead hitching himself to a seat between two of the crenels.

It was some consolation, but barely enough.

'It is not just.'

'No, it is not.'

His acceptance merely stoked my anger. 'So all ends are neatly tied. You will rule the north and stand at Lancaster's side.' I could not name him King at that moment. 'The Percy name is polished into brilliance.'

'It is and we will do the work well. I'm sorry that all this disturbs you.' He turned his head, squinting at me in the low sunlight. 'I am sorry that you scowl at me.'

I made to walk past him, although where I could take refuge I had no idea, except that he slid from his seat and caught my arm.

'I don't necessarily turn a blind eye to what Lancaster did.'

'No? You're the only Percy hereabouts who does not!'

'Let me speak.' His voice had sharpened. 'I don't sanction it. My father does, even my uncle, but I don't. I think that a sacred oath should be kept. I think that the wrong King has been crowned. But we can do nothing to change that. I acknowledge what is just and right for your family, Elizabeth, but as my uncle said – it was never a possibility.'

'It was our support that made it possible. There you were, bowing and scraping before him as soon as he had landed. And your father sold his soul for the power it would give him. Did you enjoy being kingmakers? Now you have the royal House of Lancaster eating out of your hand. The royal Lancaster arse is resting on a Percy cushion. And you will enjoy the proceeds.'

'So will you. So will our children.'

I thought of my son Hal, inheritor of all this power and prestige.

'Yes. I know that. That makes it so much worse. And I am ashamed.'

'You will forgive me if I cannot share that shame. We did what needed to be done.'

'God forgive you for it.'

I tugged my wrist from his hold and left him to survey the

rewards of his treachery. Harry had driven a wedge between us, for which I could not readily forgive him. My heart was a lead weight in my chest, and there was no one to whom I could unburden my disappointment.

Chapter Seven

Alnwick Castle: February 1400

I had a premonition as soon as Harry turned in my direction. Perhaps it was in the set of his shoulders as he walked across the bailey from the gatehouse where he had exchanged words with a courier in Lancastrian livery. His steps were slower than they might have been if it were good news, his head bowed in thought. Despite our estrangement I walked to meet with him in the centre of the space. My premonition suggested that this could set us all aflame.

'There is a burden on your soul,' I said. Now that he was closer I could see the cleft between his brows.

'Perhaps.' The cleft grew deeper, becoming more akin to a trench.

'Can I guess?' I asked. I could think of only one event to reduce him to morose introspection.

'Richard is dead.'

An unadorned pronouncement of the end of the man who had been King. Had we been expecting it? I could not claim to be baffled by the news, yet still it was there, like the shock of a bee-sting to the wrist when collecting lavender. In some strange manner, seeing Richard a prisoner in Westminster Hall, without respect, without freedom, had moved me more.

I could accept that his suffering – for without doubt he had suffered the blow against his royal dignity – was now at an end.

'Where?' I asked.

'Pontefract.'

'How?'

'They say that he refused food and starved himself to death.'

My frown matched Harry's. Surely Richard deserved more than this bleak catechism but we seemed to be locked into it, unwilling to open the floodgate for emotion to taint the air around us. I imagined that Harry would not be without some level of regret while I felt that sharp severing of the cousinly bond. I remembered Richard, so lost and alone, his future so unclear. Now it had been decided for all time. But was it by his own choice?

'I doubt it,' I replied. 'What is Lancaster saying?'

'That it is unfortunate that Richard found the need to curtail his own life.'

My thoughts turned bitter as unripe sloes. So Richard was dead, an astonishingly fortuitous event, removing from Lancaster a serious source of opposition, the man who had the one claim to be the God-anointed King. Richard was no longer alive to provide a figurehead for insurrection. It would solve many problems for the usurper.

I surveyed Harry who was simply standing, regarding the distant courier who had remounted and was about to leave. Between us, in so short a time, another wall had been erected by this death. A wall which at present neither one of us was prepared to scale.

'Does anyone believe it?' I asked.

'The cause, or the event itself?' He did not look at me.

'Not the event. Lancaster will be quick to bring the body

to London, on show to prove his sad demise.' Poor Isabelle, who would never see her heroic Richard again unless it were in a coffin. 'I meant the cause.'

Harry shook his head; we were in agreement on this point. As tenacious as he was of his own honour, Richard would have clung to life and fought to have his crown restored. His death must be put at Lancaster's door.

A silence had fallen between us.

'I thought you would wish to know,' Harry said eventually. 'Before you hear it from servants' gossip.'

'Yes. Thank you.'

He turned to walk away, then stopped. Now he looked at me, deliberately, directly.

'Do you want my advice, Elizabeth?'

'Do I?'

'No, but I'll give it anyway. I know that for you Richard's death will further open up the whole question of who should rule. You cannot even pretend that Richard might, by some miracle, be restored. Don't allow your Mortimer ambitions to take control. It could be dangerous. It could be catastrophic.'

'My Mortimer ambitions are already alive and well,' I responded.

'That is what I am afraid of.'

Alone, I worried at it, as I would worry over a length of knotted embroidery thread until all was smooth, fearing all the time that nothing would ever be smooth again. I felt sorrow over Richard's fate. More than sorrow. He was of my own blood, my own heritage, my mother's cousin, although my own life had never run along a close path with his. Did I regret his death? Yes, but I would never revere Richard. He had been as savage as any man in his anger, as Philippa had discovered with Arundel's brutal death.

But grief at the death of my royal cousin was not my overriding emotion.

A grim acceptance was all I could manage, as I determined to light candles for Richard's soul; his death had turned for England, and for me, a whole new page that was yet unwritten. Who would do the writing there, and what would be recorded? With Richard dead, and thus no hope of his restoration, the Earl of March should without question take the crown. My dedication to my nephew's cause, already whipped into life when Lancaster had the crown placed on his own head, had with Richard's death become embedded in rock, as solid as one of Alnwick's great towers, a formidable bulwark against any siege. If Harry thought to win me round, he would discover that I was equally impregnable.

As Harry disappeared into the distant barbican, all I could envisage in the coming weeks was hot dispute. Troubled at the potential for clash and division, I turned towards my family and took myself to discover Bess where I could hear her with Dame Hawisia in the herbarium. Dame Hawisia, skilled with cures and potions, was a Percy through and through, of some ancient lineage, and now of advanced age. Already ensconced here at Alnwick when I had arrived as a child, her loyalties were to Harry and Harry alone, which I had long accepted. A law unto herself, she ruled the nursery with a rod of iron and a cunning tongue.

My daughter was being instructed in the properties of the herbs most frequently in use to augment dishes and soothe all manner of ills. I thought it too cold to dwell long, when the herbs were in winter starkness, but, well wrapped in hood and cloak against the cold, Bess was laughing; Hawisia was scolding, wielding a knife against a tough rosemary stem. It warmed my heart when Bess ran to me, dragging me into her lesson, a sprig of pungent juniper in her hand, its berries dark with immeasurable power for those who could make use of them.

'Dame Hawisia says to drink these berries in red wine will stop poison from killing us,' she announced. 'But we must pound them first.'

She made me smile, banishing for a little while my melancholy. 'I doubt we'll have much need of that. Not much poison around here.'

'It will also stop the flux,' she informed me with solemn relish. 'Tom in the stable had the flux last week, until Dame Hawisia dosed him. He swore at her.'

'Then we must pray for Tom's soul. Tincture of juniper is a good remedy to know.' I enjoyed her enthusiasm. 'Dame Hawisia will show you how to make it.'

Bess ran off to pester Dame Hawisia. She would make a good wife for a great magnate at some distant date in the future. Seeing no insecurity here, my heart settled a little and for a time Richard's death was set aside, allowing me to step into more tranquil pathways. But not for long.

So Richard was dead and the Percy lords flourished in reflected Lancaster glory, even as we slid with much rain and high winds from old year into new. To my utter disgust, my Mortimer nephew's claim to the throne remained merely a simmering pot pushed to the back of the hearth, ignored by all. But not quite all. I should have expected one source of interest in our household.

'Mother.' Hal was standing at my side on the raised dais in the great hall, fresh from the practice field, wanting information.

'You are filthy,' I observed, keeping my distance. I was

dressed to welcome a delegation of Percy allies, my embroidered damask incompatible with dust and sweat and other unrecognisable substances.

'I know. But will I be King of England one day? Is it my right to be so?'

It took me aback, this question that I had not foreseen; that needed some careful thought. And a gently worded reply for so young a boy. I beckoned.

'Sit there,' I said, watching him take his place in the great armed chair that the Earl or Harry used to overawe the tenants. I pulled a stool to sit next to him as he shuffled into place, thinking that my decision had not been of the best. The chair would need a thorough clean. 'Who told you that?'

'Dame Hawisia. Is it true?'

'What did she tell you?' I asked.

Hal's eyes were bright as his father's might be when faced with some conundrum. 'My grandmother Philippa of Clarence was the daughter of the old King Edward. I knew that. But Dame Hawisia told me that I now can claim the crown. Because King Richard is dead, I should be next.' He thought for a moment, grasping for the facts. 'Because my grandmother was the daughter of King Edward's second son.'

Sighing silently I answered plainly. 'You have your grandmother's royal blood, but the claim is not yours. It belongs to your cousin Edmund of March.'

'Why?'

'Because –' how to explain – 'because Edmund's father, your uncle Roger who died in Ireland, had a stronger claim than I do.'

'Because he is a man.'

'Yes.'

Hal thought again, rubbing the carved lion on the chair. 'If my cousins Edmund and Roger died, would I then be King?'

Dame Hawisia had been unconscionably chatty.

'No. It would be your uncle Sir Edmund Mortimer.'

'Oh.' He studied my face. 'So Dame Hawisia is wrong.'

'Yes.'

He considered again. 'I am a Percy.'

Such pride. 'But you are a Mortimer as well as a Percy.' I too had my pride. 'Do you mind not being King?'

Another long consideration. 'No. I will be Earl of Northumberland one day and ride against the Scots, as my father does.' He looked at me under his lashes. 'You did not mind me asking?'

'No. I should have told you.' I ruffled his hair, laughing as he ducked his head. 'But now you should go and tell the sergeant at arms that you have returned to your lessons. And you will ask pardon for your absence.'

He stood and bowed. 'Yes, madam.' Then ran to the door.

But at the door he stopped and shouted.

'Do I tell Dame Hawisia that she was wrong?'

'No, I will.'

Just for the blink of an eye, I saw the defiance in him that he had inherited from his father; he would be more than pleased to inform Dame Hawisia of her twisting of the truth, until he read my raised brows, bowed and ran. Leaving me to decide: how much do I tell him? Certainly Hal was of an age to know the power of his descent from the Mortimers, and why Lancaster's claim to the throne was false.

Smiling a little, sending for a servant to clean the chair, I remembered my mother, Philippa of Clarence. It was she who had laid the foundations of my Mortimer ambitions, instructing me in the power of my Plantagenet royal blood, instilling in me her own importance as only child of King Edward's second son Lionel. Explaining that we stood in line to the throne, in direct descent through her and her father Lionel, if ever aught happened to bring the line through Richard to an end.

'You will remember this,' she had declaimed, drawing me to sit within the curtains of her bed. Had she known that she was dying? I had not, but her words held a grave solemnity for me as a child of ten years. 'You will allow no one to persuade you that a woman's blood is inferior. If Richard dies without an heir, then your brother Roger should, by the legitimate laws of inheritance, succeed him. Do you understand? It is for you, Elizabeth, to keep this knowledge safe.'

I promised, and she had kissed me. It was the last conversation with her that I remembered. My mother had spoken with a conviction that I must hold fast, for she addressed me as if I were full-grown. It would be a slight on my mother's memory, on her fervour, on her final wish as death approached, to deny her birthright.

But Hal was still young and deserved to enjoy the excitement of learning to wield a sword without being burdened by thoughts of whom he would wield it against, of whose blood would stain the blade. Nor did I like interference from the household, even though this busy tongue had as much status as any Percy. Before the Percy guests arrived I sought out Dame Hawisia in her own domain in one of the distant towers where she sat surrounded by leather bags of herbs. I challenged her.

'It is not good that you plant in my son's mind that he should be King of England. It is not his right, as you know full well. It belongs to his cousin.'

Dame Hawisia scattered dried leaves of thyme on a piece

of old document and made patterns with her forefinger as she replied.

'I will tell him what I think he needs to know. If any mischance should befall your Mortimer nephews, my lady, then your Percy son should know that he stands very close. Your brother Sir Edmund has no son to inherit. And now that King Richard, God bless his tortured soul, is dead, how close does that make your son to wearing the crown?' Oh, she was sly. And well informed, not merely in potions and portents.

'*I* will tell him what he needs to know, Dame Hawisia. And when.'

'Yes, my lady.'

As she looked up, I saw in her eye that she would do as she wished. Any dictates from me were adeptly avoided. But I knew the way to curb her wilfulness.

'My lord Harry would not approve of your filling his heir's mind with dangerous doubts and dreams. Hal will be Earl of Northumberland. There is no doubt of that, and it will be enough for him. You would not want to risk Harry's displeasure.'

Dame Hawisia might be cunning but I could match her. Her eyes were hooded as she returned to her pattern-making. Harry's name would keep her silent and I would be the one to decide when Hal should know more of the complications of England's inheritance, a complication that was becoming increasingly bloody. For barely had we celebrated the birth of the Christ Child than the country had been cast into a ferment with a plot to wipe out King and heirs and restore Richard, before his tragic death, to his rightful throne.

The Revolt of the Earls, plotted for the great tournament at Windsor on the Feast of the Epiphany, was dispatched with speed and some bloodshed without our involvement, but its repercussions were cruel. Alianore's brother Thomas and her uncle John Holland, both heavily involved, were removed from this life by an axe. Constance's husband Thomas Despenser also lost his title and then his head. Constance, forcefully widowed, would not, I imagined, be regarding King Henry with any degree of cousinly warmth. Nor would Alianore, who had never had much to start with.

My own thoughts hummed with the intensity of a beehive in spring, and not a happy humming. Here was death doled out by Lancaster to those who had attempted to unseat him before he could establish his authority over the kingdom. How fast, how effective he had been in crushing those who dared plot and scheme. It was a warning of the dangers for those who dabbled in treason. It should be a warning for me. For one of the few times in my life, my head ached with the circling vortex of right and legitimacy, driving me to resort to Dame Hawisia's infamous tincture of pennyroyal, harsh on the tongue but soothing to the senses.

Yet it did little to banish my megrims; there was no restoration of warmth between Harry and myself. The heady atmosphere that kept us company might have subsided from boil to simmer but Harry was unrepentant of his support for Lancaster and I was unwilling to make concessions. At best we avoided each other; at worst we enjoyed sharp exchanges, as now, where we were in the muniment room, Harry scratching his signature with an air of despondency.

'You have been prowling for the last half-hour,' he said.

'I cannot sit.' Yet I stopped in front of him. He was signing documents appertaining to the East March. Without any pleasure. He would rather be riding round it but a bout of hostile weather had kept him at home.

Irritable, restless beyond measure, I riffled through the documents on which he was working, picking at the Percy seals until their wax edges crumbled and Harry slapped his hand down on them to deter me. I withdrew, but not far, contenting myself with scraping the dripped wax from the candle sconces and dropping it onto Harry's documents.

When he looked up at me, reprimand ripe on his tongue: 'I have a wish to see my two nephews,' I said.

'Why?'

'Because of this.' From my sleeve I took a sheet of parchment and held it out. I had received a letter, confirming my worst fears, and those of my sister by law.

'Who is it from?' Without taking it.

'Alianore.'

'Let me guess.' Now he threw down the pen and looked up. 'King Henry has invited the Mortimer lads to court. For some unspecified length of time.'

'Yes. I see it's no surprise to you either. Read it.'

I recalled our concerns at the coronation that my two nephews would remain royal wards but now under Lancaster's constant supervision, and here was the confirmation in Alianore's careful script that did not fully reveal the panic I knew she must be feeling. The death of her brother and uncle had shaken her.

The King has requested that Edmund and Roger should visit with him at Windsor, and it will not be a brief visit. Since the Revolt of the Earls, it seems to me that he sees shadows under every bed, in every corner. He has informed me that it is his intent that they be brought up with his own youngest sons, as befits their birth. I am allowed to keep the two girls, but my sons will be lost to me.

And then as an afterthought:

I pray that education is all he intends for my sons. How can I believe in his magnanimity to his own family when he was prepared to destroy his Holland connections, close as they are? I accept their treason, but the King's vengeance was excessive.

Can I refuse? Alianore had asked at Westminster.

'Can she refuse?' I asked Harry.

'She could. I'm not sure of the repercussions if she did. Henry might arrive on her doorstep with an armed escort to invite them in person.'

'Do we allow it?'

'We can't stop it, and it's probably too late anyway. Henry is their King with some distant cousinship. They are his wards. If anyone can intervene it is your brother Edmund, as head of the family in your nephew's minority. We have to trust in the King's high principles.'

'Ha!' I doubted that Edmund would remonstrate with Henry. As for the King... 'I have yet to see a man with high principles where his power is being threatened.'

'What is your brother Edmund saying?'

'Nothing that I am aware of.'

'Sensible man! And here's something you should know, since we are talking of principles and power. The King has given us partial control of the Mortimer finances.'

'Has he?' I think I sneered.

Harry fixed me with a level regard, clearly striving for patience. 'The King has given the finances into our care to stop them falling into the hands of any man who would use the money against him.'

Without doubt I sneered. 'So we have done remarkably well out of Lancaster's control over my nephews.'

'We have. Better that we should benefit than some. At least we'll not squander it, using it to hold the north in peace.'

I was driven to make another circuit of the room, principally to escape Harry's cold acceptance. By now Alianore's refusal of agreement to the visit was probably an irrelevance. My Mortimer nephews, their estates portioned between Lancaster's friends, their finance in Percy coffers, would already be ensconced with the royal offspring in Windsor Castle.

Again I stopped in front of my husband who had once more taken up his pen.

'I wish to see my nephews.'

'Tell Philippa to go. She is nearer to Windsor than we are by a good few miles.'

'Philippa says she is ailing.'

'Elizabeth...' Harry sighed, drawing the pen through his fingers, leaving smudges of ink and grunting when he observed it. 'They will be safe enough. They were as healthy as all young lads, and twice as annoying, last Easter when we saw them. They need some discipline and I expect they'll get it at Windsor. Your brother is too lax to take them on and it's time they were placed in some noble household. They will thrive as royal wards, I expect. And besides, you can't go. The roads will be awash.'

'Things have changed since last Easter.' I needed to assure myself that my brother's sons were still healthy and well treated. 'And the roads will be less awash by next week.'

'I doubt Henry will smother them in their beds.'

I leaned, my hands splayed on the desk, forcing him to look up at me.

'How do you know?'

'I don't. And neither do you.' And when I still held his gaze with mine, an unspoken weight between us: 'I know what you are thinking,' he said.

'And so you should.'

For here was the rub, as Harry knew as well as I. With Richard's demise, the way for a Mortimer heir had been effectively opened up. Except that Lancaster's fist, with Percy support, was even more securely wrapped around the crown. If Lancaster could obliterate Richard, what hope was there for two young boys now under his dominion, boys with the strongest claim since Richard was dead?

Harry thought for a moment.

'I doubt a child of nine years poses the same challenge to the King's authority that Richard did, a man who had already worn the crown. I doubt he'll harm the boys. Now stop interrupting me.' And as I marched to the door: 'I forbid you to travel all the way to London to pursue a problem that does not exist.'

'Forbid me? Will you lock me in the cheese cellar?'

'Don't tempt me.'

My worst fears had been stirred into hot life. It would be the simplest of tasks to remove two dangerous if youthful claims to the throne, and we would know nothing about it until it was done, as we had known nothing of Richard's demise by unknown means at Pontefract. Before I opened the door I stopped, and leaned with my back against it.

'You could escort me, of course.' I hoped that he would, even though it would be a chilly escort with Harry's present mood for company.

'I've more valuable demands on my time than to arrive on the King's newly brushed doorstep again. I was there last month when he called a parliament that had nothing better to do than discuss the possibility of an English invasion of Scotland. It was a waste of my resources in men and money. I'll not travel all that distance again to investigate if your nephews have improved their manners.'

He was packing rolls into a small travelling coffer, which gave me all the indication I needed.

'Where are you going?'

'To Bamburgh. To make sure they are still content with my new overlordship.'

'Why would they not be? They would not relish you with an army come to impose your will if they disobey.'

Harry ignored this. 'Do you want to come with me?'

'No.'

'Then you might restore your sweet temper while I am away.' Sometimes he had a tongue sharper than a honed sword.

'I doubt it.'

'So do I. I might find a need to extend my absence and visit the outlying Western March.'

'You will do as you please.'

Down in the bailey, he swung himself into the saddle. Since we proceeded to make our farewells at a distance of a tilting yard, thus lacking any intimacy, whether real or sham, it was not the happiest of partings.

Chapter Eight

I allowed him a day before I made my move. The Earl was at Carlisle. Worcester was at Westminster raising money for a beleaguered king who was discovering more opposition than he had expected. With no one to ask questions I ordered my coffers packed and an escort to be ready at dawn, gave a verbal message to our steward, whose mouth firmed in a line of disapproval, said my farewell to my children who failed to persuade me that they would wish to accompany me, and set out. First south, past the great fortress of Pontefract where Richard had been incarcerated and done to death, before heading west for the Welsh March.

If I was uneasy at Harry's reaction when he discovered what I was about to do, I was not prepared to admit it. I would think about that on my return when I must steel myself to make reparation. For now, for a little while, I would be Elizabeth Mortimer. As we approached the wild lands of the Welsh March, urging my mare into a gallop I rode the wind with none but my bland-eyed escort to overlook my actions or question the wisdom of such reprehensible behaviour in Lady Percy. I would be selfish and irresponsible. And I laughed aloud, wishing in that moment that Harry was with me so that we might ride together, tasting the heady brew of our love and this unexpected freedom from matters of power and conflict. Oh, I wished it so, that we could be drunk on the sweetness of the mew of the buzzard circling above, the glint of sunshine on my harness fittings. I wished that our thoughts could once more weave together, our love a thing of wonder rather than an obstacle to be skirted round as my will clashed with his. I wanted him to be here with me, to smile across at me, to touch my hand, to promise all things in compassion and desire.

But Harry was not with me. Compassion and desire had been subsumed under the demands of Percy and Mortimer hegemony. I imagined what he would say if I could magic him to my side.

'By the Rood, Elizabeth. Will you dabble in every pot like some old crone, muttering curses?'

Which made me laugh again, with visions of Dame Hawisia and her potion-making, but it brought me to my senses. My days of selfish irresponsibility were long gone.

I slowed to a sedate pace, savouring the slopes and summits of the welcoming hills, for I had lived at Ludlow even after my marriage to Harry, not being of an age to take on the physical responsibilities of marriage and there being no Percy lady at Alnwick to undertake my upbringing. Then all had changed, within a year tragedy striking our household when my mother died, followed by my father within the next twelvemonth. At the age of ten years it was considered of value for me to go and live with my new family in the north. Now I was twenty-nine years old, with much experience beneath my girdle, mistress of the Percy households, and at odds with the Percy heir.

Which cast the cloak of duty once more over my shoulders, and as I came within the walls of Ludlow Castle, despite the warmth of familiarity, the anxieties that had set me on this course returned four-fold. My freedom had been short-lived indeed. I too doubted that Lancaster would wilfully do away with the boys, but I needed to show him that there was at least one Mortimer who had an interest in their welfare. Since Harry could not be moved, I knew perfectly where I needed to come for help; my younger brother Sir Edmund Mortimer, the most powerful of the Mortimer family in the minority of our nephew. Here he was, come to accompany me across the outer bailey to the inner gate.

'Did I know you were coming, Elizabeth?' my brother asked with speculative appraisal of me and my impressively armed retinue. His smile held a weight of suspicion.

'No.'

'Is Harry not with you?'

'As you see.'

Sliding to my feet, escaping from a cursory embrace, I wasted no time in words of polite queries after his health. 'Have you any commitments for your time over the coming days that can't be put off?'

'I always have commitments. The Welsh are always a nuisance, and becoming increasingly so.' His eyes narrowed a little. 'Why?'

'I want you to escort me to Windsor.'

'God's Blood, Elizabeth!'

Enjoying this caustic reuniting, I smiled at my younger brother, for his own sake and because he reminded me of Roger who was dead. Handsome and affable, dark-haired and dark-eyed as all Mortimers, he would prove to be good company when I had won him round. Brave in battle, if sometimes rash, Edmund was cut from the same rich cloth as Harry, skilled in the use of arms. I reached up to kiss his cheek, for he had the height of the Mortimers.

'Does that mean you are not willing?' I tucked my hand within his arm, encouraging him to walk from the inner bailey into the privacy of the living accommodations, appreciating the solid feel of him beneath the smart houppelande with its full sleeves gathered into embroidered cuffs. Edmund had as much an eye for the fashion of the day as had Richard, extravagantly toed shoes and all.

'You look exceptionally well escorted without me. The Percy lion will give any band of brigands pause for thought. And now that your family is in the ascendant, shining as brightly as the stars, who will waylay you?'

'That is indeed true,' I agreed, ignoring the cynicism. 'The wages for our loyalty to a Lancaster King are mighty. But I want you to come with me. I think I might need your authority as head of the Mortimer family. It will give my request some level of substance.'

We had made our way into the great hall, and from there to the great chamber and its associated rooms, the work of our Mortimer ancestor, the first Earl, before he had met such an unfortunate traitor's death. Without doubt he had an eye to comfort in these spacious rooms, which looked tidy enough but more sparsely furnished than I recalled, perhaps lacking a woman's touch. 'Have you no thought for a wife yet, Edmund? It's time you were wed.'

'Which has nothing to do with your visit.' The grip of his hand demanded my attention. 'Does Harry actually know you are here?'

I hedged. 'He knows my intentions.'

'Ah, but he doesn't know that you are here. I don't want him coming after me with sword and lance. Even his tongue has an edge.'

'I will abjure you of all blame,' I assured him.

'So let me guess,' Edmund said as he relieved me of my cloak and hood, sending the steward for ale to wash away the dust of travel, while I sank onto a cushioned stool with a sigh of appreciation for a seat that did not move. 'It is your intent to see nephews Edmund and Roger.'

'Of course. Alianore is anxious.'

'Why? They're safe enough. Alianore is always anxious.'

'Alianore is grieving the loss of her brother and uncle,' I remonstrated. 'And how do you know they are safe?'

'Why wouldn't they be?'

'No one seems to have any concern for this sudden change in their arrangements.' I saw the slide of what I might have thought to be guilt as he turned to take the cups and flagon from the servant. 'I know that they would soon be taken into a noble household to polish their manners, but this is different. This is Lancaster, following his own devious policies, whatever they might be.' I saw Edmund brace himself to reply, and touched his wrist as he approached with the cup. 'Just take me to Windsor and exert your Mortimer charm. I need some peace of mind, even if you do not. It astonishes me that you should have allowed it to happen without any remonstrance. Why could they not stay here, under your jurisdiction? They can learn chivalry and good manners and military skills from you as well as anywhere else.'

'They can't, because the King ordered that, as royal wards, they should not. He said they should be under his authority.'

'Exactly.' I took the cup of ale and sipped, enjoying the fine brewing. 'Richard was under his authority too, and look what happened to him. And I don't like it. Now take me to Windsor.'

Edmund decided, through long practice, not to argue.

While we travelled I learned of Edmund's adventures over the past months. He was familiarly loquacious, comfortable in explaining his change in loyalties. They did not surprise me. He would always take the expedient route to solidify Mortimer power, and indeed I could not take him to task for it. It was not easy territory to hold against Welsh and border raiders but Edmund made allies where he could and kept a formidable band of retainers to deter those who were not open to friendly gestures. On Roger's death it was Edmund who had taken on the mantle of Mortimer leadership until our nephew was of an age to do it himself. Not without lands of his own, his admiration of our tragically killed brother made him more than willing to take on the protection of the Welsh March. Still unmarried, he was without heirs so that I chivvied him again about a possible bride.

'There is no haste,' he said. 'I am not burdened by years.'

'So I see by your taste in garments,' I said, running my hand down the sleeve of rich wool, doubtless woven from his own sheep and dyed an eye-catching viridian, which would certainly take the eye at King Henry's court. 'But life can be short,' I added. Our brother, our parents, had all died young, not one of them with more than thirty years to their name.

'I will live a long and happy life. Did the signs at my birth not predict it?'

There had indeed been strange portents, although I had no recollection of our father's stables running with blood so deep that the horses splashed through it up to their hocks. I did not know what my mother had made of it all on the birth of this child, when the scabbards of swords and daggers filled with blood and axes turned red. All foretold the future of an eminent soldier, in Edmund's mind, when only a dagger tucked into his cradle within the coverlet would halt his howls as a restless babe.

'So to ensure a long and happy life, I suppose you threw in your lot with Lancaster at the earliest opportunity,' I remarked.

His reply was irritatingly unemphatic. 'I saw no reason not to. No different from you in the north, leaping to join his banner. You marched all the way to Doncaster; I only had to go as far as Hereford. I joined the Bishop of Hereford there, in bending the knee. Lancaster was inclined to be gracious, as he would be since Richard still wore the crown and Lancaster needed all the help he could get.'

I pulled my mount to a standstill to take a breath after a long uphill stretch. 'Why did you do it, Edmund? Surely you of all people should have had our family interests at heart.'

He replied with a little heat and in some detail, such that I turned my head to watch the play of discontent that enlivened his features, adding years with lines between his brows, indenting the corners of his usually smiling mouth.

'Don't lecture me about substantive Mortimer claims, Elizabeth.' He made a brisk gesture with the flat of his hand as I opened my mouth to do just that. 'I agree. I agree with you about right and legitimacy, but Edmund's too young and I've no mind to be regent until he comes of age. I've other worries chasing me from morn till night. There are rumours of insurrection in Wales. Were you aware of that? Owain Glyn Dwr is considering himself to be worthy of the title Prince, and aims to extend his arm over the whole of the province. We'll have incursions into the March as soon as the weather improves. I'll wager my manor in Dorset on it. What would young Edmund do about that, if he were King? Our new King Henry will give stronger resistance than Richard ever did, and I'll fight at his side to keep these marcher lands safe. With Richard we may as well have handed them over and saved ourselves the bloodshed. Look how bad it was in Ireland. Lancaster, on the other hand, won't give in without a fight. It would be a foolish man who chose the Earl of March over Lancaster who is experienced and already blooded in battle.'

That it was all true made me feel no better about it. Lancaster enjoyed an exemplary reputation. Yet still I was reluctant to give his argument weight. Surely right and justice mattered. If kingship did not rest on true inheritance, then the whole structure could be destroyed overnight. Of course I realised the futility of such an argument, the sheer emptiness, for Richard had been the true King. He should never have been deposed. But Richard was dead, and the claim of a Mortimer King must always take precedence over Lancaster.

Edmund must have seen the consternation writ large in my expression. 'Let it be, Elizabeth. Forget right and justice. Enjoy the peace and the power as long as it lasts under our Blessed King Henry, long may he reign.'

'I can't forget it. It smacks of cowardice to do so. And I doubt there'll be much peace in the north. The Scots take every opportunity to breathe down our necks.'

'And the Percy dragon does not breathe back? I swear there is never peace where the Percy family is involved.' Edmund leaned, grasped my bridle, and pulled my horse on into a brisk walk, our escort following at a discreet distance. 'Now tell me about my nephew and niece. It is a constant source of astonishment that you and Harry ever had a chance to conceive them.'

I knew what he meant. Harry's absence was legendary, yet he had miraculously found enough time to spend with me to father a son and a daughter, conceived in the gaps between his gracing a goodwill mission for King Richard to Cyprus, his appointment as Governor of Bordeaux, leading raiding parties from Calais and raising the siege of Brest in company with his uncle Worcester. When not engaged in warfare, he went in company with my cousin Henry, then still the Lancaster heir, to flex his restless muscles on the tournament field at St Inglevert where their exploits became the talk of Europe. It had been a relief to me, and a delight, when he was appointed Warden of the East March and Governor of Berwick. At least the latter two placed him somewhere in my vicinity at Alnwick, or within the possibility of my visiting him, which Cyprus did not.

So for the next few miles, content to be deflected into less abrasive conversation for a little time at least, I told Edmund of our son Hal, for whom Harry was planning a future as a great knight, and our daughter Bess, who would one day be much sought after as a bride with her Percy and Plantagenet lineage. They were the joys of my life when Harry was not at home to distract me.

Of late there had been altogether too much distraction.

Windsor enveloped us in luxurious accommodations, although I noted the heightened defences at gate and wall after the abortive threat at the Epiphany. The guards were watchful and doubled in numbers. To my regret King Henry was not present.

There was no need to call on Edmund's familial authority. Our nephews Edmund and Roger were presented to us without delay for our inspection, in the apartments set aside for John and Humphrey, the younger of the royal sons. The young Mortimers were well fed, well clad and growing like young colts. Moreover they were acquiring the polish of royal manners too, as they bowed their greetings with some flamboyance not always evident in the March.

'I told you I would not be an asset to this journey,' my brother muttered, returning the bow, running an eye over his nephews, then leaving me to make of the visit what I could while he hunted out some refreshment and congenial company.

'Are you comfortable living here?' I asked, wondering how best to get the information I required.

'Yes, madam.' There were no doubts to be read in Edmund's spritely demeanour. 'I am learning to use my sword. I practise with John, the King's son. He is more skilled than I but says that I improve every day.'

'I have a new hound,' Roger added, 'called Rollo. My lord the King says that he will give me a horse of my own, when I have grown as high as this.' He spread his fingers a hand span above his head.

Nothing wrong with Roger either.

'I hope that you are still learning to read and write,' I asked, encouraged against my will.

'Yes, madam. After Mass, every morning.' Edmund was adamant, if unenthusiastic.

'Are you free to ride out from the castle?'

'Yes, madam. Yesterday we took the hawks out along the river.'

'Are you guarded?' I tried.

Edmund's brow wrinkled as he considered. 'We always have an escort, and servants to do our bidding.'

'Are your doors locked?'

Edmund glanced at Roger as if he could not see the reason for such a question. 'No, madam.' He looked as if he would rather be hawking now than being questioned by his aunt. After a few more desultory queries about their health and the quality of their freedom, they left me to return to the admired company of the two Princes John and Humphrey.

Edmund and I remained at Westminster for two nights, my own ears and eyes alert for any evidence of malpractice. There was none. Edmund fought with them in mock combat, encouraging their skills with sword and bow. There was no lock on their chamber door, or not one that was used. It was clear that the Mortimer youths were given the same consideration as the young Princes.

'What did you expect?' Edmund asked as we prepared finally to leave. 'Chained to a wall?'

I did not know what I expected, other than to be reassured that they were safe and without restraint.

'I don't fear for them here, Elizabeth,' as we turned our horses to the north. 'There are some who might make use of them.' For the first time I detected a shadow of unease in my brother. 'They are as safe here as they are in Ludlow or Wigmore. Perhaps safer.'

'Who do you suspect?'

'Best not to say.'

'But you will.' I bent an eye on him. 'Secrets were never a strong point with you.'

He smiled. 'Then I'll tell you what I fear, and you will not repeat it.' The smile had rapidly faded. 'There are some who would take every opportunity to be gained from espousing the Mortimer cause, merely to increase their own power. How better than to raise a rebellion in the Mortimer name, to use the lads for their own ends? I will not, but there are some who might.'

'Who?'

Edmund was surprisingly and maturely stern. 'You don't need me to tell you. It's close enough to home for you to detect the signs.'

He would say no more; much like Harry, Edmund was not one for enigmatic warnings so it worried me, but there was no point in my trying to move an immovable object.

There was much political wisdom in his warning, and it showed me a landscape that I had not given cognizance to. There might be some magnates who would find the boys of great value if they wished to remove Henry of Lancaster, magnates who might be even more dangerous to the future of my nephews, using them as pawns in the game of power that they would play out at the Royal Court. There was one close family that might see a Mortimer rebellion sliding perfectly into the pattern of their own ambitions.

I considered the three Yorkist cousins of ours: Edward of Aumale, Richard of Cambridge, Constance Despenser.

But that was not Edmund's meaning.

It's close enough to home for you to detect the signs.

The thought kept me company all the way to Alnwick after I had parted from Edmund. The lives of my nephews had suddenly taken on a major significance. There were power-hungry magnates far too close for comfort, who might be capable of more deceit than even I had given them credit for. As for what I had discovered at Windsor, many would say that my concerns should have been laid to rest but still I could not find comfort in Lancaster's protection of the boys. Yes, I could trust him not to allow the boys to fall into malignant hands, but he might still find it an advantage to not have them there at all. To remove two dangerous pawns might come well within his remit.

Now all must be shelved, for there was a Percy for me to face.

Alnwick Castle

If I expected the explosion that awaited me, I was not to be disappointed. My father by law, if he had been in residence, would have said that I deserved it. My brother had parted company with me, expressing similar sentiments. Now I had to face the wrath in full flow.

'In God's name, Elizabeth!'

At least my husband waited until we were out of earshot of most of the household. I had arrived home in the midst of a storm, to be welcomed by an even greater deluge of temper.

'I return home from Bamburgh, expecting to find you here, or at least at Warkworth if the mood took you, only to discover a message with my steward that you had gone to visit your brother in Ludlow. When did you ever find an urgent need to visit Edmund? And then when I sent a courier hot-foot, having more than a little concern for your whereabouts, they told me that you both had gone south. To Windsor. Of course you had. I should have known. Before God! Do you have to meddle at every opportunity?'

He was stripping me of my dripping cloak with ungentle hands.

'I was not meddling.'

'You were. There was no need for it.'

My hood was removed and shaken, spattering us both with water drops.

'As there was no need to send a courier to dog my steps,' I said with suitable calm, wiping the rain from my face, wishing my hair had not come loose from its pleats. Here was an occasion for dignity. 'I told you I wanted to see my nephews. You were unwilling to escort me. Edmund volunteered instead.'

'Offered his services, did he?' Harry's face exhibited scorn. 'I wager you berated him until he gave in.'

Which I did not deign with a reply.

'Do you even think that I would worry about you? That the weather would close in or a band of robbers descend on any passing traveller who wore a cloak as good as that one?'

He nudged it with his shoe, where he had cast it on the floor in a heap of damp fur and a jewelled clasp, value or no.

'I took an escort. Your livery would frighten off any self-respecting bandit. And now you know how I feel when you go off to battle. And I don't send a courier on your trail to spy on what you are doing. I recall Otterburn, Harry. Have you forgotten? Have you ever considered how anxious that made me, when you were taken prisoner and not released for a year?' I was tired and had fragile control over my temper. 'You thought your presence at Bamburgh was more important than my peace of mind. Were they delighted to see you?'

'No. Not noticeably. But they made me welcome because they could do no other. We had a brief discussion about improving the defences, which they reluctantly agreed to implement. I've put my own man in charge.' He took a breath. 'You are deflecting me from my righteous anger.'

'No, I am not. You obviously had a more satisfying out-come than I did.'

I sat down, wincing a little, uncomfortable in damp skirts.

'You deserve to be uncomfortable.' Harry did not retreat. 'So were the nephews in perfect health?'

'Yes.'

'Were they actually enjoying themselves?'

'Yes. And now I am tired.'

'And know as little as you did when you set out.'

'Yes.'

'How's brother Edmund?'

'Hand in fist with Lancaster. Like you.'

'Like any sensible man in the land. You can't blame him.' His temper was subsiding, but not by much. 'So what have you found out that gave you no contentment?'

'That my brother is of the same mind as you, and my nephews are happy enough, surrounded by hounds and horses and their royal cousins,' I admitted bitterly. 'And their manners were good. I should of course be gratified.'

'Was Henry there?'

'No. They thought he was at Eltham, but he was expected.' I paused, eyeing him, considering the effect if I allowed my tongue full rein. 'My brother Edmund said better the King to take care of them than some self-seeking magnate who would use them to increase his own power.'

'Did he now?' I had all Harry's attention. 'Like me, perhaps?'

'Like you. Or more like your father. A Mortimer King with a Percy as regent, through my blood connection, might suit the Earl very well.'

'Is that what you think? After all the trouble my father went to to get the crown for Lancaster?'

'I don't know. I don't know what I think.'

'Nor do I. You can't accuse us of supporting Lancaster in one breath, then intending to use the Mortimers against him in the next because you happen to be my wife. Or perhaps you can. It's woman's thinking and too complex for me.' He came to sit beside me. 'If I touch you, will you strike back?'

'Yes. I might. Lancaster has made them his wards, as we thought. They will remain under his jurisdiction, in whichever castle he chooses.'

The shadow of Richard and his death spread its wings over me again. If the boys ever became a threat to King Henry through the attentions of some ambitious lord, their lives would be worth nothing. Lancaster would not hesitate to rid himself of the threat.

'We can't change it,' Harry was saying. He had not touched me.

'We could try.'

'You are unrealistic and unreasonable.'

'As you have just said. I am a woman.'

'God preserve me from all difficult women. I swear you are my bed of nettles, Elizabeth.'

Which was as disparaging a verdict as I could ever recall.

There was no reconciliation between us.

Retiring to my rooms I chivvied my serving women, ordering up hot water and a bath, as if I could scour away the events of the last half-hour. I could not of course and my mood remained unsettled until, cleansed and dried, my hair combed free of tangles and anointed with a mix of dried rose petals, cloves, nutmeg and galangal, I wrote to my sister Philippa.

We are not dwelling in a paradise of love and esteem. Harry is vocal in his alliance with our treacherous cousin of Lancaster. The hopes for a Mortimer King are dead and buried. I am finding it hard to accept this so our exchanges have the quality of a saddler's bodkin.

I find myself wishing for the equable days when Richard wore the crown and Lancaster lurked in the courts of Europe, earning his living at the tournament.

I am sure that you would condemn me for so weak a betrayal of our own blood.

I retired alone to bed with no one to appreciate my perfumed hair.

Chapter Nine

Alnwick Castle: June 1400

Within a year of his being crowned, and after much careful planning that was not at all to the approval of the Earl of Northumberland and Sir Henry Percy, our new King Henry invaded Scotland. At Alnwick I bade Harry farewell as I had so many times before and prepared to watch as the Percy banners and retainers headed north in support of their King.

'Too much damned royal interference in our lands for my liking,' growled the Earl. 'To have the King camped hereabouts and planning new incursions tramples on our toes. We'll deal with the Scots to our own advantage without his beady eye on us.'

'God keep you and bring you home safe,' I said formally to Harry who was preparing to mount, interested that the Earl was already becoming jaundiced with this royal alliance.

He eyed me. 'I've had a warmer Godspeed.'

'I've had a more loyal husband.'

'If I die on the battlefield, you'll regret such a hostile farewell.'

'If you die on the battlefield I promise I will make amends when I kneel at your tomb. I have no portent of your demise.'

He kissed my cheek for form's sake. I watched him go,

my mind still furious with him and his betrayal, my heart beating with love for his departing figure.

Undoubtedly I loved him. As he disappeared in a cloud of dust, I recalled the early days when I did not, our paths crossing infrequently when Harry's brought him to the gates of Alnwick or to Warkworth. We exchanged greetings, asked after each other's health, gave gifts at New Year, supped together in the great hall, then he was invariably collecting his horse, his weapons and his retainers and was off again with a fleeting kiss to my cheek and a promise to be home soon, much as today. Our life was one of border warfare, the frequent raids into Scotland to seize land and livestock being fixed in Harry's lifeblood. I found myself a neglected bride with an absent husband.

When was it that I had decided I wanted more than this from Sir Henry Percy?

Oh, I recalled as if it were yesterday rather than the span of a dozen years, when he left me to go to Newcastle, directed there by the Earl because of an imminent threat from the forces of the Scottish Earl of Douglas. Helping him to shrug his way into a padded gambeson, I found myself thinking that I would rather be stripping it off him. It took much control not to curl my fingers into his hair before he crammed his helm onto it. I had grown up. I was seventeen years old.

So when did Sir Henry Percy decide that he had more than a passing liking for me, that I was more than just another young female in the Percy household?

I had no idea. Harry was not one for soul-searching nor for putting emotions into words unless it was impatience, when his diction became colourful. Thus the source of his love for me was an enigma. Action was more in his line than discussion and confession.

In the end it was all a matter of fate and some careful planning on my part after a lengthy absence that had filled me with fear and a physical desire that refused to be buried in daily routine. It was after the battle of Otterburn that resulted in Harry's being taken prisoner in a clash of forces that went terribly wrong, resulting in a long year of worry until I would see him again. Harry's younger brother Ralph had been returned to us speedily because of the state of his thigh wound, but Harry had to wait for the princely sum of three thousand pounds to be spent on his restoration, raised by the Earl to recover his beloved son and by King Richard who in those days valued Percy loyalty.

So Harry came home, to much rejoicing and ballad-making of Harry's fatal battle with the Earl of Douglas...

Percy wi' his guid braid sword that could sae sharply wound
Has cut the Douglas on the brow till he fell upon the ground.
The wound was deep, he fain would sleep right by the braken-tree
He has laid him doon a' wounded sair beside a lilye lee.

My heart rejoiced too as he dismounted, as healthy as he had been when he set off to do battle. Allowing the household to flock and welcome their long-lost son, I waited, feasting my eyes. He was all I recalled, heroically proportioned, as handsome as a fighting-cock in glossy plumage. His hair gleamed. So did his smile. I was awarded a kiss.

And I wanted him in my arms, in my bed.

'Elizabeth. You have grown. I swear you came only to my shoulder when I left.'

'You have been away many months.'

His eyes narrowed. 'You have grown more beautiful too.'

'Thank you.'

I was impatient. He was distracted. I followed him to his chamber, dismissing his servants. I sat on his bed, hands demurely clasped.

'Did you want me for something?'

'I have come to renew my acquaintance with you,' I said.

'Well, here I am. What have you been doing?' he asked, attention fixed on unbuckling his brigandine.

'Waiting.'

He looked up sharply. 'Waiting for what?'

'You.'

'And?'

'To become your wife.'

He tilted his head. 'You were shy when I left, as I recall.'

'Not shy. Perhaps I did not know my own mind well enough.'

'And you do now.'

'Indubitably.'

A crease appeared between his brows. 'How old are you?'

'Eighteen years. You should know that.'

'I should?'

'Yes. I am Elizabeth Mortimer and your wife in name only.'

His gaze was arrested, taking me in from my neat coif to my shoes, and all in between. I had dressed particularly carefully. Had I not had a year to consider it?

'Then, wife in name only, come and be my squire.'

I pushed myself to my feet to help with loops and latches and difficult buckles, all with the usual coating of dust.

'Were you badly injured in the battle?' I asked lightly. I had found that my hands were not as steady as I would have wished.

'A mass of cuts and bruises. Nothing like Ralph.'

144

'Who is well recovered now. You, Harry, look sleek and well tended.'

'I was made welcome by Sir John Montgomery at his manor at Eaglesham.'

'Were there no daughters in this household at Eaglesham,' I enquired dulcetly, 'to devote themselves to your needs?'

'No. I was the enemy.'

'A most attractive enemy.'

He glanced down at me, as I glanced up.

'You have acquired a flirtatious turn of phrase, wife.'

At last I did curl my fingers into his hair. While Harry gripped me by my shoulders and kissed my mouth in quite different mood from his greeting in the bailey.

'Have I neglected you?'

'On the whole… I was still catching my breath, my blood hot.

'It was *indubitably* wrong of me.'

'I think you will not neglect me today.'

'A forward wench.'

'I have been practising.'

His brows rose.

'In my mind, you understand.'

He found the need to kiss me again.

Then decided that I was the most effective squire he had ever had.

So I climbed into bed with the Northumberland heir. Behind the curtains with their rampant Percy lions, all was most satisfactory. Finding as much delight in me as I did in him, Harry's energies were prodigious.

'I am not a castle that needs to be besieged,' I observed when I could breathe again.

'Are you not?'

'I have capitulated. I will still have capitulated tomorrow and the next day.'

'Good. But a good commander always inspects the defences.'

His inspection made me laugh.

'I did not realise how fortunate I was to capture a Mortimer bride. I must stay at home more often.'

My heart swelled with love for him.

'I like this verse,' I said, singing softly against his hair.

Up then spake Lord Percy fair, and Oh but he spake hie
I am the lord o' this castle, my wife's the lady gay.
If thou'rt the lord o' this castle, sae weel it pleases me
For ere I cross the Border fells the ane o' us shall dee.

'I regret the end of Lord Douglas, but it is a relief to me that it was not you who died.'

'It is a relief to me too. You should know. I bear a charmed life.'

It seemed on that day that we had both been touched with the hand of some magic. How could such magic have become so tarnished?

I need not have expended any emotion whatsoever on Harry's fighting for his life against the Scots in some major battle, which illogically made me crosser than ever. By the autumn we were settled back into the usual round of petty squabbles and minor insurrections. King Henry's invasion of Scotland was abandoned, chiefly through his lack of money to pursue it and Scottish refusal to even consider King Henry's claim of overlordship. A minor clash at Fullhope Law brought an end to it, the Percy forces returning home with no significant losses and their banners in good form. The English invasion had become a fast retreat, leaving the borders once more under Percy supervision. So the King went home in a state of disgruntlement, while the Earl and Harry donned their authority as Wardens of the East and West March with more than a little self-satisfaction that the King was out of their hair.

Relieved I might be that Harry had returned with no significant injury, but he and I stalked around each other, my memories of marital magic pushed further into the distant past. We were not hostile, but coolly tentative. I sensed him watching me for a weakness in my armour. I refused to give him one.

'I rejoice in your return, my lord.' My outer mood was much as it had been when he left.

'Pleased to hear it.' Harry stood, legs braced, hands fisted on hips as if addressing a cohort of retainers. His eyes were keen on my face. 'Have you had cold weather here?'

'No. Why?'

I did not see the sharp wit being honed at my expense.

'It was the ice on your tongue, madam.'

'No, sir. It has been uncommonly warm!'

'So that accounts for it. Your welcome has the aridity of a drought.'

Nor to my chagrin did he give me a chance to retaliate, marching off to deal with some minor affair of horses and weapons. So the air in the Percy household remained chill.

Until letters arrived, delivered from the south, all three by the hand of the same courier. Two for me and one for Harry. I read the one from Alianore first since it promised more interest, being full of her thoughts, if tragic ones; her dis-satisfactions, her sons still domiciled at Windsor, her gnawing bitterness over the loss of her brother. But buried within the domestic minutiae was a nugget of information that I sensed would be more important. And probably dangerous. It had, I remembered, troubled Edmund who had seen this coming although I had barely considered it in my concern for the health of the Earl of March.

'There will be trouble in the Welsh March,' I said. Harry's head was bent over his own document.

We had not talked of it before. My thoughts had not been with Edmund's worries and Harry's vision was towards the north.

'I know,' he said. 'Owain Glyn Dwr, newly styled Prince of Wales.'

He held the letter out, as I held mine in exchange. Harry's letter, far more formal than mine and in a clerkly hand, bore the royal seal, but they had the same message, clear enough from the first line dictated by the King. Owain Glyn Dwr had proclaimed himself Prince of Wales, heralding imminent Welsh incursions into the March, the Welsh lord staking his claim for territory he considered to be his. The attacks had probably already begun. There would, I realised, be much stepping on Mortimer toes.

'Why is the King telling you?'

'Read on.'

So I did, my eyes stopping at, and rereading, the reason for this document being sent to Alnwick.

'Henry wants you,' I observed.

'Yes.'

Disillusion descended, thick as syrup from overripe cherries. 'What has he offered you this time, to tempt you to move your campaigning from north to west?'

'Read on again. Your regal cousin is feeling generous. Or desperate.'

So I did. It was a magnificent gesture. It was power. It was more than a worthy honour. Harry would become Justiciar of North Wales and Chester, exerting royal power in the King's name throughout the province. Strategic castles had been offered to him to enforce his authority: Chester, Flint, Conwy, Caernarfon and Beaumaris. They rolled silently over my tongue. Harry would have control of the county and lordship of Anglesey and the custody of the Mortimer lordship of Denbigh, perhaps in repayment for the crown taking back control of the Mortimer estates and finances which had recently occurred. Here was a debt that my Lancaster cousin was paying in full.

'What do you say?' Harry asked.

I did not hesitate, making no attempt to mask disdain. 'I say that you would be a fool to refuse this.' It was a monumental gift of power that the King had made, but then he saw the value of keeping the Percy lords compliant and effective in his name. 'Does this not win you entirely and for ever to the Lancaster cause?'

'It might. If I have enough money to achieve what he wants me to achieve. I have my doubts about the state of the royal coffers and parliament is not of a mind to be too open-handed. How will I pay for this bold strategy in the west? Out of my own pocket, I suppose, until the crown can raise the gold. But it's a gift I can enjoy, to extend royal authority into Wales. And I know the reputation of the Welsh lord Glyn Dwr well. He is a worthy opponent.' Harry was smiling. 'I'll enjoy crossing swords again with a fighter of such renown.'

He was already involved, envisioning campaigns and battles against the newly proclaimed Prince Owain Glyn Dwr. The Mortimer cause was sliding further and further into obscurity. Alianore was not wrong in her complaints that her sons had been forgotten.

Meanwhile Harry cast Alianore's letter from him. 'Does your sister always write at such length about nothing of interest?'

'Yes. I suppose that she does. If you accept the King's offer, it will take you from home for months at a time. The extent of your authority will be vast for one man.'

'Do you think I am incapable?'

'Never that. You'll have ridden round every castle within a week.'

'Have you read the final comment?'

I did so. If the arrangement of castles was a sign of King Henry's high regard, this was an incomparable honour. The young Prince Henry, Lancaster's heir, now of an age to don the royal cloak of leadership, had been placed under Harry's guidance.

'I am suitably impressed.'

'So am I. Let's hope he has a sure grasp of warfare.'

No. There would indeed be no support for Mortimer interests. Harry would have no time from cock-crow to owl-hoot to be other than servant to Lancaster and his heir. I tried not to acknowledge how much I would miss him.

'Will you miss me?' he asked.

I avoided his mischievous attempt to plant a kiss on my coif, taking a stool set some distance from him.

'Why would I not?'

'Because you still blame me – or the Earl, which comes to the same thing – for easing the crown onto Lancaster's brow.'

'Yes, I do.'

My eyes held his, intransigence as strong in him as it was in me. My heart was sore with it.

'Where are the days of our love gone?' he enquired mildly.

'They are mired in betrayal.'

'Or in Mortimer ambition. I didn't wed you for this, Elizabeth.'

'You wed me because your father told you to.'

'I see that this is a lost cause.'

'It can never be anything other.'

'Which makes me look forward to campaigning in Wales, away from domestic combat.'

This hurt more than all the rest. At last, Harry's glance dropped to the second letter on my lap. 'You haven't read it yet. It may give you some better news about something.'

'It will be from Philippa.'

It was her husband's seal, but easily recognisable. I broke the wax and unfolded it, to find two documents, one enclosed within the other, the outer one written, briefly, in a hand that I did not know. A clerk of Sir Thomas Poynings, I realised. A sudden sense of disquiet made me look first at that single sheet. I skimmed down, then dropped the letter to my lap where it lay with Philippa's own as yet unopened letter.

I looked up at Harry.

I must have uttered some sound of distress for he instantly abandoned the royal commands, covered the ground in three easy strides and dropped to his knees beside me, gathering my hands into the shelter of his as if we had never exchanged a cross word.

'Tell me,' he said.

What he had read in my face I had no idea. I felt cold, beyond any feeling at all. I could not speak, my throat gripped with pain.

'Your hands are freezing,' he said. 'I'll read it myself if you wish.'

'She is dead,' I said abruptly. 'Philippa is dead.'

'Oh, my dear girl.'

'I did not know.'

'You could not have guessed.'

'I knew that she was unwell, but not that it was a danger to her life. I thought that it was one of the fevers that afflicted her when she was a young child.' Guilt joined hands with the sorrow, that I had not taken more concern, instead casting it aside as Philippa trying to gain attention.

'Was she carrying a child?' Harry asked.

'I don't know. She was well enough at the coronation.'

No tears, no outer grief must be allowed or I would weep on his breast, but it was a hard task. My sister had lived no more than twenty-five years. It made my breath catch a little.

Upon which Harry was moved to take me into his arms. And I wept.

When he had dried my tears he said, 'Now you should read her final words. They may give you comfort.'

He left me. And so I did. The letter had in mind, I quickly realised, the letter that I had written to her, of my sorrow and acrimony with Harry.

To my most dear sister.

I have a need to write to you. I am unwell which is proving to be lowering to my spirits. Who is to say how many years are still to be numbered to my life?

Your letter troubled me. This is what I would say to you. I do not believe that you are aware of your own good fortune.

I have in my short span of years had three husbands to my name yet I have never known the joys and pangs of love. My marriages were not made for love, nor did it grow. I have never been fortunate to carry a child of my own, on whom to lavish the emotions of which I think I am capable. I need not tell you of the losses I have suffered. I have hopes of this marriage with Thomas, but my fears over my health are lively.

Will you take this advice from a sister who is younger than you and many would say had far less knowledge of life?

Knowing you as I do, I can imagine the strains in your own marriage. Do not, I beg of you, allow Mortimer ambitions to destroy the love that you have been so fortunate to discover. I envy you. I always have, for who could not? I would that Arundel had had such glamour as Sir Henry. Although his care for me was prodigious, the age difference of thirty years was difficult for us to bridge with anything other than a mild affection. Do not take your love lightly, Elizabeth. Do not allow the bold Hotspur to go to war under the cloud of your displeasure. How would you live with your loss if your last words to him were angry ones?

You are more fortunate than you know.

Tears were already making smudges on the page.

When I am restored to health again, you may forget my melancholy as a product of a bitter woman. Meanwhile I look to see you at court, when we can exchange gossip, despise Constance, and hope for better days.

Your loving but regretfully morose sister,

Philippa

Duly chastened, I sat with Philippa's words on my knee, absorbing her grief and disappointment at the lack of a child, at the lack of any marital tenderness other than respect.

I thought about Harry, about what was standing between us. My ambitions, as Philippa knew. My damnable Mortimer ambitions. Would they destroy our love? They would grind away at it if I allowed it, until there were no smooth edges. I could not expect Harry to compromise; it was not in his nature, but always to drive on towards his goal. He might have the glamour of which Philippa was envious, but he had a will forged for the old gods by Hephaestus with fire and iron.

I sighed.

Having everything Philippa had died wanting, I was risking all that she would have seized with both hands and rejoiced over. Acknowledging it, I knew what I must do, although I was no better at compromise than Harry. I must find him, make my peace with him. But it was Harry who returned to find me.

'Well?' He did not approach but stood beside the door, one hand still on the latch. I could feel his eyes searching my face and wished I was not so tear-stained.

'I'll not show you the letter,' I said. 'She was very unhappy. She would not want you to read it.'

'It is between the two of you. I'll not pry. Will she be brought back to Wigmore for burial?'

'No. It is Sir Thomas's wish that she be laid to rest at Boxgrove Priory.' I bore down on the regret that she would not be restored to past Mortimers. 'I have something to say to you. I would be pleased if you would listen.' Even though he angled his chin, I placed Philippa's letter on my stool and walked across the room to him. 'This has been ill-managed by me. I cannot ignore the rights of the Earl of March, but I should not have allowed them to drive a rift between us. I understand your reasons for being in alliance with Lancaster. I understand and I must accept that he is King because he was chosen to be so.'

Harry took my hands, and I allowed it, threading my fingers with his, smiling a little when he asked: 'Are you feeling quite well?'

'I am in excellent health. But listen. Philippa says that I am not aware of my good fortune. She is right, of course. It is so easy to accept the happiness that greets me at the beginning of every day. It is far too easy to take it for granted and I should not. I know now that it would be a terrible thing if I allowed our love to fade and die, or even to be hacked about through recriminations. If you decide that you no longer love me, it will not be on my head. So I would say this. I will not oppose you. But please remember sometimes that I have loyalties with which you might not agree.'

'I will remember.'

'And I am sorry for making you my enemy.'

'You are never my enemy. If you fall out of love for me, it will not be on my head.'

'So we are in agreement again.'

'It seems so.'

'The household will be relieved.'

He drew me into his arms and we stood together, absorbing the closeness which had been absent for so many weeks. His chin rested on my head.

'Do you miss your brothers?' I asked. He rarely spoke of Thomas and Ralph, both younger than he and both dead, Thomas more than a decade ago when fighting in Spain, Ralph who had survived the battle at Otterburn only to be laid low in Palestine little more than a year ago. Harry was the only surviving Percy son. No wonder that the Earl's eye rested on him with such pride and optimism, the one glittering gem in the Percy coronet.

'Yes.'

'You don't speak of them.'

'Which does not mean that I don't recall them with a severe sense of loss. As you will remember Philippa, even when you do not speak of her,' he said gently. Then, when I did not comment: 'I still have to go to Chester and the Welsh March.'

'That I know.'

'Our duty – Percy duty – is to the King and the realm.'

'I understand. Philippa says that I should never send you off to war without telling you that my love for you remains constant. I must not risk your dying without your being aware of it.'

'So now I am aware. But I will not die. I will return to you.'

'And I will thank God, even though I declaim hourly at your absence.'

'We have had enough declaiming for a se'nnight. Kiss me instead.'

So after a sweet reunion, Harry departed to be all things to King Henry in the Welsh March. I remained at Alnwick, crushed by the loss of my sister, but with the restoration of a lightness in my heart.

This would be Philippa's legacy.

Chapter Ten

Alnwick Castle: Late June 1402

When the appalling news arrived, disconcertingly from the west rather than the north, any serenity I had managed to stitch together since my sister's death was destroyed in a heartbeat. It was delivered by word of mouth, by a Mortimer courier, no one having time or foresight to write it down. I stood and listened, weighing every word, overlooking the need to ply the exhausted messenger with ale and food. The details of his telling, sparse as they were, made my skin creep with dismay.

'Repeat it,' I said, my heart constricted.

And he did. It made the news no better. It was shatteringly bad.

'Has the King been told?' I asked when all was at an end, and I discovered that my fingers had curled themselves into fists to beat off the flood of dismay. I straightened them, flattening my slick palms against my skirts as if such an action could assuage the pain. It could not. The pain would live with me into an unquantifiable future that I could not contemplate. I needed no lessons in England's hostilities to know that this catastrophe would require a miracle to resolve it.

'Yes, my lady. A messenger was sent. We believe he is at Berkhamsted.'

If I had expected news of a battle, it would have been from the north. We had been troubled by Scottish raids in both the East and the West March for the whole of that summer. Harry, no longer Justiciar of North Wales because it now suited King Henry to place the authority in Wales into the hands of the young Prince, supported by my brother Edmund and the rest of the marcher lords was restored again to his duties in the northern March, to deter the threat of an invading Scottish force.

'Do you regret it?' I had asked. 'Losing your authority in Wales?'

'Not so much as you'd think,' was all the reply I could extract from him. 'I like to see recompense for my efforts when I'm left to pay for them. There was precious little support or gold from King Henry.'

And that was all the explanation I could dig out of him.

Living in the saddle from one week to the next, Harry proceeded to collect another array of scars and abrasions. With the Earl also frequently absent in the March, mine was the ruling hand at Alnwick where I collected all the information I could, from couriers, from travelling merchants, from tattered groups of mummers with questionable skill, bent on earning their next meal. All enabled me to absorb the echoes of ripples throughout the realm.

All enabled me to worry constantly.

How I missed Philippa's letters. There would be no more confidences, no more moments of joy and reconciliation. No more insights of information and concern. Too young to die, now she was lost to me. Edmund and I were all that remained of Philippa of Clarence's royal children born and raised in the

Welsh March, an area that was undoubtedly in ferment with tales emerging of attacks sweeping down over the hills in the more than capable hands of Owain Glyn Dwr. Edmund would be girding his loins in support of King Henry, not reluctant to pit his wits and his strength against Glyn Dwr. By now he had an ally in Prince Hal who had proved to be more than capable of holding his own. At fifteen years he had blossomed under Harry's care, emerging as a born soldier. The Prince and Edmund and the other marcher lords would one day, when Glyn Dwr was defeated, hold the March in peace.

Such had been the meat in my daily gleanings. This new development was not what I had expected. It was nothing less than a disaster for my brother Edmund.

'Who has taken up the reins of the authority in the Welsh March?' I demanded.

The messenger shrugged. Of course he would not know. The young Prince might already be collecting a force to over-turn the disaster, if he was even half the youth that matched with Harry's description of a gifted commander in the making.

I dispatched the messenger, almost dead on his feet, to find sustenance while I sat alone for a handful of minutes to assess the extent of the disaster. There was nothing I could do except wait for Harry's return. Not that there was anything Harry could do in the circumstances, but I was in need of his advice. With this dire turn of events in the March, my brother's future was unfathomable. Even worse, I could do nothing to remedy it.

My throat thick with fear, I sent a messenger north to find Harry anyway.

By the time Harry returned to Alnwick, the Mortimer courier was long gone, and my anxiety had grown out of all proportion, but it was obvious that my own messenge had failed to hit its target. Harry was ignorant of the catastrophe. Harry was full of good humour as he and the Earl, together with the Scottish lord George Dunbar, turned renegade to fight under the Percy banner, rode in with their forces to make inroads into the ale I had provided.

Our retainers were in good heart. As the ale was passed around, the songs began. Raucous. Crude. Jocular. Soldiers, young and old, relieved at a safe return, revelling in what had obviously been a victory, now looking forward to a few days of food and drink and the telling of tales of courage and fear.

Once I had
Yellow locks, ringleted.
Now hair grey and sparse
Sprouts upon my head.

Removing his helm, one of our retainers upon whom the years were pressing hard, dug his fingers into his scalp, his hair flat and matted with sweat, as the rest joined in, repeating the sad loss of youth with ear-shattering enthusiasm. Until Harry took up the next verse, tunelessly it had to be said, but full of passion as he bemoaned in dramatic fashion, his fist hard against his heart:

I would like
Glossy plumage, raven-hued,
Not this bristle
Of sparse grizzled hair.

Harry's locks, far from grizzled, shone damply in the sun. His retainers lifted their cups in mock salute and ribald comment.

'Some've us have no need for raven hair.'

'Some've us do well enough with russet.'

How they loved him, revered him. They would follow him to the gates of hell if he asked it of them. I watched the faces of these outspoken men of the north. They were free with their complaint and denunciation, but their loyalty was beyond question for a man of the calibre of Hotspur. They would follow him and fight for him to the death. My heart, already under attack, was swollen with my love for him. Unexpected tears gathered like a fist in my throat.

'The Scots riffraff ran fast enough from Hotspur's bristle,' Harry's youngest squire added, bursting with pride.

'They didn't see yours, lad.' Harry clouted the lad's shoulder. 'They'd have fallen on their swords in despair if they had.'

The young squire, with barely a growth on his cheeks, flushed as he was buffeted by those around him. While, grinning, Harry launched into the last verse which we all knew well enough.

Courting is not for me,
For I beguile no girls.
Tonight my locks are grizzled
Not tangled yellow curls.

He knew I was standing behind him. He did not even turn when I placed my hand on his arm, but clipped me to him in a soldierly embrace. What point in worrying him with my news, for which there was no immediate remedy?

'What need have I to beguile girls?' he shouted to the fast-drinking crowd.

'You dare not, your honour. Your lady would attack your collops with a knife.'

'Who's to say she hasn't already done so?' I asked in all innocence.

Harry enveloped me in a sweaty hug and kissed me, raising a cheer which developed into the much loved ballad from a score of throats.

The Percy out of Northumberland, a vow to God made he
That he would hunt in the mountains of Cheviot within days three
Despite the mighty Douglas and all that with him be…

The roar of the voices was thunderous…

'We caught them,' Harry informed me, face flushed with victory and pride.

'Who?' It was not a question that needed to be asked, but it would get me a fast account of what had happened. Harry was well, weary, not over-clean, his clothing in need of severe attention, but apart from that full to the brim with his achievements.

'A Scottish raiding party at Nesbit Moor.'

'So you beat them.' I knew that I must let him talk it out before giving my own news. I was well versed in men newly returned from a fight. The light of battle had barely died in his eyes.

'It was a good battle, sharp and bloody, and we took hostages. It won't stop the attacks across the border but it will make them think twice for a few months,' said a new voice, that of the Earl of Dunbar who had walked across to join us.

Dunbar was as enthusiastic as Harry and I managed to grant him a smile. George Dunbar, Earl of Dunbar, was a man with old age in his sights but lacking in neither energies nor accomplishments on the battlefield. Nor was he lacking in pride, a trait common to these northern magnates, but his lofty conception of his own status was higher than most. It unnerved me that he was fighting for the Percy interest against his fellow Scots, his defection coming from a territorial dispute with the Scottish crown and the rejection of his daughter as a Scottish royal bride.

'I think they'll be back before a few months have passed,' the Earl of Northumberland growled.

'They'll be back within the month,' Harry corrected, punching Dunbar's shoulder. 'I need a rest and a bath. My backside needs not to be in contact with a saddle for at least a week. Come and welcome your husband home, Elizabeth.'

Instead, I pulled him away from Dunbar and the Earl. I neither trusted nor liked the Earl of Dunbar, whose loyalties were suspect, and I had a fair idea of the Earl's opinion. 'I doubt you'll have time for a rest.'

'What's happened?' He was suddenly on the alert, as if a herald's trumpet had blown to summon him to arms. The flush faded from his cheeks, leaving his face lean and intent as at last he sensed my anxieties.

'There's been a battle in the west. At Bryn Glas, north-west of Wigmore.'

His brow furrowed in thought. 'I know of it. Not a place I would choose for battle. All hills and valleys, the perfect place for an ambush.' His attention was now fully on me, gripping my hands, sensing the horror that had built within me for some days. 'What happened at Bryn Glas?'

'It's Edmund. And it's not good news. On the King's request, my brother called out his own retainers and the men of Herefordshire to push back Glyn Dwr. They met at Bryn Glas, where Rhys Gethin, one of Glyn Dwr's captains, had positioned his archers on the top of the hill when Edmund was marching up the Lugg valley. Edmund was beaten. It was 'a desperate outcome.' I moistened my dry lips. It seemed that I had lived with this for a lifetime. 'It is said that the Welsh women defiled the bodies of the Englishmen killed.' Distress was beginning to take over as I recollected all I knew.

'I can imagine. But what in God's name was he doing to get himself beaten?'

'I was told that Edmund decided to take them on by launching an attack up the hill, to displace them.' Even I could see the disadvantage in that. I swallowed hard. 'I was told that perhaps close to one thousand men were killed by Welsh arrows. I know not the truth of that, but it was a notable victory for Glyn Dwr.'

'God in heaven! Did Mortimer know no better?' Then: 'Elizabeth.' Harry was surprisingly gentle, as if the thought had suddenly sprung into his mind, as he remembered the recent loss of my sister. He was now stroking a hand down the length of my arm, as if I were a mare that needed soft treatment. 'What of Edmund? Is he dead?'

This was not gentle. I had lost my sister; now it was uncertain whether Edmund still lived. 'Not that we know, but nothing is certain. He was taken prisoner, we think. The messenger did not know where. Probably into one of Glyn Dwr's refuges in the mountains of Snowdonia.'

That was the worst of it. I had no knowledge of where he was, whether living or dead.

'Well.' Letting me go free, Harry drew his hands down his cheeks, considering the possibilities as I knew he would. 'We'll know soon enough. If Edmund is alive, Glyn Dwr will send out word for a ransom. All we have to hope is that he survived the attentions of the Welsh harpies and kept his genitals in one piece.'

'So I pray.' I was grasping Harry's sleeve, feeling the

surge of energy there, encouraged by it even though it had not changed the outcome of the disaster. 'Rescue, so the messenger intimated, is impossible, by some minor force of arms. Glyn Dwr's base in the mountains is remote and well defended. It is not to be possible, unless the King will consider a full-scale invasion.'

Harry grimaced. 'Does the King know?'

'He was told.'

'But we don't yet know what he is doing. He can't ignore it. King Henry needs Mortimer in the March. The young Prince has much promise, but he needs good men under his command. Although what Edmund was thinking...'

'What do we do now?' I gave him no opportunity to continue his damning of Edmund's tactics.

'If he is a prisoner, and we presume he is or his body would have been returned to Ludlow, Glyn Dwr will be more than keen to ransom him. He needs the gold. That's what I would do.' He pressed his lips to my brow in a preoccupied salute. 'All is not lost. What we have to do now is persuade the King to raise the ransom. It's cheaper than an invasion in the long run. I don't see why he can't be persuaded.'

'Do we ride south?'

'We do indeed. I should have known there would be no rest. The Earl and Dunbar can keep the northern March in check while we'll have conversation with King Henry. By God, he owes me.'

'What does he owe you?' I did not know what he meant, but it was not a priority. 'I will come with you,' I said.

'Of course you will. I never thought otherwise.'

The Earl was less than enthusiastic. 'Why waste time and energy over a lost cause?'

'Why should it be lost?' I challenged. 'Do I leave my brother at the mercy of the Welsh?'

'You'll do as you wish,' he replied, compassion as lacking as enthusiasm. 'But if you manage to wring any ransom money from our King it will be a miracle worthy of St John of Bridlington himself.'

King Henry had been busy. We met up with him and the Earl of Worcester, together with an impressive force at Lichfield. The King was looking harassed but determined, falling immediately into details of the massed attack that he intended against the intransigent Welsh. A cold fury inhabited him, his words, his brisk actions, as we met outside his tent. His planning was meticulous, as with everything he undertook. His forthcoming marriage to a Princess of Navarre had been put aside until better days.

'I've a mind to crush this insurrection before winter sets in,' Harry announced when we had barely dismounted, reminding me of his vision in the days at Doncaster. 'I have one force gathering at Hereford under Arundel and Warwick. I'll lead a second myself from Shrewsbury, while my son Hal will lead a third from Chester. I'm weary of these constant incursions. We'll go in with a three-pronged attack and lure Glyn Dwr from his bolt hole.' His jaw was tight with passion. 'Once I have him in my hands, he will not see freedom again. So I swear by the Holy Trinity.'

Harry, after acknowledging his uncle, was content to ask questions and give advice. There would be no role for him in this campaign. My cousin seemed to have no thought of why we were here in Lichfield, rather than keeping the Scots at bay in the north.

'Henry,' I said at last, when a brief pause developed in the planning. 'We are here to talk about my brother Edmund Mortimer.'

For a moment a line appeared between the King's brows, then it was gone. 'Forgive me. I should have commiserated. You will understand my preoccupation with Glyn Dwr's predations.'

'I do understand. But mine is my brother's future. His life, if that is under threat.'

King Henry's reply was immediate and far from conciliatory. 'A pity Sir Edmund's men proved fickle when under fire from the Welsh archers. If they had shown more backbone I would not be faced with this added complication. I hear that the troops Mortimer had raised from Maelienydd betrayed him in the thick of battle, going over to the Welsh.'

Startled by this unexpected attack on a loyal soldier, I pursued my objective. 'Whether they were fickle or overcome by a stronger force is beside the point. My brother is now a prisoner in their hands.' So much we had learned. Edmund was alive and imprisoned, and Glyn Dwr was offering his life for a substantial payment.

'Edmund Mortimer hadn't the sense but to attack uphill, without cover, under a barrage of archer fire. He deserves to be a prisoner for his foolhardiness,' the King retaliated with a soldierly absence of compassion.

Harry silenced me with a glance, even though he had expressed the same disgust at Edmund's lack of tactics. 'What do you plan to do, my lord?'

'Rescue him if we come across him.'

'You will offer a ransom, of course, for my wife's brother. Glyn Dwr will be willing to negotiate.'

The King's response took me aback in its complete rejection of any such plan. 'By God, I will not. The money I have to hand will be spent on this expedition, and on your defence of the north. You'll get what's owed to you. But I'll not let it run through my fingers by ransoming Mortimer.'

I sensed Harry stifling an equally curt reply; although he seemed to move easily from one foot to another, his response was less than agreeable. 'We have seen little of this coin so beneficently offered so far, my lord. You are full of promises but there is nothing to show for it. When you gave me authority in Wales, I promoted the siege of Conwy Castle, with your son, at my own expense. It cost me all of two hundred pounds, and I have yet to see any recompense. Surely there is enough money in royal coffers to redeem the life of a marcher lord of repute.'

A taut silence hung in the air between them.

'It is difficult, Sir Henry. Sufficient money is not easily come by—' Worcester, solidly formal, attempting a benign influence over all. And failing when the King interrupted.

'You will be paid eventually, Percy. Even though I did not care for the manner of the outcome at Conwy.'

Harry's expression had darkened at this overt criticism. 'Because I negotiated a conciliatory agreement to end the siege?'

'Because you allowed the Tudor brothers, traitors both and cousins of Glyn Dwr, to escape from Conwy with their lives.'

'In exchange for nine of their accomplices who were put to death. It ended the siege cheaply and effectively. If you had thought to put a trustworthy garrison into Conwy, it would never have been captured by the Welsh, which brings us to the inescapable conclusion that there would never have been the need for a siege in the first place. The Tudors took it while the English garrison was at prayer.' Harry's temper was rising to a dangerous level, his choice of words unfortunate. 'God's Blood, man! Complacency in a garrison is hard to forgive. And now, my lord, you are uncommonly free with your blame. Would you have been happier if I had left Conwy in Welsh hands?'

'It would never have ended in negotiation if I had been in command.'

'Well, you were not, my lord. And it did. Effectively, I would say.'

This was disintegrating into a morass of disrespectful accusation and counter-accusation on both sides. I might know nothing of the events at Conwy but it had left bad blood between Harry and the King. The possibility of persuading my cousin to rescue my brother was fast disappearing in a cloud of ill will.

Harry was not finished. 'And what's more, my lord—'

I interrupted.

'Are you then saying, Henry, that you will leave my brother's fate in the hostile hands of Glyn Dwr?'

'If I have to.'

'So you care nothing for your marcher lords and my peace of mind.'

'You know enough about border politics, cousin.' His ire was turned on me. 'He's in no danger. Edmund Mortimer is too valuable for Glyn Dwr to kill. Why worry? He can wait on my pleasure, when I have the money to spend on him.'

I thought as things stood that would never be. 'But he's not valuable at all if you won't pay the ransom.'

'I won't pay because I can't. As soon as I have Glyn Dwr in my hands, then all will be resolved.'

'If you are ever fortunate enough to discover Glyn Dwr's stronghold.' My own temper was alight, leading me to some equally ill-advised comment. 'I would not wager my 'rings on it.' I had not thought that the King would be so intransigent.

'Perhaps you should sell the rings, which I anticipate being of some value if they are Percy heirlooms, to raise Mortimer's ransom. Or perhaps you would be even better advised to get your husband to talk to Glyn Dwr. He has a closer relationship with him than I have claim to.'

It was bitterly said, a sour twist to my cousin's mouth.

'My lord…' Worcester placed a warning hand on the King's arm but was shaken off, while I looked at Harry, expecting him to deny it. He did not.

'Sometimes it is better to talk to the enemy rather than threaten him with a mailed fist.' Harry's jaw had clenched again.

'If you had taken him prisoner rather than indulging in some cosy exchange of views to your joint advantage, it would have saved me a deal of trouble. All I got out of it was a wagon of worn armour and a parcel of Glyn Dwr's Welsh servants. What good is that to me? And now you wish me to spend money to remedy Mortimer's mistakes. I'll not have gold pouring into Glyn Dwr's coffers, to be pouring out again for that Welsh magician's vicious pleasure in slaughtering my subjects. Mortimer can remain where he is until Glyn Dwr is beaten. That is the end of the matter.' But it was not the end. Eyes cold with fury, Henry added: 'If you saw fit to treat with Glyn Dwr, I would see it as treason.'

Harry's response came swift and sure. 'Do you accuse me of treachery, my lord? If so, say it plain.'

There was a hiatus of held breath.

'Are you with me or against me, Percy?' the King demanded.

'Do I have any choice, my lord?' was snapped back.

'None. Since I have an army at hand in full military

array, and you only an escort, formidable as it might be. But I have to be sure that you will remain loyal when you have returned to your northern lands, out of my sight and hearing, when it would take you no time at all to raise your banner against me.'

'My lord. I beg that you would consider...' Worcester's calm was vanishing like mist in the morning sun, while I was horrified at this sudden disintegration into hot rancour.

'Do you doubt my loyalty?' Harry took a step forward that could have been called threatening. 'After all I have done to promote your power and your hold on this land that was not yours until three years ago.'

'No one doubts your loyalty, Sir Henry.' Worcester still attempting to smooth out the unsmoothable, but at least it seemed to bring the King back to the need for conciliation.

'Forgive me. I doubt everyone's loyalty. It seems to me that I am under attack from all sides,' he said, more equably now, breathing hard. 'Loyalty is in the quality of the support I get, not in empty words. I made you my Lieutenant in North Wales, giving you control of a handful of my castles. Does that have the stench of mistrust about it? Would I make a man I did not value my representative in so perilous a province? I would not.'

'Yet you paid me nothing to cover all my expenses accrued in your name. How should I feel valued?'

'I gave you my son, into your care. How would I give a man I did not trust the guardianship of my precious heir?'

'Yet you use the word treason easily enough.'

'And I will again, if given due cause.'

I could not believe how quickly we had become submerged in belligerence. It seemed far too extreme, for Lancaster to threaten, for Harry to issue a challenge that my cousin would not be where he was without Percy backing. For Worcester to see the need to stand between them. The King still glared his displeasure. I glanced at Harry who looked equally recalcitrant as he made his parting shot.

'Then there is nothing more to say, my lord. You do not value your friends highly. I'll take my empty words and go home.'

'I value Percy friendship very highly.' I watched as the King again grappled with his ill humour. 'Will you add your forces to mine? To drive into the centre of Wales? That would be proof indeed.'

Harry's lowering brow was pure Percy magnate. The Earl could not have done better. 'Not if you want me to hold the north as well, my lord. Our victory at Nesbit Moor will not go unpunished by the Scots. I'll spend the money I have on the defence of the north and my own lands. We will await news of your success in Wales.'

Before we turned to go, for clearly Harry was not intending to linger to exchange pleasantries: 'Where are my nephews?' I asked.

Their safety had become even more paramount to me if Edmund might not survive.

'Safely tucked away behind the walls of Berkhamsted. With my younger children. They are safe there.'

'Safe from whom?'

The King marched away. Worcester raised his hands in some quality of desperation and followed him. But not before imparting some unsettling information.

'You should know, Harry – the King has confiscated all Sir Edmund's plate and jewels, if you were hoping to realise some ransom money from them. He is very thorough over all matters of finance.'

'Which is as close to a death sentence for my brother as a rook to a raven,' I said.

'It is,' Harry agreed, 'if the Welsh Prince is of a mind to test the thickness of your brother's neck.'

'So what was all that about?' I asked as we rode north, our failure a constant irritant like pollen on the wind. I was remembering the dangerous spark of fire between Lancaster and Percy.

'Nothing worth talking of.' Harry's face was grim, as it had been since we left Lichfield.

'The King all but accused you of treason.'

'He did. And he was wrong. I met with Glyn Dwr, that's all.'

'So what was it, that wasn't treason?' I would not let him slide out of this.

'I tried to open a negotiation with Glyn Dwr, to bring him back to the King's allegiance. He was not unwilling, but Henry was not of a mind to grant a royal pardon or even a lull in the fighting. Or his Council refused – it came to the same thing. It was considered neither honourable nor benefitting the King's majesty, to treat with so great a malefactor. The Council would rather have Glyn Dwr dead. So my attempt at conciliation was thrown on the midden and the taint of treason was attached to my name for suggesting a meeting of minds in the first place. That's all I have to say on the matter.'

What more was there to say about the failure of our venture? All was as clear as light through a crystal: the young Earl of March still locked away, however comfortable his sojourn, with Henry's children. Edmund a prisoner somewhere in the Welsh mountains without hope of ransom. I could see Lancaster's scheming as easily as if he had written it down for us, although I disliked what I was reading. He had no intention of ransoming Edmund. I doubted that he would ever make much of an effort to rescue him. My heart was sinking lower by the mile, until eventually as the towers of Alnwick came into view Harry turned our conversation once more back to the political.

'You see what the King's doing, don't you?' he asked.

'Yes. I see it.'

'It's in King Henry's interests to hope that Edmund never emerges from Wales with his skin intact. Or his head attached to his body. Henry will be toasting Glyn Dwr and a job well done if Edmund conveniently disappears. Our King has decided that on this occasion a dead Mortimer is of more value than a living one.'

All true, and the bleakest of résumés. Richard was dead. The only cause to champion, for those disaffected from Lancaster, was that of the Mortimers. Who was there to raise the banner, to fire the hearts, if the Earl of March was locked up and Edmund somewhere lost in Wales? Who was there to lead a Mortimer campaign against Henry?

'He'll never release my nephews, will he?' I said.

'I doubt it. I wouldn't, in Henry's position. He's got what he wanted, hasn't he? A handful of useful sons to rule after him and all opposition removed. If he can bring the downfall of Glyn Dwr in Wales, arrange the silencing of your brother one way or another and keep the Percy lords happy in the north, his troubles are solved.'

I considered. Well, I would ask, even if I did not like the answer.

'Would you be prepared to defy him? To negotiate with Glyn Dwr again, for Edmund's release?' Clutching at distant hopes, when Harry had awarded me another lengthy silence to work out my emotions against the familiar scene of hills and woods and the rooks that rose noisily at our approach.

'No. It would be senseless.' He must have felt my anger, my despair. 'Tell me what you see, Elizabeth. Tell me the forces that stand against us.'

I thought.

'King Henry has an army in the field and the Scots are looming in the north. Glyn Dwr has the Welsh tribes behind him and is wreaking havoc in the Welsh March. While we are trapped in the middle...'

'Exactly. If we are careless, we'll be caught like a sword blade between hammer and anvil, and distorted out of true alignment. We can't risk that. Edmund has to pay the price for his crass response to Rhys Gethin's crafty planning at Bryn Glas. The Percys will hold the north and not dabble in events that don't concern them. Which on this occasion means Mortimer affairs.'

'But what if...'

I was still reluctant to abandon the cause, even though I could not argue against Harry's brief but masterful assessment of our position. The ill feeling between us had long mellowed but the Mortimers remained as sour dregs in the bottom of our cup of happiness.

'You have to resign yourself to it, Elizabeth. The King won't rescue him, and neither can I. As for the Earl, he won't give it a second thought.' He considered briefly. 'As it was pointed out to me, it would be treason to go against royal commands.'

'Would you care? It was treason to support him against Richard.'

'I know.'

It was not dissimilar from trying to extract juice from a rock-hard quince.

'Is it true that the King has not paid you for your service to him?' I asked.

'It is true.'

'So you say that we cannot afford to ransom Edmund ourselves.'

'It cannot be done.'

Which sharpened my response somewhat. 'It seems to me that it could be done if anyone had the inclination. All men are the same. As long as a man has power in his hands, then he will let sleeping dogs lie.'

'An excellent picture. This is certainly a Welsh dog that should be left to sleep. Or perhaps a dragon, allowed to slumber in its Welsh cave.'

I would have the last word. 'Once you made Lancaster King.' I remembered Philippa's thoughts. 'You could unmake him.'

'To what purpose? I'll not raise a rebellion in the Mortimer name. We have a war of our own to fight, and I would rather not be fighting one with King Henry as well.' He pulled his horse to a standstill, which forced me to do likewise. 'I would rather not be at war with you again either. The dust has only just settled from the last sharp skirmish. Can we make a permanent peace, rather than a truce that will fall apart at the first hurdle?' He stretched out his hand to close over mine on my reins. 'My heart is with you, Elizabeth. But my head says to leave well alone. So should yours.'

I sighed, seeing the rightness of it, desiring eternal warfare no more than he did.

'I cannot,' I said, stubborn to the last. 'It matters too much.' Philippa's wise words were discarded.

'Then we must agree to differ.'

Expression hardening, eyes hooded, when he removed his

hand from mine it felt as if he was indeed withdrawing his love. I was even more bereft when he kicked his horse into a canter, leaving me to follow with the escort at my own speed.

My heart was a solid weight in my chest for this was my own fault. For once Harry had been willing to compromise, and I could not, closing the door on our negotiation, with no encouragement for further improvement. There was no one to blame but myself.

Chapter Eleven

Alnwick Castle: September 1402

'Birds of ill omen,' Dame Hawisia muttered, clutching some ancient talisman of dubious nature to her black-garbed chest. 'I know about this. There's bad things coming, mark my words.'

In those days, in that autumn, we were troubled by rooks and jackdaws roosting in the crevices of the towers. They were always there, come in for shelter as the weather grew colder, but they had arrived in far greater numbers this autumn than I had ever seen them. Their raucous cries, their droppings fouling the stonework, just the vast mass of them as if in some malign collusion, made the household wary. Black feathers drifted down. And with them black thoughts.

'Nothing of the sort,' I responded smartly.

Walking along the wall walk, I determined that I would not be intimidated in my own home; by a Scottish army at our door perhaps, but not by Dame Hawisia's declaiming of soothsayings and predictions.

Hal ran ahead, ever a bold lad, to dislodge the birds with hoots and wheeling arms, sending them circling into the air in a grim cloud of disapproval, but Bess stayed close to me.

'They will not harm you.'

'They look at me,' she said.

Her childish features, still soft, were patterned with fear. It beat against my heart.

'We can soon stop that.' I picked up a piece of flat stone dislodged from the parapet. 'How good is your aim? Can you throw this? Can you throw it as far as Hal?'

Without question Bess took it and threw, a commendable attempt for so small a child, so that it smacked against one of the crenellations, causing Hal to duck and the rooks to depart in a clatter of wing and claw.

'Excellent!' I praised her, removing a feather that had lodged in her bodice, tucking her hair into her coif. 'See how brave you are. As brave as Hal. Your father will allow no one to harm you. And nor will I.' It pleased me to see her smile.

'The birds won't harm her. It's what they predict that brings the trouble,' remarked Dame Hawisia, lurking at my side. 'Don't say I didn't warn you.'

But what did they predict? Superstitions and fears ran rife in the household, from the arrival of the Scots in battle array to a swarm of rats in the cellars. In the end I sent two of the ostlers – with an enthusiastic Hal in tow and a brace of falcons – to discourage the birds from roosting, but without too much effect. They continued to congregate with their sharp eyes and sharper beaks. They made me shiver.

'They won't go until the ill prediction has come to pass.' Dame Hawisia continued to enjoy the attention when my household asked for her interpretation.

'That's as may be, but I don't want to hear you speaking of it to Hal and Bess.'

'I would do naught to frighten them.' She stalked from my presence in a black swirl of anger.

'I am not frightened,' Hal assured me with shoulders squared.

'I am,' admitted Bess.

Were we not all afraid? Sometimes in the night I woke to feel terror sitting on my chest, like one of the malevolent imps painted in the chapel to warn us of what would await a sinner in hell. It is only fear of the unknown, I chided myself, trying to catch my breath, for I would not burden Harry with my nightmares. Still they remained, even in daylight, as the black birds flew across the sun, making fluttering shadows against the stonework.

I could do nothing to reassure Bess other than distract her with a visit to the mews where the hawks were moulting. My own present anxieties were nothing to do with either the Scots or the rats, but with the wellbeing of Harry in the north. When the dusk call of the white owl screeched between the towers every night for a week, it made me imagine souls in torment.

'Elizabeth!'

The vast bailey into which I had emerged some time ago was filled with a rough mingling of Northumbrian, Scots and French voices. One rang out in a bellow above the rest. My relief was a live thing. The feathered omens of death had proved false.

'Elizabeth!'

Deciding that it would be politic to respond, I began to push through the throng, accompanied by our steward who was prepared to smooth my path. I really had not needed to be summoned. Harry was home.

Our lives, as indicated by the Earl, had returned to the normal run of affairs, of attack and retreat. Nor had Harry been misinformed about the all-pervading miasma of war in the north. Before the end of the campaigning season, the Scots, their pride damaged by the Percy victory at Nesbit Moor, launched a reprisal over the border. In the early days of September they crossed the Tweed, raiding as far as the Tyne and almost to our doorstep, resulting in immediate retaliation from the Earl and Harry and Dunbar.

I heard nothing of Edmund's fate.

But now they were come home to celebrate a fortuitous victory, and the anxiety of a waiting wife was draining from me like snow-melt in April. Our retainers were jubilant if sore-headed from their ale-fuelled celebrations. So many faces that I knew. There would also be those missing, those who had not returned. Even a victory had its price to pay, and this had been a more major conflict than the skirmish at Nesbitt Moor.

Harry was safe. Harry was alive and come home.

I made my way towards him, taking note that we had prisoners, a cluster of men, disarmed, surly, but glad to be alive, high born by the gilded and incised quality of their armour. They would be ransomed of course, for they were of the highest of Scots blood. Our steward pointed them out to me.

'The Earl of Fife, son of the Regent of Scotland, my lady. Then Lord Montgomery, Sir William Graham, Sir Adam Forster. And there, by their heraldic symbols, three French lords, fighting in the name of Scotland.'

A valuable hoard, I agreed, for families were rarely slow in paying for the return of their menfolk.

I considered them, where they stood in a lightly guarded group, moved by the thought that some lady of the household would have welcomed Harry and seen to his comfort after

Otterburn. Some unknown lady would have tended his wounds, given him clothing and food, hot water for bathing, for was he not of the most noble birth and reputation? Had she asked if he had a wife at home who would worry about him, a family who would be willing to raise money to see him safely home? I would do the same for these prisoners, for it was my duty and my pleasure. They were the enemy but would have fought with distinction, thus it behoved us here at Alnwick to receive them with chivalric dignity, in recognition of their bravery.

I passed by the Earl and George Dunbar, acknowledging both, but not stopping. Harry, the one man in all the melee whom I needed to see, had dismounted and was speaking with a man who had been lifted down from a horse-drawn litter, clearly unable either to ride or to rise from his makeshift bed. It never grew any easier, this constant departing and returning from battle. He looked up, his gaze fierce beneath the travel grime.

'Elizabeth.' He held out his hand to draw me forward for whatever the divisions between us in the privacy of our own chamber, they would not be made public. 'I found this Scots gentleman lying in the heather. Allow me to make you known to Archibald Douglas. The Earl of Douglas will make his home with us for a time. We will make him as comfortable as we may.'

I regarded him, a young man perhaps lacking a few years of Harry's age, but his face, what I could see of it, drawn with exhaustion and pain. Tied around his head to cover half his face was a filthy bandage. His armour removed, his clothing, clearly borrowed, was in a parlous state.

'You are right welcome here, my lord,' I said.

I knew of the Earl of Douglas by repute. He was a worthy

adversary in the March, although not always the most successful of leaders on the battlefield.

'Not through choice, my lady.'

His voice might have been cultured beneath the Scots burr if it were not so racked with the humiliation of defeat and an inability to stand on his own feet. The fourth Earl of Douglas would not enjoy this lack of dignity.

'That I know.' I was tolerant of brusque and suffering prisoners of high blood. 'But we will soon see you restored to health. I doubt you will be with us long. Someone will want to claim you.' I smiled down at him, placing my hand over his where it gripped the crude covering. 'Despite your lack of good manners.'

He managed a faint smile. 'My thanks. I would not seem churlish.'

'He's churlish because he's been punctured like a colander,' Harry observed. 'Five arrows found their mark in him. It's a miracle he's alive to be churlish.'

'I understand. I see you lack compassion too from your victor.' I frowned at Harry. 'A prisoner in pain does not necessarily have good manners. Even when he needs to win my good offices on his behalf.'

Now Douglas managed a grating laugh. 'You need to keep me in good health if you want a financial return on my skin.'

'We will do what we can.'

What I could only interpret as fear impressed the muscles beside his mouth.

'Can you restore my sight to me? I think that is beyond any man's miracle.'

I gestured to Dame Hawisia for her to approach. 'This is Dame Hawisia who will do her best for you. She has a reputation as a cunning woman.'

Death and blood and pain. But this year's prisoner could be next year's friend. I knew the chivalric code, as did Harry, as I gave orders to the servants to carry the young lord of Douglas into the castle. He was a man of land and power and family who would be more than grateful for his safe return, even without sight in one eye if it proved to be beyond remedy.

The Earl was at our side, as Archibald Douglas was carried away.

'An excellent haul of prisoners, Douglas particularly. They'll be pleased to get him back.' His lips thinned into a smile. 'It will make amends for the lack of payment from the King. Your recent complaints to him have had little effect, Harry.'

'No effect whatsoever. I never thought it would,' agreed Harry, who seemed less concerned as he observed the potential income around us. 'This will defray all our expenses.'

'Douglas will fill your purse with gold,' the Earl acknowledged.

Surprising me, overwhelming me, a wave of grief struck so hard, so much that I turned on my heel and followed the source of our gold into the castle. Archibald Douglas would be ransomed and returned to those who loved him. My brother would remain unransomed for all time.

'Elizabeth.'

This time I took no notice of Harry's call. All emotions under restraint, I saw Douglas put to bed, his bandages replaced, then took refuge in my still room, looking for something that would give him respite from the pain of the wound to his eye. The Scots lord had been right. There would be no saving the sight but I could give ease from his physical agony if not from his heartache.

I pounded and mixed, stirred and blended to no avail, despite the raw scents of comfrey, marigold, knapweed and mouse-ear hawkweed. It might ease the pain of wounds gained in battle but there was no ease for my pain, only a sharp sorrow that had made me shiver. My connections with past, present and future seemed to be wearing thin, thinner by the day. I had lost Philippa. Roger was long dead. Edmund was captive. I did not even know if he was wounded although there had been no news that he had suffered in the battle. If no one would rescue him, would I lose him too if Glyn Dwr decided to make an example of him? A public execution might put fear into the marcher lords.

And then there was Harry.

Straining the pounded leaves and stem of St James's-wort, I mixed the potion with careless application of the spoon; then, having to mop up the drops I had spilt, thought that I would have been better to leave it to Dame Hawisia. Harry had no sense of how I felt. All he could think of was the amount of gold that could be used on the next expedition against the Scots.

I would not weep. I would not weep.

Even this morose young man whose face was disfigured would be restored to his family. Did he have a wife? A sister, a mother, who comforted each other in their sorrow?

In that moment of pounding herbs into a salve I felt alone and without comfort.

The door was pushed open.

'They said I would find you here.'

Harry slouched in, leaning back against the bench, picking up leaves and pots, then pushing them aside when I did not respond. I could sense him frowning at my unresponsive back. 'Do you not have someone to do that for you?'

'Of course. But I can do it just as well,' continuing to keep my face turned from him. 'The Earl of Douglas's eye will be beyond saving. I'm sure you know that. But we can reduce the swelling and save his life. His other body wounds will heal, terrible as they are.'

'Thank you. He was a worthy enemy under atrocious fire.'

'I would hope some lady would do the same for you in similar circumstances.' I smacked his hand with the spoon when he dipped his finger in a puddle of the decoction. 'It will purge you faster than the flux if you taste it, so I warn you.' When he would have touched my cheek lightly, with a laugh, I pulled away. 'You are safe returned, for which I am glad.' How dry and unemotional my words sounded. I remembered reunions in the past when we had fallen into each other's arms. Now I was cold with grief and he was wary.

'I might risk the purge if you were of a mind to welcome me home.' He grimaced, wiping his fingers down the breast of his doublet. 'I was hardly put in danger. It was not a battle that I enjoyed.'

No, he had not. There was something troubling him. The usual euphoria was strangely absent.

'Was it not a victory?'

'Oh, yes. But nothing to my glory.' He brushed it aside, a thought that he did not wish to consider, as if it had played on his mind for too long. 'There's something I need you to know.'

'I know what it is.' Since his thoughts were still with the battle, I went back to my pounding and measuring. 'The Earl said it clear enough. The ransom for these Scottish lords will pay for the lack of financial appreciation from King Henry.'

'No. That's not it, although it's true enough.' Harry caught my hand, stilling it on the bench. 'Listen to me.

The Earl's ransom will provide an answer to one of our problems.'

'Only one? We seemed to be beset by problems before you went away.'

'Put that down.' He took the spoon from my free hand. 'Look at me.'

I did as I was bid but my soul was still heavy.

'Do you have a purpose for this vast sum?' I asked. 'Another campaign against the Scots?'

'I do have a purpose. Here is our means—'

'I am not interested in your purpose and your means. Did you know this? One of Dunbar's captains had what I could only think was a pleasure in telling me. Did you know too? My cousin Henry has managed – by some unfathomable means – to raise the money to ransom Lord Grey of Ruthin, another of Glyn Dwr's captives. It was an exorbitant sum, but my cousin managed to count out the gold coin with barely a shudder, because Grey is useful to him in the March. Yet he will not ransom Edmund.'

Harry was arrested. 'I did not know.'

'Well, now you do. So don't tell me how you will spend your ransom money on yet another campaign against the Scots.'

Freeing my hand from his, I made to leave the room, carrying the pot of liquid, until Harry, lounging no longer, stood in my way; he took the pot from me, set it down with a thump that threatened the perfection of the vessel, and closed the door.

'You are more difficult than a score of imprisoned Scots. This large sum paid for the release of Archibald Douglas by the grateful hand of his grieving royal wife and children is our means of ransoming your brother.'

I stood quite still. Taking in what he had said. What he was still saying.

'If the King will not do it, Elizabeth, then I will. Here is the money to hand, in the form of Archibald Douglas, whom you...'

I will not weep. I will not weep.

I could not speak.

'Elizabeth...'

'Thank you. Thank you.'

'I know it hit you hard.'

'I thought you did not care how hard it hit.'

'Of course I care.' He took me into his arms and I allowed it, even though we were squashed between workbench and cupboard. 'You have been so angry.'

'I know. And today I felt alone.'

'You are never alone. And when I am not with you in body, you have the spirit to know that I love you and will return.'

'You rejected my concerns. You abandoned all my arguments that my nephew should be King.'

I felt him sigh, his breath stirring my coif, puffing fragments of pounded herbs into the air. 'I did. I still do. He is too young. And before you talk about regencies, who would you have as regent?'

'You?' I would even appeal to his own sense of family pride.

'Or Edmund. Or one of the York litter,' Harry said. 'Have sense, Elizabeth. That should stick in your craw as much as it does in mine. A more ambitious family I have yet to meet, and a more untrustworthy one. England is too unsteady to gamble our future on a nine-year-old boy and a clamouring pack of royal cousins. At least Henry can lead an army into battle. And he's powerful enough to hold the pack at bay.'

'I know all of that, but the longer he is King, the tighter his hold on the realm will become. I thought you were dissatisfied.'

'I am. More than you will ever know. But not enough to follow your path.' He huffed again. 'Will this divide us for ever, Elizabeth? Will you not at least meet me halfway? I can't support the Mortimer claim, but I can restore your brother to you.'

I wept a little after all.

'I have had a thought,' I said when I had dried my tears on my sleeve.

'I knew you would. That the King will not like it.' Our minds were moving together again. 'I have an easy solution. We'll not tell him until it's done.'

'Is it not treason?'

'I expect it is. But we'll be forgiven fast enough. King Henry needs us.'

We stood for a moment in perfumed unity, dust motes falling silently in unceasing glitter from the sun, all the worries and heartache dissipating as our breathing fell into a familiar rhythm. We were at one again, and I would allow nothing to destroy that.

'And another thought,' I said, for my mind could not finally rest. 'What will the Earl say, if you use the money to ransom Edmund?'

Harry seemed untroubled. 'Douglas is my captive, not the Earl's. I am free to dispose of him and the resulting payment as I see fit.'

My heart was light, lighter than it had been for some time, when Harry released me, retrieved the pot and placed it in my hands, folding my hands around it as if it were the Holy Grail and he Sir Galahad.

'And now you had better take this foul-smelling draught or potion or whatever it is to our prisoner. Or we will have no Earl of Douglas to ransom.'

Yes, my contentment was much restored but in the coming days the black birds still kept their vigil on our towers. The white owl continued to swoop and screech. Dame Hawisia scowled and muttered about unseen and unknown horrors to come. Harry's presence strengthened me, but still I shivered when the rooks descended in their menacing cloud.

The Earl of Douglas was dosed and asleep. Hal and Bess had been reunited noisily with Harry; Bess's rook-induced fears magically dispelled with the return of her glorious father, Hal keen on hearing every detail of the campaign and explaining his lack of fear when the black birds troubled us. Now the children were restored to their own household while Harry was in the armoury, taking note of the notches that marred the once fine blade of his favourite sword. It would need a smith's skill to hammer it again into battle readiness.

'It has been well used,' I said, leaning beside him, much as he had leaned beside me in my herbal still room. I had brought wine with me, pushing a cup towards him. Perhaps he would be persuaded to tell me about this battle, what it was that had not pleased him.

'Not as well as you would think,' he said.

I waited. He would tell me in his own good time.

He found no enjoyment in what had been circling in his thoughts. The statements that came were crisp and laconic, as if he were giving a report to a senior commander. 'It was at Homildon Hill. You know the place. The Scots took up their position on the hill. It was in my mind to order our cavalry to charge head-on and dislodge them.'

'Much like Edmund at Bryn Glas.'

'Much like Edmund.' His lips twisted before settling into a rueful smile. 'I was suffused by memories of my inglorious capture at Otterburn in the moonlight. I would have my revenge. It was the obvious way, or so I thought – to attack and scatter the enemy.'

He lifted the sword, as if he saw an enemy against whom he would use it, so that light shimmered along its disfigured blade.

'Yet you did not.'

'It was the Earl who refused. So did Dunbar. The use of archers was Dunbar's strategy and he has a persuasive tongue. Nothing to be gained in a mounted attack uphill, he said. Use archers instead. So that's what we did and all I could do was sit tight and wait out the effect of the arrow storm against our foe. Oh, it worked. It worked gloriously well.' Carefully he placed the sword down, leaning on his hands to study the still-fine engraving. 'All was confusion, disarray and ultimately death with arrows raining down upon our enemy, but I felt cheated.' He stopped and looked fully at me. 'All my life I have been raised to think of battles being won by knights in armour, fighting with all their prowess, to prove their strength and courage in battle. Knight against knight until the strongest won. I did not expect to sit at the rear and allow archers to do my fighting for me from a distance. Yes, we won. It was a superb victory. My father and Dunbar celebrated. But for me it was a humiliation. Do you understand?'

'Yes.'

Knowing Harry, of course I understood.

'And Dunbar was crowing his triumph.'

'I understand that too.'

Thrusting the sword aside, he drank morosely.

'You must learn patience in your old age,' I said. 'You do not always have to charge at the enemy.'

'Old age? I am in the prime of my life.'

He was thirty-eight years old.

'Prove it,' I said, and my thoughts were not on the battle-field.

'By God, do I believe what I'm hearing? I won't do it!'

Harry's roar could be heard from some distance. The windows were open, the weather mild and we had moved to our preferred home at Warkworth. There, following, was the softer rumble of the Earl's voice. I could not hear what he said, but Harry's reply was clear enough, even more forceful than the first.

'And I'm not of a mind to travel all the way south to explain why I will not!'

I had been speaking with Archibald Douglas who was concerned at the perennial slowness in setting up an exchange of prisoners. He was strong enough now to sit in a chair, lightly clothed in one of Harry's tunics, but he had indeed lost an eye when an arrow had penetrated the guard on his helm. His sight would always be compromised, but he accepted it with an astonishing degree of equanimity. The arrow wounds scattered about his body were healing fast.

I sat at his side on a cushioned stool in the private garden, helping him to while away an hour. He was not one for reading and time hung heavily for him, much like Harry if some ailment kept him abed. We were enjoying Dunbar's absence, having discovered that his habit of pronouncing majestically on every issue raised in conversation was unacceptable to both of us.

'You must be patient,' I said when we had exhausted our criticism of Dunbar.

'If only I could ride.'

'You cannot yet.'

'Hotspur would let me try.'

I grinned. 'Hotspur does not oversee your convalescence.'

'So I know who rules here at Warkworth. Much like my wife at home.'

'She will miss you. And you have children?'

'Four. The youngest born the month before Homildon Hill.'

'Tell me about your royal wife. Lady Margaret Stewart.'

But his thoughts could not be distracted. 'I can ride. And I'll fight again. I'm not the first knight to lose an eye and I won't be the last. If you can get your husband to chivvy the negotiations.' He cocked his chin at the clash of will beyond our pleasant refuge. The Percy lords were in one of the ground-floor chambers in the Grey Mare's Tail Tower, attached to the east wall. 'Although now might not be the best of times.'

'Perhaps not.'

I decided that I might investigate. Harry's temper tended towards volatility, but what had stirred him to this? I doubted that it would be Worcester's doing since his visits were always equable pools in the torrent of everyday life. Yet here was a very public display of disgust being exhibited in one of the main antechambers where a messenger stood at a distance in proximity to the door for a fast departure, the Earl with the delivered message in his hand and Harry stalking the floor, his bright hair aflame. The messenger, I noted, was a royal one. The message bore King Henry's seal. Worcester simply stood by the window, arms folded, chin lowered to the furred neck of his tunic.

'What?' Harry demanded as I entered.

'The whole household can hear you,' I said. 'And probably in Alnwick too.'

'I care not. I will not do it.'

'What will you not do?' I opened a door into a more private chamber, its windows offering views of the river rather than the bailey. 'It might be more politic to discuss it in here, if you are going to be rude about the King again.'

Harry stalked through, the Earl and Worcester followed, Worcester with a wry smile, while I directed the messenger, much relieved, to make a fast retreat.

'He overreaches himself. He oversteps his right. This is not tradition. It is not justice. He might demand, but I am under no compulsion to obey.'

So this was King Henry's doing. 'Will you allow me to read it?' I asked the Earl, holding out my hand for the offending missive.

But the Earl crushed it in his hand. 'Henry orders us to send our captives to London. All our captives.' His mouth shut like a rat-trap. The document was cast to the floor.

I looked to Harry for further enlightenment but I could already understand his anger.

'We are forbidden by the King to ransom our own captives.' Worcester's soft voice made all plain.

'Which he can do, I suppose,' I said, my eye on my husband who still fumed. 'Because he is King.'

My calming words had no result. Not that I expected one.

Harry thumped his fist against the armoire in passing, making the door hinges squeak. 'Has it not always been the law of the battlefield? Of war? That the victor ransom his prisoners personally, to their comfort and his own financial advantage? King Henry will not fulfil his monetary obligations to us. He will not ransom Mortimer. But he denies our right to raise money from our own efforts on the battlefield where we have fought in his name.' He scooped up the crushed document, tossing it from hand to hand, the seal already shattered in the Earl's fist. 'Here he demands that we turn our prisoners over to him. God's Blood! I'll not do it.'

I slid a glance towards the Earl, whose expression was shuttered as closely as a storm lantern.

'I expect the King will summon us to meet him in parliament, escorting our prisoners. He has called one for the last day of September.' The Earl tried to look mildly contemplative, but failed. 'We will be expected to be there.'

'He'll not see me there, by God! Or my prisoners.'

'I don't agree with you.' The Earl cast himself into a chair by the window, his brows a solid bar above his nose. 'I think we must comply.'

Harry looked as astonished as I. It was Harry who responded with unfilial heat.

'Comply? You will go along with this travesty of justice? What are you saying? Will I see you marching south to deliver your prisoners to Henry's door? I suppose you will kneel in cowardly gratitude at the same time!'

'I will give him the courtesy due to my King. I will consider the wisdom of acceptance. It will stir more trouble than it's worth if we don't.'

'More trouble? How can there be more trouble?'

'If we stand against him, he'll bolster Westmorland power against us. I'll pursue no policy that will encourage the King to extend Westmorland's control or put more castles into his hands.'

'He's not wrong, Harry,' Worcester advised. 'If Westmorland gains more at your expense—'

'Let him try,' Harry broke in. 'There'll be no bending of my knee on this royal command. I have tolerated too much for too long...'

'Now is not the time to demand more.' The Earl pushed himself to his feet to approach his son. 'I warn you, Harry...'

'Warn me? Warn me of what?'

The Earl visibly took a breath; his voice mellowed but the atmosphere in the room retained the temperature of the smith's forge. 'It is in my mind to take my own prisoners to Whitehall and bend my knee – as you put it – before his royal demands. I suggest that it would be best for everyone if you – and your prisoners – were with me.'

'You might suggest it, but I will not.'

'Will you defy me too, as well as your King?'

Never had I seen father and son in so headlong a clash of will, like autumn rams fighting for supremacy on the northern hills.

'I will, sir. You can make my apologies to our puissant King. I see what this is. Henry has an itch that must be scratched. His campaign in Wales was a disaster, however he might write it. All he got out of it was a herd of miserable cattle, sore feet and waterlogged tents, including his own that was demolished on top of him in a gale. A shame one of the tent poles did not knock some generosity into his stubborn head, I'd say. He'll not allow our success at Homildon Hill to be lauded in comparison with his failure. He intends to share in our glory, and he wants the money. I see what he wants. He would get Douglas from me.'

'Then let him have Douglas,' Worcester sighed, 'and win the King's everlasting gratitude.'

'Oh, no. I've done enough to win the King's gratitude to last me a lifetime.' Harry cast the letter at his father's feet. 'Take the rest if you will, go and bend the knee and smile as he strips you of your ransoms, but Douglas does not go. And neither do I.'

The Earl inhaled visibly once more.

'I command you, Harry. You will do as I bid you.'

'Command? You will command me? Then you are destined to be disappointed, my lord.'

'I doubt the Earl of Douglas is well enough to travel,' I said, pouring a merest drop of oil on this blistering confrontation.

'Good.' Father and son still faced each other like boar and hunting dog. 'If you feel you need an excuse, my lord father, tell the King that our noble prisoner was like to die on the journey. Douglas stays here.'

Harry marched out, in no better mood than he had marched in. Worcester decided to follow him, leaving me to face the Earl who was no less angry but with all the control of age and experience that had escaped his son. For the first time I detected the merest plea in his eye as he addressed me, but it was well hidden, his voice still raven harsh.

'It would gratify me, Elizabeth, if you could use your powers of persuasion to bring him round to what is only good sense.'

'On this matter I doubt that I can. You saw how he reacted. He will not give Douglas into the King's hands.'

The Earl's lips thinned into as close a sneer as he would allow.

'And you are obviously hand in glove with him. Perhaps I should expect no less. Are you guilty of such self-interest? We all know he wants the money to rescue your brother.'

Of course he would have worked that out for himself even if Harry had not told him. I made no apology.

'Then if that is self-interest, I agree. No one else is moved to help Edmund Mortimer. If Harry will do it, I'll not oppose him.'

'No, you won't oppose. You'll bend his ear with subtle wiles. I don't like it.'

'I don't suppose that you do, but are you so surprised? You know that your son has always been restless over Lancaster and the Mortimer claim. He feels that Henry led you on with oaths and fair words with the sole purpose of winning the Percy family to his side. He feels it sorely. Nor has the King been generous in payment for your service against his enemies, which rankles even more.'

'So he will defy me and the King.'

'On this matter of prisoners, yes, he will. He is his own man. He doesn't need my subtle wiles to lure him on, as well you know. When did he ever not know his own mind? In the past it has been a trait that you have admired in him, has it not?' I watched as colour rose in the Earl's face. 'You must accept his decision.'

'We'll see if the King is as understanding.'

He turned away from me. And in anger I spoke: 'I think you should pray that his rebellion against the King does not go further than the matter of who ransoms the prisoners.'

The Earl turned slowly back to face me. While I frowned, baffled at what I had said. The thought had come into my mind, as sharp and as lethal as the arrow that had destroyed Douglas's sight, and I had expressed it before I had given any thought to its meaning. Where did I foresee this stand against the King taking us? Why should it necessarily become a more treacherous disagreement than one over money owing and the tradition of ransom payments? Some sense of danger had prompted me, but of what I was uncertain, and immediately regretted allowing the Earl any degree of access into my mind.

'What do you mean by that?' His eyes were opened wide.

'Probably nothing.' But I had seen, in that moment, a looming danger ahead, for all of us. My heart thumped with some strange anticipation.

'So why say it? Women's logic. Worth nothing.' And then, in direct contradiction, 'Go and talk to your husband. See if you can make him see sense.'

'I will talk with him, but I promise no outcome that will please you, my lord.'

I curtsied with effortless grace, my spine stiffening as I heard his parting delivery.

'We might all benefit if you could put the future of the Percy family before Mortimer politics.'

I would not rise to it. Nor did I have to, for Harry, casting an eye over an ailing horse, was no more open to advice than when he had defied his father.

'It is a matter of chivalry and the rights of tradition. I'll not do it. Don't bother to repeat my father's views, Elizabeth, if that's what you were about.'

'I will not. I am honoured that you will support my brother.'

'Support? It's a fine line between regretting his predicament and condemning the reason for it. Your brother was a fool to get himself captured in the first place, but I'll not let him languish for ever as Glyn Dwr's captive. Who knows what ideas he'll absorb when having to share a table with Welsh rebels from morn till night, for I doubt he'll be consigned to a cell.'

Which was the end of our conversation, Harry returning to his investigation of the animal's foreleg which, the groom advised, had a heat in it. I suppose that I had understood why the Earl was so ready to comply, to protect his interests against royal inundations. Lancaster might well increase the power of Westmorland at Percy expense. Sometimes the Earl was more realistic than Harry.

But Harry had no intention of being a cog in the machine of royal finance.

What danger had I seen? A thought that returned to haunt me. I did not know.

Chapter Twelve

As expected, King Henry summoned his parliament to meet on the last day of September at Westminster. True to his word, the Earl left Warkworth in the week prior to this in a foul mood, unaccompanied by his recalcitrant son and without his son's personal captives.

'No good will come of this.'

It was directed towards me, the Earl pulling on his gloves, as much as it was to Harry who looked upon the departure with studied dispassion.

'No good will come of our grovelling before this King who does not know our worth.' Harry expressed his usual views. 'If he will instruct his Council to pay the moneys owed to me, I might change my mind. Until then, I stay here. So do my prisoners.'

There was no chance of that eventuality. Even Worcester had been brutally honest in his comments on royal coffers.

'Empty as a beggar's purse, unfortunately.'

'He'll not fill them with the results of my battles,' Harry snarled.

'I'll tell him what you say, although I'll wrap it up in softer terms,' Worcester said.

'I'll not anticipate a friendly reply.' The Earl had the final comment. 'As long as the King does not call me to answer for your sins.'

'Your shoulders are broad enough, sir.'

So the Earl rode south with Worcester, and his prisoners too. But not Archibald Douglas who remained in our company to recover his strength. Or such was the rumour we allowed to spread as we awaited the Earl's return. In fact, his multitude of wounds were well healed by the time the Earl rode back alone into the bailey at Alnwick, prisoner-less, his mood grimmer than on his departure, the long ride home having done nothing to drain the poison from whatever had happened in the royal audience. He sat, glowering in silence over the dishes and cups until, by the end of the meal, Harry lost patience, dismissing the servants with a jerk of his chin.

'Will you tell us, or will you sit in a dark cloud for the rest of the day?'

'Oh, I'll tell you.' The Earl downed the dregs of yet another cup of ale. 'I had to present myself to the King and parliament in the White Hall. With my prisoners, all in a magnificent parade as if the King had captured them himself. They knelt. Twice. King Henry was enthroned in suitable glory. It was all very amenable.'

'Did he notice my absence?'

'Yes.'

'Did he take note that Douglas was not there?'

'Yes.'

'And he was accepting of it?'

Archibald Douglas sat in silence at my right hand.

'No.'

'What did he say?'

'Not a word. But his displeasure sat on his shoulder as heavily as the fur he was wearing to impress his magnates.'

The Earl showed a tendency to lapse again into brooding silence, until Harry prompted: 'Did he then provide a feast to welcome such men of high standing?'

'He did, with all grace. I was the one to receive the lash of his tongue, because you were not there and neither were your prisoners. Your disobedience brought naught but humiliation for me. I was summoned again next day. To say it was stormy would be too mild.'

'I expect you held your own. Will he pay what he owes?'

'He will not. He says he has not the money.' Pushing aside his cup at last, the Earl stood, resting his fists on the table, turning his eye on his son. 'The King says that he wants to see you. I made no excuses for you. If you continue to defy him, it will be on your own head.'

Harry exchanged a glance with me.

'What do you think,' he asked with a slight smile. 'Do I go and face my nemesis?'

'I think you must make up your own mind. It will not be a comfortable meeting but it might clear the air between you. If you can keep your temper.'

'Then I'll go.' He stood, stepping to face his father. 'I don't need you to defend me. I'll go and defend myself. If he wants me to continue to uphold his interests in the north, he must give me more than pretty assurances that my efforts will be rewarded.'

'Take Douglas with you,' commanded the Earl.

'And will you?' Douglas asked for the first time.

Harry did not even take the trouble to answer, leaving me to reassure the Scots lord.

'You will remain here,' I said. 'If necessary you will suffer another relapse from your atrocious wounds.'

With something suspiciously like a grunt, the Earl followed his son from the room.

Harry was still simmering as he made preparations to depart.

'I'll not offer to accompany you,' I said as he cast an eye over his entourage.

'To beg forgiveness from your cousin? I think not!'

'That would not be my intent. Merely to keep the peace between you.'

Answering a compulsion, I took hold of a fold of his sleeve. Harry would be in no physical danger and yet... I was uncertain of what it would mean if the hostility I had seen between Harry and the King at Lichfield grew even greater. To have Harry and the King at daggers drawn might have unforeseen repercussions. How tangled my thoughts on that day. I would in my heart support my Mortimer nephew against this Lancaster King, but to anticipate violence between Harry and King Henry filled me with fear. Which was a grave contradiction, for to do one would necessitate the other. I desired one, but feared the other.

'Keeping the peace between us is a thing worthy of ridicule, my love. Your logic is as lacking as Bess's.'

I could explain neither to myself nor to Harry this sudden anxiety that pervaded this leave-taking. 'Be careful, Harry,' was all I could say.

'Of what?'

'Of making a bad situation worse.'

'I don't intend to kill him.'

'Of course you don't. Will you tell him how you will use the ransom?'

'I doubt I will need to. He is no fool. But if you mean, will I offer the information, then no, I will not. I am no fool either.'

'Then even more I would say – take care. I would rather I did not have word that he had locked you in the Tower for some treasonous utterance.'

'I will be all sweetness and harmony.'

I kissed him.

'If you are, it will be for the first time.'

Warkworth Castle: Late December 1402

Harry did not return but I received a message. The brief content of it, in Harry's scrawl, gave me cause for concern, together with the fact that he had chosen to write it rather than give it verbatim to the messenger, even one as trusted as Morys, a discreet individual who was usually in the employ of Worcester.

'Where is he?' I asked Morys.

'Still at Westminster, my lady.'

'Is he in good health?'

'He is, my lady.'

'So he's not under lock and key.'

'No, my lady.' Morys's eye did not quite hold mine. 'But he is, if I might say, somewhat agitated.'

'And what is it that has agitated him this time?'

'I could not say, my lady. But he had conversation with the King.'

I opened the note. There was no greeting.

Take an escort and go to Ludlow where I will meet with you. It might be best if you do not discuss this with the Earl. You are

*travelling for a family matter. Don't waste time. Whatever you
hear, don't leave Ludlow until I arrive.
Yours in haste.*

More enigmatic than Harry's usual style of making all
plain. A dispute over royal debts and prisoner ownership
would not take him to Ludlow of all places. I was intrigued.
What had happened in London to pre-empt this visit to the
Welsh March, unless Harry had finally persuaded the King to
ransom Edmund and I was requested as a solid family link in
negotiations between all parties? It might be natural for me,
related to all, to open discussions with Glyn Dwr to release
my brother. It could not be, in the present circumstances, that
Harry was planning on starting the negotiation to ransom
Edmund himself. Until Douglas was returned to his grateful
family and we had been rewarded for it, there was little
point in approaching Glyn Dwr. Nor could I truly believe
that the King had changed his mind and decided to waste
much-needed gold on rescuing Edmund.

Obedient to my orders and taking Morys with me, I made
my familial excuses, bade Douglas farewell, and set off in
clement weather so that we travelled fast, the children who
accompanied me enjoying the adventure and the change of
scene. Even so Harry was there before me, his mood edgy as
he took my bridle, looking up at me after a brief acknowledgement of Morys, with no real welcome.

'You took your time.'

'I came with amazing speed.'

He cast a jaundiced eye over his heir and his daughter. 'It
might have been better if you had not brought them.'

'Why not? If you don't give me warning of the purpose of
this visit, you cannot expect me to see into your tricky mind.

They will enjoy a visit to their mother's ancestral home. It will be good for them to see that Percy is not the only name of importance in their family.'

He appeared to consider this and his scowl was smoothed over as he helped me to dismount.

'You could kiss me in welcome,' I said.

'I could.' Which he did, on one cheek and then the other.

'You could greet your children as if you were a loving father.'

'I could.'

Which he did, inspecting a laughing Hal as if he were a Percy retainer, commanding him to march, lunge and parry with his dagger, lifting Bess to a high seat on the mounting block as audience to the whole procedure.

'And then you can tell me why I am here. And what you said to Henry.'

'More pertinently, what Henry said to me.'

So things had not gone well.

'What did he say?'

'I'll tell you later.'

We walked together into the great hall, turning into the old solar block where Harry had made his accommodations, the children running ahead. Despite the lodging of a lively disquiet, since Harry was not prepared to unburden himself, I would wait. I was highly skilled in waiting.

'Why are we here?' I asked. That I needed to know.

'Because of rumours coming out of Wales.'

'Has anything changed? If Henry won't ransom Edmund, and you haven't raised the money yet for Douglas, are we not still waiting to see if Glyn Dwr will behead my brother out of pique or consign him permanently to a dungeon?' A sudden horror twisted the anxiety. 'He's not dead, is he?'

'No, he's not dead. But here's the sting in the serpent's tail. I have had an invitation from Glyn Dwr to join him to discuss something to my advantage.' The earlier frown returned, became more pronounced. 'It behoves us to discover exactly what your brother and Glyn Dwr are about.'

'If you were invited, that still does not explain why I am here.'

His countenance lightened in a smile.

'Because you are the perfect excuse, my beloved, for an innocent visit. Because you are a caring sister. You are concerned for the health of your brother, if anyone questions why we might be journeying into the fastness of Glyn Dwr's princedom, and you have persuaded me to escort you to have conversation with him. I am simply an indulgent husband, bowing to the whim of his distraught wife.'

'Anyone who knows us will be aware that I have signally failed to persuade you to do anything you did not wish to do.'

'And nor would Edmund render you distraught. But let us on this occasion hope that we can pull the wool over all eyes. I will try to look persuadable and you might weep into your kerchief.'

Leaving Hal and Bess in Ludlow, we journeyed to the west into the mountains of Wales to where we had learned that Glyn Dwr was to be spending the winter at his main stronghold of Sycharth, a short distance over the border. I might have been afraid that we would become a ready target for his Welsh archers but Harry was phlegmatic. We had been invited. Our escort was small but well armed and our Percy banners were flying. We had added Mortimer flags too, gold and blue stripes showing boldly against Harry's blue lion.

'You admire Glyn Dwr,' I observed, hoping for some

insight into this Welsh warrior who was claiming the principality as his own, and shedding blood to do it, before I had to share meat with him.

'I do indeed.' Harry grinned, happy to reminisce. 'Our paths first crossed before his rebel days when he was fighting for England against the Scots. We met at Berwick when I was still young – barely twenty years old and willing to be impressed. He could wield a sword like one of King Arthur's knights of old, and with the same glamour. Now with years on him, he is still a man of courage but also with a grave dignity.' His smile faded. 'Now I also admire his conviction in his Welsh blood and his right to rule. We parted on good terms after Conwy, spending the days, and the nights, talking about armies and campaigns. We had much in common and I regretted being unable to bring him back into the English fold. He would have done so with the slightest encouragement from the King,' he mused, more willing to talk about their meeting than he had been previously. 'Henry damns me for not taking him prisoner at the time, or even killing him outright with a knife between his shoulder blades as soon as he turned his back.'

'I doubt it would have made the Welsh more peaceable.'

'It would have removed a dangerous element from the scene, but he has sons to follow in his footsteps, and I had not the occasion to do it. Nor would it have been right. We had agreed to a negotiation, not an assassination. He could have clapped me into one of his cellars if he had wished. It was a matter of trust between two knights. As I told the King, it was not in keeping with Glyn Dwr's rank for me to use the oath of fealty as a trick to ensnare him, to then strike him down as soon as his confidence was won. Such a deed is not in my nature.'

Sometimes Harry, who could ride into battle with bloody sword, surprised me with his level of chivalric sensitivity, but I forbore to comment, except to ask: '*This* isn't a trap, is it?' The hills pressed down on us, the croak of ravens and the mew of raptors accompanying us as if to warn us of what awaited. 'You don't expect us to be massacred before we get there, as the enemy? Glyn Dwr may not be as chivalric as you seem to be.'

'I wouldn't have agreed to bring you if I had thought I was putting your life in danger. They'll not kill us, whatever the outcome. I would be more valuable as a hostage, and so would you, but I don't fear that either. As for Glyn Dwr, he has a stripe of chivalry as wide as this never-ending mountain range beneath his black urge to kill anyone who stands in his way to dominance over Wales. He'll not shed your blood, nor would he consider a ransom. Who would pay it? Not King Henry. As for me, your royal cousin would consign me to permanent captivity.'

Abruptly, Harry's words were cut off. Whatever it was between him and the King still disturbed him enough for him to keep it between his teeth.

'The Earl your father would find the gold somewhere to bring you back to his bosom,' I offered, to disperse the cold anger. And indeed raised a smile.

'Ah, but would he pay for you?'

'I will put that burden on your own heart. So we could all end up as hostages, a family Mortimer gathering. Now there's a thought to cast me into depression.'

He leaned over to squeeze my hand.

'What is it that worries you?' I asked.

'Naught but what Edmund might have promised his host.'

It was an interesting point. I did not believe that Edmund's busy doings had caused the set of Harry's jaw but I replied equably.

'We will soon discover, for good or ill. I don't believe Edmund would be lured into treason.'

'Who knows what Edmund would be lured into, with the right incentives?'

We gathered a Welsh escort on small mountain horses toward the end of our journey but they kept a respectful distance, like well-trained sheep herders ensuring the delivery of the flock, although their bows were well in evidence as we arrived at Glyn Dwr's hall in the midst of a hailstorm. Even the deluge could not hide the impressive defensive position of this place known as Sycharth. High on a hill that had been sculpted by the hand of man long past, it was a place of woods and running water that I thought would have held much appeal on a day of sun and mild winds. Constructed by craftsmen, more timber than stone, more manor house than castle, it was superbly protected by two moats over which we crossed to reach the gatehouse. This was the home of the Welsh Prince, a palace of wealth and good taste, hemmed in by its church and mill, the pigeon house and fishponds. I imagined deer ran free on the hills beyond.

'Impressive,' I said as, closely escorted now, we entered beneath a carved gateway.

'Let's see what our welcome will be,' Harry replied as he helped me to dismount.

Received with grace by numerous servants, our drenched outer garments removed from us, we were drawn into a chamber where wine and a fire awaited us. And so did our host, Owain Glyn Dwr, whom I surveyed with interest as he bowed with words of smooth appreciation for our arrival.

Here was no crude Welsh robber and rebel. Here was a lord of wealth and culture. But then I was not surprised. Had he not been raised as a young boy, before he was at odds with the King of England, in the household of the Earl of Arundel, Philippa's husband? He had training in the law as well as in weapons. Anyone who expected a rough-hewn peasant or wild brigand from the Welsh hills would have been foolishly naive.

He met us alone. No Edmund, no family, no servants. He poured the wine himself with an ease at odds with his status. Here was a confident man who smiled his pleasure at our arrival.

'You are right welcome. I am gratified that you risked the journey, Sir Henry. It is an honour to welcome you too, my lady. The Mortimers hold a place in my heart since I had the pleasure of knowing your sister, albeit briefly, when I was honoured with Arundel's friendship until his death. I regret his passing, and the manner of it. As I regret hers.'

He was tall and dark-haired, rugged of feature and striking to look on. Older than Harry but still with the stature of a soldier in breadth of shoulder, he had the accents of a great lord, and an educated one, used to being obeyed in his own domain.

I found myself smiling when he took my hand and saluted it with gallantry.

'Do the Mortimers indeed hold a place in your heart, my lord? Or only in your plans?'

Which lit an answering smile and a mischievous gleam in his eye. 'I have many plans that are dear to me, that are far-reaching. But you need have no fear for your safety here. Either of you.'

'I have no fear,' Harry remarked, taking Glyn Dwr's hand

in a firm clasp when it was offered. 'You invited me. I think you have too much honour to kill a man in your own hall, with your invitation tucked in his sleeve.'

Harry too could be as smooth as silk, and equally confident.

'I know those who would have no qualms in dispatching Hotspur and leaving his body to the crows, but I am not one of them,' Glyn Dwr replied. 'As you say, it was a request from one man of honour to another. You will come to no harm here. Now, on a battlefield is quite another matter...' The light in his eye deepened. 'I presume you did not inform your King of our proposed meeting.'

'No, I did not. I was called traitor after our previous attempt at a lasting pardon, so I saw no need to open myself to further infamy. And there were other matters between the King and myself that took my attention on my departure from London. The subject of our meeting here did not arise.'

There it was again. What had Henry said to him – or what had he said to Henry! – that he could not shake off, even now? But Glyn Dwr was addressing me.

'I have enjoyed the company of your brother, my lady, and look forward to making your acquaintance.' He bowed. 'My people will show you to your rooms. Then we will eat and afterwards we will talk business.'

Which stirred an urgency in the air. We were welcomed as innocent guests yet I would wager there was no innocence in Glyn Dwr's mind. We would do well to remain on our guard despite his considerable charm.

'Why are we here, my lord?' I asked, since Harry made no move to do so.

'All will be made known to you. I wager it will not be to your discomfort, lady.'

After a rapid attention to our attire, we congregated in

the great hall where all was seemly and of quality. The food was plenteous and cooked with sophistication, much taken from the estate but with touches of a master cook in the Sycharth kitchens. Pike and carp from the fishponds, pigeon and venison from the estate, but also peacocks and cranes, washed down with best Salopian ale and French wines. I detected herbs and spices in the piquant sauces, worthy of my own still room. Around us the tapestries were rich in content and colour, mostly hunting scenes, the furnishings worthy of those at Alnwick and Warkworth, the conversation about court matters at home and abroad. Glyn Dwr had a knowledge and a web of connections which any leader would envy. His wife, Margaret, daughter of Sir John Hanmer, an English judge on the King's Bench, had a gentle dignity and firm opinions, not to be overawed by her husband's newly acquired title. Their four daughters were raised in the manner demanded of a noble household, courteous and well spoken, as were a cluster of sons although his heir Gruffydd was absent on his father's business. While Iolo Goch, a Welsh lord who joined us as a guest at the board, was a writer of verse and singer of songs, of much repute.

Yet, wary at being seduced by this regal graciousness, I was not ready to be won over. Why were we here? What was in Harry's mind was impossible to tell as he drank, conversed, discussed with aplomb and enthusiasm. Mostly it seemed about the breeding of stalwart horses fit for the tournament field and the value of archers to a man intent on destroying an enemy that outnumbered him. Not a word about the present situation passed any lip, as I exchanged opinion with Glyn Dwr's daughters and the Lady of Sycharth on the quality of linen, on child-rearing, the necessary contents of a still room and the recipes used to enhance the preserved fruit.

And here of course, in the midst, was Edmund. Edmund who was smilingly at ease, participating in the general conversation as if he too were an invited guest and had that right. Here was no prisoner under restraint. But then I should have expected no less, since Archibald Douglas sat at our board at Alnwick and Warkworth as an honoured guest. When he greeted me there was no anxiety at his confinement, only an unsettling dark secrecy when his eyes touched on mine.

There was music, singing in Welsh, in soft Welsh voices, from a group of minstrels. Our patience and good breeding were astonishing. Until: 'It is time for discussion, my friends.'

With a smile Margaret and the young girls left us and, reluctantly, Glyn Dwr's sons, followed by the servants, leaving the four of us and Iolo Goch. I would remain. Nor was there any suggestion that I should accompany the female household.

'Let me tell you of my hopes and dreams, that are indeed far-reaching.' Glyn Dwr raised his cup as if in a toast. 'Although I think none of them are new to you. I am a man whose lineage straddles the border of Wales and England. I am descended from the ancient Princes of Wales but my grandmother was an Englishwoman of some note, as is my wife. I trained as a lawyer at the inns of court in London. I served as a squire in the household of the Earl of Arundel. I fought for the English against the Scots at Berwick back in 1384. None of which is new to you.'

'Yet you have sworn enmity to this Lancaster King. You are proclaimed Prince of Wales. You will wage war against him to achieve your hopes and dreams,' Harry said.

'Indeed. I was promised a charter from your King to make me Master Forester and Warden of Chirkland in the Marches. I was deceived. I was never to receive such authority. The only way to possess what should be mine was to fight for it.'

'I think Grey of Ruthin had a hand in your decision.' Harry's brows rose as he encouraged our host to talk.

'More than a hand. Grey of Ruthin, God rot his English soul, threatened to burn and slay and pillage through any part of the March that I held.' Glyn Dwr shrugged self-deprecatingly. 'I admit, I retaliated in kind. A rebellion in the making, you could say, but I'll not take such words from any man. I have too much pride. You know what happened. Ruthin denied his threats, but I'd not trust in him. I was encouraged by my Welsh supporters to take Wales back from the English thieves and rule it as a Welsh prince. Do I not have the blood of the ancient Princes of Wales in my veins? So the fire was lit in me.' He laughed softly, as if at some memory. 'Despite some initial defeats, living as a fugitive, I have consolidated my support and am now in a position to hold the English King to account. This land is mine and I will fight to achieve recognition.' He paused to survey the three who made up his English audience. 'That is my stand. To take back Wales from English dominion.'

'And I admire your ambition,' Harry replied after another pause in which Glyn Dwr motioned to the Welsh bard to refill our cups. 'I might even have sympathies for them. I know what it is to be tied by unbreakable loyalties to the land and estates of my birth.' I saw as his eyes narrowed a little. 'But I also consider myself tied by oath to King Henry. You must be plain, sir. Why am I here, invited to sup with a self-sworn traitor?'

For the first time since the meal had ended Edmund spoke up.

'We know that you are in serious dispute with King Henry.'

Harry's glance flashed a warning not to tread too closely

into personal matters, yet he agreed. 'I think that by now the whole realm knows of it. If they do not, they are deaf.'

Unabashed, Edmund continued: 'We know that you have not been paid for your services to the crown.'

Harry's mouth curved with a depth of cynicism. 'Are you offering to make good my losses? I doubt that you are capable of it. Your own resources are much depleted after Henry's pillaging of your coin and plate.'

With a silencing gesture when Edmund would have responded vociferously on the matter of his stolen property, Glyn Dwr took up the general thrust. 'No, I think we are not able to recompense you. But we can offer you a different incentive.'

'An incentive to do what? And who is offering it?'

I glanced at my brother, whose eyes were trained on his hands cradling his cup, his expression superbly innocent. Had Harry noticed? Of course he had. It had been like a herald's call to arms. *We* can offer you an incentive. Not *I*, but *we*.

What had Edmund done?

There was another little pause. I could not yet fully see the direction we were taking, although enlightenment was building. I looked again at my brother, who now had his gaze trained on his host. Anywhere but on me.

'You have spoken very little this evening, Edmund,' I said.

He looked up, a gentle smile touching his mouth. 'I am a guest here. The offer to be made is not mine.'

'I was under the impression that you were prisoner?'

'I cannot fault my lord Glyn Dwr's hospitality.'

'Henry will never ransom you,' Harry said, dragging the discussion back to practicalities, 'so don't set your heart on it. He would rather you disappear into the Welsh hills, or indeed into an unmarked grave,' he added brutally, 'than return to stoke the Mortimer cause into flames. One less Mortimer is to his advantage.'

Edmund looked between the two of us.

'My ransom is no longer a matter of importance.'

Once again I could feel the expectation in Harry, as he absorbed what was as clear as if written in blood on the fair cloth under our hands. Yet Harry's clasp around his cup remained loose, his body relaxed in his chair as he waited for either Edmund or Glyn Dwr to make the grand revelation.

'How can you be freed if there is no ransom paid?' It was I who asked the question. 'You need to use plain words, brother. We are dancing in circles.'

Edmund pushed himself to his feet, to go and stand before the fire, his back to the leaping flames that outlined him in red-gold.

'Then I will be plain for, as my host says, it is time for truth. I have been well received by my lord, even though I caused the death of his men. As he killed mine. The affair at Bryn Glas was a tragic day for all; for me a disaster. But my lord Glyn Dwr and I have talked.' Now Edmund's gaze, bright with assurance that was not that of a captive, swept all present. 'We all know the true direction that we should take since Richard's death. The wearer of the crown, if not Richard, should bear the Mortimer name.'

'I would not disagree.' I must be careful here. To talk treason discreetly with Harry was one thing. To speak openly in this company was quite another. I glanced at Harry who remained unmoved by the dramatic announcement. 'You were ready to support our Lancaster cousin, Edmund, justice or no. What has changed?'

'I have made my decision.' Walking towards me, Edmund stretched out a hand to close his fingers around my wrist, an intimate gesture between brother and sister. I could read the thought in his mind before he spoke the words. 'I want you to consider the value of joining hands with me, and with my lord Glyn Dwr, to achieve the rightful inheritance of our brother Roger's son.'

I studied his face, still youthful, for was he not still a mere twenty-five years, but the lines of determination were strong. Here he saw a pathway to his own ambitions, for as uncle to the future King during the boy's minority, he would be in a position to exert supreme power. Who would have a better claim to be regent? But I saw that it would also be a difficult, dangerous path. One that could bring bloodshed and pain to all involved.

But was he not right? The old conflictions returned multiple-fold. The crown should be Mortimer; my nephew should rule in place of Henry of Lancaster, and I would never deny it. But to join the ranks of the Welsh insurgents in a combined enterprise against the English throne of Lancaster was no simple decision to make. That was the offer that Edmund and Glyn Dwr were making.

Troubled, releasing my wrist from his hold, I regarded my brother, dispatching all emotion from my voice. 'So you are going to throw in your lot with the rebels.'

'I do not see myself as a rebel, my lady.' Glyn Dwr did not take my accusation harshly. I thought he was understanding of my conflict.

'No, you would not, of course.'

And was I too not of a mind to be a rebel? The opportunity shone brightly.

But what of Harry?

'Don't judge me, Elizabeth.' Edmund sat beside me again, drawing his stool closer so that he could lean persuasively. 'I am going to fight for my lord Glyn Dwr against Lancaster. I will write to my tenants to inform them of my intent. We will fight together to restore my nephew to the crown that is his. And when he becomes King of England, my lord Glyn Dwr will have all his rights in Wales recognised.'

Treason indeed, already planned, already envisaged.

'You have gone so far?'

'I have gone as far as I can go. The letter is written. It only has to be sent.'

'And I cannot dissuade you.'

I had no wish to see Edmund end his days at the mercy of an axe on Tower Hill. But did I wish to change his mind? Within me a sense of justice wrapped warm hands around my heart. It was right. That Edmund was willing to fight for it filled me with a strange awe that my brother would be so moved. Would I be willing to join him in his treason?

'You cannot dissuade me,' he was saying. 'I was hoping to persuade you to put your blessing on this venture.'

His words might be addressed to me, and yet his whole concentration was now on Harry. My signature was not the one that he wanted. I would be of no use to him in the battlefield, whereas Harry and the Percy retainers as an ally would be invaluable. But the Percys were King's men, were they not? They would not betray the man they had helped to bring to the throne. I looked at Glyn Dwr who was leaning back in his chair, allowing Edmund to speak for himself. At Harry who was watching, listening, every sense raptor alert.

'I wish you would listen to reason,' I heard myself say.

But what was reason? My heart cried out to give Edmund my blessing in the name of my dead brother whose son had been robbed, and my dead mother whose Plantagenet blood was of such high esteem.

'I will not change my mind.' For a moment his face softened infinitesimally, before returning to its stern mood. 'I have committed myself in the strongest possible way. I feel it an honour to accept my lord's offer of his daughter Catherine as my wife. We will be joined in blood as well as in our battle for justice. For my lord Glyn Dwr and for our nephew the Earl of March.'

Which announcement sent all my thoughts awry. This was no lightweight hop from one side to another. Edmund was attaching himself to the Welsh Prince's gleaming meteor. Here was no casual alliance but one sealed in blood and legal entanglements of marriage. And Edmund knew it.

'I suppose I should congratulate you in finding a wife,' I managed to say. 'She is not the one I would have chosen for you. Nor would our father. I mean no disrespect, my lord Glyn Dwr, but you must see that it is so. Edmund could be putting his head into a noose with this strategy.'

'Alongside mine, if King Henry gets his hands on us.' Glyn Dwr remained impressively unmoved. 'Will you support us, or will you turn evidence against us, my lady?'

Harry's hand, clamped hard on my arm, stopped me. His voice was low, without any intensity, as if he were asking for another cup of wine.

'Why am I here?'

A question to which we still had no answer. Nothing had yet been directly asked of him, although an intelligent man could surmise with much accuracy. He directed it at Glyn Dwr, not my brother. That was where the power lay.

Glyn Dwr pushed away his cup, flexing his hands as if at

last the moment, for him, had come when he would spread bare his hopes and dreams before us.

'We thought you might consider joining us, with your retainers, to destroy the Lancaster King.'

Harry's voice was harsh. 'Why would I? What would be the advantage to me? We are Kings of the North. To put it crudely, what would I get from abandoning Lancaster for Mortimer? What's in it for me, to throw in my lot with a foresworn Mortimer and a Welsh rebel, saving your grace? I might be at odds with the King for any number of reasons, but that does not mean that I will sign my name away to treason. Better to renegotiate with the King than wager my life on a chancy uprising in the hills of the west.'

I expected Glyn Dwr to react in anger; instead he leaned back and began to speak with all the cool formality of the trained lawyer that he was. 'You are, by your own presence here, in severe conflict with Lancaster. I'll not give him the honour of the title King, for it should never have been offered to him. But it was, and now we must put it right. Lancaster will never be satisfied until his hold on this country is complete. Is he not chipping away at your power even now, encroaching around the edges? I know he sees Westmorland as a worthy rival to you.'

When Harry made no reply, Glyn Dwr continued, an energy beginning to infuse his voice. 'Join with us.' He extended his hand, open, face up as if offering a gift of great worth. 'Together we will be invincible. You from the north, Mortimer and I from the west. Edmund of March will be King. We will hold the country together in a tight fist until he comes of age. Right will be on our side, and until he is old enough we will give him good counsel through his aunt and uncle.' Glyn Dwr acknowledged me with a bow of his head. 'He will reign in peace, for who will there be to fight against him? All true English and Welshmen will know that he has the blood royal. And I, as Prince of this principality, will swear my allegiance to him. You, my lord Percy, will continue to hold the northern Marches in the name of the King as you have always done.'

Harry was standing, looking down at his host. Precipitately I rose with him, thinking from his stance that he would decline and announce our departure.

'Richard is assuredly dead,' Glyn Dwr said, 'whatever the rumours that he is alive and well in Scotland. He is dead and buried. The crown belongs to the Mortimer boy. Join with us and make it happen. Let us drink to our success and a new King, a new royal power.'

But Harry did not pick up the cup; he cocked his chin.

'I will give some thought to your offer, my lord. Meanwhile I will accept your hospitality for the night.'

Neither condemning nor accepting.

'Will you not give me your thoughts, Sir Henry, before you leave this place?'

'I will. There will be no doubts between us when I go.'

But then the calm in the chamber shattered, as if Glyn Dwr had been suffused with light and passion, with the heat from the fire and the magical portents of old prophesies.

'Join with us, Sir Henry. The dragon from the north and the wolf from the west, as told by the old prophesy of the mighty Merlin. Together with the Mortimer lion we will shatter this kingdom that has trampled on justice and honour. We will overthrow the moldewarp, the mole. Make this alliance with us, Sir Henry, and we will see a Mortimer on the throne before the year is out.'

I knew the prophecy, of course. The Prophecy of the Six

Kings. We all knew of it, by repute the mystical imaginings of the magician Merlin when King Arthur asked him to foresee the ultimate fate of his kingdom. Merlin had warned that the dragon, the wolf and the lion would combine to sweep aside the King that was the mole. The sixth King. The King that would be King Henry. I did not think to hear it as a foundation for a campaign, and it troubled me. This was making a magical prophecy into a political tool, Glyn Dwr being quick to harness it to his use in his discussions with Harry.

'There are strange stars in the heavens that presage our good fortune,' Glyn Dwr said as if he saw my lack of conviction in Merlin's prediction.

'As I will avow,' Harry agreed.

Iolo Goch, silent and watchful throughout, spoke for the first time with all the weight of a man of knowledge of such affairs.

'A blazing star has been observed, my lords, my lady, every night from February. It is a thing of wonder and without doubt it presages an event of great power. There was a star in the east to announce the birth of Christ, was there not? There was another star to announce the coming of King Arthur. It is my reading of events that this new comet heralds the rising of Owain Glyn Dwr, Prince of Wales. How can we fail, with such magnificence in the heavens?'

'So you see,' Glyn Dwr added. 'We have a cause and we have a great star to stand witness to our success. Even at my birth these major events were foreseen, with stars and comets and the earth itself shaking.'

'As my own birth was announced with blood,' Edmund added.

'Join with us, Harry Percy.'

Again Glyn Dwr held out his hand, as if to make an agreement, but Harry made no move to take it.

'I will consider your offer, my lord. I will give my answer in the morn.'

As we left the room, Harry holding the curtain so that I might pass through the door, we were followed by the soft voice of Iolo Goch breaking into song.

See ye that blazing star,
Ye bards, the omen fair
Of conquest and of fame,
And swell the rushing mountain air
With songs of Glyn Dwr's name.

The melancholy tune followed us all the way up the stairs.

Chapter Thirteen

We retired to our well-appointed chamber, the bed enticing with its soft covers and curtains stitched with golden dragons, but we were not there to sleep despite the weariness of the long journey culminating in the uneasy tensions of the meal and Edmund's change in allegiance. Glyn Dwr might be urbane but what we had discussed would disturb the whole order of things. His final incandescence had illuminated the chamber with his visions of the future.

'Which daughter is he going to marry?' Harry asked inconsequentially.

I sat on the bed.

'I don't know. If it's the eldest, she's the fairest of the four.'

'Then I can see why he is so enamoured. They are all comely.'

'Enough to throw down a wager to King Henry?' It nipped at me with rat's teeth, even though I was stirred by the possibilities that had been placed before us. 'To cancel his indenture to the King through a marriage to the enemy? Many would say it's a dangerous ploy for a man of sense.'

'We could argue that your brother was never a man of sense. He should never have lost the battle of Bryn Glas.'

Accepting that Harry's measuring standard was invariably what happened on a battlefield, I sat more comfortably and thought, unwinding my hair from its caul, drawing my comb through its length; actions that might appear to be languorous but my mind was not. A Mortimer crown was suddenly not such a distant vision after all. An exhilaration crowded into my throat as a whirl of possibilities presented themselves, if we should march in step with Owain Glyn Dwr. It would of course be Harry's decision, when and how he wished to make it, and I would not destroy our new-found harmony by pre-empting his train of thought. Even so, with the fall of my hair masking my eagerness, I allowed the future to emerge speculatively bright in my mind.

Until Harry came and sat before me, taking the ivory ornament and applying it himself so that my imagination set at rest for a little time, I sighed with pleasure, struck as ever by his gentleness when I had not expected it.

'She is not as fair as you. Whichever one it is.'

'Thank you, even though untrue.' I had long accepted my limitations, but Harry seemed not to mind my dark hair and grey eyes, nor my straight nose and determined chin, although they were not the stuff of chivalric song. 'I thought you might be seduced by soft Welsh voices.'

'I prefer your harsher tones. I know where I stand when you are displeased. Even your hair has a will of its own.' The remnants of the pleating had caused it to curl around his wrist as he combed.

I laughed a little, leaving him the silent space to broach the crucial subject. Which he eventually did, sooner than late.

'Well, my wife? Here's a critical proposal for us to con-template.'

'Tell me what you are thinking.'

He stopped applying the comb, holding it loosely in his two hands that seemed far too powerful to wield so fragile an object.

'We have been rebels before.'

'We thought it was justice,' I said, playing the hand of the devil.

'What we have done once, we can do again.'

'If we consider it just to do so.'

'Yes. If we consider it just.'

'Even if it is treason.'

'It was treason last time.' Harry slapped his palm down on the body of the fire-breathing dragon that rampaged over the bedcover, stitched painstakingly by some past Welsh lady. The fall of his hair hid his expression from me. 'We did not question the rightness of it. Or not overmuch. I think we crowned the wrong King in that year, seduced by Lancaster's show of piety at Doncaster. Those damned relics that blinded us all.'

'And we were blinded by your father's determination.'

'That too. But I cannot put all the blame at his door. It is at mine too. You know that I have always agreed that it should be Mortimer. But...' He grimaced down at his hands that were now empty, but scarred and abraded, as if lacking a sword.

'But it was easier to support Henry.'

'Yes.'

'And now, it is not.'

'Now it is not.'

'Why is it not? What has made this sudden difference?'

I needed to know, to be sure in my heart that Harry truly wished to step from loyal subject to rank rebel once more. Far more dangerously now, for Henry of Lancaster was the

228

military leader that Richard would never have been. If we stood against Henry, it would be a true battle, steeped in blood to determine the victor.

And I knew that I wanted it. Despite all the dangers and the threat of failure. Despite the looming possibility of death for Harry, of disgrace for me and for our children if we travelled this treacherous road, I wanted him to take that step to champion the Earl of March. Perhaps it was something in this place, this room, in Glyn Dwr's domain that gave dissent such a glamorous power. How could we fail? What would we not risk to remedy a great wrong? Right and justice were indubitably fighting on our side and would bring us victory. I could not anticipate death. I could not foresee disgrace. And if indeed it swept us up in its craw, then we would accept. We were free to make that choice. Once again fervour began to beat in my blood, in my mind.

'You know all the reasons,' Harry said. He began to pace, ranging the width of the room, then the length, as I knew he would. The honesty surprised me. 'We have always had expectations. Percy ambitions are pursued with sword and banner. The Percy lion will overcome all obstacles. We removed Richard because he had begun to undermine our authority in the north, did we not? But Lancaster proved no better. Yes, he awarded us grants, titles, wardenship of the March, control of castles, but with them came greater responsibilities when the Welsh and Scots reacted against Henry's rule. We should have seen it and did not, blinded by the largesse. Yes, we had power, but we were left with expensive border wars that made demands on our purse strings, with no recompense from the King. We ended up paying for the defence of a realm whose King could not meet its costs. Do we accept it? Or do we resist? Do we take steps to secure our power under a Mortimer monarch?'

He wanted an answer.

'I say we put a Mortimer on the throne. But it is not my agreement that is needed in this house.'

'There is no goodwill left between us, you see,' Harry continued as if I had not spoken. 'Lancaster blamed me for negligence over the fall of Conwy, of my refusal to take our Welsh host prisoner rather than talk tactics. He had no respect for my right to ransom Douglas myself. What does a subject do when his King has no respect for him? When that subject was the one to place him on the throne in the first place?'

He returned to sit before me, taking my wrists.

'Our power is on the wane, or will be within the coming years. What will be left for our son to inherit? Ralph Neville is the new beneficiary. My role as Justiciar of Wales has been given to Prince Henry with no recompense for me. Do you know what our grateful King plans? To set up a commission to oversee the release of all the prisoners from Homildon Hill because we, the Percy lords, could not be trusted to act honestly in our dealings with them. And the illustrious head of the commission will be Ralph Neville. I would wager my best horse on it. Nor is he the only one to have ambitions along the March.' He paused. 'I see the Percy lion laid low. Do I sit at ease in Alnwick and allow it to happen? It is not in my nature. Better to ride and face the enemy and demand retribution.'

'Or change the King.'

'Or change the King.' He raised our joined hands to his forehead, his hair falling over my wrists.

'And then there is...' Harry shook his head, releasing me. 'Nothing. Do we not have sufficient reason? Henry of

Lancaster is not the next in line. Edmund Earl of March has that claim. And when he's King I'll make damned sure that he does not interfere with battlefield matters and ransom rights!'

'I think the Douglas ransom rankles most for you.'

'By God it does!'

He was on his feet again, hunting for ale or wine, discovering a chased silver flagon in a cupboard beside the fireplace. Talk had made him thirsty.

'So we become rebels.' I nudged a little.

'We become restorers of justice. Mortimer justice.'

It seemed to be settled. The air shimmered a little in the heat from the fire. My heart shimmered within me too.

'Will the Earl agree?' I asked, refusing the offered cup.

'I don't know.' Harry shrugged one shoulder in a habitual gesture of rejection. 'I expect he can be persuaded if Neville is breathing over the boundaries of his lands.'

Abandoning the cup, Harry pulled me to my feet.

'Let us do it,' he said, as much fire in his eye as there had been in Glyn Dwr's.

'It will be a long path. A dangerous one.'

'We will follow it together and make the Earl of March the King of England, in his mother's illustrious Plantagenet name.'

We clasped hands as if we were combatants making a pact for the future, united in our visions at last. But we had never been combatants, merely lovers pushed in different directions. We would no longer be divided.

'Have you a true conviction?' I asked.

'I have.'

'Then you know that I will stand with you whatever the outcome.'

'I know it.' The lines in his face softened. 'It is a heavy

mood for such a remarkable chamber. I feel we are being crushed with magnificence.'

'And Welsh songs of death and glory from the pen of Iolo Goch.' Suddenly overcome by the return of our unity in mind and heart, and a need to be even closer, I stroked the tips of my fingers down his cheek. 'Lord Owain has a fine voice. Do you suppose that he sings to Margaret in their chamber?'

'It is just the sort of romantic thing he would do. Until she tells him to shut up and go to sleep. I've never met a man who could talk as he does.'

'You prefer a man of few words. Like yourself. Unless temper strikes.' I kissed his mouth. 'You never sing to me.'

'You would not want me to.'

'No, but I would like the sentiment.'

Sitting once more on the bed in this softer mood, Harry pulled me into the crook of his arm. 'I remember no songs.'

'Which is untrue. Am I to leave here, comparing you unfavourably with a Welsh Prince? Or even with Edmund? Sing to me "A Song in His Lady's Absence". It is a sentiment I understand well enough.'

'Well, I'll speak it, if you will imagine the notes. I am in a mood to be sentimental. Too much Welsh music and Welsh ale. And too much politics.'

So in a complete reversal of mood, one of the traits I loved about him, Hotspur began some of my favourite verses, his voice soft, his chin resting on my head, my cheek against the measured thud of his heart in his chest. There was nothing wrong with his memory. In his voice a sadness, a melancholy, as if he knew what it was to be parted from the lady he loved. As indeed he did, as I knew what it was to be parted from him.

Now would I fain some mirthes make
All only for my lady's sake when I her see:
But now I am so far from her
It will not be.

Though I be far out of her sight
I am her man both day and night, and so will be:
Therefore would as I love her
She loved me.

'As I do,' I said.

'As you do. Do not interrupt. I am in melancholy thought here.'

When she is merry then am I glad,
When she is sorry then I am sad, and cause is why:
For he liveth not that loved her
So well as I.

Silence fell around us. Just the drift of ash on the hearth, the faint beat of the wind against the shutters. Our breathing. There were tears on my cheeks as the lament caught at my throat. All the haunting beauty of the words, all the yearning loneliness of it. I made no attempt to hide them, instead I turned my face against Harry's breast.

'Thank you.'

'Did I live up to your expectations?'

'And beyond. There is none to compare with you.'

His kiss was deep and long.

'Let us essay this magnificent bed and pray that the dragons don't keep us awake.'

It was not the dragons.

Next morning, not long after a grey dawn, Harry was closeted with Glyn Dwr while I had conversation with Edmund, the first time that I had been alone with him since the news had reached me that he was a prisoner and his life under threat. All past anxieties were now abandoned, just as I cast aside, for that one moment, all thoughts of future conspiracy, as I simply walked towards him and drew him into my arms. Edmund laughed. Then hugged me in return. We stood for that one moment in silence, in reconciliation, mending the dangerous abyss that had opened up in our lives. Until we stepped back and exchanged a smile with not a little self-consciousness.

'Anyone would think that you were worried about me,' Edmund observed.

'No, of course I was not. I knew you would survive.' Did he notice the catch in my breath? If so, he allowed it to go unremarked, which pleased me.

'So you didn't come with Harry to ask after my health?'

'No. You are quite capable of taking care of yourself.' I fought against the rush of emotion, astonished at its power, as I recalled fears that we might never meet again, and deliberately turned my conversation into more pertinent and perilous paths. 'Are you sure you know what you are doing, Edmund?'

As if Harry and I had not had the conversation of the previous night, and made our decision, but I knew in my heart the stronger of the two characters in this newly forged alliance, locked tight with a prospective marriage. Edmund might well be blinded by Welsh magic.

'She's a wife such as I would choose,' he said. 'I consider myself fortunate.'

'I didn't mean the marriage. She's attractive enough –' I

234

had discovered Catherine of the four fair daughters – 'but are you content to harness your future to Glyn Dwr's cart?'

Edmund's handsome face darkened at what might be seen as an attack on his judgement. As I suppose it was. His jaw jutted.

'It might be that he is harnessing his to mine.'

I was not convinced by that jut of the jaw. Glyn Dwr had agreed that the Earl of March would be King, and as King would confirm his own recognition as Prince of Wales. But would this well-mannered Welsh lord be satisfied with that? He was a man of ambition and considerable presence. I thought Edmund naive if he believed his host was interested only in furthering Mortimer claims, with his own ambitions pushed onto a trencher to the side. Would he want more than the principality of Wales? And there would always be the issue of who would hold the regency for my young nephew.

'Have you been put under pressure to make this alliance?' I asked since there was no one to overhear.

'I don't understand you.'

'It would be, for you, the clear straight path to freedom. There will be no need for ransom. Here you get marriage and release in one neatly tied-up package, as long as you sign your soul away to Glyn Dwr's dream.'

'Yes.' His eyes narrowed.

'As long as you do as Glyn Dwr bids you.'

'Which might be what?'

'More power than you have considered. Power at your expense. Does he guarantee the return of your Mortimer lands in the Welsh March, or does he have an eye to those for himself? And who do you see as regent for young Edmund?'

'Of course the land will be mine again. And will I not make a fine regent?' His eyes narrowed further in a less than friendly stare. 'Or does Sir Henry see himself in that role?'

There was antagonism here which I tried to sweep away. I had done ill to stir it up perhaps but I could not neglect this abrasion, allowing it to become a weeping ulcer. 'All I say is – beware of this Welsh lord with a persuasive tongue. If I made an agreement with him, I would ensure that it was written down and sealed in the presence of witnesses, and not all Welsh ones.'

'You are too sceptical by half. You don't like him.'

'I don't know him. But I think I do like him. I see nothing in him to dislike, unless it is the knowledge that he set out to charm us.'

'It's not charm that has won me over, Elizabeth. It is pragmatism given the circumstances. What choice is there, for me or for you? We should never have given our allegiance to Lancaster in the first place. Look at how he repays me, even though I knelt before him in Hereford. He will consign me to the Welsh hills to the end of my days. He will keep young Edmund more prisoner than free. So we'll put it right. We will pin our rising star to our nephew's banner, and I will bring to fruition the great portents at my birth, of blood and battle and victory.' The tension was strong in him as he voiced the familiar sentiments. 'Do you not agree? Does Harry not agree after your night of tearing apart Glyn Dwr's plans?'

I saw the fervour in him, muted in the morning light, and so I relented, as a good sister should.

'At this very moment I expect Harry is shaking hands with Glyn Dwr and planning a campaign,' I said. 'We have all been subverted by his glamour.'

I was rewarded with a smile that made me realise why

Catherine would not be averse to this Mortimer husband. 'We'll not regret it, Elizabeth. I swear it. England will rise again, a new age, a Mortimer age.'

His enthusiasm was infectious, making me smile too. 'So it will. Good fortune, Edmund. Enjoy your new bride.'

'And good fortune to you. We'll soon be in the thick of a battle.'

I feared it was true. But there was no turning back. And were we not right in our judgement?

Thus we became traitors to the crown.

We returned to Ludlow, where Harry proved to be intro-spective, despite being home and comfortable before a fire in one of the private chambers, our decisions made. There he lounged, a hound at his feet, a cup of ale in his hand, as if the weight of the world bore down on his shoulders. I thought it was not what had passed between him and Glyn Dwr. Watching him, trying to read his introspection, I decided that it went back much further, to what had been said between him and King Henry, whom he had resorted to calling Lancaster. What had passed between them? Was it some insuperable clash of will between Harry and the King, of which I had been graced with only a trenchant summary, that had persuaded Harry into joining hands with Glyn Dwr?

I put down the Book of Hours that I had opened, since conversation had not been forthcoming. Dousing all but one of the candles so that the hounds and stags in the tapestries faded into the shadows apart from their gold-stitched eyes, I sat at his feet, which usually engendered some response, even if of a caustic nature.

'Something's eating at you, Harry,' I observed.

Silence, the Percy gaze on some distant scene.

'Harry!' Less lightly.

He looked down at me. 'It is all decided. When the time is right we will raise our forces in the north and march to join with Glyn Dwr. Together we will lure Lancaster...'

If I did not stop him I would have a full-scale campaign described to me, an efficient smokescreen to deflect me from whatever it was between Hotspur and the King.

'What happened between you and Lancaster?'

'Nothing but a difference of opinion over Douglas's future and whether our parsimonious King owed me any money at all for my services to the crown.'

'I don't believe you.'

His glance was quick. A hesitation, barely recognisable as one.

'Something was said,' I drove on. 'Something thrust you into Glyn Dwr's arms faster than an arrow from a Welsh bow. Oh, I knew all the reasons for your disenchantment. But it was more than that. Something was scratching at you. It still is. I'd rather you told me than pretended all was as it had been before your visit to Westminster. Is it still to do with Douglas's ransom? I would not have thought...'

'By God, Elizabeth, it sticks in my gullet!'

Ah! 'What was said?' I asked.

I stood, replenished his cup and smoothed his hair in passing. He was not pacing tonight. This was a matter of deep reflection, of some bitter memory. I returned to stand behind him, my hands on his shoulders. He leaned his head back to look up at me.

'I asked for payment for my work in the March.'

'And Lancaster of course said no.'

'He said no. As he always does. He asked if I had brought Douglas with me. I said I had not. That I would ransom him myself since there was no money coming my way from the King. I said that this time I would not take no for an answer. Perhaps it was not the most politic statement I have made, but I said that it was his duty to repay me, and I would not accept his refusal.' He gave a harsh laugh. 'He lapsed into Latin, as smooth as any damned lawyer. *Aurum non habeo, aurum non habebis.* I have no gold, you will have no gold.'

I was fascinated, horribly so, my fingers stilled. 'So what happened?'

'I said that I expected he would have plenty of gold to spend on his new bride and his marriage feast.'

'And?'

I walked round to kneel before him. For a brief moment a rueful smile touched Harry's mouth before it vanished.

'What happened? That's easy enough to tell you, but by God it dented my pride. His royal fist connected with my jaw.' He rubbed it as if it could still be felt.

I had stiffened. 'He hit you.' I could imagine the scene, throbbing with male arrogance. 'Tell me you didn't hit him back.'

How dangerous was it to strike a crowned and anointed King? Or would it have cleared the air between them, like two young pages scuffling in the dirt of a practice field? But they were not youthful pages. They were King and subject. They were Lancaster and Percy, one as proud and ambitious and obstinate as the other.

'I raised my fist,' Harry admitted. 'I'll take a blow in cold blood from no man, King or commoner.'

'So you hit him.' It was both shock and intrigue. 'Surely not a common brawl, Harry.'

But that was not it either. Harry's brow became lined with fierce furrows.

'No. No brawl. Are we not who we are and above that? I lowered my fist before I could do any damage, but my King drew his dagger against me.'

I waited, breath held, fingers pressed hard against my lips. Here was danger indeed. This is what had been eating at Harry through all the hours spent in Glyn Dwr's company. This is what had stood at his back, breathing dragon-fire, when he had made his decision to toss his future into Glyn Dwr's hands.

'Did you do likewise?' I asked. I could already envisage royal troops at our door, to arrest Harry for an armed threat against the life of the King.

'No. I don't say that my hand did not move towards my sword hilt. The temptation was to retaliate, steel with steel. But in my own defence, I stepped back from him.'

I tightened my grip on his arm. 'What did you say to him?'

'I said that I would not clash with him in a chamber at Westminster. But I would in the field.'

There was nothing I could say.

'It lay there between us,' Harry admitted. 'Like a stain on the tiles.'

'A stain in blood.'

'If you wish. Then I walked out, before either of us could say more or inflict any further harm.'

'A challenge then. And it has burned in your memory ever since.'

'By God, it has.'

'Did Henry pick up the challenge?'

'How could he not? I was not ambiguous. Nor will I be. I'll prove Hotspur on the field of battle if I have to. And this time we will crown the right King.'

I sat quietly for a little while, considering what had spurred

Lancaster into making so ill advised an attack on Harry. Both men of self-esteem but Lancaster should have known that a Percy must be handled with care. Physical violence, unprovoked except by words, would achieve nothing but hostility. Yet who knew better than I how provocative Harry could be when thwarted or abased.

'Were there any witnesses to this?'

'No. Thank God. But I'll withstand Lancaster's demeaning of my rank and my blood no more. Our friendship is at an end.'

'So that is why you agreed to Glyn Dwr's alliance.'

'It played its part. I have done with Lancaster.'

So there it was. I knew the best and the worst. The humiliation would have been too much for a man of Harry's breeding to bear.

'Do you blame me? For throwing in my lot with this Welsh renegade, whose ambitions might well dispense poison to all of us?' he asked with a wry curve of his lips, leaning forward to pinion my wrists in his clasp. 'I thought you would.'

'How can I?' I asked. 'And now it is done.' And on a thought, something I should have asked long before, even though I knew the answer as plain as he: 'What will happen if we lose?'

'What happens to all traitors? It will not be pretty.' He must have seen the stark acknowledgement in my face, before I hid it. 'But he'll not take extreme measures against you, my dear one. Are you not his cousin? Besides, who says that we will lose?'

I had no recollection of a more uneasy wedding ceremony.

How could it not be uneasy with this royal bride, against the baldly expressed wishes of the French King, come here to bolster King Henry's undesirable reputation as a false usurper? The King might have his four sons from his first marriage to Mary de Bohun to safeguard his throne, but now he needed the justification of a woman of European rank and status. So the widowed Duchess of Brittany with her impressive Valois and Navarrese connections was here to be wed under the soaring arches of Winchester Cathedral, surrounded by the King's family, loyal counsellors and powerful magnates, of whom at least one family had branded itself traitor in intent if not yet in deed.

How would the foreign Queen fit into the mosaic of this new House of Lancaster? I could find it in my heart to be compassionate, given the upheaval in the country, but she was a woman of more than thirty years and considerable experience, quite capable of creating her own role as Queen Joanna of England when she was finally crowned.

I assessed the quality of the guests around us. Many would say that it was an hypocrisy for us to attend, to smile and express good wishes, when we knew that one day, not too far distant, it might come to a clash of cold steel on a battlefield. I had no guilt; nor did Harry. We celebrated, disguising our disillusion with this monarch as effectively as a group of mummers disguised their true faces with bright masks, but behind the masks the Percy family seethed with discontent.

Harry and his father had not mended their dispute over the affair of the prisoners from Homildon Hill. Harry had no pity for the Earl's humiliation at the King's hands; their conversations were short to the point of ill manners. As for this marriage, any good wishes Harry offered to King Henry were less than enthusiastic. Worcester kept a still tongue and dour expression while King Henry was saying nothing about past differences. Ransoms and prisoners were not spoken of, all laid aside until Henry Beaufort, Bishop of Lincoln, had tied the royal marital knot.

It all festered like fat on the surface of a rank pottage.

'Smile, Harry.' I applied an elbow to his ribs within the pretext of realigning the links of his jewel-studded chain. I was rewarded with a direct regard in which there was no humour.

Yet within my heart there was a fulfilment of something that I had believed lost to me. Harry and I were restored; our future as clear-cut as the ruby pinned in Harry's chaperon. And so was our love jewel-bright. It was a warm glove worn over a cold hand in winter. It was a cup of honeyed wine on a frosty morning.

The choir sang, the Bishop pronounced, the congregation in damask and fur shuffled in the cold, anticipating the coming feast until, ceremonial at an end, Lancaster and Joanna exchanged a tender salute, and then he was presenting her to the silk-and-fur-clad subjects. There was no smile on Harry's face.

'What will your uncle of Worcester do?' I asked, watching Worcester's urbanely smiling greetings to his new Queen.

'He will fight with us, of course.'

Unlike our hasty departure at the King's coronation, we joined the guests for the feasting.

'It casts a hefty doubt on his claim to be short of money, doesn't it? Enough roast cygnets, venison and rabbit here to feed the whole of Winchester.' Harry pushed aside a dish of stuffed pullets, the grease glistening in the candlelight. 'As for the quantity of birds, their feathers could stuff a mattress for the wedding night.' He wiped his fingers disparagingly on a napkin. 'I trust the bride approves of this extravagance for a party of magnates who would rather be elsewhere.'

'Enjoy the meal, my lord. We may never be guests here again.'

As I dipped my spoon into a platter of pears in syrup, hypocrisy was indeed a sour taste in the mouth, but I knew our decision had been the honest one to make. I knew it even as we raised a cup to toast the royal pair. It was difficult to wish the bride a long and happy marriage.

As we prepared to leave I saw Constance making her determined way in my direction, with who knew what conspiratorial thoughts in her head.

'Let us hurry.'

'Why?'

'I have no wish to know what is in Constance's mind, nor for her to make any attempts to read mine.'

We made our apologies and started for the north. Constance's concerns remained unknown to me, and to my relief Alianore was not present, still no doubt furious over the permanent destiny of her Mortimer sons. Harbouring treachery was wearing on the nerves. As for the royal bride, before our departure I curtsied, keeping a curb on my tongue and a welcoming expression. She was tall and gracious, a handsome woman possessing much composure and considerable presence, which would be expected of the Duchess of Brittany. It did not surprise me that Lancaster had considered her a fitting Queen for England.

'I have heard much of you and your family, Lady Percy. It

is good to meet with you. The Earl of Worcester has been a welcome escort on my journey here.'

'The Earl of Worcester has been highly complimentary of your ability to weather a storm at sea, my lady,' I replied, for did she not deserve a welcome from me? 'It has been a marriage much anticipated by all.'

She touched the fingers of her right hand to the magnificent jewelled collar bearing the motto *Soveignez* – Remember Me – that rested on her breast, one of the royal wedding gifts bought with money that Harry thought would have been better spent on a body of archers for Percy use.

'Perhaps you will visit with me,' she said, 'when I am settled in London.'

'I would be most gratified, my lady.'

Her glance sharpened. 'Yet I see caution in your eye, Lady Percy. Will you tell me why?'

So she was a woman of some intellect and perspicacity. I should have expected nothing less.

'The world of politics is an uneasy one, my lady.'

Turning her head, she sought out Harry standing gloomily silent on the edge of a little group of wine-quaffing magnates.

'Sir Henry Percy has an abstracted air about him.'

'More like rank disapproval than an abstraction.' I could see no reason to deny it, allowing my regard to move to King Henry who was exchanging good wishes with the ageing Bishop of Winchester who had been too ill to conduct the marriage service. Seeing the direction of my gaze, the bride nodded.

'Ah, I understand! There is some disagreement. But if our lords are at odds, it does not necessarily mean that we may not have sensible converse. Are they at odds?'

'Yes.' I would be as forthright as she, but I sighed a little.

'It may be that we cannot converse intimately to any degree, my lady.'

Her touch on my arm was light.

'Then we will see. There is much for me to learn since I know not the politics of this realm. Mayhap you are right.' She smiled. 'But indeed, I hope that you are wrong.'

'I fear that I am not, my lady.'

She turned from me to speak with Worcester, leaving me with some reluctant liking and some regret.

Chapter Fourteen

Alnwick Castle: March 1403

'Persuade him,' I urged Harry.

'And how do you suggest I do that, since we are barely on speaking terms?'

I did not know how, only that it was essential, for without the concurrence of the Earl of Northumberland in this enterprise, all could fall by the wayside. Glyn Dwr might glitter with present success, the spring weather luring him from Sycharth to attack the Welsh March once more, doubtless Edmund at his side, but to take on the English crown alone and topple Lancaster from his throne would be beyond his powers, as even he would admit.

'You must have some notion,' I persisted.

'I will do it, in my own good time. But don't interfere.'

I knew better than to do so. I would leave it to Harry, even though my fingers itched to become involved. There were couriers, there were letters received and dispatched. There were raised voices, raking through all the old arguments of where Percy loyalty should lie, until I was weary of it. All I could see was our facile agreement with Glyn Dwr and my brother being ground into dust beneath the Earl's intransigence.

'Tell him we'll go to war without him,' I said in the end in a moment of unfortunate flippancy.

'I'll not. And nor will you.'

So I did nothing until the Earl of Worcester led his smart entourage beneath the entrance to our formidable barbican, and Harry summoned me from my morning tasks.

'So now come and watch. And listen, faithless one. This is how it is done.'

'And what would we be doing in the Postern Tower?' I asked as I accompanied him across the bailey to the distant corner of the curtain wall.

'Indulging in nefarious alliances, if I am not mistaken.'

Thus the three Percy lords met in the privacy of the Postern Tower where no one would disturb them, as they had so many times before. Northumberland. Worcester. Sir Henry. They were dressed for leisure, great magnates taking their ease in leather and fine wool. Three powerful and wealthy men with family interests to discuss. No weapons; no elements of war were present. A brindled hound curled by the hearth. And one Percy wife sat at the window, astonished that we had ever come to this point of agreement.

The Percy magnates clasped hands.

No oath made, no words of intent spoken. A silent Percy agreement that was unshakable. Owain Glyn Dwr had his alliance. The Earl of March had his army that could bring him to the throne.

I watched them as I dispensed cups of wine to seal the intent, for there were no servants present.

What had, in the end, persuaded the Earl? What had finally tipped him over the edge from royal counsellor into treason? A dislike of Lancaster's high-handedness. A detestation of being called to account for his son's behaviour, the humiliation of it all when Harry was his own man and followed his own inclinations. The royal expectation that the Percy family would continue to protect the north at their own expense. It had been wearing away at Percy pride for many months now.

Yet nothing would have finally spurred him into this hand clasp more than our cunning King recently transferring the captaincy of Roxburgh Castle from Harry to the Neville Earl of Westmorland; another dent to Percy hegemony in the Scottish border. Oh, King Henry was generous in return; the Earl of Northumberland and his heirs were granted a tract of land covering the greater part of southern Scotland, claimed by the English crown. Until a Percy looked below the surface of the grant. This land that was to be ours had yet to be captured from the Scots. At Percy expense.

'We are being used as pawns in Lancaster's clever game, with Westmorland as his knight,' was all the Earl said. 'We'll be pawns no longer.'

And perhaps the Earl enjoyed the vision of himself as the dragon, sweeping down from the north to join with Glyn Dwr and Mortimer to call the King to account. It was a dramatic picture that he would surely enjoy.

Why Worcester? Covertly I watched him in communication with his brother and nephew. A quiet, contemplative man whose loyalty to the crown was as strong and apparently immovable as the stone walls that surrounded us. The most unlikely of plotters. I did not know why he had thrown in his lot with this insurrection. I could only hazard a guess since he never explained, but I presumed that it was Percy blood being stronger than any water that Lancaster could offer, however jewelled the cup.

So it was done, with a hand clasp and a silent toast, while

my mind was full of an image for the future. The Great Hall at Westminster, hung with the gold and blue of Mortimer banners and cloth of gold. Edmund Mortimer, Earl of March, crowned King Edmund. Beside him the Percy lords in velvet and ermine and gold chains. Sir Edmund Mortimer too. And Prince Owain Glyn Dwr, a most valuable ally. A tight-knit family that would rule England well through my mother Philippa's royal blood.

And I? I too stood in the Mortimer and Percy throng, striking in coronation robes. There would be no official recognition of me, no chain of office, no staff or sword of power, but I would have the ear of those who counselled and advised. I would have a voice in my nephew's education in his early years, to make of him an impressive man and King. I knew it could be done. When Richard had first been crowned at ten years, who had played a firm hand in those early, dangerous years? His mother Joan, Countess of Kent, held no position on the Royal Council, but her voice did not go without a hearing. A woman of strong will and royal ambition, she had been a force to be reckoned with in the regency. So would I be. So would I have a presence in the midst of these magnates. Was it not my right?

It was a powerful image, blinding me to what would have to come before such magnificence could be enacted.

'Are you satisfied?' Harry asked in the end. The Earl and Worcester had climbed to the wall, looking south, still deep in planning, while Harry and I walked back to the practice yard where Hal's noisy efforts with sword and shield could be heard. 'You look like the cat finishing off the cream.'

I ran my tongue over my lips. 'And the cream was superb, more than you will ever know.'

'I know it well enough.'

There was more than mere satisfaction or anticipation of the coming call to arms in Harry's stance. It would help him lift the lingering guilt over Richard's death from his shoulders, and perhaps from mine too.

If, later, I contemplated anything of that meeting in the Postern Tower, it was that Dunbar was not one of our number. Dunbar who had been hand in glove with us in so many campaigns of recent years. But then, he was not a Percy. It did not concern me.

The only question now: when would it happen? What would give our conspiracy the order to start, to blossom into an enterprise that would fire the whole kingdom?

Spring merged dulcetly into summer; as we waited, the Percy family went about its normal occupations of making excursions into the territory of the border Scots. While for me, a small distraction: a letter, one I would normally have relished but which now with rebellion hovering seemed so unimportant. My eye skimmed where once it would have absorbed every detail.

To my dearest sister Elizabeth,

I had hoped to meet up with you at the Winchester wedding but we did not travel. Affairs here in the Welsh March are too unpredictable and my lord Edward was not in a celebratory mood.

I read on, seeking out gems from Alianore's wordy communication. Her husband's refusal to attend the wedding was hardly news, or unexpected.

Glyn Dwr is at large with the fine weather. We have recently lost

our castles at Usk and Caerleon and have not the money to raise a
force to reclaim them. At least he has now turned his eye on bigger
fish and has ambitions to capture the royal fortresses. We hear that
he has taken Carmarthen.

So our Welsh prince was not waiting on Percy involvement.
He had a driving force within him as strong as Harry's.

I could all but smell Alianore's unease in the next para-
graph. It seeped from the ink.

You will know about Edmund's volte face, of course. I wish that I
had conversation with you so that I might know your own mind.
I cannot deny his willingness to support the Mortimer claim, but
to do so in the company of Glyn Dwr, who is our sworn enemy in
the March, is quite another spoon in the dish. I cannot speak of this
with my lord. He damns both of them since he wants no success for
Glyn Dwr, and sees no possibility of any for Edmund.

We are not a happy household.

Do you support our brother in this outrageous marriage to the
Welsh girl? What does Harry say?

What indeed? I had not told her that we had joined the side
of insurrection, nor would I until it became reality. It would
not do for the King to be warned by casual gossip. Besides,
nothing might still come of it. We might have debated an
alliance with Glyn Dwr over a pot of ale, we might have
clasped Percy hands in alliance, but we had yet to raise our
banners in support of Edmund and Glyn Dwr. Harry and
the King might yet mend their crippled fences.

I read rapidly down the rest of the sheet. Family affairs for
the most part. The two boys still at Berkhamsted; at least the
King was considerate enough to send Alianore regular reports

on their health and education. Plans for the marriages of the two girls. Alianore's hopes for another child, for a son for her marcher lord. The King was at Kennington, planning further campaigns, rumours of foul moods abounding. I presumed I knew the cause of that.

> *I trust all is well with you.*
>> *Your sister in love and family,*
>> *Alianore*

Disappointed that there was so little here that I did not already know, I was in the action of folding the sheet to peruse again later when the final scrawl caught my eye, as if it had been added as an afterthought. And in it two names, entirely familiar to me, which made me stop and read the final lines in the letter again. And then a third time.

So Alianore's news was not without its interest after all. I kept the information in my thoughts. The involvements of Constance of York I cast aside. But the machinations of the Earl of Dunbar, a man I had never warmed to, were an entirely different matter.

Alnwick Castle: Late June 1403

I was on the wall-walk, taking some much-needed air after a fraught hour, looking down to where Harry, still mounted, was looking up. Apprised of his coming some hours ago, outside the walls was a surprising array of soldiery, close on a hundred to my eye, while within, in the bailey, Harry's personal retinue jostled for room. This was not to be a lengthy sojourn but a brief stop on the way to somewhere that was causing Harry concern. I cast my mind over any recent news. There was nothing to stir alarm in me, other than the usual rumblings in the west where Glyn Dwr was on the offensive.

'Where are you going?' I called down.

'I, my lady, am going to Chester.'

I walked down the stairs, lifting my skirts from the dust, pushing aside a hound with my knee. The last I had known of Harry's doings, he was deep in the siege of the peel tower of Cocklaw to the north, no doubt frustrated into outbursts of temper by its stern resistance, and shadowed by Dunbar who had returned to our company. Who was not, as far as I could see, here with us today. So Harry had rid himself of his shadow. I was unsure whether this would be good news or bad. Meanwhile, he was casting an eye over me.

'You look as if you have been in an argument.'

'I have.'

'Is that why two of my best ostlers are at this moment sitting in the stocks?'

'It could be.' I had spent an hour giving jurisdiction in a number of disputes in the Percy household. 'A fight over a kitchen wench that disturbed everyone, with a black eye, a probably broken nose and some smashed jugs and beakers. They were still crying their innocence when I dispatched them to sober up and lament their sins.' I frowned over to the little crowd that had gathered by the stables. 'I expect you will be inundated with demands for justice from their fellow ostlers.'

'They'll get short shrift from me.' Harry's scowl sent them hopping out of his sight. 'You are lord of Alnwick when I and my father are absent.' All delivered in a carrying voice so that no one would be in doubt of it. Not that my authority was ever questioned. I accepted it – so did the household. But sometimes it was hard for these northern menfolk to accept a decree from a woman, and not a Percy by birth.

'If I had given judgement, I would have kept them confined twice as long.' Harry continued to frown at his offending servants.

'You don't know how long I have condemned them to their humiliation,' I advised. 'They will still be there at cockcrow tomorrow, until I decide to release them.'

He laughed.

'Why Chester?' Now I was on a level and conversation at a normal volume was possible as I stroked my hand over his horse's gleaming flank with one hand, my other on his gloved hand in silent greeting. We were all suffering from the heat. 'I have heard nothing other than that Glyn Dwr has taken Usk and Caerleon from Edward Charleton, who is not pleased. The King is at Kennington.'

'Not for long, I wager.' Harry had dismounted, beating summer dust from his jerkin, having dispensed with his heavy gambeson, passing his gloves to me. 'By God, I've had enough of sieges and this sweating heat.' He held out his hand to a passing servant, relieving him of a leather bottle of ale. 'My gullet is parched, and dry with useless negotiation. God's Blood!' He drank, wiping his mouth on his sleeve with smeary effect. 'Give me a battle any day where we can make an impact. A siege draws my blood like a physician's leech.'

Beyond the walls I could now hear the approaching bleat of sheep and the low of distressed cattle.

'You seem to have provided us with meat for a twelve-month.'

'And that's all I've got out of weeks of campaigning. It makes me have sympathy with Lancaster's last abortive campaign in Wales.' He stooped to rub his cheek against my coif in a little intimacy that stole with delight through my blood. 'We need a plain battle, to draw the Scots into the open and bring them to heel, but they've withdrawn behind their walls. Much as I'd do in the circumstances, but thrice-damned Cocklaw drains us like an ulcer on the arse.'

So he had not enjoyed the lack of action. But I still did not know why he would march across the country to Chester.

'Where's the Earl?' I asked, since he had not returned with his son.

I moved to stand at his horse's head, taking the reins as Harry, in the absence of a squire, began to unbuckle the saddle.

'Still north in the borders. The last I heard he was writing yet another missive to King Henry to grant us moneys for our efforts, calling on all their past friendships. A last-ditch stand that will achieve nothing, even if he kneels at the royal feet and bends his forehead to the dust.' Harry's mouth twisted into a sneer. 'All Lancaster has to hand, that was not spent on the dower of his foreign Queen, will have been sent off to the Prince to hold Wales in subjection and rid himself of Glyn Dwr. Not with any great success if Charleton is suffering from incursions.' The unbuckling was complete; a squire arrived to take over.

'And where is our friend my lord of Dunbar?' I enquired, in the light of my enhanced mistrust of the man, thanks to Alianore's busy writings.

Harry pointed somewhere vaguely north. 'I'm not right certain. And neither do I care too much. At least he is not dogging my footsteps. Elizabeth – I need to talk with you. But first, here's someone you will be pleased to see.' I raised my hand to acknowledge Archibald Douglas who had just ridden in and dismounted, his scarred face immediately responding in a smile. 'I've released him, by the by. He's a free man.'

'But still riding in your retinue.' I tucked my hand in Harry's arm to lead him out of the fray, my curiosity getting the better of me. 'Presumably it is in his interests. What have you promised him?'

'We have an understanding. I've promised him the town of Berwick if he and his men will support my cause.'

So this was serious indeed. I kept my reply measured, as if Harry giving away a prize possession was an everyday occurrence. I wondered if his father was in agreement, or even if he knew. I had the impression that father and son communicated less than in the past, despite the tacit pledging of joint support.

'Which Lancaster will not like,' I observed.

'Lancaster will not be in a position to object.'

'Quite a cost for you to pay, for Douglas's allegiance. Will you really give up Berwick?'

'Yes, I will, if we can win the day. I can't stay long.' We were into the relative cool of the entrance hall. 'Will we ever have this conversation?'

Harry's immediacy began to destroy my composure, the blaze of excitement as bright as his hair. This urgency in Harry was a new thing. There was a shimmer of energy around him, a fire that had been lacking over the months since our meeting with Glyn Dwr, or at least when in my company. It now seemed to me that his planning had come to fruition.

We were alone in a shadowy corner of the hall, where there were seats set for those who wished to take their ease beside a painted screen, the noise distant, the light muted when Harry faced me.

'Lancaster might be sitting tight,' Harry said, 'but Glyn Dwr is not. He's on the move against royal strongholds. His home at Sycharth has been burned to the ground before being looted by the Prince. He'll not be best pleased.'

The news jolted me. I recalled the surprising elegance of his home, loved and furnished over the years, the breath of history in its walls. I recalled the welcome we had received, and was regretful that it had been reduced to ashes, momentarily wondering where Margaret and her daughters had taken refuge.

'He's taken Carmarthen. So Alianore says,' I said.

'Has he now? Even better then, that I should shake out the Percy banners and make my allegiance clear to all. We should wait no longer.'

'Why now?' I asked, out of curiosity, refusing to allow the sudden spurt of fear to surface. What had changed in recent weeks? Nothing to my mind, but something had set its spur to Harry. And I should of course have guessed.

'I've had my bellyful of sieges and it gets us nowhere. We sit and watch. We fire arrows and they fire back. We negotiate with no end result. That's no life. Within a decade I'll be too old to mount a horse and draw a sword. Better to live my life to the full now, to drain the cup, than to wait until it contains a few paltry drops.' His gaze that held mine was uncommonly solemn in its utter conviction. 'If we are going to act on our proposed allegiance, it should be now. If we believe in the Mortimer cause, then why hold back longer? I vowed to do it, and so I will.'

A frisson of excitement, of achievement, that at last it would be done. But there was the hook of fear.

'You will join Glyn Dwr in open rebellion,' I said. 'You will actually do it.'

He rubbed his hands over his face before raking his fingers through his hair. I thought it had been a difficult decision, but there was a relief in him now that it was made.

'I'm going to Chester to muster an army powerful enough to hold Lancaster to account. The Cheshire archers will readily join me. Still many believe that Richard is alive and well in Scotland, despite Lancaster exhibiting his body to prove the point that he is dead and now buried. I can use that to my own advantage in a rising against Lancaster. The men of Cheshire have a loyalty to me.'

Would he have asked my opinion about this dangerous move? Probably not. And yet I might have hoped that he would. Restless, moody, robbed of action in the field, even now longing to be on the move, he was reduced to twitching a tapestry into line here, moving a chess piece indiscriminately on a board set out for a contest if anyone was of a mind to sit and play while I sat and watched him. These chessmen had not been used for many a month.

'We'll do it, Elizabeth.' He was returned to stand before me for a little while.

'Thank you,' I said. 'You know right well what is in my heart.'

'Why would I not fight for my Mortimer wife?'

He linked his fingers with mine, halting long enough for me to be able to carry his hand to my cheek in a gratitude I could barely express.

'But will you have enough support?' I asked, anxiety keen in the fact that I should ask at all. 'To face both Lancaster and the Prince in the March? Young he might be, but you have said he is as able as any when it comes to tactics and strategy.'

Harry's shrug was an easy gesture, full of confidence. 'He's good but we'll be better, with a force that cannot be brushed aside. I'll march south through Yorkshire and recruit from my own lands as I go. I hear that the Archbishop of York and some uncertain clergy will not be averse to a Mortimer line of succession. My uncle Worcester will meet me in Chester. My father will follow from Tadcaster when he has raised his own tenants. We will send out letters under our own seals to call in all men who question Lancaster's right.'

'It is all planned.'

'It is all planned.'

In that moment I did not know whether to be horrified at how far and how quickly it had all come together, or grateful that at last my family would achieve the recognition that belonged to it. Harry was oblivious to the fluctuations in my mind, nor did I burden him with them. Indeed, I was angry that now, at the last, my own convictions were found to be resting on a shaky foundation. It was so easy to foresee the future, the wrong King replaced with the right one. It was so hard for a woman to send her lord off to war, knowing the risks, accepting them but dreading them too.

'I've had a siege in which to let my mind plot and plan,' Harry was explaining as he flung himself astride a settle. 'I'll join forces with your brother and Glyn Dwr, and with such power at our disposal, Lancaster won't be able to withstand us. We'll take Shrewsbury, garrison the castle, and then we'll hold the March.'

He was still sidestepping the mention of conflict in the field, so I would ask the plain question: 'Do you envisage facing Lancaster on a battlefield?'

'Yes.'

I waited, considering the terrible destructive quality of a battle, cousin against cousin, Plantagenet blood against Plantagenet blood; but that was not a matter to exercise

Harry's practical thoughts. He was already seeing some far-flung battlefield on which he could deploy his troops.

'We'll have a substantial force, but it will be the archers who hold the key.' I saw that he had thought it out, seeing a battle at the end of this. My fingers were linked tightly beneath the folds of my skirt. 'I saw that at Homildon Hill,' he continued. 'The archers had such devastating power, the knights were barely needed. I have to say it went ill with me on that day, but so it was. It's the only way. And no better time.'

There it was. A battle, subject against King. Treachery, plotted by the kingmakers in the north.

'Were you going to ask me what I thought?' I managed a smile.

'No. I thought I knew what you thought. But I will, if you wish.'

Hitching my skirts I went to sit opposite him, face to face.

'And if I advise against it?'

'I'll listen. As I've listened all my life.' He leaned to touch my cheek in a moment of unutterable tenderness. 'You won't change my mind, though. You know that.' His smile was wry. 'For good or ill, when my mind is latched to a plan, it is hard to dislodge.'

'Like a tick on a hound. Impossible, I would say.'

'Nor do I think you would wish to. These are merely foolish fancies at the eleventh hour, Elizabeth. You are as committed as I.'

I thought about the future that we could not see, of all that might go wrong. All that could be achieved. But to send him off to battle with no word of warning would be a lack in me as a wife. Yet what need for me to worry? This was no different from all the other times Harry had ridden from my door to fight. An arrow fired during a siege would be just as fatal as a sword thrust in battle. This was his métier. This was what he must do with all the extravagance of which he was capable.

'Well?' he asked, jaw tilted.

'Go and join Glyn Dwr and fight for what we believe in.'

'I will, in your name and my own.'

'Amen.'

There was the lightest of scratches on the reverse of the screen to catch our attention.

'Hal?' Harry asked.

'Probably. But he usually applies his fist unless his tutor is watching him. He has not yet learned the power of discretion.'

But it was not our son, rather Dame Hawisia who appeared to destroy our privacy.

'Do you need me?' I was reluctant to be disturbed by some household matter over which our steward could ably decide.

Dame Hawisia shuffled around me to where Harry still sat. 'I came to see my lord Harry.'

'Then come, for he will not be with us long. My lord leaves for Chester.'

'I have come to read the signs for you, my lord.'

I sighed, while Harry grinned. Dame Hawisia read the signs with great frequency for any who would listen and reward her with a coin.

'I care not for signs, Hawisia,' he said, although gently enough. 'Unless it be the great comet that we have all seen and interpreted, for so Hotspur will dash across the battlefield to bring King Henry to his doom.'

Dame Hawisia's mouth disappeared into a mesh of

wrinkles as if she consigned such signs in the heavens to perdition. 'Yet I would read them, sir. If you will permit me.'

'If you wish.'

I sat again, expecting Dame Hawisia's usual preparations for scrying which I should perhaps have discouraged if the maids had not enjoyed being told of their future lovers' good looks and abilities to seduce them into bed. A bowl, a ewer of water, a bag removed from her sleeve to scatter the contents on the surface in which she would draw patterns with her clever fingers. But none of that. Yes, she extracted what was needed from her sleeve but this was round, small, wrapped in soft leather. Unwrapping it she held it in her hand.

'What is it?' I enquired. I had never seen it before.

'A shew-stone, my lady. For heavy predictions. If you will hold it in your hands, my lord, so that your essence might warm it.'

The stone was dark and hard, even darker in this shadowy place, like some species of quartz that emitted no light, but Dame Hawisia had no doubts in her skill to show Harry his future. While Harry did as he was bid, holding it between his palms with good patience, I considered the advisability of this. Good news would be welcome, of course. But what if it was not? Yet I could hardly snatch it from her and deny her this moment of Harry's attention that she so rarely enjoyed these days. I found myself smiling. It was only an old woman, desiring to exhibit her skills, becoming the centre of her lord's interest. A woman who would read good fortune for her nurseling of years ago.

While Dame Hawisia muttered to herself, I remembered what I had been told of the portents at Edmund's birth, that I was too young to recall for myself. Burning signs in the heavens, like flaming torches, the earth shaking as if to signal some event of vast importance. Had we believed in the potency of these signs in nature with the flocks calling from the fields, the goats running amok? Perhaps his association with Glyn Dwr, who seemed to have been blest with similar signs and wonders, would confirm the glory of his birth. I doubted Dame Hawisia would see in her shew-stone anything as shatteringly dramatic for Harry.

'As long as you do not see my death today, mistress,' he said. 'I have far to travel.'

Harry handed her the warmed stone. Curiously, it had darkened even further in colour so that it almost glowed on the old woman's palm, emitting a sense of ancient power.

'No, my lord. I have read the stars from the day of your birth. I see an end, but it is not today.'

He laughed, disbelieving. 'Then tell me when, and I will make preparation.'

'No, I forbid it,' I said with a sharpness. 'I don't think you should call on powers that we might not trust.'

The signs at Edmund's birth had been seen by all, open to interpretation, but this shew-stone had elements of the devil in its softly glowing surface, its dark magic. I knew not what Dame Hawisia would see in it. Nor did I wish to know what patterns she had seen in the stars that foretold the day of Harry's death. But Harry remained smilingly disinclined to worry, his glance to me mischievous. He had known her all his life and loved her.

'What do you see? Tell me quick, before my wife calls a halt.'

'Do not mock me, my lord. Did I not warn you that you would be taken prisoner at the battle of Otterburn?'

'So you did. And that I would spend many precious hours

in boredom locked in a castle. Which was uncannily correct. So tell me what I can expect in the coming campaign. If I am taken prisoner, is it another castle, another month or two of life without action? Will we have to look for another ransom?'

I could not return the bright glance in my direction. At the last, I did not wish to know…

'No.' I said again: 'No. I think you should not, Dame Hawisia…'

'Let her. It will do no harm, and give her much satisfaction.'

She smiled in triumph, bending to look into the heart of the quartz. Smooth-edged, it glimmered in the soft gloom with what seemed to me a malevolence.

'I see a battle. I see archers and horses. I hear cries of pain and death.' She tilted the disc.

'Who wins?'

'Too much darkness.' She looked up, eyes suddenly fierce. 'But I'll say this, my lord. I see your ploughshare drawing its last furrow.'

I sat up, every muscle tense.

'Where is this?' Harry was asking, as if he had no belief in it, whatever the reply.

'You will perish at Berwick, my lord. I see it here. Your sword will leave your hand for the last time at Berwick.'

'At Berwick? Am I in old age, retired to the fortress at the edge of the March, surrounded by my children's children?' His regard was kindly, with more tolerance for the old woman than I could muster.

Dame Hawisia's face was stark with deep etched lines, her eyes sunken in her face like the dark pools on the moors to the north, reflecting no light, no indication of what was below the surface. Her tongue licked over her dry lips, and again, as if she sought for words to describe the vision that had opened for her.

'I do not see the time, my lord. Only the place. The spirits are not communicative.'

'Then I must take care not to draw my ploughshare anywhere near Berwick.' He gave her a coin. 'My thanks for your concern, Hawisia. Fortunately I've just promised to hand Berwick over to the Earl of Douglas.'

'I only say what I see.'

'I know it. And value your care.' And when she turned to go, the shew-stone once more secreted in its leather wrapping: 'Take care of my wife while I am gone.'

The old woman stopped, back stooped, to look from one of us to the other. Then her eyes met mine, as inscrutable as ever, but it was their very lack of expression that caused me to shiver, a goose walking over my grave.

'It is not my lady who will need care,' she said before shuffling off through the archway towards the buttery.

For some reason to which I was not made privy, Harry decided to spend the night at Alnwick. One more night, just the two of us in the great chamber, our world enclosed by the curtains of the great bed. We said all that was needed to be said, our love expressed in words and a physical joining worthy of the Stella Commata, that had recently blazed in our night-skies or so Harry said before he fell into sleep. I agreed with him, for the power of the stars was with us.

Before he slept, Harry traced my brows with the pads of his fingers, taking cognizance of my nose, my cheeks, my chin, my lips.

'What would you do if I died?' he whispered in the darkness.

'If you died, I would want to die too.'

'So that you could be with me.'

'So that I could be with you.'

'I won't die, I promise you. I will carry your image into battle. I can think of no better safekeeping for me, to know that you will be waiting when all is done.'

My senses were raw with emotion as I reciprocated, tracing his beloved features as he had traced mine.

We rose with the early dawn, Harry eager to be on his way, breaking our fast with our household, our private farewells done, my role merely that of Lady Percy, ministering to all with food and warm words of encouragement. I walked through the great hall, speaking here, exchanging opinion there. It was a moment full of bright hope, until it was time to go and, in the bailey where Harry's horse awaited him, my heart was wrung with a deep sense of loss that was a physical hurt.

Then the children were there, attracted by the noise, their apologetic tutor, a man of some learning and much patience, giving up on a lost cause.

'I thought you would not mind, sir. In the circumstances...'

'No.' Harry clapped the young man on the shoulder. 'I would have come to them, if they had not come to me.'

I let them have his undivided attention for those final moments. I had no right to demand all his time, yet it was hard to be unselfish, experiencing a sharp need to snatch at every moment; it was so before every campaign, but this one held such an extreme element of uncertainty as Harry prepared to challenge the King by force of arms.

'Do you go to battle, sir?' Hal glowed with worship of his father. And who would not? Harry's surcoat gleamed with the azure lion, prancing on a golden field, as did the pennons and his banner. No one would be under any misapprehension that here was Sir Henry Percy, resplendent and riding out to war. The hero-light was on him. 'Do you fight? Will you be gone long?' Hal's questions were endless.

'I do. I will. And then I will come home. But first, before I set even one foot beyond this gate...'

'You have a riddle,' Hal crowed.

'Now how would that be? And if I chanced to have one about me, how would you have guessed?'

It had become a habit, a recognised moment of foolishness between father and son, a simple riddle such as a mummer might employ, growing more complex as Hal grew. And for the victor – and was not Hal always the victor? – a prize. I knew why they had disobeyed their tutor. Who could resist a prize from a great lord, even a fairing of little value?

'If you have learned your letters,' Harry warned, amazingly stern.

A craftly means of ensuring that our son spent as much time at his books as with his horse and his swordplay.

'I have, sir.'

A slip of parchment, torn from some document, probably a rent return, exchanged hands. I read over Hal's shoulder, as he traced the words with his finger.

> I work long hours and must obey my lord,
> I break my rest and loudly shout at dawn.
> I am rung right well
> To make sorrow or joy for those who hear.

It was simple enough, neither beyond his reading nor his understanding. Harry had chosen well.

'It's easy.' Hal tucked the parchment into his sleeve, as he had so often seen Harry do with a message or a document. 'It's a bell. A bell. Like the one in the church that rings out for Matins. And for the passing bell when someone has died. The lord is the priest who rings it.'

'Clever! Then you shall have your reward.'

From Harry's sleeve appeared a bright, newly wrought dagger, a lion snarling cunningly within the hilt. It found its way with rapidity into Hal's grasp.

'It is too much, Harry.' This was no fairing. It worried me a little that my son was growing so fast. Perhaps it was past time that he was sent to some noble house to learn all he would need to know as a Percy lord about the art of war as well as chivalry, all that had not already been trained into him by his father and grandfather.

Harry smiled at me. 'He is of an age, and will be older when I see him again. I may not be back to celebrate the day of his birth. It is a good gift.'

Which Hal, engrossed in the sharpness of the blade, acknowledged with a perfect, formal little bow. He was indeed growing well and time passed. He was almost ten years old now.

But Harry had turned to our daughter.

'And who is this lady, dressed to say farewell to her lord?'

Bess, who at eight years was still too young for dignity, was hopping with excitement, her cheeks pale with anticipation. She could read her letters better than Hal and was quick to take in the words of her riddle, delivered in a traditional question. I thought that it might be too simple for her now but she studied it with all seriousness.

A winter miracle.

Water becomes bone.

Can you not stand in it without your feet becoming wet?

What am I?

Bess stood on tiptoe, pulling on my sleeve so that she could whisper in my ear. I nodded. 'Ice,' she announced. 'It is ice. Like the puddles in the bailey at Alnwick on a December morn.'

'So it is.' Harry crouched before her, arms resting on his thighs. 'How fortunate that I have a gift for you too. Your lady mother says that you have need of one. And I think that you will like this.'

A string of beads, pulled slowly, magically appearing from a purse at Harry's belt. A paternoster, which I took and wound around Bess's neck. She looked down at it, her face full of delight and even awe as her fingers stroked the smooth coral and the sun glinted on the gold. Her own paternoster was little more than a trinket of carved wood. This was a gift fit for a lady indeed.

'Is this for me?' Its value gleamed in the light.

'It belonged to your Neville grandmother,' Harry said. 'You did not know her, but she would be pleased for you to wear it.'

I made no comment on its value, except to say: 'Coral is a great prize. It wards off the evil eye.'

'So it does.' He looked up at me as he received Bess's kiss on his cheek. 'But I think you will do that in my absence.'

'And for me?' I asked, in the spirit of the moment. 'Have you no riddle for your long-suffering and neglected wife?'

He was standing, taking his gauntlets and his helm from his page. No journey was safe in this country now. He would not ride without his gambeson today. 'You are a constant riddle in my life.' He touched his lips briefly to my cheek. We had already said our own private farewells and this was a very public place. 'This one comes into my mind often: *I saw a woman, solitary, brooding.* Are you as quick as your daughter in guessing?'

But I knew the answer. An old riddle used against men who had no will of their own.

'I am no hen!' I said.

'No, you are not. You are my heart. As is always so.'

Then: 'Listen,' Harry said, drawing me aside at the last. 'If I am taken prisoner again, as at Otterburn, and must needs be absent until ransomed – God save me from it – I have appointed William Clifford as guardian to our son. I know he will be safe in your care, but Sir William will stand for him if necessary.'

I knew Sir William Clifford well, a stalwart soldier from a Yorkshire family, at present Governor of Berwick in Harry's name. But what he could do that I could not baffled me. Yet now was no time for unpicking Harry's plans.

'If you wish it,' I said.

'He will report to you if necessary.'

But before I could ask why he might consider it necessary, Harry beckoned Hal and whispered in his ear. Before long our son was back, carefully carrying Harry's great sword wrapped in linen.

Harry took it from him, passing it to his squire, gripping Hal's shoulders in thanks.

'When I return, you will be my page. And one day this sword will be yours. I carried it at Otterburn and at Homildon Hill. It will serve me well in battle again. It will serve you too.'

'God keep you.' Harry was preparing to mount. I had to say it; it needed to be said, and I was brusque: 'Alianore says we should not trust Dunbar.'

'Alianore with her usual, if long-winded, perspicacity is correct,' Harry replied. 'A wolf in wolf's clothing.'

'So you knew his loyalty was damaged.'

'Yes, I knew. He is looking to Lancaster for the rewards that he has failed to seize in our company.' Briefly there was a grim shade around Harry's mouth before it melted into a fierce smile. 'That's why I gave him the slip at Cocklaw. I needed his presence no longer. And as for you, my lady Percy. Look for me within a month, two at the most.'

At the last, on a whim since I had no belief in such trinkets, only in the skill of the wearer, I pinned a ring-brooch to the thick padding of his gambeson. An old gem, it had belonged to my mother, given to her by her father, and before that a gift from her grandfather, the old King Edward the Third, so with much age on it and probably carried into many battles. It was worn, the gold soft, the engraving blurred and the claws that held the gems uneven but if any of my jewels held power, this was the one. I knew the words by heart.

This which you have fastened on saves you either by sea or in battle.

It had not saved my father but then he had not worn it in Ireland.

'What is it?' Harry asked, squinting down.

'A token to preserve your life.'

'Rather I'll put my faith in my sword and my horse.'

'Wear it anyway,' I said. 'In my name. In my Plantagenet blood.'

'And you will be my talisman.' His reply was gentle and

without artifice. 'For you are all to me. My life's length and breadth and height. God keep us both.'

'Amen.'

For a long moment our regard held. Then another brief embrace and he rode out. I could not go and watch; instead I sent Hal with one of my women.

'Watch until you can see him no longer. Then come and tell me how brave your father looks.'

I could not see it for myself. I knew it.

Back in the hall – although why I should have returned to that once intimate corner beside the screen I did not know – when I moved the chess pieces into their habitual watchful positions, ready for battle, I noticed. Harry had moved the King, knocking the little carved piece with its shield and sceptre so that it rolled onto its side. And perhaps it was not so indiscriminate after all, for he had moved it into direct attack from an opposing knight with its lopsided gait. For a little while I stood and just looked. Such a contest would be bloodless on a chess board, apart from loss of a little pride in defeat. Standing the King back on its base, returning the knight to its position, I prayed that the one developing in the west would be just as painless to rectify.

And which figure here was George Dunbar? I picked up one of the two knights on the side of the fallen King. Alianore had rumours of his double-dealing, that he had sold his soul to Lancaster in exchange for the return of his lands along the border and the lordship of Allandale if he could ever recapture them. If that was so, he would not be joining Harry in his rebellion. But would he join Lancaster? My instincts said that he would. I had never had any admiration for Dunbar, no matter how much praise his military skills evoked.

Should I have said more to Harry? I thought not. He

understood Dunbar very well, and if Dunbar was now in the pay of Lancaster, to weaken the Percys in the north, then Harry had been forewarned. Perhaps he always had been a questionable element in our midst, yet he had fought well as a good ally. Self-interest could wreak havoc with rock-solid loyalties, as we must all accept.

But now Harry was gone and I would follow him in my heart, with every breath in my body, to put right a foul wrong. But what would be the cost of failure? Treason led to a bloody end. For those who fought. For all of us.

I would not contemplate that.

We would be victorious and Edmund of March would be crowned King Edmund of England.

Not two days after Harry had ridden south, my lord of Dunbar was demanding entrance at our barbican with the air of a man who had come to the end of a hard journey. His mouth was set in a firm line when I received him in my hall, as was my duty. Nothing could fault his courtesy despite the urge to spit at his feet.

'My lord.' I approached, extending my hand.

'My Lady Percy.'

Dragging his hat from his matted hair he bowed, shoulders stiff, armoured as ever in self-worth. I waited to see what he would say, how he would explain his arrival. As I expected, he was as slick as a pool of wax from a newly snuffed candle.

'I missed Sir Henry after the siege at Cocklaw. There were rumours that he was suffering from a dose of the flux. Concerned for his health, I followed him.'

It was magnificently done.

'Sir Henry's health is, as always, exceptional.'

Which was received by the faintest tension in his jaw. 'Has he been here?'

'He has. You have missed him, by two days.'

'Where has he gone?'

I gave no recognition of the brusque demand. 'He has ridden south, my lord.' I would give him no help. 'Can we offer you and your retinue hospitality? You appear to be in need of at least a good meal and a night's sleep in the comfort of a bed.'

'No.'

'Are you perhaps in a hurry, my lord?'

Reading something that I had hoped to hide in my cool response, the Earl of Dunbar summoned up a smile and true chivalry. 'Forgive my want of manners. I'll not impinge on your generosity, my lady.'

'Where will you go?' I enquired. 'The Earl is still somewhere in the March and would no doubt value your company. Is the siege of Cocklaw at an end?'

'Yes.' I could almost see his mind working behind the smooth facade which was becoming less smooth by the minute. 'I'll join the Earl.'

'Now?'

'Yes. My thanks, my lady.'

He rode out, not half an hour after riding in. And he rode south.

'Well, Alianore,' I murmured, watching the cloud of dust. 'You were wise not to trust him. But Harry is warned. What harm can Dunbar do?'

Chapter Fifteen

Alnwick Castle: July 1403

A somnolence had fallen over the castle environs with all the fighting men gone; unsettling in its intensity, so powerful that it could be felt like the flutter of moth wings against the skin, it pressed down on us. This always happened when a major campaign was under way. Our depleted garrison kept a close watch, their voices muted. There was no raucous laughter, no drunken revelry in this fighting household. Every one of us was waiting, our senses tuned towards the south, towards the west.

But it was, on that particular evening, the heat that was so wearing, so enervating – the heat of a July day that was slow to dissipate as night fell and should have promised us respite. The servants settled the great castle into its secure night-time state with even less noise than usual. Harry was somewhere in the west; his father the Earl in his Yorkshire lands, marching to join up with his son and Glyn Dwr. Where was Worcester, now that he had irrevocably distanced himself from the King? With Harry, I hoped, at Chester, to instil in him some patience when events did not exactly fit the pattern of his desire. I prayed as I often did that Thomas Percy's equable good sense would prevail. I thought it would be needed.

But perhaps there would be no need. Perhaps there would be no battle. Perhaps Lancaster would be the one to step back from the brink and offer the hand of conciliation and some level of financial recompense. There would be no battle and Harry would come home, regretful that there had not been at least one minor clash of cold steel for him to enjoy. But I would be grateful. I wanted no bloodshed.

Momentarily I covered my face with my hands.

Was that not a wish contrary to all my desires, that of a foolish woman allowing her ambitions to be deflected by her fear for her lover's safety? It had all gone too far now for conciliatory gestures. Lancaster would never give up his hard-won throne. Glyn Dwr with Edmund at his heels would seize every opportunity to be a thorn in England's flesh along the March, a thorn that Lancaster would never tolerate. Whereas Harry's greatest wish now was to fulfil his destiny on the battlefield for the prize of the crown of England. He would win it and present it to Edmund Mortimer, Earl of March.

Was that not what I wished for, whatever the cost in blood and death?

Would you truly risk Harry's life for Mortimer glory?

I shut down the pernicious thought, as I would slam the lid of a clothes press to keep out the moth.

The sun was almost set, dropping fast now over the garden where we lingered, my women and I, into the heavy dusk of evening until the moon would rise over the stonework with its silver haze. All embroidery had been laid aside, all books of valiant tales closed. Where was the sun setting, the moon rising, on Harry? Was he perhaps at Ludlow, taking advantage of Mortimer hospitality, or somewhere with his tents and soldiers? Somewhere the Percy banners and pennons would drip as limply as the great banner on the tower above me.

I sighed slowly, silently. It was not my place to speak of what was in every mind, to stir more concern. Our menfolk had returned from the great conflict of Homildon Hill with few casualties. They would fight bravely and effectively again, for there would be a battle. I knew it in my bones. It would be soon. But when and where? The outcome of this rampaging hostility was beyond my knowing.

Blessed Virgin, keep him safe. Give him tolerance. Grant Henry of Lancaster the foresight to act generously. Let my brother Edmund be wise in his allegiances. Give Worcester a benign influence on the proceedings. May the Earl be speedy in his march across country. Keep them all safe from harm. And those who would fight in obedience to their overlord, bring them home safe too to their women here in the north.

My fingers moved restlessly over the smooth beads of my paternoster, lingering on the carved gauds. Never had I prayed so fervently or so uselessly. It would be a hard task for the Blessed Virgin to bestow such indiscriminate blessings when there was blood in the air.

I must pray for a miracle, I decided. After Compline I would light candles, filling the chapel with them whatever the cost and the Earl's frown at such expense, and ask the Blessed Virgin to achieve the unachievable, for with the Holy Mother nothing was impossible. The Earl need never know.

'It is so hot.' One of my ladies, fanning herself with a broad leaf plucked from some aromatic shrub.

'Too hot to do anything but sit here in the plaisance,' I admitted. 'Play something for me.' I was in no mood to pick up the lute for myself.

Obediently and with some skill she set her fingers to the lute strings and began to sing. Words I knew so well and could have sung for myself. Words I had last heard...

Now would I fain some mirthes make
All only for my lady's sake
When I her see;
But now I am so far from her
It will not be.

The plangent notes struck hard against my heart, as did the memories of Harry at his most tender.

'Not that one.'

Without demur, used to my present megrims, she changed to a livelier stanza: her fingers busy on the strings, she sang a new song to stir the heart's-blood, much in fashion when knightly courage was admired.

What is he, this lordling, that cometh from the fight?
With blood-red raiment so terribly arrayed...

I could not bear the image, however chivalric the words, however heart-rending the notes.

'Nor that one.'

I could taste the resulting silence around me that pressed down even more heavily.

'Do I sing to the Blessed Virgin, my lady?'

I nodded. What could be better than a petition to the Holy Mother to soothe all troubled hearts?

Blessings upon you, Heaven's Queen,
Folks' comfort and angels' bliss.
Unblemished Mother and virgin pure...

I closed my eyes, allowing myself to be comforted a little along with folks and angels, conscious only of the perspiration along the line of my hair, the soft murmurs of a pair of ring-doves roosting in an overgrown arbour. No weather this for marching. No weather for riding in armour *à outrance* towards the enemy.

A sound caught my attention so that my head snapped round, but there was nothing other than the sweet notes and sweeter voices as my ladies joined the singer.

> *Bring us out of care and dread*
> *That Eve has brewed for us in bitterness.*

The sun had dipped at last below the horizon. It would be a fair night, the moon rising ghostly in the light sky, like the blue lion on gold, shimmering in the heat. I closed my eyes again.

> *Lady, mild and gentle, I cry to you for mercy.*

The lute-playing had come to an abrupt halt.

'Blessed Virgin come to our aid in this hour of fear!'

The whispered plea from the singer also hushed into silence, so that I sat up and followed the line of her sight. The moon hung large and full, a shadow pacing slowly across it, when there was no cloud in the sky. A rounded shape ate at the substance of it, like some ferociously hungry creature, so that the light in the garden grew imperceptibly dimmer. A strange dimness though, with hard edges, deep shadows.

What strength did this strange magic portend as an omen? First the star Stella Commata, blazing out in the heavens to herald some great happening. And now this, the moon steadily obliterated by a malign shadow, creeping ever onward until the world around me grew dark as pitch, my women fading into mere shadows, the glint of their jewels and my own crushed as the light died. I watched, every sense alive to things I could not see. The somnolent hum of bees had died away, the guards on the walls stood immobile. The doves had fallen silent too.

All to be replaced in my mind by distant but strident shouts and alarms, calling me to stand in concern, turning to face west, even though in the confines of the walled garden I could see no distance at all.

'What is it, my lady?'

'Nothing. Nothing.'

My voice was hoarse. Of course there was nothing. I had no gift of second sight to envisage what I could not see.

Esperance Percy!

The Percy battle cry. Did I hear that? Or was I guilty of some imaginative mishearing, in the still dark, of a cry I knew well?

Henry Percy King!

It took my breath. This I had never heard voiced. Was it my mind playing tricks on me? My beads fell unnoticed from my fingers into the grass.

The moon was quite gone. The dusk intense. The noise and voices I might or might not have heard ebbed away until all was silent again. But the terrible menace remained, holding me in thrall.

'My lady?'

Something about my stance had alerted my women. My shoulders were stiff, every muscle tense.

'It is nothing,' I said again, dismayed at the dry creak in my voice. 'We must become used to such portents in the time of upheaval. See – the lady moon is returned to us unharmed and undrenched with blood. All is as it should be. The Holy Mother will not be deaf to our petitions.'

The shadow, still moving, began to reveal the moon once more and with it the flutter of moths as above me a sliver of moonlight grew into a perfect arc, touching the flowers with silver. It should have been beautiful. It should have been reassuring. Instead it was sinister. My senses were flat and cold, much as the emerging face of the moon, as I turned back to my women, the muscles of my face strained when I smiled. But smile I did, for they deserved reassurance. They too had menfolk marching in Harry's force.

'No more music. Let us go in. There are tasks to do before we retire and we will meet for Compline.'

But first I sought out Dame Hawisia where she sat by the fire in the kitchen, eyes closed in dreaming. 'What did you see in the shew-stone?' I woke her without mercy. 'What did you not tell him?'

She blinked at me with the return of understanding. 'I do not recall, my lady.'

Crouching, I held her so that she must look at me, trying to gentle my hands on her frail shoulders when it was in me to shake her into memory.

'Look at me and tell me that you had no premonition of disaster.'

'There are disasters on every page of life.'

I could wring nothing from her, see no terror in her face, merely the confusion of an old woman. Perhaps she had indeed seen nothing, or in truth did not recall. And before God, Harry was miles distant from Berwick.

That night I could not sleep, every noise plucking at my senses like a page's first attempts at a lute. Finally I rose and returned to the garden alone, as if I would find some reassurance. I did not. The moon was pale now, sinking to its daytime rest, while I was full of foreboding.

My mercurial, ever-changing Harry. Yet he was my constant, the one certainty in my life. My keystone. No one else could ever be that. Without him, what would my life be? I would be only half alive. *You will be my talisman*, he had said. *You are all to me. My life's length and breadth and height.* As he was mine.

All I could do was wait.

I picked up the paternoster beads from where they had fallen, forgotten, in the grass and crushed them to my heart. They were icy to my touch.

When the news came, as it must, delivered by a battle-weary Archibald Douglas, his scarred face seamed and drawn with exhaustion and grief, it was not a surprise to me. He stood before me, his hands open and stretched towards me as if making an offering to some all-powerful deity.

'You know what it is that I will tell you.'

'Yes.' I could barely make my lips form the word.

'I can give you no solace. Except to say that he died bravely.'

'Yes.'

Breathing was so difficult. Thinking was well-nigh impossible. Was it even within my power to exist in this wasteland of emptiness?

He had died bravely. I would have expected no other. How would he not die with courage deep-set in every bone and sinew of his body? I stretched out my own hand to touch Douglas's fingertips. It was all I could do. Words were beyond me. And then, when he had told me the dread burden of it all: 'Have you brought him home?'

'It was not possible. Forgive me...'

Then he was gone about his own affairs, leaving me with a paralysis of heart and soul and mind that crippled every emotion but the one that hurt most and from which I would never be free.

I had lost him.

The sun shone with benign warmth, the world stepped on its measured way around me. Late roses spread their blooms rampantly over the trellis in the plaisance, while blackbirds flocked to eat the early damsons. The bees were busy again. The castle came awake. So much light and life around me. But darkness and death were the sum total of my experience in the bitter days that followed. All the beauty was obliterated in a dark river that swirled about me with no mercy.

Blessed Virgin come to my aid. Do not, in your mercy, hold your compassion from me. Holy Mother take away this anguish.

Would I ever be free of this pain? It built and built in my breast, like a wolf's howl in the northern forests. My eyes were sore with lack of sleep and shed grief.

Harry never did meet up with Edmund or Glyn Dwr. He never did take possession of Shrewsbury where Prince Henry held control. He never did make the crucial crossing of the River Severn as he had planned. Nor did he fulfil that terrible destiny, that on the field of battle he would wrest the crown from Henry of Lancaster and thrust it into the hands of the young Earl of March.

Harry Percy was dead.

Hotspur was dead.

I crushed my hands over my lips to silence that howl of grief, that refused to be silenced.

Yes, he fought, so I was told. Over the fields to the east of Shrewsbury, rich with the crops of peas that entangled and hampered the horses, Harry made war. Yes, he led his troops in brave attack, a final great charge when all were weakening around him. Some said that he should never have done it, but I knew him. He would not step back when there was still a chance of victory.

Esperance Percy! Esperance Percy!

I could imagine the great cry thundering across the plain from so many voices. Could I not hear it in my heart, my head, as it filled every space within me? I could see the blue lion of the mighty Percy lords held above him, gleaming on his breast, so that all would know that this was Hotspur, come to fight for what was right, against a King who should never have been.

He fought as I knew he would, as if the gods of old, of myth and legend, had lent him all their strength, all their old glamour. He would have been one of the brave number to stand alongside the heroes of King Arthur's magical court.

Should he have made that final charge?

Who was to know?

Henry, my cousin of Lancaster, was responsible for my lord's blood being so wantonly spilled. In his fear and his cunning, Lancaster hid behind others in his royal livery so that he would not be a marked man. Harry never hid. The Percy lion flew above him until the end, so they say. My glorious Harry. My courageous Hotspur, battle-hardened after thirty-nine years, yet the Percy lion had fallen and was trampled in the mire of the battlefield.

Should he have made that final disastrous charge? The thought returned again and again. Perhaps not, but he would have been unable to withstand the fervour in his blood or the defiance of Lancaster's challenge. He was ever too impetuous, with no one at his side to hold him back.

No one did. Not Worcester who was there at the battle, fighting at his side. Not the Earl who was not there. Not thrice-damned Dunbar who betrayed us all and fought at Lancaster's side because Lancaster offered him lands and annuities that would never be achieved as a Percy ally. Why did Worcester not offer temperance? Why did Worcester, the master of negotiation, not stand between Harry and the usurper?

Harry Percy King!

I had never heard such a cry in battle, but now I did as I took to my bed where it snatched me from sleep. I had never heard it but there were some who brought their swords and arrows to his service who would not have been averse to a Percy King. Many who spurred him on to his terrible fate.

And so he died in a welter of blood and vicious hand-to-hand combat. What was it that destroyed his life? The blow of an axe? A sword's lethal edge? Perhaps an arrow, penetrating the face guard of his battle helm. I would never know who killed my brave Harry, whose hand was responsible for the fell deed. I did not know nor ever would, for I never saw his body in the aftermath. In the bloody confusion of battle, perhaps it was the chance arrow that he had feared so much. He had been wise to fear the arrow storm after Homildon Hill.

I could not speak with Dame Hawisia, who had been a false prophet, leading me to rest in the assurance that he would not die. *You will die in Berwick*, she had said. But he would not set foot in Berwick. His great sword would fall from his hand in Berwick, she had said.

'My lady...'

There she was, wringing her hands.

'I cannot speak with you.'

I turned away. I could not bear to look at her, much less speak with her.

Harry was not taken prisoner for ransom this time. There would never be another aftermath of battle when we could buy his redemption. It was a rout, they told me, the treacherous Dunbar fighting for Henry despite all the battles that he and Harry had shared in the past. There was no honour. Dunbar saw Lancaster as the path to his aggrandisement in the northern border; Dunbar looked to Lancaster as the source of his future restoration, whereas the Percy power stood in his way. Harry dead would play perfectly into his hands.

Beware Dunbar. How accurate had Alianore been.

So much I could not grasp of those final days. But who defiled his body? That I knew. I knew and would never forgive Henry of Lancaster for his foul deeds. Harry's body was rescued by his faithful retainers who would not let it lie to be hacked and mutilated. Thomas Nevill, Lord Furnival, discovered my lord's body and took it with all care to Whitchurch to the north where it was buried in holy ground. He searched the field, the carnage, with such diligence, so that my lord's body might not be despoiled by more than the wounds of the battle.

But Lancaster had not been satisfied. Lancaster would not allow his enemy's body to rest undisturbed. My heart wept in despair, for Harry's body had been snatched back into the hands of the usurper.

Holy Virgin. Remove these images from my sight. Let me not imagine the evil that was acted against him.

Could Lancaster not agree to parley? To negotiate? Did it have to be this battle to the death? Could something not be resurrected from the collapse of that first fine friendship between Harry and Henry of Lancaster, on the tourney fields of France?

But Harry would not have wanted reconciliation.

287

The voice whispered it in my mind.

It had all gone too far for that. Their friendship was long dead.

Some said that Lancaster fought at the forefront of his men rather than hiding behind his liveried minions. They said that he too was brave. My mind could not encompass it. What is bravery in the one who slew the man I loved beyond death? They said he shed tears over Harry's body when he was found on the battlefield but I think it was said to comfort me. I doubt he would have wept. Lancaster did not discover Harry's body in its death throes.

God damn him! I damned him with every breath.

All that remained at the end of the day was a field of bloody corpses, both men and horses, amidst the trampled peas, with Worcester bound to his horse and taken to Shrewsbury Castle to await his inevitable fate. The head of Lancaster's once loyal servant, Thomas Percy, was mercilessly dispatched to adorn London Bridge, his body sent for burial to the Abbey church of St Peter at Shrewsbury. No such compassion was shown to Harry. Lancaster's vindictiveness took my breath in his need to send a powerful statement to any who would rebel. To Glyn Dwr and to Edmund. Beware all who dare rise in rebellion against the Lancaster King. Here is Sir Henry Percy whom you will know as Hotspur, defiled and humiliated.

My heart shivered with the horror of it.

I wept hopelessly. There would come a day when I could weep no more, when it would not be politic for me to weep, but for now the tears flowed. I would never again hear his voice nor see him ride towards me. I would never see him beat the dust from his clothes or gulp a cup of ale after a dry campaign. I would never see the smile that lit his eyes when they rested on me. I wept for Hal and for Bess who would have nothing but a distant recollection of their father, that would fade as the years passed. At least I had the bright memories to fix in my mind.

Why had I not known the moment he was robbed of life? How was it that I could continue to hope that all would be well and that he would come home to me? I had betrayed him in my hope, when I should have been on my knees in grief.

One day I must take up my life again. Was I not a Mortimer, inured to pain and loss? Was I not a descendant of Kings? But not yet. Not yet.

What would you do if I died?

If you died, I would want to die too.

I had lost my love, the centre of my life. It seemed to me that there was no longer a reason for me to rise from my bed at dawn. Why would I wish to live? Harry was gone from me, from all of us, for I was not the only one to feel the pain. The household at Alnwick groaned with it, and I groaned too. For one thing I knew. The Earl was not in the battle. He and his troops had never fought. He and his troops had never arrived, never marched beyond his lands in Yorkshire.

How much of a betrayal was that of his son and heir?

I would never forgive him. My heart was closed against him, my soul encased in a cold demand for vengeance.

May God cast His judgment on the Earl of Northumberland.

Alnwick Castle: Early August 1403

Our men, what was left of them, returned piecemeal, desolate in defeat, trudging towards the barbican but with no joy of homecoming in their faces. There were few without injuries. No soldiers' light-hearted or crude banter today, they limped with the weight of the world on their shoulders and on their hearts. I knew the faces. They were men dedicated to Hotspur's cause, whatever it might be, wherever it might take them. Once they would have sung about the prowess of their Percy lord, or their loss of hair with old age, joking in their achievements. Now their lodestone was despoiled. He would draw them to him no more. He would no longer charm and encourage and lead by his valiant example. They were alone and abandoned.

As was I. I had lost my own lodestone.

But now I must welcome them back in Harry's name. As Lady Percy it was my duty and my care.

A page almost fell from his horse to come and stand before me. In his arms, lifted from one of the wagons, was a wrapped package. He raised it on his two hands with all the reverence of a priest elevating the Host, before placing it at my feet, his head bowed.

'What is it, Hugh?'

Did I need to ask? On his knees, he turned back the cover, as gently as if he would reveal a newborn child. Thus it took me no time at all to recognise what he had brought for me, the blade chased and gilded, the hilt plain with its soldier's grip. Almost I bent to pick it up, but seeing the face of the page, now lifted to mine, ravaged with loss and guilt too, I did not. I must leave it in his care for now.

'Was my lord's sword rescued from the battlefield?' I asked.

And realised it could not be. It was unused, the edges fine, the metal gleaming, as if it had just come from Harry's hand in our armoury. No signs of battle damage here. I could not believe that he had not used it in anger against Lancaster.

'No, my lady.' There were tears marking pathways through the grime on Hugh's cheeks.

'You must tell me.'

He gulped, wiping his face on his sleeve, as he allowed the words to burst from him in a cataract of despair. 'My lord bid me help him gird on his sword on the day of the battle, when we knew that Lancaster was facing us. We had taken up our position when we learned that Lancaster was to the south, at Haughmond Priory. But I could not. It was my fault.' The tears began to fall again. 'I had left the sword in the village where we had spent the night.'

'You must not grieve, Hugh. You did not cause his death.'

'They say that I did, my lady.'

It was Harry's best-beloved sword, the one that always came first to his hand, the sword that had brought him success at Nesbit Moor. He would not have been pleased, but I doubted he would have vented his anger on the child. Some sharp words perhaps, before discovering a different sword to take into battle. But the page was overwrought from too much blood, too many terrible sights.

'No,' I said gently. 'Your lord would not have blamed you. You must not distress yourself. Come. Stand up and—'

'No, my lady. You do not see. Not at all. Because of the place where we spent the night. It was the house of William Bretton. It was all my fault that my lord died on that foul field at Shrewsbury. He was hacked to his death because of me.'

'I do not understand you.'

It came as a mere whisper. 'The house was in a place called Berwick, near to Shrewsbury.'

'Ah!'

'Sir Henry talked about a soothsayer,' the page continued, the words still falling from his tongue in a stream, 'who had predicted that he would perish at Berwick, but that he had believed it to mean Berwick in the north. Until I left his sword beside the door in that manor house. So my lord knew that his life was drawing to its end. He knew he would lose the battle.'

I raised the boy to his feet, fighting hard to smile on him. 'My lord would never believe that he would lose a battle because of one misplaced sword, no matter what a soothsayer might foretell. He had too much faith in his own powers to fight off the enemy. Did he chastise you?'

'No, my lady.'

'He would not. He would never blame you for a moment of forgetfulness. Nor will I.'

I wiped the tears with my thumbs, making even more smears on his face, as I struggled to control mine. No, he would not. But I understood. And I understood how any soldier would not lightly cast off rumours of ill omen. Grief racked me, that he should have ridden into battle with this storm crow on his shoulder.

'I went back to the Bretton house after the battle. They had put the sword aside, but I reclaimed it in the name of my lord, to bring it home.' The child delved into the breast of his tunic. 'I should return this to you too, my lady.'

He held out the ring-brooch.

'Did Sir Henry not wear it?'

'He would not. He said it was too valuable for battlefield games, and that the gems were insecure, but that I should return it to him after the battle.'

So he had fought without even my protection.

I took it, gripping it hard in my palm so that the edges gouged my flesh. And said to the page: 'Take the sword, Hugh. Clean it as if your lord would use it again, and then take it to the armoury where a place of honour will be found for it.'

One day it would belong to my son, when I would tell him

of Hotspur's glorious fall at Shrewsbury. Watching Harry's page go with his burden, I stood and welcomed back our men, organising care and food, potions and nostrums where needed for wounds and bruises, all governed with a strong hand.

Only later did I go to the armoury where I picked up the sword. I wept over it, undoing all the page's good work.

'Henry Percy.'

I said his name aloud, an incantation to summon up the dead.

There was no reply. The steel cold under my hand, Harry's question returned to me:

What would you do if I died?

And my response:

If you died, I would want to die too.

But I could not. I was compelled to live on without him in this vast barren landscape.

Chapter Sixteen

I was waiting for him. I had chosen to seat myself in the high-backed chair on the dais, the position of power that he was wont to use when giving judgement. My hands were pressed flat against the carved arms in anticipation when the Earl marched into the great hall of Warkworth Castle. He halted, abruptly, immediately schooling any thoughts that might be visible in his expression. No one had warned him that I was here. The Earl of Northumberland was come home.

Slowly I rose to my feet. Today I would give judgement.

'In God's name, why did you betray your son?'

If there was any grief in him, it was well hid from me. I did not wait for a reply, for I had travelled swiftly and with purpose to be here at Warkworth for this denunciation. I took another breath. The simple act of communication might be almost beyond me, but I would say what was in my mind.

'Why did you not take your retainers and fight with your son on the battlefield? You failed him. Where were you when he made his last charge at Shrewsbury? He is dead, and I swear you are not without blame.'

At least I had had the sense to wait for him where we would not be overheard, but self-control was hard.

I had known he was coming. The uneasy town of Newcastle, with a weather eye open to Lancaster's whereabouts, had refused to allow the retreating Earl and his army to enter, so here he was taking refuge at Warkworth; an old wolf retreating to its lair where it could lick its wounds and recover. To fight another day.

Except that there were no wounds. He had not fought. He had never been at Shrewsbury.

Here was the mighty Earl of Northumberland with his forces returned home, banners flying, heraldic motifs brilliant in the sun; not tattered and blood-soaked, utterly diminished as those brought back by the remnants of Harry's army, but gloriously unsullied. The only fighting his military force had done was to attack Newcastle when they were kept from the ale and food to be found within its walls. Now the bulk of the army was disbanded, but here was the Earl with his shining personal retinue, proclaiming his authority in his own lands.

Northumberland. Proud, selfish Northumberland, the crafty, self-serving King of the North. Northumberland the Faithless.

I tried not to sneer but all the years of decorous good manners were cast aside when he stood before me, hands clasped around his sword belt, head raised as if in pride at his achievements.

I took a step to the front of the dais.

'You were to lead your forces to the Welsh March. Harry relied on you to make all speed and protect his flank, yet you did not. I know that you did not. You never marched further than your own lands at Tadcaster. And because you left Harry to fight Lancaster alone, today he is dead.'

My voice rang out to fill the spaces around me. In spite of my intention to temper my voice, I was past discretion. This was for all the world to know and make judgement. I cared not that those who had eventually followed the Earl into the hall and so come within hearing stared at me with shock akin to fear.

The Earl's eyes on mine were as cold as his voice. There was no guilt that I could see, there in their flat gleam where sunshine angled through the high windows to paint him in strips of light.

'I do not have to answer for my actions to you, madam.'

'You must answer for your culpability before God, but do I not deserve an explanation? Today I am a widow. My children are fatherless and we are all tainted with treason, our lives now in Lancaster's gift. A captive traitor faces death and I swear Lancaster will have it in his mind to hold us up as examples to those who plot insurrection. All because you did not bring your troops to protect your son against the royal army at Shrewsbury.'

He turned away, ostensibly to give his cloak to a page whose eyes were wide with astonishment that Lady Percy should upbrade the Earl in his own castle.

'We are traitors anyway in the eyes of Lancaster,' he said. 'As soon as our banners were raised against him we were traitors.'

Now I swept down from the dais to face him on a level.

'But Harry would not be a dead traitor if you had fulfilled your promise. If the battle at Shrewsbury had been won, we would not be traitors at all.'

I gripped his sleeve when he would have pushed past me.

'Don't deny that you were complicit in this whole under-taking. I know that you were party to the planning, for I have seen your name signed on the letters to Glyn Dwr. You had an army at Tadcaster in campaign order. You told Harry that you had every intention of marching. Why did you not?'

I struggled to keep the despair from my voice when it

threatened to overwhelm my anger, while the Earl shook off my hand.

'Where is my grandson, my heir?' he asked.

'Here with me. I'll not let him or my daughter out of my sight.' Harry might have left his son under the immediate care of his old retainer Sir William Clifford at Berwick if aught should happen to him at Shrewsbury, but I had done nothing yet to contact him. Hal was mine to protect, and I would, with my life.

'Thank God.'

If I saw any relief in the Earl, I brushed it aside as an irrelevance, returning to my tirade of blame and apportioned guilt, my hands tightening into fists.

'Would you willingly send your son to his death? I know there was a rift between you over the fate of Douglas. I know you disapproved of the depth of Harry's quarrel with Lancaster. I know that you resented having to carry the blame in his name when Lancaster took you to task. Would you truly place the burden of your humiliation at Lancaster's hands on Harry's shoulders? I cannot believe that you would do so heinous a thing.'

I watched the tightening of the muscles in the Earl's jaw, the flicker of his gaze at last away from me. So my words had moved him, but to guilt or defiance, I could not tell.

I continued to belabour him with my anger. 'Did your glorious son, in the end, go to meet up with Glyn Dwr without your consent? If it was your intent to punish him, to teach him the need for duty and obedience between father and son, your lesson was a tragic one. There is no redemption for your son. What use a lesson, if it cannot be learned and acted upon? Before God, you demanded a high price for your own pride, and Harry paid it.'

'I had no argument with my son,' he snapped back. 'Unless it was the speed with which he gave battle. He lacked patience. He should have waited when he saw that it was impossible to meet up with Glyn Dwr. He forced the confrontation with the King at Shrewsbury – and on this occasion it cost him dear.'

'So why did you not move more quickly? You must have seen the difficulties. You tell us often enough of your skill at battle tactics. You could have been there. I have seen you cover the breadth of the border within two days of rigorous marching.'

'How could I?' He faced me now, his anger as bright as mine, his authority as fine as the metalled gambeson with its incised studs patterning the breast. 'I was in no position to march. You know nothing about my situation in Yorkshire or you would not make such ill-judged accusations. Be silent, woman.'

'I will not. My widowhood gives me every right to speak out.'

When the Earl's mouth shut like a trap on an explanation he would not make, I no longer tried not to sneer. The rumours over past days had coated him in the slime of treachery.

'I have heard it whispered,' I said, allowing my own voice to drop into the little space between us, 'I have heard it whispered that you were crafty-sick, my lord, in some distant part of Yorkshire, so that you could not be reached. I have heard it said that you took refuge, claiming a weakness that kept you from your saddle. A malady that would render you far too ill to appear on a battlefield.'

The Percy chin was raised. He would not remain silent under such taunts. 'The whispers, if they exist, which I doubt, are nothing but malicious arrows delivered to wound me and destroy my reputation for veracity.'

'What veracity? And it is a positive arrow storm, my lord. What was your crafty-sickness? An ache to your head? A wrench to your ankle? Perhaps it was an ague that kept you abed for a se'nnight. Or was it a fever? You look in excellent health now, my lord.' I drove on before he could make denial. 'Or was it that you were too afeared of losing your power? To take a stand on the battlefield against Lancaster would be deleterious indeed. Perhaps you had decided that Lancaster would be a safer bargain as an ally than Glyn Dwr and the Mortimers after all.'

'I have no fear for my power. It is as strong as it ever was. I have an heir and I am still at large to rebuild where inundations have been made. King Henry and I will come to terms.'

He called him King Henry, not Lancaster. My ire once again burned bright.

'Your desertion of your son was shameful.'

'There was no shame. My son conducted himself on the battlefield with great honour. His name will be renowned for all time as a mighty warrior.'

'His death need never have happened.'

The ageing eyes were dull now, without emotion. 'But he is dead. I have lost all three of my sons, and Hotspur was my best-beloved. Do you think that it was in my planning? If you do, then you are a fool. Now leave me. Go and look to the health of your son, for he is all we have between survival and destruction.'

It was our final word. I knew no more than I had before. But forgiveness was not within me, nor was pity for a man who had lost all three of his sons, and this the finest. I did not think that he had made much of an effort to reach Harry's side, whatever the reason.

The outcome of that terrible battle, for Harry, rattled on and on in my mind. There was no forgiveness for anyone until it could be put right, as much as it ever could. My powerlessness ate at me, gnawed at my very bones. I expect that I was impossible to live with.

With something akin to an ill-tempered truce, the Earl and I waited on events, watching the road to the south, expecting any day to see a royal army approach to encamp outside Warkworth with foul intent. News came thick and fast, none of it good. Lancaster had marched north to Nottingham. Then Pontefract. Lancaster had cannon, sufficient to batter and force Warkworth into submission. Lancaster burned with anger against those who had dragged his kingdom into the horrors of civil war, Englishman fighting against Englishman, with much killing. Every morning upon waking it was my first thought: would this be the day that we were forced to face our treachery? If we did not surrender, we would be subjected to a siege, and if my cousin was intent on applying his cannon, we would face defeat and all it implied.

I should have known it. I had known it. But all I had seen was the righteousness of our cause. I still saw it and had no guilt. I would face the consequences of my Mortimer name and blood, as had Harry.

And yet, even though I was robbed of the one fine strength in my life, with no heart to fight, my life was still driven by the sense of duty that had been engrained in me from my birth. I must ensure the safety of my son. His inheritance of the earldom must be secured against all odds. There was also another burden, more terrible, on my soul that could not be relieved until I had paid my final debt to Harry.

So we waited as the days of August trickled past, but instead of an army, we received one of our own men, to throw himself from his horse and demand immediate talk with the Earl. I left them to it. It could not tell me anything I wished to know or could not guess at. If it was Lancaster's final approach then so be it.

'You will not need me,' I said.

'I will send for you.' The Earl glowered at my lack of grace.

'But I might not come at your demand.'

He could arrange to repel the siege without me.

Fewer than a handful of minutes had passed when, without knock or request, the Earl thrust open the door of my chamber, his whole body taut with urgency. At his side his hands were clenching and unclenching, while beside his mouth a muscle twitched. The lines on his face were sere and hard.

'What now?' I asked, my attention caught. He had not sent a servant but had come himself, even though he would consider it a servant's task.

His reply was harsh. 'Get your travel garments. Organise your children. I've arranged the horses.'

'Where am I going?'

'Alnwick. I need you to be gone from here within the half-hour.'

Already he had turned his back on me to depart.

'Why?'

As he looked over his shoulder, for a moment a vestige of panic touched his eyes but then they focused on mine with all the old authority of the Earl of Northumberland.

'Our King has a desire to heap further humiliation on us. He has sent Waterton and a tidy force with very specific orders. They were riding fast and not far behind my courier. I need you and my grandson to be gone. And before you stop to argue the case, his orders are to arrest you, Elizabeth, and your son. His intent is to stamp out this insurrection, and to do so he must have control of those who bear the Mortimer name and Mortimer blood. I'll not have my heir under lock and key with the Mortimer boys at Berkhamsted. Or worse, in the Tower, the crime of treason hanging over him in his father's name. Get your cloak and one woman to accompany you. Alnwick will be safer than here. You'll be well out of here before Waterton arrives.'

'Surely the walls will protect us.' I was fighting against the quick surge of fear.

'I know not if he has one of the royal cannon with him. We'll not risk it.'

I needed no second telling, already stirred into action to collect necessities for the short journey, my mood grim for there was no case to argue. I would not have my son fall into Lancaster's hands, neither would I allow myself to be taken prisoner, which I had never expected. When I met my cousin of Lancaster again, I needed my freedom. I had a bargain to make with him. As a prisoner I would be powerless to determine the outcome.

'At Alnwick give instructions to open the gates to no one. I'll send an escort with you but I can spare only a token force. I'll stand here and welcome Sir Roger Waterton. His information was good. He knew you and the boy were here. But we'll foil him.'

We were mounted, Hal ablaze with excitement, Bess stoically determined – for I would not leave her at Waterton's mercy while I was impressed by Lancaster's determination to wipe out all traces of opposition. I would never have believed that he would lift his hand against me. I had been wrong.

'I'll come to you when I know what the King intends.' The Earl held out his hand. 'Take care of them.'

I found myself placing my hand in his in tacit recognition of the importance of this agreement between us, although my reply was acerbic enough. 'And myself?'

'Of course. You are the royal mother of my heir.'

A truce indeed. I almost forgave him.

'When you get to Alnwick lock the gates and open them for no one but myself.'

We rode hard and fast, no great distance, less than a dozen miles, and a good road, but far enough without protection to feel Sir Roger Waterton dogging our steps. If he had sent out scouts, anticipating such an escape, then we would be vulnerable. I found myself praying silently that his confidence in his success would overrule any such necessity. Perhaps he had hoped that we would not be warned.

We rode without caution, ignoring weary limbs and compromised breathing. This was a need for speed; the fox must outrun the hounds. Every noise, every shadow, every innocent merchant or pedlar on the route, made my heart thump. There were few travellers but we stopped to exchange the time of day with no one. They shrank back to let the Percy banners pass.

What would I do if Hal was taken prisoner? I could do nothing if my own freedom was curtailed. The mighty earldom of Northumberland was at risk; I must reach Alnwick in time, for Harry's sake, for Hal's. For my own.

At last. The day was dipping into soft dusk as we drew

rein before the massive barbican. Soon we would be safe, the children delivered into the hands of their household with orders given to the captain of the guard to prepare for an unfriendly visit. I found that I was shivering with the fears that I had suppressed throughout that long day.

Perhaps I had not truly realised, until my own freedom and that of my son was threatened. Perhaps I had not tallied the full cost of treason for those on the losing side, but then had we not thought ourselves to be invincible? We had not seen failure but only the weakness of Lancaster, the increasing number of those who would turn against him and make alliance with us. Now I had to face the reckoning. To take me into custody, as well as Hal and even Bess, would rid Lancaster of an ongoing Mortimer menace. But he would also have designs on the power of the Percys, and who would own the mighty Earldom of Northumberland. With the heir in his hands, Lancaster would be able to pipe the tune to which we must all dance.

And what of the Earl? I had no compassion but I recalled his demeanour as we had ridden out. A little stooped, greyer, his face palely drawn beneath the marks of determination to resist. He would never give up the earldom this side of the grave but there was a desiccation, a weariness about him that I had not seen before, as if his life juices were being drained from him.

Which caused my breath to catch. Did he weep for Harry? He would not tell me or allow me to know. Surely there was some grief, some sense of loss within, some softness within that hard carapace.

I had no compassion. Harry was dead and Hal under threat. It was a relief when the great gates of Alnwick closed at my back. Had Harry seen this eventuality? I set about contacting Sir William at Berwick. I would need all the help I could get.

No army appeared on our horizon. No Waterton with his royal command to haul me into Lancaster's presence. No William Clifford either. Instead, on the following day it was the Earl, hot on my heels.

I was at his stirrup before he dismounted where I was immediately aware that all his old energy was back; he tossed his helm to a page and stripped off his gloves, ordering the steward to bring ale and meat to the hall as he pushed his hair from his brow. Much as Harry would have done.

'Well, my lord?' I was striving again for courtesy.

'Waterton arrived, as we knew he would, but without the cannon. I told him he was wasting his time, that you were here at Alnwick and the gates shut against him. If he wanted to escort you and the boy to London he would have to wait for the King and the cannon to force a hole in our walls or starve us out.'

'And he went away without recourse?' It sounded an unlikely outcome. 'I see he did not shackle you and drag you south to answer to Lancaster.'

'There was a negotiation of sorts.' I kept pace with him as he entered the hall. 'King Henry invites me to York.'

I halted. So did the Earl.

'*Invites* you. Is it a trap?'

'I doubt it. The King has a surprising streak of chivalry under his Lancastrian skin. If he invites me, he will not condemn me unheard.'

Which was a true enough reading, once I would have thought. Now I was not so sure. 'And will you go?'

'I will. Am I not a loyal subject?'

'Whose son died in blatant insurrection, sword in hand.'

The Earl finished draining a cup of ale, wiping his mouth on his sleeve, once more the tough border warrior.

'Whose son died as a result of deliberate royal provocation. But provocation can be healed if the King has a mind to it. I will answer the King's summons and sue for mercy, acknowledging him as my King.'

'Does he promise he will spare your life, if you make suitable submission?' I watched the tinge of colour creep into the Earl's gaunt cheeks. 'Will he promise the Earldom of Northumberland for your heirs for ever if you are full of remorse?'

'I will do all that is necessary.'

My courtesy was at an end. 'Make sure you do not wear away the paving with too much kneeling, when you lick his royal boots.'

'Enough…!'

I did not wait to hear the outburst of anger. Had I not spoken the truth?

Thus the Earl rode south to York, where it seemed that Henry of Lancaster had made his base while he dealt with the intransigent north, and I went with him, bearing a dread mission that grew in its enormity with every mile we covered. Sunk in introspection, the Earl did not question my movements, even though I gave no explanation. I did not have to. We both knew what awaited us before we even came into Lancaster's presence.

We took a small private retinue, no armed force; we were in the mood for subjection, and much else.

I would risk my imprisonment. If Lancaster were willing to offer a truce and safe passage to the Earl, I did not think he would be so graceless that he would imprison me, and my son was safe, left behind with Sir William behind the strong walls of Berwick. Now I would risk all, to appeal to my cousin's mercy. I needed to see him, to argue my cause, and if he would not, if he remained unbending – for who would blame him if he turned his back on the wife of the man who, a friend turned enemy, had sought his blood on a battlefield – then I must destroy my own pride. If I must grovel on my knees before Henry of Lancaster, then that is what I would do. I would join the Earl in abject abasement.

Micklegate Bar, York: August 1403

Here were the walls of York, by which time the lurking dread in my mind had reached the black, sweating consistency of a storm cloud. Before Micklegate Bar, the vast fortification guarding the road into York from the south, I drew rein. So did the Earl, my silent companion, and our escort. Our horses fidgeted to move on, but we held firm, our retinue uneasy, eyes sliding from what awaited us.

'This is what we achieved,' I said. 'This is our bane, and will be for all time.'

Slowly, holding my breath, I raised my eyes. Had we not made a deliberate detour to enter the city by this particular gate? We had been forewarned. Never, knowing exactly what I would see, had I needed such an effort of will.

'Look up, my lord of Northumberland. If I can look up, so can you.'

But he already had. I could not fault his courage.

I controlled my mind, my throat, my belly as I forced my muscles into obedience to look up to the crenellations that topped the defences dominating the entrance to the city. My lips were pressed hard together, my hands curled into fists around the reins, nails digging into my palms, but I kept my back straight, my head proudly raised. I would commit this deed with all the honour of my Plantagenet blood.

What would a King do with the head of a traitor, killed in blood? He would take that head and display it in all prominence to warn others of what might be their fate if they too lifted a sword against the crown. He would make an example of the owner of that head. A humiliation. A deliberate bringing low of one of the proudest of families.

Could I bear to look on this remnant of the man who had meant all to me?

Harry's head had been impaled on the barbican. Or what there was left of it which had not been ruined by carrion and weather and the passage of time. The remnant of skin was grey, the hair lank. I looked no further at the power of carrion beaks against the soft flesh of eyes and mouth. Aware of the destruction I would have covered my face with my hands, blocking my sight, but that would have been the way of a coward. I forced myself to look. He had died for my cause at Shrewsbury. The least I could do was acknowledge it. I would not hide from the truth.

'This is the cost of your failure to march to Shrewsbury,' I said.

There was no reply. The Earl's face beneath the rich folds of his chaperon was almost as grey as that of his son.

It hardened my heart against Lancaster. Had this been deliberate, to place Harry's head here so that we must ride beneath when we obeyed the royal summons? If his purpose was to intensify my grief then he had succeeded more than he could possibly have imagined. I was rent with pain.

The Earl bowed his head in formal acknowledgement of his son. So did I.

Where the rest of his body was, I did not know. That was in Lancaster's remit, to make the country cower in fear. We rode on beneath the barbican, so that we could see its dread burden no more. But I could sense its presence. Wherever I was in this tainted city, I could sense Harry's degradation.

'Well, my lord? I see that you accepted my invitation.' Lancaster's watchful eyes moved from the Earl to take me in as I rose from my curtsey. 'Perhaps I am surprised to see you too, Elizabeth.'

He had taken up residence at Friar's Manor, accepting the palatial hospitality of the Order of the Franciscans as he had once before on his way to invade Scotland when Harry had ridden willingly enough at his side. Awaiting us in a room furnished with exquisitely carved chairs and tapestries that impressed on us the sufferings of Christ, Lancaster proved to be as uncompromising as I had expected when we made all necessary recognition due to the man who wore the crown. We would not antagonise him by denying respect in these first minutes, but this would be a difficult meeting. I could expect no less, yet I did not fear for our safety. As the Earl had said, we had been invited with safe conduct.

Plainly clad in wool and dark damask, more soldier than monarch, Lancaster dominated the room and the meeting, his words directed at the Earl, as was the spike of his anger.

'I gave you office. I gave you authority in my name. I gave you lands. I gave you what moneys I could spare, although you will deny it. I gave you castles to hold in my name and yours.'

He paused, his fingers, rigid in his anger, splayed on his hips.

'And how did you repay me, Percy? You and your son raised arms against me. You raised your flags in battle against me and drew your swords. You would take the crown from me and set up a Mortimer in my place. On my throne. A Mortimer with Percy advisors. Do you expect a gracious meeting? I can think of no reason why I should not confine you – both of you – to some cell to live out your days there. Except that I said I would not. I invited you here to allow you to speak.'

All delivered on a level, with no explosion of passion. He had had time for his ire to cool, to be replaced by cold recrimination. Now he raised a hand to snap his fingers for a servant to provide a stool for me. He made the Earl stand. The servant was dismissed. What more there was to be said would be said in private.

'Have you nothing to say to me?' he demanded.

'In my own defence,' replied the Earl, as calm as Lancaster, magnificently deferential, 'I did not actually raise my standard against you, my lord.'

'So they were not Percy standards Waterton counted at Tadcaster? Or before the walls of Newcastle?'

'They were mine, my lord.'

'But you say you were not complicit in rebellion with your son.'

'No, my lord. I was not complicit.'

'It is not what I hear.'

The Earl was solemn in his denial. 'The common gossip is false. Those who would scar my reputation as a loyal subject do me an injustice, my lord. I had no intention of taking the field against you.'

'You had not agreed to join forces with your son and Glyn Dwr.'

'I had not.'

I could not bear it. Every word was a nail in Harry's coffin, a coffin that had been denied him. Was this to be the Earl's defence, that he had been entirely divorced from it all, as if he had had no communication with Edmund or Glyn Dwr? I could see the plan forming in his devious mind. He would argue that he had no army ready in marching order at Tadcaster, that he had not been in agreement with Harry's march to Chester. I had spent the miles from Warkworth considering how the Earl would answer Lancaster's accusations. Now I knew the worst of it.

'So perhaps you will explain to me why you had an army under your command when Westmorland and Waterton crossed your path in Yorkshire.' Lancaster was determined to pursue the truth, as I forced myself to concentrate on the nuances in this confrontation.

'They mistook my purpose, my lord.' The Earl remained steadfast in his original premise. 'My forces were to keep the peace in your realm. Did you not give me the office of Warden of the March, to achieve just that? And I have achieved it, as you know, my lord, mostly at my own expense. The country is uneasy, ripe for uprising. That is the reason for the existence of my army in my Yorkshire lands. Also, my lord, as you will know, I need those troops to win the lands along the Scottish border you so graciously granted to us.'

'I did indeed give you that office, and the promise of those lands.' There was no hesitation in my cousin, and no softening either. 'I believed that of all the families of England, I could trust the Percy blood, so closely connected with my own. But perhaps you would also care to explain to me your involvement in a plot that forced me to fight a bloody battle against my own subjects, in my own land?'

'I was not party to it, my lord.'

Lancaster barely hesitated. 'I find it impossible to believe you.'

Whereupon the Earl sank to his knees, head bent in what I knew to be a parody of regret, but how well he did it, the ageing magnate on his knees, plainly clad in abasement, appealing to his King.

'I put myself at your feet, my lord, in awe of your mercy. I knew nothing of this rising. The plan, the construction of it and the intended outcome, if it was to promote the Earl of March as a threat to your throne, was the work of my son alone. I had no involvement in it. I held no meeting with the Welsh rebel or with Sir Edmund Mortimer, although I know, to my regret, that my son did. I for my part knew nothing of it until I heard of your victory on the battlefield. My son disobeyed me when he took the field against you, my lord.'

Whereas I had not flinched from observing the brutal wounds inflicted on Harry's head, now I closed my eyes. I could not bear to look at the Earl. Excuses I had expected. Wily arguments, of course. Even a pitiful demand for forgiveness. But this. This I had never expected.

'I find that hard to believe also,' Lancaster was observing at the edge of my consciousness. 'A marvellous division in Percy ranks? I think not. If your brother and your son raised their standards in Glyn Dwr's cause, I think you would be neither ignorant of it nor far behind in joining forces with them. You three were ever hand-in-glove.'

'It is so, my lord. My son was always impetuous. His marriage to the Lady Elizabeth encouraged him to look to the Mortimers as a possible claim to the throne in your stead.

I warned him that it was dangerous. I advised him against it in the name of loyalty, but to no avail.' His face turned fractionally to where I sat, as rigid as one of the saintly figures in the tapestry behind me. 'Perhaps the lady is not entirely blameless in this. She would encourage my son in his defection to the Mortimers. It was her closeness with her brother Sir Edmund Mortimer that drew my son into the Welsh net with Glyn Dwr.'

So he would throw me to the wolves as well. My chest was tight, my breathing shallow, my throat too dry to swallow. What sort of betrayal was this? Far worse than Harry challenging Lancaster to fight for the crown on equal terms. The Earl had just repudiated the close regard between father and son, and stabbed me in the back.

'As for my brother of Worcester,' the Earl was continuing, 'I regret his decision to throw in his lot with my son. I did not believe him open to such persuasion.'

When Henry slid a glance in my direction, I spoke up for the first time through that appalling denunciation during which the Earl had abandoned his son and brother and implicated me. I would be honest too. I stood to deliver my verdict.

'I knew what was planned, my lord. I both knew and approved. I did naught to stop Sir Henry when we met with my brother Edmund and with Glyn Dwr. It needed little persuasion on my part, but you should know that I supported the rightness of the Earl of March to wear the crown. If you are looking for blame in this, you cannot exonerate me despite the closeness of our blood. Sir Henry and I stood shoulder to shoulder, hip to hip, and I will not beg for mercy on my knees. My nephew should be King of England.'

'Well, at least we have truth here.'

'You have the truth from me, sir. I will leave it to your judgement to assess the worth of Northumberland's confession.'

'Stand up,' Lancaster ordered. And when the Earl was once more on his feet: 'You will come with me to Pontefract, my lord of Northumberland.' The smile on Lancaster's face was like a crack in an icy pool, unnerving in its chill. 'There we will decide on your punishment, for your *lack* of involvement in insurrection. I will leave you with your daughter to enjoy the outcome of this interview. I doubt it will be pleasant for either of you.'

Perhaps I saw pity on his face.

'As for you, Elizabeth, I will consider my policy for your future. You avoided Waterton sent to arrest you, and yet here you are of your own volition. It makes me wonder why. Perhaps you might come and tell me in an hour, in the chapel after Matins.'

I bent my head in yet another obeisance, to hear him add: 'Royal widows, Elizabeth, are always valuable.'

I shivered inwardly.

Then the Earl and I were alone. I could not look at him.

'I despise you,' I said. 'I despise you for what you have just done.'

His reply was immediate and harsh as he put out his arm to prevent me walking past him.

'Why would you? You should be thanking me from the bottom of your heart. I'll not put myself into the King's hands by inviting blame. My inheritance and that of my heir – your son – depends on King Henry's being willing to overlook my past demeanours. What would you have me do? If you are content that I make your son's inheritance unviable, I'll go back and tell the King that I had put my name to the alliance.

Is that what you would prefer? Our credibility destroyed and the Earldom with it?'

'I would rather you treat your son's name with honour, not with ignominy. To achieve your *credibility* you have smeared your son's reputation in filth.'

'I have not. He was impulsive, too much so for his own good as he proved again and again. It's no secret, and I'll not apologise to you for using his weakness to Percy account. When I die, your son will become Earl of Northumberland. If I must forswear Harry to achieve it, then I will do it.'

If there was any truth in such bitter reasoning, it was beyond my acceptance. Without thought, without control, I lifted my hand and I struck him, the flat of my palm against his cheek, the sound sharp and hard in the room.

The Earl was as shocked as I, until he recovered, and sneered.

'A woman's blow!'

I was aware that my hand curled into an unwomanly fist. Would I have struck again? I did not. The Earl raised his hand as if he would strike me back.

'Would you dare?' I said, not even flinching.

His hand fell away, the force of my blow bright on his cheek. I might regret my lack of restraint, or even my humiliation of a man of supreme arrogance, but contempt remained a bright flame to consume all past respect.

'You might have turned your back on your son, but I never will,' I denounced him. 'I repudiate you. I damn you for what you have done here today.'

My blood running cold with a fury that I must restrain, I went to my meeting with Lancaster, knowing I would face a contest that I must win, not only for my freedom but for the reason I had come here today. We met in the chapel; all the memories crowded in of the chapel in Doncaster where this had all begun, Lancaster taking his oaths and drawing us into this fatal denouement. Where Lancaster was on his knees in his personal communication with God, standing as I entered, signing the cross on his breast.

By the time I had made my own genuflection to the altar, he was facing me.

'Well, Elizabeth.'

He would not immediately be accommodating. I knelt before him, when I had sworn that I never would. My cousin's words fell over me in all their cold clarity.

'Is this to beg for your freedom? To allow you to return to the north, or to the Welsh March, where you will pick up the sword that has fallen from Hotspur's dead hand? Are you not satisfied with his death, and those of your Percy retainers? The battle was such that I would never wish to face again, with all its blood and destruction of brave Englishmen, on both sides.'

It was a cruel picture that he drew, as he held out his hand to raise me to my feet.

'No, my lord.' Our eyes were on a level. 'I think you know what I will request.'

'I think I do. And why should I comply? Your husband was a traitor. What's more, he destroyed a friendship that I held dear. My admiration for him was so strong that I would give my son and heir into his care.'

'I ask because I think it is in you to have compassion on a brave man who fought for you, who spent his time and his energies for your cause. Your friendship was forged at the tournament where you would have learned his strengths, and also his inability to turn aside from a difficulty. You would have known his belief in what was right. He would fight for that to the death.'

'And I loved him well. Until he turned against me.'

'Until he turned against you, because in the end he believed that yours was not the rightful claim and that you broke your oath.' My mouth was dry, my lips stiff with the words, but I had planned them well and I would say them. 'You are the victor, my lord. I think it is in you as the victor to hear my petition. For the sake of Henry Percy's son, I ask it. It is not fitting that all remains as it is.'

'It is fitting that my enemies see the results of his treason.'

'And now they have. You allowed the seemly burial of Worcester at Shrewsbury. Have mercy, Henry. Allow me to put my lord to rest.'

'I said that Percy's head would remain on Micklegate Bar as long as it can last the predations of time and carrion.'

'Have mercy, my lord. On me and on the friend that Sir Henry Percy once was to you.'

I was kneeling again, head bent as the silence pulsed against the bare walls in that holy place. Then at last, when I had given up hope:

'Very well. I will allow it.'

I sighed. 'I doubt that you will accept my thanks, but I give them.'

'Where?' he asked. 'Where will it be?'

'In his own country.' I thought for a moment. 'Warkworth, perhaps. He loved that the most.'

Once more I was brought to my feet by his hand on my arm. 'I will do it, but hear this, Elizabeth. I want no shrine to Percy rebellion. If I discover that you have set up some monument to Percy power, I will come and destroy it.'

I held his eyes with mine. 'As you destroyed his first burial.

They said that you wept on the battlefield on finding him. I suppose that was a lie.'

'It was a lie. I might weep for many things, but I did not find Hotspur's body amongst the terrible melee.' I could see the bitter memory newly engraved in his face. It was a far cry from the man who had celebrated at his wedding, a mere handful of months ago. 'You have what you wanted,' he said. 'I won't ask for your loyalty.'

Which did nothing but rekindle my anger as I recalled one of my main grievances. 'Nor will you get it. You bought Dunbar.'

'He did not take much buying.'

'Was he always your man? Was it always a ploy, to have him in your service, to skulk and watch to report back on what the Percys might be doing?'

'I like to think he was my man.' Henry lifted a shoulder in a careless shrug. 'What would you have me do? A King buys friends where he must.'

'So that's why you now allow Dunbar to style his new herald with the name Shrewsbury. In memory of a battle in which he took the field against those who thought he was a friend. Before God, I did not think you would be so insensitive.'

But Lancaster's patience with me had drained. 'If you wish me to carry out my promise of a moment ago, attacking me is not a good way to keep my compassion.'

'No, it is not. You have my gratitude.' I all but choked on the words, but I made them. He could have denied me, after all.

'All I ask is that you use my compliance wisely, that you retire to live in peace while you consider how many died at

Shrewsbury because of you, and because of Hotspur's futile Mortimer cause.'

I bowed, and turned away. Then stopped, looking back at him.

'Could you not have stopped the battle? Did you desire my lord's death so much?'

'Do you think the blame lies at my door?'

'Yes.'

I thought that he changed his mind over what he would say. 'I did all I could.'

'But not enough.'

Chapter Seventeen

Warkworth Castle

Lancaster kept me at York for the turn of two weeks, perhaps to impress on me the ultimate power he had over the rest of my life, before allowing me to return to the north. We had no communication during that time other than the polite and very public exchange of niceties at meals when he deigned to keep me company. What was there to say between us? But he carried out his promise to me, and most speedily.

It was a trying time.

At least I was spared having to tolerate the Earl's company since he was sent on to Pontefract to await Lancaster's coming.

But now I was free and with the lapse of time the sad cavalcade of Lancaster's organising had arrived at Warkworth before me. By the time I dismounted I knew that all restitution had been done by those household officials loyal to the Percy name. It helped in a little way to assuage the raging sorrow and the anger that Sir Henry Percy should have been dealt with as brutally as a common criminal.

I dismounted, stiffly, our steward immediately at my side, his face grim but with a certain fevered satisfaction. Before I could even ask:

'He is here, my lady. Two days since. We have made arrangements in the chapel. I thought that would be what you would wish.' He swallowed hard, for a moment his eyes bright with moisture, his voice raw, but his command was superb. Stronger than mine, I suspected, for I was weary. 'All is restored. We have put all to rights.'

'Praise the Blessed Virgin.' I sighed in a semblance of relief that Lancaster had been true to his word, at the same time as I felt a need to clutch my steward's arm, exhaustion striking home. 'And I have the final piece of the whole, to make all well. Or as much as we can make it. I think nothing will ever be well again.'

He kept hold of my arm as if he feared to let me go.

'If you will give it to me, I will see to it, my lady.'

'No. This is what I must do myself. But you have my thanks. Come with me, if you will.'

He led me towards the open door which led into the old keep.

'Where is the Earl, my lady?'

'With the King in Pontefract. From there he will be sent to London to answer for his sins before parliament.' I was sorry for the sudden anxiety I had caused this loyal retainer who stiffened beside me.

'The Earl will not be incarcerated. The King will release him, I expect, when he has made him suffer enough. It is good news, you understand.' I could never see it as good. 'He will be allowed to speak in his own defence.'

Our steward was reassured. 'Good news indeed. Meanwhile I will do all in my power to serve you, my lady. I know that yours was the determination that made this possible. The whole household knows the debt it owes to you.'

I rewarded him with as much of a smile as I could summon. He slid his grip from my arm to my hand to lead me into the great hall.

'You are cold. Will you rest first, my lady, and take some wine? Your chambers in the west range are all prepared.'

'No.' I felt that I would never be warm again. 'My mind will not rest, nor will it until we have brought Sir Henry home. This must be done now.'

Signalling to the page who, anticipating my need, had already collected the burden wrapped in the blue Percy lion, holding it as if it were as precious as the bones of St John of Bridlington, I followed the steward across the hall and into the chapel where a bier had been erected before the altar. It had been covered with a banner that fell in seemly folds to the floor on all sides, shrouding the uneven shape below it with grace. One candle cast its faint gleam on the golden stitching, the rest was hid in discreet shadows beneath the simple arches. All was still, as if waiting for me and what I had brought with me. Even the candle flame burned straight and true. There was no movement in that place. No life.

'Light the candles,' I said. 'All of them.'

'If it is your wish, my lady.'

'I saw him in life, I will see him in death.'

There was our priest beside me, anxious, putting into words the steward's concerns. 'But my lady, it was no ordinary death. It may be better that you do not—'

'I know what I will see. I owe it to him to do this since he died far from me and without my knowledge. I will put my seal on his death by being witness here in the holy place that he loved.'

Between them steward and priest lit the candles on the altar and in the wall sconces, before, reading my mind, the steward lifted a stand of them forward so that the bier would be illuminated as if with heavenly glory.

'Thank you.' I drew in a heavy breath, steeling every one of my senses against what we must do. 'And now we will complete our task.'

For Henry of Lancaster, my cousin Henry, to make an example of a Percy traitor, in his wisdom had defiled Harry's body. Blessed Virgin, had he no pity? No pity, as he had made abundantly clear. Only a limitless demand for revenge.

Lancaster may have wept in the aftermath of the massacre, but he had been struck by the value to him of Harry's death. From that final resting place in Whitchurch, in a quiet corner of the Welsh March, my cousin Lancaster had my lord's body exhumed, the corrupt flesh rubbed with salt, to prevent further corruption before it could make the impression Lancaster desired. My lord was placed carefully, sitting upright between two great millstones at the High Cross in Shrewsbury, so that all who passed by might see and be afraid. Thus was the great Hotspur finally brought low in public view.

Until, that is, Lancaster decided that the rest of England must be reminded of the penalty to be paid by traitors. Harry's head was sent to York, to greet us, set on the spikes of Micklegate. And then the unforgivable butchery, when Lancaster ordered the foul dismemberment, quarters dispatched to London, to Bristol, to Newcastle and to Chester. I could think about it now without vomiting. Messengers were sent out to proclaim his death through the country, and here was the evidence. There would be no convenient rumours that Harry Percy, my beloved Hotspur, was still alive.

Richard's body had been left intact. There was no grace in Lancaster's treatment of my lord.

But now we would make restoration.

The priest turned back the glorious cloth to reveal what lay below, and although my belly quailed, I was astounded at the length to which our people had gone. Flesh had succumbed from time and weather and the dread attentions of crow and raven, from the mishandling of those who had no compassion, from the wounds on the battlefield, but those allotted the task had masked the ruined limbs in clothing. Percy motifs shone out in the candlelight, disguising the depredations below. They had put boots on his feet and gauntlets on his hands; a tunic covered his breast. My breath caught again at the dignity they had awarded him.

Now I took the bundle from the page and between us we unwrapped the one part that was missing.

I took it in my hands, retrieved as it had been from the ignominy of Micklegate Bar, cleansed as much as had been possible. Remnants of that deep red hair were still visible, the skin drawn tight over the carapace of his skull. Carefully we placed it in its rightful position, then drew the covering over all, the candle flames a blessing again on the gilt and the embroidered damask.

'Sir Henry Percy, returned to his own, as it should be,' I said. 'My well-beloved Hotspur, made whole in death.'

We bowed with all reverence.

'What do you wish, my lady?'

'I will keep vigil.'

'Where will you wish my lord to be interred?'

It was a difficult decision that I had been refusing to face.

'I will decide.'

Lancaster's advice and threat rang loud in my ears.

They left me.

Through the pall I touched his hands. The length of his arm, his feet, the curve of his breast where an attempt had been made to reconstruct what had been destroyed by Henry's doing. Then, drawing away the cloth once more to view the whole, I knelt at his side. This was not Harry, merely the structure that had once enclosed his heart, his mighty spirit, his vivid mind. He was not here. I imagined him riding his favourite horse across the northern hills, the breeze lifting this hair about his brow, rippling the pennons of those following him. His hands guiding his mount with such assurance, his banners flying overhead. That was Harry, not this carapace. But this needed to be done and so it was, as I wished it.

I knelt in that cold place, without tranquillity, without serenity, and kept vigil for him who was my love. He would not be left alone.

Eternal rest grant him, O Lord,
And let perpetual light shine upon him.
From the gates of hell,
Deliver his soul, O Lord.
May he rest in peace.

Then in the deep silence I decided where he would be buried.

Once determined, it was not difficult to achieve despite my status as widow of an attainted traitor. Alone, clothed in black from head to foot, my face and hair veiled, I stood in the chapel set aside for this moment, the most secluded, the darkest, offset from the high altar, the one least likely for pilgrims to visit within the splendour that was York Minster. And here was one of the priests who approached, leading a small cortège that carried an unadorned coffin.

'My lady. Do we have permission for this deed?' he asked

after a deep bow, his plain dark robes, as if he too were part of my plotting, merging with the shadows.

'We do.'

'His Grace the Archbishop asks that he might see the permission.' The cleric, a man of some standing by the quality of his vestments, but nervous of these present events, hesitated, then explained as if I would not be aware of something so germane to the pattern of my life. 'It would not be politic for the church to displease the King at this juncture.'

'Let the Archbishop keep the permission. It is genuine. The King will not deny its existence.'

The document changed hands. I did not need it. I knew the words by heart.

Whereas of our special grace we have granted to our cousin, Eliza-beth, who was the wife of Henry de Percy, knight, the head and quarters of the same Henry to be buried. We command you that the head aforesaid placed by our command upon the gate of the city of York be delivered to the said Elizabeth...

The seals were Henry's. The signature was Henry's. The royal will was Henry's. It would not be questioned, and if I had needed proof that the Mortimer cause was in tatters, this was it.

'It is the King's wish, and mine, that this be kept secret,' I said.

'As it will be, my lady. The Archbishop understands.'

So he should. Archbishop Scrope had in the not so distant past given Harry his blessing in his rising. But Harry had been the one to pay the price with his life, while the Archbishop was carefully disguising any past disloyalties with a semblance of rectitude.

'Shall we proceed?' My voice was clipped, for which I made no apology.

Harry would be buried here in York. Not Alnwick or Beverley, where other Percys had been laid to rest. Not at some centre of Percy power. Lancaster had forbidden me to create what might become a shrine to so dangerous a subject, luring others who could not settle in this reign. If I did so, he would tear it down.

Thus Henry Percy, called Hotspur, would be placed here beneath an unmarked slab with which Lancaster could find no fault. I would ensure that Harry would sleep in as much peace as it was possible for him to achieve; the slab would become worn and indistinguishable from any others with the passage of feet of those pilgrims and worshippers who found their way to this chapel. And if, one day in the future, there was a change of climate, I would construct for him a tomb as fine as any in England, with an effigy to proclaim his magnificence.

There. It was done. The coffin in place in the darkness of the vault and the slab lowered so that there was no sign of what we had encompassed.

'I have enough gold to pay those whose silence must be bought,' I said.

The cleric understood. He bowed his acknowledgement.

So at last Sir Henry Percy was laid to rest with no fanfare, no mourning, no choir, no prayers other than the basic committal to the grave.

'Amen.'

Mine was the only voice to echo that of the uneasy priest.

I would know where he was buried. I would know, and one day when they were older, I would bring my son and daughter here.

Beneath the black veiling I wept. There was no one to see or to wonder.

From York it was my intention to return to Alnwick where Bess awaited me in the care of a distraught Dame Hawisia and a devoted flock of household retainers, but first I must divert from the route. My heart lifted, for the first time in days. Hal, bearing Harry's blood and Harry's spirit, was doubly precious to me.

'I have come to see my son.'

Sir William Clifford bowed.

I was at Berwick, with only one constantly playing theme in my mind, like the chorus of a minstrel's song, repeated over and over until the hearer would happily dispatch the singers to the most distant corner of the outer bailey. So this cadenza played and replayed. We would lose everything. Castles. Power. Integrity. If that was all I cared about. I had lost Harry too. All I had left to me of that bright presence was his lineage through his son and daughter. I had a need to take Hal under my wing, to ensure his safety and his education as he grew to be the fine heir of all that was left of the Percy inheritance. There would be little of it unless Lancaster showed compassion. It would all depend on how repentant the Earl was prepared to be, to win King and parliament into allowing some vestige of Percy authority to remain.

And so, in Berwick, I stood in the private chamber of Sir William Clifford, appointed guardian when Harry rode to war. I had taken him by surprise.

'I wish to see my son,' I repeated, when Sir William made no move to send for Hal, only dismissing the soldiers with whom he had been conversing while he rolled up what appeared to be a plan of defences. I waved aside the offer of a cup of ale. I did not wish to stay, merely to reassure myself of Hal's safety. It was in my mind to leave him here behind the impregnable walls of Berwick with Sir William until the future was clearer for all of us.

'My lady.' Sir William's expression was beyond deciphering. 'The young lord Henry is not here.'

'Not here,' I repeated, as witless as a popinjay.

I did not understand. Had he been sent back to Alnwick? Or even Warkworth? But why would Sir William do that, letting the boy out of his direct line of sight? Berwick was as strong a fortress as any, and it had been Harry's final arrangement for his son. It must be honoured.

'No, my lady.'

I frowned. 'Is he, then, at Alnwick?' Perhaps Alnwick was safer, stronger.

'No, my lady.' Sir William cleared his throat. His eyes did not quite meet mine. 'He has been sent to Scotland. The young lord will already be there. Did you not know?'

Scotland! I was mentally groping to make sense of this.

'Why? On whose authority?' Oh, but I knew, in that moment I knew whose hand was on this scheming. 'My lord appointed you as our son's governor. Why would you send him to Scotland?'

'My lord the Earl decided it would be safer to have the lad out of the King's clutches.' Sir William was gruffly consoling. 'After the attempt of Waterton to take him into custody, you understand. It may be that the King would decide to take the lad as security for the Earl's future good behaviour. I could see no harm in it, and would of course be overruled even if I had. The young lord Henry has been sent into the care of Sir David Fleming and Bishop Henry Wardlaw. He is Bishop of St Andrews, as you will be aware...'

'I am well aware.' I felt the blood draining from my face. 'The Earl had no right to send him without my knowledge.'

'He thought it for the best, my lady.'

For the first time in my life my senses swam. The close heat in the room pressed down on me, the flames in the fire flickering uncomfortably in the edge of my vision, so that nausea rose to compromise my dignity. My knees were weak and my sight dimmed. Not even when I had forced myself to look on Harry's head on Micklegate Bar had I been so affected as I was at this sudden shock, the spaces around me closing in as if they would force me to my knees.

I felt Sir William's hand on my arm.

'My lady. You are distressed.' Leading me to a stool, pushing me to sit, thrusting a cup of warm ale into my hand: 'Drink, my lady.'

And I did, forcing the shadows back so that I could see the truth of what had been done.

'Thank you. I am merely tired from long travel.'

And I am heartbroken.

'I thought you would know. I thought the Earl would have told you.' His words were intended to comfort, but they did not. 'The Bishop of St Andrews has custody of the young Scottish heir, Prince James, to undertake his education. The Prince is a year younger than our young lord. They will be good company for each other in Wardlaw's household.'

'Yes. I expect they will. Thank you, Sir William.' I placed the cup down. It was not his fault, after all.

Of course Hal would go to some great household to learn what needed to be learned about chivalry and knighthood that he could not learn from Harry, a final layer of polish and culture. It would always have been so. I knew and accepted. But not to Scotland, without my knowledge or my permission, all resting on the Earl's insufferable ambition to safeguard the future heir. He had neither informed me nor consulted me, and I was powerless to change what had been done.

I could not forgive him the betrayal of Harry. This heaped further blame on his unrepentant head. I despised him for his lack of compassion, for his over-weaning self-gratification.

Sir William was speaking again.

'My lord the Earl thought he must safeguard the heir, with the tragic passing of my lord Hotspur. We are all much weighed down with sorrow.'

I looked into his kind face, seeing the heavy lines, for he too was grieving. His use of the familiar name for Harry brought tears to roll down my own cheeks. I was incapable of preventing them.

'Forgive me…'

'You can mourn too, my lady. It is a time of despair for all of us. Who would condemn you for shedding tears over the death of so great a man?'

But I was already wiping away those tears.

'I have mourned my lord Hotspur when I buried him with all the dignity that our King denied him. Now I have lost my son too.'

For did I not see the consequences of Hal's being taken under the mantle of the Scottish court? He would remain a pawn in their hands against future negotiations with England. I doubted I would ever see him again.

'You have your daughter.'

'Yes.' I stood. I must return to her.

Except for Bess, I had lost everything I loved most dear.

We suffered. Of course we did. Lancaster was in no mood to allow us to make easy recompense for the rebellion.

Worcester's execution would not wipe away our sin; Harry's death and a bent knee from his widow and his father were not enough to turn Lancaster's vengeful eye away from us. The Percy shadow in the north was far too ominous to overlook.

There was really no doubt of the Earl's complicity in the plot, no matter how smooth his explanations; the number of men under his command at Tadcaster was the proof of it in Lancaster's eyes. The Earl was forced to put his seal to documents directing his officers to surrender all the castles held in his name at the same time as all knights and esquires of the northern counties were required to swear an oath of loyalty to Lancaster. Stripped of his lands, his castles, his offices, the once mighty Earl of Northumberland fell from the heights of great magnate to the depths of disgraced pauper.

Except in his own mind.

The Earl bore a charmed life when made to answer for his treason before parliament in London, where he begged forgiveness on his knees as if his pride had been stripped away too. At Lancaster's insistence he was reconciled with Dunbar and Westmorland with another magnificent pretence of amity behind the cold eyes. Parliament was inclined to be lenient to this once great warlord. In terms of the laws of arms, it was decided, he had never unfurled his banners against the King, thus he was guilty of trespass but not of treason. A fine was imposed, which Lancaster promptly forgave, accepting the Earl's renewed allegiance instead. Even the Percy lands and castles were returned to us, but it had taken much self-sacrifice on the Earl's part. He had done much kneeling.

So the Earl returned home to Alnwick, on the surface humiliated and isolated, bereft of his powers as Warden of the March. Silent, morose, he locked himself in and claimed infirmity to avoid all contact with the world beyond his gates, even refusing to appear at the Royal Council when summoned to do so. An onlooker might conclude that he had paid highly for the Percy decision to oppose Lancaster as King, but I was no mere onlooker. I saw what was behind the facade of the grieving, infirm Earl of Northumberland, mourning his son and brother in his northern lair. Brooding on the fact that he was no longer Constable of England or Warden of the March, and that the one to benefit had been Ralph Neville, Earl of Westmorland. Behind it all was a man still plotting. Couriers came and went constantly, but, sworn it would seem to secrecy, did not speak with me.

'What are you doing?' I asked, frustrated at my not knowing. 'Still thigh-deep in treachery?'

'What would you have me do?' he growled.

'Safeguard the interests of my son. Keep Lancaster's forgiveness so that the heir can one day come home. It is his inheritance you are playing with. If you are not careful you will drop it in the fire and all will be consumed.'

'You should know. You are an expert on dabbling with treason, my lady!'

Which effectively put an end to my questions, as he had intended. Had I not dabbled? Had I not risked Hal's inheritance, flagrantly ignoring the possibility of defeat? But then there had appeared to be no overwhelming risk; Percy, Mortimer and Welsh Glyn Dwr had seemed invincible.

How were the mighty fallen.

So the Earl sat like a spider in his web, spinning I knew not what while I lived out a solitary existence, burying my grief in the routine tasks of managing the great household. I did them instinctively because I had to; I did them with ease because it was second nature to me. To receive guests and ensure hospitality, to welcome petitioners, to discuss the provisioning and feeding of those who depended on Percy charity. All without enthusiasm or any involvement of my heart. It seemed that my life had closed in on me so that I was a prisoner within the walls, yet I had no desire to break free. It would have been a simple task to leave Alnwick – for what kept me there? – and I might have been happier for it, with all its memories, but I had no desire to escape my despair.

While the Earl plotted, I struggled against the hopelessness of searching for Harry in all the places where he might be, but where he was not. I knew he could not be there, but some foolish hope lived within me. Striding from the stable, grooming his favourite horse. Running up the steps to stride along the wall-walk towards me. Sitting at ease in a corner where the sun might creep in and lull him into a brief doze. Watching his men practise their archery from his habitual tower vantage point, eagle-eyed for any slackness. Walking into my chamber at the end of a long day to take me into his arms and assure me of his love.

He should be in all those places, doing any one of those things, but he was not.

How many times within a day did the thought come to me: *I must remember to tell Harry*?

But Harry was not there to be told.

And yet in the depths of my desolation, a cold duty came to me, a realisation that drove me to reach out to Percy connections, Percy loyalties. My son was lost to me, but my daughter was not. Bess's safety, her future position in a family that was not tainted with treachery, occupied my thoughts. And here was one step I could take. Here was the one remedy against her present vulnerability. In a strange way, knowing well that Harry would have approved, I enjoyed the negotiation entailed in bringing my plans to fruition. I made as certain as

I could that in the coming years Bess would be surrounded by those with power to protect her.

Thus I attended a wedding. A winter wedding.

If I could have said that my heart rejoiced on this auspicious occasion, when even Dame Hawisia smiled her approval, it would have been a lie. My heart remained encased in the black ice that crunched beneath the horses' hooves of our guests, the celebrations tearing at me anew for they did nothing but paint my isolation in even broader strokes. Every day I was assailed by a crippling loneliness.

It was held at Warkworth, the Earl refusing to travel far from Alnwick, but keen to be seen to smile on this alliance between his granddaughter Bess and John Clifford, Baron Clifford and Lord of Skipton, a local lord of some power. It was a good marriage, the Clifford family estates running close with ours, their interests in the north matching steps with ours. I watched the ceremony unfold with its hearty mix of gossip, celebration and solemnity, aware of nothing but the scarcity of Mortimers and Plantagenets in the crowd. Edmund would not come, of course, immured as I had learned with his new family and Glyn Dwr in Harlech Castle, nor would my royal cousin of Lancaster, but at least I had Alianore, escorted by her marcher husband. She beamed indulgently on the youthful couple.

'You were no older than your daughter when you came to Alnwick to be wed to Harry.'

I was in no mood to be indulgent towards happier days, but I responded in kind: 'And Harry was no older than John Clifford.'

Deliberately I pushed aside the memories that were particularly sharp on that day. I hoped my daughter would be as content as I had been. She would be fortunate if she discovered love in any of its degrees. Within the week she would travel to live in the Clifford household where she would be safe, a Clifford rather than a Percy, whatever befell the rest of us. I imagined that Harry would approve of this alliance with a stalwart Yorkshire family. It made me smile with brittle acceptance. The Clifford ranks had no difficulty in accepting a Percy bride. The Earl was still a figure to be reckoned with in the north. Perhaps if he sheathed his sword and obeyed the summons to appear before the next Royal Council, Lancaster would forgive him rather than merely tolerate him, and restore some of his erstwhile powers.

'How is Hal?' Alianore asked after the vows were exchanged.

'Since he is enjoying his education at the side of the Scottish prince, I imagine he is in excellent health, his talents blossoming. News of him is sparse, but what I hear is good.'

Would this be the rest of my life? Living through the lives of my children, grasping at infrequent news? It assuredly would unless I married again. Or unless I looked once more to the west, to Edmund and Glyn Dwr, involving myself in their still simmering ambitions. There yet remained a cause to be fought for, to restore the crown to my Mortimer nephew. I fidgeted with my gloves for the day was cold. At that moment I had no heart for it. I had no heart for anything, much less a hopeless cause. And then, when I least expected it, the sealing off of all my senses behind a wall of loss and grief was shattered.

John Clifford and Bess were standing together, for a brief moment alone. Bess asked a question, head tilted, chin raised with all the Percy pride available to a nine-year-old child, making some broad gesture with her hands. John, adult at sixteen, laughed, replied, patting Bess on her neatly coifed

336

head and stooping to kiss her brow, before he took her hand to lead her into the hall where a feast had been prepared and there would be dancing.

It was as if a fist had struck me below my heart. The memories flooded back, of Harry accepting me with the same easy affection when I wed him. Had he tugged my veil into place? Had he kissed my brow? I thought that he had. My throat tightened, my eyes pricked with tears, which I blotted with the fur edge of my sleeve, turning away from Alianore. It was as if all my senses had come back to life, thawing beneath the warmth of that young friendship, and it was painful as feeling returned.

Meanwhile Bess responded to some comment with a secretive little smile which had just the hint of roguishness. She had grown up in the past year without my noticing it.

'It is permitted for the little bride's mother to weep,' Alianore said, ever watchful, steering me away from prurient eyes.

'There is no need for weeping,' I said, jaw clenched against any inclination. 'I expect he will treat her well. He would not dare do otherwise, for I am sending Dame Hawisia with her. Bess will have all the Percy support she needs, and more, in the Clifford household.' A memory again intruded, gnawing at my control. 'What's more, she will be able to dose them all most effectively against the flux with juniper berries.'

I shook my head when Alianore looked puzzled. I could not talk of it. Instead she asked: 'And what of you?'

I would be alone, a vessel without sails or rudder in a storm.

Alianore tucked her hand beneath my elbow, pulling me along until we stood on the edge of the crowd in the shelter of a buttress where the wind could not freeze us.

'What do you hear of events along the Welsh March?' she asked, low-voiced.

I had no interest. 'Very little.'

'Probably because you haven't been listening. It is mooted that there will be an attempt to rescue my sons.'

'Impossible.'

'Not so.'

For the first time in so many months, the tiniest flame of my interest was aroused.

'A plot?' I asked.

'If you will.'

'Are you involved?'

'No. I cannot be.' Her eyes rested on her distant husband, in conversation with a dour Clifford coterie. Mine followed.

'He would not approve,' I observed. Edward Charleton, with an eye to his own lands, valued his loyalty to Henry of Lancaster. He would not risk involvement in any enterprise that would endanger this, not even to rescue his wife's Mortimer sons.

'He might, but what he doesn't know he won't grieve over,' Alianore admitted, accepting what could not be changed. 'He is loyal to the King and opposes Glyn Dwr's ambitions. I doubt if Edward will ever join hands with the Welsh lord in anything but a thin-lipped truce.'

'Tell me what you know,' I invited.

'I can't tell you more. But I expect you'll know before it happens.'

I frowned. 'Who will lead it? Not Edmund.'

'No. How would Edmund get his hands on them to rescue them? Nor could Glyn Dwr.' She turned her back on the crowd. 'Who, Elizabeth, do you know who would be ambitious enough to attempt such a bold move, stealing them away from under Lancaster's nose?'

Our eyes touched, held, before looking away, as if recognition would implicate us too. I could think of some who might. I could think of one of my acquaintance who had kept close ties with the court, whose ambitions were unfathomable, who might not be averse to stirring more flames of rebellion. But indeed, I did not think it would ever happen. Who would be so foolhardy as to ignite Lancaster's wrath? He had proved himself more than ready to protect his uneasy inheritance and with four sons to share his burden it would be a brave or a foolhardy man, or woman, who would issue such a challenge.

Harry would. Harry would do it.

Harry was both brave and foolhardy.

But Harry was dead.

'Who,' Alianore demanded with an interesting spite, 'would have no hesitation in following her own probably immoral desires?'

'You can't say that, Alianore.'

'Oh, but I can.'

'Just because you don't approve of her present manner of life.'

'No, I don't. Her immorality is a disgrace to us all.'

Since her tone had become more astringent, I drew her further into the shadow of the wall. 'Hush...'

'I will not hush.'

'If your brother wants her as his mistress, it's as much his fault as hers.'

'I'll not disagree.' Alianore proceeded to condemn her brother as heartily as his lover. 'I don't have to agree with his choice of female to warm his bed.'

'Do you believe it? That she will involve herself in a Mortimer plot?' I asked, interested to know where her thoughts were travelling, seeing the need to direct her concentration away from her brother's lust for a woman who was not his wife.

Alianore sighed a little, turning to face the crowd once more. 'No, I don't think that I do. It is merely wishful thinking.' Her glance became keen and distinctly judgemental. 'I thought you should be warned. You have been wrapped around with your own affairs for far too long. I thought it time that you emerged to see what was going on around you. Have you abandoned our cause? Has Harry's death robbed you of your dream to achieve a Mortimer crown? For shame, Elizabeth.'

'Am I so self-indulgent?' I said, shocked by her unexpected attack.

'Terribly so!'

And I nodded, suddenly of a mind to agree. 'It is time that I stepped out into the world again. Let us go in and toast John and Bess and smother them with gifts.'

'And for a little while we will forget that a Mortimer rescue might cause us all more upheaval than we would wish for.'

I doubted that there was anything to forget. It would not happen.

Chapter Eighteen

Alnwick Castle: January 1405

I was wrong, and Alianore distressingly correct in her assessment of my abandoning of the Mortimer cause. Matters had been developing, as I was to discover when a soft, leather-wrapped package arrived for me with the New Year, enclosing a length of fine damask, delivered by a smartly liveried retainer who had journeyed some distance with an escort.

'What do they want?' said the Earl, taking note of the striking livery of silver and red quarters with their gold fretwork as the courier was dispatched to the kitchens for sustenance and a fire to thaw his hands and feet. It was cold weather for travelling.

'I have no idea, my lord.' I hid the letter which the courier had also passed to me, draping the fine cloth, which I had just released from its wrapping, over my arm. The dark blue was flattering to my colouring, as was the sumptuous pelt of fur that had accompanied it. Some thought had gone into the sending of it. 'Just a New Year family gesture, from my cousin.'

'Cousinship does not necessarily dictate so much effort. Or expense.' The Earl's speculation was tinged with suspicion. 'I did not know you were close enough with the York branch of your family to exchange gifts.'

'Nor I. She has not received one from me.'

The letter from Constance, Lady Despenser, once Countess of Gloucester, now flagrant mistress of Alianore's brother the Earl of Kent, burned in my palm.

'Well, that family will want something. When do they ever not?' He ran the back of his hand down the length of the sable, perfect for edging the heavy embroidered silk. 'Expensive. I doubt she expects you to intercede for her.'

'No. I have no one's ear. Nor does she require intercession. She is quite capable of interceding for herself to get restitution of her husband's land and her own dower.'

Constance was still suffering from her dead husband's treachery in the Revolt of the Earls, which was common knowledge; I did not mention the brief conversation between myself and the courier in that first moment before the Earl encroached on our privacy.

'My mistress expects a reply, my lady,' he had said.

'Then I will give one.'

I would not be hurried. Not by Constance of York.

'By word of mouth, if it pleases you.'

'Yet your mistress is willing to put her own thoughts in writing.' My fingers closed around the letter, still deep within the cloth.

'My mistress is a woman who drives her own path through life, my lady. It is only a New Year's greeting, and of no interest to any man.' His smile was unpleasantly ingratiating. 'Or to any lady other than yourself.'

Ingratiating he might be, but it was enough to spark my interest.

Making my apologies to the Earl, I retired to my chamber

where I handed cloth and fur to one of my women and set myself to read. And I read again, considering its content. Yes, it was a festive greeting, hoping that I would enjoy the gift. She had been thinking of me in my widowhood, praying that I would be soon restored to calm equanimity, able to look to the future. Perhaps I would visit the Royal Court. Perhaps I would even consider taking another husband. I was hardly too far gone in years. Nor was she.

I know what it is to suffer the loss of a husband for sins against the crown.

Which was true enough. Constance's life had undergone much upheaval when she had lost her own lord in the aftermath of the Revolt of the Earls. Thomas Despenser, once Earl of Gloucester, had ignominiously forfeited his head, when seized by a mob loyal to Lancaster in Bristol as he attempted to escape to France. But was this widow-like compassion enough to account for this more than friendly overture where none had existed before? I had my suspicions, being well aware, as was the rest of the court, of where Constance's sensual eye had travelled since her husband's head fell.

Yet the content of the letter was completely innocuous.

It was that which worried me. I did not think that Constance would send me a gift of sable pelts of such good quality without some purpose.

I looked again at the final sentences, trying to read through Constance's carefully constructed lines.

It is my intention to travel to the Despenser lordship of Cardiff next month where I will meet up with some old friends from the Welsh March. I can hope that you too will be there so that we might renew our cousinly friendship. Who knows what the outcome will be? If nothing else, we will raise a cup of wine to toast Hotspur's brave exploits at Shrewsbury and commiserate on his death. I know that you will act in his memory and bring our meeting to a good fruition.

I sat for a long time, tapping the document against my knee. So little explained, so much hinted at.

If nothing else we will raise a cup of wine to toast Hotspur's brave exploits at Shrewsbury.

A dangerous statement, all in all, when Harry's brave exploits had been treason. So what was her intent in this meeting with old friends in Wales? I had the impression that she believed me to have more knowledge than I actually had. She did not realise my self-imposed isolation. Even Alianore knew more than I of what might be afoot along the Welsh March.

But a reply was needed. I sought out the messenger, his frozen features pink with warmth and ale and warming flattery from the kitchenmaids. I sat across from him at the scrubbed board in the kitchen, to the discomfort of my servants, who retired to gossip behind the pans waiting to be scoured clean.

'Here is my reply for your mistress. Say this. I will give this matter my close attention. I am gratified that you felt so well disposed towards me that you should send a gift, and an invitation to enjoy your company and that of old friends in Wales. I will consider that too. Can you remember to repeat that?'

'I can, my lady. I have much experience.'

Of secrecy. Of scandal, I expected. Constance's name was coupled with that of Alianore's brother in an illicit union, becoming mistress of Edmund Holland, Earl of Kent, within a very short time of Thomas Despenser's death. All the reason for there being no love lost between Alianore and Constance. For a brief moment I was taken up with Constance's predicament. If she was expecting marriage from Edmund Holland, she a widow of four years' standing and he as yet unwed, it seemed she was destined to be disappointed. Perhaps even Edmund Holland baulked at a too-close York alliance, and he would need to discover a wife with money, which Constance did not have. I could almost feel compassion for her.

There was neither scandal nor compassion in my reply, which seemed hardly worth the sending. And yet it left me with much to contemplate, not least that this opaque communication might be all plot and no substance. One thing to see a possibility and a desirable outcome; quite another to put it into action when the King was awake to every danger. I had committed myself to nothing but I would wait and listen.

Before my daughter's marriage, I would have rejected any suspicion, but my mind had come alive, Alianore's warning directing my sight towards political events. There were new players, it seemed, in the game to make a Mortimer King. If Constance decided to busy herself in Mortimer affairs, who better to achieve it, for Constance's reuniting with Lancaster after the treason of her late husband, however genuine the reconciliation might be, had given her entrée to the Royal Court. It would not be impossible for her to arrange an escape for the two boys now ensconced at Windsor, boys no longer but now young men who would not be averse to some grand adventure which would lead to their escape and freedom.

What would Harry advise? Harry would not advise me to sit and wait at Alnwick. He would already be ordering his horse to be saddled and his retinue to arm themselves.

A new thought came to displace Constance: was my brother Edmund involved in this? Before I committed myself to anything, I needed to know what my brother had to say for himself. Furthermore, if there was a conspiracy, why had I been kept in the dark?

It was good to be involved again, my mind once more racing to absorb new events. As I had once before, when I had defied Harry's wishes, I left the north, despite the January cold. Firm ground and lack of snow made travel relatively easy. If there was a conspiracy unfolding there was only one who would know and who could be trusted to tell me the truth. In the recesses of my mind there was a frisson of excitement. One day Alianore and Roger's sons might be free.

The Earl scowled at my preparations for I intended to travel in some style.

'Where are you going?'

'Ludlow.'

'Why?'

'I need a change of scene. Of air.'

'Nothing wrong with the air here in my lands.'

'None at all. But I have a desire to see old friends.'

I noticed how I had picked up Constance's phrase. It was in my mind, and could not be shaken.

Settled in the fur-heaped comfort of the travelling carriage I resurrected the image of Constance as I had last seen her; a woman of self-will, of keen ambition, of self-regard. And how charming she could be. Within months of Despenser's death, Constance had persuaded Lancaster that she was a woman to be trusted. How much had she smiled on her cousin to wring from him the confiscated property belonging to her husband, as well as jewels and plate and the custody of her son? A woman of considerable talent, she even had her dower rights restored to her, despite being a traitor's widow. There was no doubt in my mind. If there was some means of taking the Mortimer heirs from their royal imprisonment in Windsor without Lancaster's knowledge, she would have more opportunity and more chance of success than anyone I knew.

But why would she? Why would she wish to become involved in so tortuous an affair that had already cost Harry his life? Only if, anticipating victory, it meant political influence for her and her brothers Edward of Aumale and Richard of Cambridge. Which raised an alarm in my mind as clamorous as the church bells in the town through which we travelled. Would I want my nephew to fall into their hands, to be crowned King with Constance's brothers as counsellors? Would I wish to be involved with this York conspiracy, even with the allure of ultimate Mortimer enhancement?

Aumale had been one of the Epiphany plotters, the only one to retain his head and his position at court without punishment. Which smacked of ill-dealing, for who had informed Lancaster of the plot, to allow him to take such rapid means to foil it?

No, I did not trust any of them. For once the Earl and I were in agreement.

It was a relief to be on the move, yet I could not bring myself to draw back the curtains when we rode past Shrewsbury and its blood-soaked land. Instead I buried my face in the cushions, eyes tight shut against the vivid images that obscured all good sense. At least the dread noise of battle did not assail me as it had in my garden when the moon had been blotted out. One day I would make my pilgrimage, but not yet. First I must discover what it was that I did not know.

Before my expected arrival I had sent a message on to Harlech, asking Edmund to meet me. When the great English fortress had fallen to Glyn Dwr in the previous year, after the loss of his lovely home at Sycharth the Welsh prince had moved his court, his military headquarters, his home and all his family, including Edmund, behind its substantial walls. I had barely moved into my own familiar accommodations at Ludlow before Edmund rode in with nothing more than a small escort, without livery or consequence, a private individual out and about on his own business with nothing to draw attention to his estate.

'I hope this is important.' His first words as he dragged off his cap from his flattened hair, regarding me with an expression that was not particularly fond. I suspected that he had only come here through habit, obeying an elder sister. The tone of my summons I realised had been peremptory. 'It's dangerous my being here. Lancaster would give a glittering reward for my head.'

'I've not come for your head,' I said without sympathy. 'I've come for information and you are the only reliable source I know.'

'To ask after my good health? That of my wife and children, perhaps? How we escaped by the skin our teeth when Sycharth was burned down around us?'

His gaze was strangely speculative, such that I felt my face flush at my lack of good manners as I walked beside him towards his own chambers. Edmund and Catherine now had two daughters but I would not be drawn to enquire. I spoke frankly as we climbed the stairs.

'I will ask after them when you tell me what you know. I've had an astonishingly vague but complex letter from Constance Despenser under the guise of an expensive New

Year offering. There seems to be some conspiracy, for which Constance wants my blessing. I think she presumes I would be well informed about it. Which I am not.'

'Why do you not announce it to the whole castle and beyond?' Edmund growled. 'Then everyone will know of it!'

Accepting this criticism, I closed the door, leaning back against it. 'So they will know more than I do!' When Edmund's eyes slid momentarily from mine, it confirmed all I suspected: 'And if there is a conspiracy involving my family, of which I am indeed ignorant, why do I not know of it?'

Edmund chose to answer my initial question, depositing cloak, gloves and cap in a heap on a nicely carved coffer that had once belonged to our mother.

'Yes, there is a conspiracy, as you put it,' he admitted, now sure of our privacy. 'The plan is to release the boys from Windsor and bring them here, under the protection of myself and Glyn Dwr. It is all arranged. Constance will oversee their escape and escort them west.'

'To Ludlow?'

Would it not be the obvious place for Lancaster to seek them out in a fit of rage?

'Or into Wales, if it is deemed safer. Constance will take them initially to her own lands near Cardiff.'

'So you are the old friends she says she will meet up with.' Before he could reply: 'Why am I ignorant of this, Edmund? If it were not for Constance I would have known nothing of the venture until our nephews were at large. When was it decided to construct this plot without telling me?'

Edmund sank onto a settle beside the fire which I had had lit to warm the cold room.

'Before God, that was a cold ride. Come and sit down rather than glowering at me.' He grasped my wrist and pulled me beside him, touching my cheek with cold fingers. 'You look as if you have grieved long and hard, sister.' And when I pulled away, as if stung by a hornet, he sighed and said: 'If you need to know, the Earl warned against involving you.'

I stiffened under his grip for he had not let me go. 'The Earl? Since when have you been in contact with Northumberland? And he warned you against what?'

'He said he no longer trusted your judgement.'

I thought about this, extricating myself so that I could turn to look at him. 'There is nothing wrong with my judgement. Why would there be? And you believed him?'

'He said you were out of your mind with sorrow over Harry's death. We should go ahead without your knowledge.'

Was this so? Had I been so stricken that I had not been in my right mind? Yes, I had mourned to the exclusion of all else, but to hide this crucial development from me... I could not understand why.

But of course I could. Since Harry's death the Earl and I had been at odds, much of it my own doing. Would I expect the Earl of Northumberland to forgive my striking him in openly expressed disgust? He would not willingly involve me in any of his dealings. He would not willingly involve a woman in his world where decisions were made by men.

'The Earl does not approve of women being informed of his affairs,' Edmund confirmed as if he were a mirror, reflecting my thoughts back at me.

'No.' I regarded my brother. 'I struck him.'

Edmund's brows climbed. 'Which was either very brave or very foolish.'

'It was very necessary. Or so it seemed at the time.' Which brought my thoughts full circle to the other woman at the forefront of this scheming. 'The Earl will not involve me, but he is eager to engage Constance Despenser, it seems. What is her interest in our affairs?'

Edmund shrugged, leaning his forearms on his thighs, turning his head to look up at me. 'An opportunity to cause trouble for Lancaster,' he said. 'A chance to plot and connive, to take revenge for the death of Thomas Despenser after the rising. Nothing would please her more than to upset King Henry's throne and tip him into the dust. Here we have a ready-made King to hand, to draw support. So she has become a Mortimer adherent.'

I did not think my brother naive, but did he see no more than that in Constance's sudden allegiance to our cause? 'I think her motives are far darker.'

'How so?'

'A chance to take revenge perhaps, but more to hold power at a future Mortimer court. Are her brothers involved? I would not wager against it, and there is no principle other than wayward ambition between them. Is Aumale pulling her strings?'

Edmund sat up, thus allowing me to see a depth of concern in his face that had gained marks of age, beside eye and nose, in the past two years. 'I too am wary of them,' he admitted. 'But we need them. Constance has the opportunity to set all in motion. She can work for their escape without raising suspicions. Once they are free and we have removed Lancaster, then it will be a Mortimer ruler in England with Mortimer counsellors. Do you think I will bow to the dictates of Constance and her brothers?'

His urgency was infectious but I thought that he would be under considerable pressure if the plot came to any sort of fulfilment. I studied him. A man of some ability, of family pride, but I did not think that his ambitions matched those of the Yorkist offspring or of Glyn Dwr. It might well become a Mortimer rule with Yorkist counsellors. At fourteen years, the young Earl of March, lacking experience, would need advice and governance for a handful of years at least.

'Will you give your weight behind it?' Edmund was asking.

'Why do you need me?' I was surprised to feel a brush of hurt. 'You were prepared to see it to the end without me. Why do you need my weight, as you put it, now?'

'Because you are Plantagenet and Mortimer.'

'So are you...'

'And Percy. You have a wide influence, Elizabeth. Your connections are impressive.'

It was a salve of sorts, I supposed.

'Will you join hands with me in this?' He held out his hand palm up, for me to take if I wished. And I did.

'Why would I not? We have always wanted this. But I fear for our nephews as pawns, used by Glyn Dwr. Used by Aumale.'

'Better than pawns and prisoners of Lancaster. When Edmund is of an age to take power for himself, he need be a pawn of no man.'

'Or woman.' I could not imagine Constance readily stepping back from her role in this scheme of her own making.

'Look, Elizabeth.' He leaned forward again, his hands clenched on his knees. 'We are no further forward in making young Edmund the king on our own resources. If the boys are free and in our hands, it will tip the balance and win men to our cause. We need this intervention if we are to see the fulfilment of the prophecy.'

'Which prophecy?'

'Merlin's Prophecy. The Prophecy of the Six Kings.'

'Oh, Edmund! Is this Glyn Dwr's doing again?'

Of course it was. The Dragon from the North and the wolf from the west together with the lion from Ireland, all converging to overthrow the King who was the moldewarp, the common and ineffective mole. I had supposed that it had died a death when Harry had fallen at Shrewsbury; clearly it had not. So who was the conspiratorial Dragon from the North now? I remembered the coming and going of the couriers to Alnwick.

'I see it all,' I said, struggling for patience in the light of the conviction that now lit my brother's face. 'You have been in contact with Northumberland, as well as with Constance. Is that not so? Throughout the winter the Earl has been knee-deep in negotiations with you and Glyn Dwr when to the world at large he has been like an old hound, growing weaker in winter hibernation, refusing to communicate, refusing to obey Lancaster and the Council. I should have known that his isolation was a lie. Another diplomatic illness to cover his ambitions. And I did not see it happening.'

'Never mind that. Do you not believe in such mystical signs?'

'I believe that they can be made to magic any force, any future. For those of a mind to believe in magic.'

'I was destined for greatness, Elizabeth. Here is my opportunity, to take control for young Edmund. To bring him the inheritance that is his.'

'And be the power behind the throne. But only if Glyn Dwr and Northumberland allow it. Do you believe that they will? For I cannot. And how does Constance fit into this prophecy? Is she the wily serpent, infiltrating with weasel words?'

'Constance has no part in our negotiations. And how can Glyn Dwr and Northumberland not allow me my portion?

I am the Lion out of Ireland. I am Mortimer. I cannot be pushed aside.' But I saw the flush of colour in his cheeks. All was not as clear as might be. All grew more complex by the telling.

'So explain to me this.' I heard my tone harden. 'What is it that you and the Welsh Wolf and Northumberland Dragon have agreed on? Have you already signed your life away?'

'It's still only a discussion, but we will sign.' His eyes were bright as sun-washed agates. 'We are talking of dividing England between us when Lancaster is removed.'

'A division of England.' It was as if a knife had been driven into the heart of all my hopes. 'So if there is a division, what sort of a crown will come to young Edmund?'

'I will sign in Edmund's name.'

I knew immediately. There was no place here for the Earl of March. 'And what will you sign your name to?'

'Glyn Dwr will take the west and the Welsh March, Northumberland the north and I the south for my nephew.'

'How much of the south will be left after those two have carved out their portion?' I asked, making no attempt to mask my disenchantment with the whole ploy.

'A substantial amount.'

'Blessed Virgin! Young Edmund should be King of England, not some trifling amount left when the rest have gorged their fill. Nor have you the right to sign in his name.'

'Who else would sign for him? You?'

A glint of anger had developed between us. Was my brother as ambitious as the rest? Did he seek to rule England in his own name, to pass the authority to his own children with Catherine? Or would he merely obey orders? Watching him, I thought him weak and as much a pawn as our Mortimer nephews.

'You will never be accepted,' I said, digging my fingers into his arm through his sleeve, trying for persuasion rather than anger. 'You may be Mortimer but you are not the heir. Will you stand aside for your nephew?'

I did not think so. I suspected Edmund of working for his own ends, as much as the Earl and the Welsh Prince.

'I will rule for him,' I was assured. 'I will restore him when he is of an age.'

'He is much of an age now.'

'Then my own rule will be a short one.'

'But only of a third part of England. And you will have signed away the traditional Mortimer lands in the west to Glyn Dwr. You will have signed away young Edmund's birthright for a mess of pottage.'

'An extraordinarily valuable mess of pottage.'

It was a muddle of complexities, through which I could see no clear path, no outcome that would ever fulfil the hopes of which Harry and I had dreamed. But Edmund brushed it all aside.

'I know you don't like it. Nor do I, but I have no choice. You don't see what has been happening while you have been shut away in Alnwick.'

'So tell me now.'

'Glyn Dwr is in negotiation with foreign powers. We have seen French and Breton ships off Caernarvon, to help our assaults on the castle and town. Glyn Dwr has signed a formal treaty of alliance with King Charles VI of France.'

Which changed the complexion of the whole rebellion against Lancaster, such that a chill ran along the tender skin beneath my cuffs. This was treason on a grand scale, inviting the intervention of a foreign power. My anxieties tripled in that one new development.

'There is a proposition that the French will launch an attack against the south of England,' Edmund explained, each word clipped as he admitted his own weakness, 'while we attack from the west and the north. Do you think that I am powerful enough to stand against Glyn Dwr and Northumberland, coupled with France? I must accept what is possible, take what I can. And so I ask you. Will you give us your support? Will you give *me* your support?'

I did not like it. It was wrong, power falling into the wrong hands. Had Harry died for this? For England to be split into three, divided for all time? Would he have been won over by Northumberland holding the north in his own name, an inheritance for our son? The clarity of the Mortimer inheritance as I had seen it had been swept aside in a cat's cradle of warring ambitions. French intervention on English soil was even more despicable, even if understandable. What would the French King demand in payment? How much influence would he expect in the future ruling of England?

'You look sour, sister.'

Edmund was on his feet, looking down at me.

'I like it not. What does France demand in return?'

All I received in reply was a shrug.

'It will mean war and bloodshed. The battles could be never-ending. Young Edmund's inheritance could be destroyed before he can grasp it.'

'You have not been averse to war in the past. You are growing old, Elizabeth.'

'Age has nothing to do with it. My own great loss has everything.'

'Then let me try this. You have always been the strongest of us, dedicated to seizing the rights of young Edmund's birth. With the aid of Aumale and Constance Despenser,

Edmund will be free to manage his own future, whether it is to wear the crown of England or rule over a swathe of land in the south. Whatever the outcome, it will be a more formidable step than any we have achieved so far. Edmund can marry, get himself his own heirs to inherit after him. Better than living an unfulfilled life in Windsor behind lock and key every night. And if we have to curb the ambitions of some of our allies, then so we will. Will you give me your blessing, sister?'

So simply put. So clearly. The outcome so inevitable. There was really only one reply, as I had always known. I stood to face him.

'Yes, I will. He is of my blood and my inheritance. It is his right, and my duty. I cannot refuse you.'

I saw relief wash over my brother's fine-boned face, for a brief moment smoothing out the lines of tribulation. 'It will be a good outcome, Elizabeth. And who is to know what the future will bring?'

Who indeed. Had not Constance written exactly the same in her plea for my help?

'What do you want from me?' I asked.

'Stay here in Ludlow. We will deliver the boys to you when Constance manipulates their escape. Then we can put out an appeal to the whole of the marcher lords, to raise their banners in the Mortimer name.'

'Will you tell them that they will come under Welsh rule if your agreement comes to pass?'

Edmund shook his head. 'We will live from day to day. We can keep the boys safe until we have the force strong enough to remove Lancaster. Glyn Dwr from the west. Northumberland from the north. When Lancaster is removed, that will be the time to reveal the stratagem for the realm.'

I was not convinced, but it was indeed my duty to support my brother, even as I tried not to contemplate the virulent language that this scheme would draw from Alianore's marcher husband. 'If I take them in here, they will be out of Constance's hands.'

'Of course.' The austere lines of his face softened again into a smile.

I joined my hand with Edmund's, resigned to a policy I did not like but one which would offer hope for the future.

'Then let us do it,' I agreed. 'Now, since that has cleared the crucial business from the air, tell me about your wife and daughters.'

'I thought you would never ask...'

But, however self-indulgent it might be, my thoughts were not with my brother and his domestic arrangements; instead they wove around Edmund's confidences as I nodded and murmured in agreement with him. I had no faith in the altruistic natures of Constance Despenser, or her Yorkist brothers. My nephews, in their hands, would be for them a means to a Yorkist end with the crown in their sights. And then there was the shocking revelation of Glyn Dwr's seeking of alliances across the sea. French ambitions in England merely added another layer of uncertainty and fear of Gallic ambition. But surely Edmund had the truth of it, that we could not progress without the support of either York or France.

'Elizabeth!'

I blinked and made a suitable apology, turning the conversation to life at Harlech, which would distract Edmund for some time, until I became aware that he had lapsed into silence, as if waiting for me.

'Your happiness gives me great pleasure,' I said, snatching at something that might be apposite and disguise my ignorance. My thoughts had been far from Harlech.

'I'm sure it does. But I doubt you heard more than two words that I said,' he replied.

'You have given me much food for thought,' I tried again.

'Good! Think wisely,' as he kissed my cheek in farewell.

I watched him go, an anonymous traveller to any who might see and consider his rank, a man of little power or wealth. I prayed that he would travel safely, back to the welcoming arms of his Welsh wife, wondering when I would see him again. And in what circumstances.

I raised my hand, suddenly thinking to call out, to bring him back for just a little while. But I did not. I let my arm fall to my side and walked back into the hall.

Bull Field near Shrewsbury: Early February 1405

It was not a long journey, nor a difficult one except in my heart; a route I knew well, so I needed no guiding, although I took a fair escort, choosing to stay that night at Haughmond Priory, an Augustinian community established by the FitzAlan family who had had such close connections with my sister. This visit could not be made in the early dusk of February, shadows closing in on me. There were enough shadows in my life. I needed the strength that came with the bright light of morning.

'My lord the King spent the night here before the great battle.'

The Abbot was considerate of my loss, despite the passage of so many months, as if I would not choose to request a bed in the same ominous surroundings. I regarded him gravely, the compassion a balm to my troubled soul.

'I am aware of it, my lord. Will you open your doors to me and vouchsafe me hospitality, even though I am the widow of a traitor?'

'You are a Mortimer, my lady. We revere Hotspur's name in this house. He was brave in battle, bold in words, dedicated to his beliefs. You are right welcome.'

Received with kindness and comfort, I knelt in the church while the canons sang the responses for Compline, praying for guidance, for healing, for my heart to feel some resonance from the stonework that was cold and dank. *Blessed Virgin, make my path plain.* Yet I felt nothing but heartache, which was only right in this place on the edge of so tragic an occurrence. Disturbed by Edmund's visit, our exchange of information, I had felt a need to make this pilgrimage. It might help, it might not.

Next morning, waiting for the late dawn, the Abbot was strong in his consolation.

'We will pray for you, my lady. And for peace in this blood-drenched land.'

'I fear that it will take more than prayer.'

'Yet we should not give up hope. Are we not in God's hands?'

I too would pray for peace, a peace that I could not envisage. To pursue the Mortimer cause would heap further death and bloodshed on more battlefields than the cold expanse that awaited me beyond the Priory's sanctuary. My conversation with Edmund had sown, with a liberal hand, the seeds of dread over the future. The Abbot's good wishes failed to bring me solace as he wished me well on my short journey.

Now, drawing my mare to a standstill on the edge of the

battlefield, I sat, well cloaked and veiled, spine straight, gaze unflinching.

'Show me,' I demanded of one of Harry's squires who escorted me, the winter sun still low on our horizon from where it would rise only a little more.

'It was here, my lady.'

He looked pale, paler than I, for it was not his choice to be here. Nor mine, taking up my vantage point on a little rise of ground, looking out over an expanse of empty fields, the land rising to my left, behind me the town of Shrewsbury, out of my sight, but I had been driven to this place by a compulsion that would not be laid to rest until it was done. No crops now, no growth of peas to catch at the horses' legs, only bare winter earth. It was almost two years since the battle that had cast me into this dread melancholy. There was nothing now but the wind in a patch of rushes, the plangent cry of a curlew, a stand of bare trees, their skeletons stark against the pale sky.

I sat, waiting for some sign, some thought to intrude. And when there was nothing but emptiness:

'Show me where they deployed their forces.'

He did so with wide gestures and pointing fingers. 'My lord Hotspur here, to our left. The King there, come up from Haughmond. Prince Henry came from that direction, from Shrewsbury.'

I could not imagine this bleak scene peopled with knights and soldiers and archers, restless horses, banners making known the proud names gathered here. I could not imagine the voices, the cries of victory or of anguish in this silently desolate place. I had no sense of the cold, nor of hunger since I had been unable to eat at the Abbot's solicitous urging. Nothing but the emptiness of this blighted spot.

'Is this where Sir Henry led the charge?'

'Yes, my lady.'

I pushed my horse on, to follow a pathway that led down into what must have been the main arena of the battle, my senses stretching, seeking some essence of him. Since that day when he had died far from me, I had claimed his body, knelt in vigil, taken in hand his burial. All intimate actions of a wife, a widow, but with no sense that it was Hotspur under my direction. Surely he would be here in this place where he had used his fiery energies, leading his men to fight for a cause. Where he had made that final charge that brought him to his death.

Esperance! Harry Percy King!

I looked around me, ever searching. Could I envisage him, sword in hand, banners snapping brightly, spurring his horse to bring Lancaster to justice? Was his spirit still here in possession of this magnificent effort to right a wrong? Did the battle cry still ring out from Percy throats on a calm day, to heat the blood of those who might hear?

No. There was nothing. There was no essence. I was as cold as the Shropshire clay beneath my horse's feet.

'Where was the Earl of Dunbar?' I asked, although my heart was sore within me.

'Here, beside King Henry, my lady. When it seemed that the King was surrounded and might fall, my lord of Dunbar advised him to withdraw from the melee for his own safety. It is thought that Dunbar saved the King's life.'

And doubtless he had profited from his selfless support of Lancaster and betrayal of Harry. I looked away, unable to bear the thought.

'What is that?' I pointed to a mound of newly turned earth, on the near horizon before me. Beside it, busy with measuring and writing implements, were a group of men.

362

'A grave pit, my lady. My lord the King had the dead buried here rather than let them remain for carrion to squander.'

'The dead of which side?'

He did not answer. Perhaps he did not know. Touching my heels to my mount, I approached.

'What do you do here?'

They were craftsmen by their garb, skilled and knowledgeable, unperturbed at being accosted by a fraught woman in widow's garb. 'We will build a church,' one replied, coming to stand at my stirrup, looking up beneath his woollen cap. 'A fine church. It is the King's wish, to mark the final resting place of the dead with honour.'

'Show me,' I said again, dismounting.

He led me round the planning, pointing out on the diagram in his hands where he had been adding measurements. The nave, the chancel, the high altar as he saw it. 'It will be a fine place, my lady.'

'I suppose it will. Thank you.'

'It is my lord the King's intention that prayers be said daily for the souls of the dead.'

'Of which side?' I asked again.

'Both sides, my lady. All who died are interred here. Our lord the King is compassionate to all, even those who sought his death.'

I gave him a coin for his trouble. 'Build well, sir,' I said. There would be many Percy bones in this forlorn place.

I admitted to some surprise that Lancaster would have taken such care over the dead who had raised their swords against him, then accepted that I should have known what he would do. My cousin Henry had a depth of piety in his soul, an ability to forgive where many would not. I must give him his due acknowledgement.

I could not forgive.

Once more mounted, summoning the squire, there was a final purpose for me here.

'Show me where Sir Henry fell. Show me where my lord fought for the last time.'

I was led to a space that looked no different from all the rest to my eyes, but there was no remnant of him. Had I expected it? Dismounting, I stood where I was told it had happened. Had his blood seeped into the earth here? Perhaps the crops would grow abundantly because of Percy blood.

Harry Percy is dead!

I had no sense of it.

'Remind me how many of our men we lost. And Lancaster's.'

'I know not, my lady, but they say that altogether two thousand men fell on that day.'

A terrible, terrible number. Such grief and loss. So many women widowed.

'It is said that Sir Henry was struck down by an arrow when he lifted his visor, my lady.'

I bowed my head. Then remounted, retracing my steps, only to stop, to look back to where the ultimate tragedy was played out.

'You are not here,' I cried aloud, my words snatched away by the wind. 'I do not know where to find you.'

Harry was not here, there was no comfort. I had lost him. What purpose in looking back? I must look forward, however unpalatable the prospect.

What of your own culpability in bringing Harry to this end?

The wind rustled over the winter fields, coldly hostile. I shut my mind against such agony. I could not mourn. I was as frozen as the landscape around me.

Yet returned to Ludlow, I found myself weeping without

restraint. Was it possible to receive another announcement of death so soon? Was it possible to withstand yet another loss, another blow against my heart?

Alianore was dead.

Alianore, who had been as much a sister to me as had Philippa, was dead, tragically in childbed. Two daughters she had given Sir Edward Charleton, only to die giving birth to their son who had fast followed his mother into death. How vulnerable we women were in childbed, whatever the care lavished on us by a hopeful husband. I had been fortunate; Alianore's good fortune and strong will had deserted her at last.

'Oh, Alianore. I will miss you sorely.'

Our exchange of confidences, when she had been full of hope for the future at the wedding of my daughter, had been our last. Another strand in my family frayed and cut. And such a beloved strand, a twist of gold.

Why did I weep so, when every emotion on that battlefield had been buried under pure despair? Because I loved her, my sister, my friend. Far easier to mourn her than the man who had been sun, moon and stars to me. His loss was too vast to encompass. With Alianore gone, on a more human scale I was more alone than I had ever been.

But enough of tears. I was alive and there was a cause for which to strive. Washing away the remnant of emotion, drawing on the spirit of Alianore, my decision was made to act at Edmund's bidding. I would wait on events. I would play my role as duty dictated, allowing Constance to bring her scheming to fruition.

Was I afraid for myself? I did not think I was. I did not think that I cared. I would accept what fate determined, even if it brought me to Lancaster's feet once again in the cloth of degradation of a traitor. Edmund's plan was so outrageous that it might just have the element of success worked carefully within it.

Chapter Nineteen

It was in the late spring of the year 1406, a year that seemed endless to me, that Lancaster dispatched a messenger and escort to find me at Ludlow. There was no cousinly greeting, or even a written missive, but at least I had the merit of a royal official arriving at my castle gatehouse with a tidy escort; a herald no less, impressive in tabard and velvet cap, a crowned sheaf of corn stitched to glint on his breast. Far more imposing than Sir Robert Waterton who had last been burdened with this task of taking me into his custody, and who had failed.

There would be no failure for this royal herald.

I had been awaiting it. This royal summons was not exactly unexpected, all things considered. Once I had fled to Alnwick, thus foiling Waterton. This time I made no attempt to escape, waiting calmly, in insouciant welcome.

'What brings you to my door, Master Bruges? Obviously some honour, to warrant a visit from Chester Herald, in full glory. Or do I misread the situation?'

I did not misread it at all.

I received him in the great hall, grimly imposing. As was I for, forewarned of his approach, I had dressed in damask and fur. My black veils long being put aside, my hair was encased in a gilded net. My visitor would not dismiss me as a goodwife in his delivery of his message. I stood on the dais, enhanced in my royal blood, beckoning him to approach with a jewelled hand.

I need not have worried that he would despise my rank.

'Sadly, no honour, my lady, although you have my admiration.' His lips, smiling wryly at his accurate reading of my greeting and my clothing, were tight pressed as he bowed, his cap, all velvet and gold fringing, sweeping the tiles in a flamboyantly feathered gesture. 'At present I am attached to the household of Prince Henry, my lady, but today I am commissioned with this task by my lord the King.' A ripple of unease laid its hand on me, even though I knew William Bruges as well as I knew any of the royal heralds, and I knew exactly why he had found himself at Ludlow on royal command. All my fears had come to pass at last. 'You are to come with us, my lady, if it please you,' he announced.

I knew the final courtesy would hold little sway if I refused. Yet I would play the innocent.

'To what purpose, sir?'

We continued the facade, Master Bruges bowing again.

'My lord the King wishes you to be his guest at Eltham.'

'And if it does not please me?'

'My lord the King says that he is sure that you will see the value of this visit. As his royal cousin he knows you will honour him, as you will be honoured on your arrival. You will perhaps enjoy renewing your acquaintance with my lady the Queen. When the King is away, campaigning against the Welsh and the Scots, it may be that you will be good company for her. It will be a fortuitous relationship for both of you, my lord the King says.'

Master Bruges was illuminating my visit in glowing colours. At his own behest or Lancaster's? This was Lancaster

368

working hard to draw me into the royal fold, using Queen Joanna as attractive bait. I abandoned the false chivalry.

'So I am not to be taken to Eltham in chains.'

'Certainly not, my lady. I possess no chains. Nor would I avail myself of them if I had. I have confidence in your good sense, my lady.'

I sighed a little at the obvious compliment. 'And when do you wish to start?'

'Immediately. If it please you. I trust you will ride, my lady. An equipage, of whatever sort, would take more time than my lord the King would wish. There is much demand on his time.'

Once again I thought the invisible chains might be rattled if I demurred, so I abandoned my fur and gold net, had my coffers packed, instructed my household of duties to be upheld in my absence – not a long one if I was allowed a choice in it – and accompanied Master Bruges to Eltham, knowing that I was prisoner in all but name. Together with my Mortimer nephews whose release from royal captivity had been planned with such attention to detail by Lady Despenser.

They were not released. They had not been rescued. The abject failure of the scheme, the disasters that followed, kept me cold company, enabling me to make only perfunctory responses to Chester Herald's court-inspired chatter.

At the beginning, all had played out as Edmund had inti-mated, while I occupied my comfortable chambers at Ludlow, waiting on results. In the deep cold of February, Constance Despenser put into operation the first steps of her conspiracy. Employing a locksmith to make copies of the appropriate keys, Constance planned to release the two Mortimer boys from their chamber at midnight when their absence would not be noticed, to begin a long flight westwards towards south Wales and the welcoming arms of their uncle Sir Edmund Mortimer and Prince Owain Glyn Dwr. My nephews would be free.

All went to plan. The locks unlocked, horses waiting, the Earl of March and his brother rode like the wind to Abingdon in the company of Constance and her son.

But Lancaster, based at Kennington, was warned when the empty chamber was discovered in the early morning, so it was said. True to form, Lancaster took immediate steps, sending a fast-riding contingent to cut off the escape, warning the Royal Council to prevent any escape by sea. So the whole plotting was foiled by chance, by Lancaster's quick thinking and the fast riding of John, Lancaster's Beaufort brother. Before they had ridden further than Cheltenham, Edmund and Roger Mortimer were apprehended and returned to their imprisonment in a seamless exercise, without fuss or too much violence. Constance was sent to Westminster to answer for her treason before the Royal Council, where wily Constance was not slow in denouncing her brother Edward of Aumale, now Duke of York, as the instigator of the plot, going so far as to challenge him to a duel.

Even now, remembering, I was forced to admire Constance's spirit. Would I have had the courage to do what she did, facing her brother, calling on the brave knights of the realm to come to her aid and act as her champions?

Constance had not been short of knightly volunteers to fight the Duke in her name, until Lancaster stopped the proceedings. The royal Duke was locked in the Tower of London, and then sent on to Pevensey where he whiled away his time with writing of his passion for hunting, indeed only recently released, while Constance was dispatched to the security of Kenilworth. Only the guilty locksmith suffered the true penalty of treason. He lost his hand, the maker of the false keys, and then his head. There was a limit to Lancaster's spirit of forgiveness.

It was a dark thought that accompanied me on that journey; so many of my family incarcerated. Was that why I had been summoned to Eltham with such generosity, to lure me from Ludlow into the hands of a vengeful King? For sure my brother Edmund would see the inside of the Tower of London if Henry could only get his hands on him.

For with the failure of the plot, events had taken a turn for the worse in Lancaster's eye. I needed no courier to inform me of this disaster, when news ran like wildfire up and down the March. Thwarted by the recapture of the young Earl of March, the agreement of the Dragon, the Lion and the Wolf came into play, and as I had expected, the Mortimer heir played no clear role in the envisioned outcome. Northumberland would take the north, Glyn Dwr the west and the Marches, brother Edmund in the Mortimer name what was left of the south and the east.

A meagre Mortimer inheritance indeed.

This insurrection, with a lively French interference, should have toppled Lancaster from his throne. Instead it spurred him into a storm of action, driving him to slam down his mailed fist to wipe out rank rebellion once and for all. Fortune was with him. A major victory was achieved against Glyn Dwr when his son and heir Gruffydd was taken prisoner while attempting a renewed attack on the castle at Usk, and sent to London in chains. In the same skirmish Glyn Dwr's brother was killed. Facing such a disaster, with only one son remaining, Glyn Dwr retired with Edmund to the security of the great castle at Harlech where they nursed their wounds, no doubt regrouping and reorganising, dreaming of further attacks across the border, encouraged by the songs of Iolo and the Welsh bards.

All was despair and disaster. Through my misery I became aware of my companion expressing some opinion.

'Forgive me.' Reluctantly I turned my head. I had no wish to converse.

'The Earl of Northumberland is, so I understand, my lady, still in Scotland.'

'Scotland?'

His sideways glance was wry. 'So the rumours say. And it may be so. Who's to know where his hasty ambitions will take him?'

He had my full attention. 'Tell me,' I ordered. 'Tell me why the Earl of Northumberland should be in Scotland.'

The herald cleared his throat. 'I thought you might know most of it, my lady.' And when I shook my head: 'The King has leaped from victory to victory, even executing the Archbishop of York, who was unwise in leading a troop of armed citizens to join with the northern lords in the Earl's uprising against the King. The uprising failed. Northumberland was hounded from one refuge to another until he fled to take exile in Scotland.' He glanced at me again, as if deciding whether to tell me. 'The Percy castles and lands are now come under royal dominion,' he added. 'Even Alnwick has been taken. The defences at Warkworth, so they say, have all but been destroyed by the royal cannon. It's all attainder and forfeiture.' He shrugged with a casual callousness. 'If you will turn traitor, that's the penalty.'

It was a brutal telling. In the blindness of my ambitions I had not seen, or had refused to see, what would become of us. Now I could think of nothing to say; helpless anger warred with foolish loss. Warkworth was battered into submission. Warkworth, Harry's favourite home, reduced to near rubble. I could have wept for that one loss alone.

'I've given you no comfort, madam.'

None at all. There was no bright sun on my horizon. My son had lost his inheritance and his freedom to return to England; the once great Earl of Northumberland had joined him in exile. All the castles I had loved and lived in with Harry were forfeit or destroyed. Harry was dead, the Mortimer cause lost. The Percys would never again wield the power to be recognised as Kings of the North. All we had possessed, all we had hoped for, had been laid waste by our own hand or by Lancaster's. The price of treason was high indeed.

'Many would say I deserve no comfort,' I said, my voice rusty with unshed tears.

There was nothing more for me to lose, except my own freedom, which was the fear that had lived with me as I had waited at Ludlow on the King's response. Now it churned within me as every mile passed, making me deaf to Chester Herald's prattle. Since Lancaster had taken his revenge on those who had threatened him, he had turned his eye on me. In which royal fortress would I live out my days? Constance, no doubt suitably obsequious to her royal cousin and the Council, had finally been granted her freedom and restoration of some of her estates. Would Lancaster be as generous to me? I thought not.

Since he had failed to get his hands on the three main conspirators, he might consider me the next best thing. It had been slow in coming, but now it was here.

You are my bed of nettles, Harry had once said in a fit of exasperation.

Lancaster would think the same. We lapsed into silence that covered many miles. Until, driven to ask by the fear that grew with each passing hour:

'Am I to be part of the King's plan for righteous revenge, Master Burges?'

Riding through the thronged streets of London with all the noise and reek of crowded humanity, all we had to do now was seek a crossing of the Thames to arrive at Eltham. There I would meet whatever punishment Lancaster saw fit to inflict on me. I had flung myself on his mercy once, at York, but how could he be gracious when I and my family had been at the heart of a new rebellion? I could not imagine that good fortune would follow me for ever. For the first time in my life I feared that my neck might be at risk.

'It may be so,' he admitted, hacking even further at my confidence. 'It would at least solve one of his problems.' Then hesitated when he caught my horrified glance, as he realised what he had said. 'Forgive me, my lady.'

'You spoke but the truth,' I admitted. 'My loyalties are suspect. My cousin failed to take the Lion, the Dragon or the Wolf into bestial custody. Perhaps I am to be the sacrificial Lamb.'

He did not pretend to misunderstand my reference.

'I doubt he will execute you, my lady. My lord the King does not wage war on women.'

I thought that he did not look too certain. 'He kept Constance Despenser under guard,' I reminded him.

'She deserved it, my lady. But now she is free, at the King's pleasure.'

Perhaps Lancaster would consider that I might deserve it too.

I travelled the final miles to Eltham in some dread,

remembering my previous visit there, summoned by Queen Isabelle, before all had become disaster, before we had all descended into hell. Isabelle was now returned to the country of her birth, no doubt disappointed that her dowry had not accompanied her but added weight to Lancaster's coffers instead. I must wait on the disposition of my own future.

I shivered with fear.

I was received at Eltham with every evidence of grace, Queen Joanna in perfect control of the hospitality offered by her household as she took my hand, raised me from my curtsey and lightly embraced me. I thought Henry, sitting by the fire, looked drained of all energies but then he had been travelling constantly from one end of his kingdom to the other, enough to draw on his considerable reserves and on his patience, but there was no sense of threat or hostility in his inviting me into their private parlour, into their private life together. This was the life he had created for himself on the back of Percy support. This was the luxurious setting for himself and his handsome wife, and as I witnessed it, disgust tightened its fingers in my flesh.

Now, urbane, cousinly, he rose and offered me wine, talked of his children and the extensive marriage plans for his daughters Blanche and Philippa, to which I responded with mighty composure. We did not speak of Constance or her brother the Duke of York. We did not speak of my own son. Instead the Queen asked after the health of Bess and her young Clifford husband, and I asked after her own young daughters who had accompanied her from Brittany.

Until I could barely contain the irrelevance of it all. But contain it I did, behind an unsmiling but courteous facade. I would not break this carefully constructed equanimity; I would simply wait on Henry's desires. Forgiveness was an emotion that I could not embrace but I would not be ill-mannered since he was of a mind to be gracious. I would wait.

But was this all a mockery? Would he dine with me, then tell me that I would face the judgement of all traitors? My hand was clammy around the handle of my knife as we supped in the early evening, with music and erudite conversation about books and travel, candles lit against the early dusk. What did I speak of, to add to the conversation? I could not recall. When the minstrels were dispatched, my cousin turned his gaze on me at last with a speculative weight.

'I find that I have a need to discuss your future, Elizabeth.'

Here it was at last. Joanna made her departure, leaving us alone, her glance towards me holding an element of warning, perhaps of pity.

'As you wish, my lord.'

I clasped my hands together on the board before me. Then loosed them when I saw the tension in my fingers. I hid my hands in my lap.

'You have been very patient.' He offered me a faint smile that I did not return, and which he accepted with a lift of one shoulder, a grimace flattening his features as he moved uneasily in his chair. No, he was not physically well, looking older than his thirty-eight years. I thought he had experienced some difficulty or discomfort when he had first pushed himself from his chair on my arrival – and would he not have once been on his feet to greet me? – but my mind was on his words, not his health. 'I have drawn the sting from the threat to my throne, for the present,' he said. 'You know this. The Archbishop of York is dead for treason. Northumberland has taken his treacherous self to Scotland.

Your brother and Glyn Dwr are holed up in Harlech. The only weak link in my armour is…' He paused, his brow a formidable line.

'My nephews,' I supplied. 'But you have them under your hand. Will you execute them?'

'Would you think it of me?'

'I might. It would wipe the board of all challenging pawns. Your King and his Queen would be invincible in the game and carry all before them.'

Lancaster sipped slowly from the cup of wine at his right hand, his eyes never leaving my face. For a moment I thought how dissimilar he was from Harry. One governed by fire and action, rarely amenable to long planning; the other cold and painstaking in the cause of his own power. Yet both driven by enormous energies. Once they had shared a solid friendship.

Lancaster was continuing with pellucid serenity at odds with his white-knuckled hold of the stemmed goblet. 'It was not my hand that killed Henry Percy, Elizabeth. You know it was not.'

'It was your command that brought the two forces to battle. It was your refusal to negotiate that brought death to so many on that terrible day. It was your noxious order that disfigured his body, distributing it around England. It was you who humiliated his honour by exposing his body in Shrewsbury and his head on York's gate for all to pass beneath. It was you who ordered the execution of Worcester when he was brought alive before you.'

The swords were naked between us now, so that I saw a flash of displeasure cross his face before the lines were hammered back into those of prideful authority.

'What would you expect of me? How could you, with

all your Plantagenet blood, even question my reaction to an attack on my kingdom that was as dangerous as any I have faced?'

'I both know and accept the penalty. But it was you who pushed him into his treachery.'

'I thought the reason for his treachery was that I was not a Mortimer, and that he regretted helping me to the crown in the first place.' So there was the truth, laid out before us in dry and simple words. 'I do not have to answer to you for the actions I take to restore peace to this kingdom.'

'No. You do not. There will never be any understanding between us.' I stood so that I forced him to look up. How could I sit in comfort and ask this one question that needed to be asked? 'What is the future for the Earl of March and his brother? Will you be honest with me? Or will you distract me with some facile promise that you will not keep?'

I did not ask what he intended to do with me.

Henry tilted his head.

'Here is my honesty. They will be raised as members of my family.'

'But without freedom.'

'Freedom is a relative concept. I cannot turn them over into your keeping, if that is what you would wish for. They are too tempting a target for those who would use their Plantagenet heritage against me, but I am not without compassion for their situation, none of it of their making, merely of their blood. I will not treat them with dishonour.'

'Dishonour! They will stay under your control until they die.'

'There will be no dishonour,' he repeated. 'I am thinking that we should find a suitable bride for Edmund. I have put his marriage into the hands of Joanna who will discover a high-born girl of good family. I am also considering that he should join the household and come under the guidance of my son Henry. At some time in the future. They both share a love of swordplay and archery.' He paused to reach for the flagon to his right, pouring more wine for himself, pushing a newly filled cup in my direction. 'And I would be grateful if you would sit down, so that I, out of chivalric honour, do not have to stand with you.'

Slowly I obeyed.

'Thank you. Do my plans sound like dishonour? Do they point to execution?'

'No. But you might do it.'

'Out of pique? You make me sound like a temperamental woman.'

'What do you know of temperamental women? It is not an accusation that you could ever level at me. Nor do I think that your wife is capricious.'

'No. You were never unpredictable. I should have known from the start that your loyalty to me had a finite quality.' He shook his head, the lines beside his mouth still taut. 'I will treat the young Earl well. I do not fear him if I can win his loyalty.' I saw him relax, determined not to allow irritation to prevail. 'Here is the truth, and something that you seem not to have considered. The only weak link in this chain, apart from those lords taken refuge from me in Wales or in Scotland, is you, my dear Elizabeth.'

I had expected it, yet my blood was a cold river. I looked up as Joanna, unnoticed during the exchange, had returned to the room, her eyes on her husband.

'So you will execute me?' I asked with terrible flippancy, finally voicing that dread that had lived with me all the way from Ludlow.

'Many would think me wise to consider it. I might win the loyalty of your nephew by fair treatment but I doubt you will ever willingly come to heel.' His voice was tainted with the bitterness of disappointment. 'Once you were Queen of the North. What would be your ambition now?'

'I have no ambition for myself. You have cured me of that.' My bitterness matched his. 'If you baulk at execution, what about incarceration in the Tower of London? For in truth I am no hound to come when I am called.'

'It might be advisable.' He considered me, his gaze perhaps troubled. 'I confess to not knowing what role you had in the attempt to rescue the Mortimer lads. I know that you were in Ludlow. Were you involved? If so, you can expect no compassion from me.'

'Henry.' Approaching quietly, Joanna had placed a hand on his shoulder. 'You have no intention of either executing or imprisoning Elizabeth. We have talked about it.'

'Elizabeth thinks I will. She believes the worst of me.'

'Kings must suffer being misread.' Her smile for me was full of understanding.

'So what do you do with me?'

'It is not so terrible,' Joanna advised.

And I could already see it in my mind's eye; I could see it fully fledged in Lancaster's planning. They had talked of it, planned it, and now here I was, to be informed. What would be the simplest way to curb a woman whose loyalties were suspect? For centuries, how had women of influence been robbed of their freedom?

'I have planned a marriage for you,' he said, fists on the arms of his chair to take his weight as he pushed himself to his feet.

How to control a widow who might be seen as a threat.

380

If not condemned to life in a nunnery, then marriage was the perfect solution.

I did not stir. I would not flinch from it.

'And if I have no desire to marry again?'

'You are still young,' Lancaster advised. 'You could carry children for an important man. Your royal blood would make you a valuable prospect.'

'If the lord you have chosen is prepared to overlook past treacheries.'

'He will overlook them.'

Lancaster might have taken a step back from the threats of death or imprisonment, but he remained coldly calculating. As did I. I would not take a man of his choosing.

'I do not wish it.'

'I am giving you little choice, cousin. The alternative is to retire and take the veil.' He must have seen my reaction to such a future, however hard I worked to mask it. 'I thought not. You are too great a danger to me to be allowed freedom of action. I said that you were not volatile, but at the moment you are a directionless vessel. Who knows where such a vessel will voyage or founder when the winds take control. I need to be certain. Marriage to a man loyal to the house of Lancaster is the obvious answer.'

'And you have chosen this man who will be loyal to Lancaster?'

'I have.' There was an implacability in him that I recognised: there would be no moving him.

'Will I approve your choice?'

'It matters not whether you approve or resist. I will not allow you to resist. Wife or nun, Elizabeth. Which will it be?'

So I stood, everything within me denying the blackness of a future with a man I neither knew nor wanted.

'When do I meet him?'

I imagined some court reception where my potential bride-groom would make his bow before me. There might be no wooing but at least I would meet him in company where I might take time to appraise this man I was being commanded to wed. Did I not deserve an impersonal first meeting with this man of Lancaster's choosing?

'Now,' Henry said. 'He is waiting for you.'

It caused my heart to thud as panic gripped hard. Now I knew what it was like for a doe to face the hunting pack, to be surrounded by a threat that would bring her down, for her strength was waning and the power of the hounds was great. Lancaster knew I could not refuse, for I was here under his jurisdiction. He knew I would never take the veil. Yet how could I accept this planning of my life that to me was anathema?

'What has been his reward,' I asked, my chin raised, 'this supporter of Lancaster, to make him compliant?'

'I have given no reward. He has agreed to meet with you, out of love for me.'

'Ha! No man has such loyalty.'

The curve of his mouth held the true essence of cynicism. 'Perhaps you are right, but he sees the value of this alliance. Besides, he will enjoy a wife to make his home comfortable.'

'He could employ a steward or a mistress to achieve that.'

'Elizabeth.' Draining his cup, Lancaster's patience finally snapped. 'Meet with him. Speak with him. I really cannot afford to have you free to travel the country, to plot and scheme. It is either marriage, or I will arrange accommodations for you at Windsor with your nephews until I seek out a suitable convent.'

At last I bowed my head.

'Very well. I truly have no choice.'

'No. None.'

'Do you tell me who this man is, this royal minion?'

'Oh, I will let you meet him and make your own opinion.' For the first time there was a hint of malice in Lancaster's eye. 'The royal minion will speak for himself. You will find him waiting for you in the small antechamber. My steward is waiting to show you the way.'

I walked to the door, skirts swishing against the boards as the only indication of my inner fears. Marriage or a soft imprisonment, there would be little difference, my every step watched, every word I spoke recorded and reported back to Henry. My freedom curtailed by a locked door or a watchful husband.

My shoes slapped irritably against the wood.

Lancaster's voice followed. 'You cannot win against me, Elizabeth. You don't have the weapons to engage in warfare against me.'

And I knew it. All was lost for me.

Chapter Twenty

Dismissing Eltham's steward in a somewhat peremptory fashion, I stood outside the chamber, one hand pressed down hard against the door so that the grain of the linenfold bit into my flesh. Here was my future, for good or ill; this man would direct my life to his liking and his advantage. Would he be objectionable to me, some despicable knight without culture or even kindness? Lancaster might consider this to be the worst form of punishment, of degradation, to give me into the hands of a man I could not even respect. I shivered beneath the weight of my garments, grimacing at the knowledge of my hem heavy with dust, for had I not travelled to Eltham in them? I was not garbed for meeting a bridegroom.

But then it would not matter what I wore. This was no wooing, on either side.

Soft footsteps sounded behind me, a servant, sent by Lancaster I presumed, who in heightened suspicion was taking nothing for granted. He opened the door for me, ushered me within, then bowing, closed it. No flight for me now. Remaining with my back to the door I stood motionless and regarded the man who waited, my heart beating hard so that it seemed the whole room echoed with it. Candles had been lit here, a multitude of them. My proposed bridegroom, by chance or design, was illuminated in a glow of gold.

He was standing at the far side of the room, his back turned to me, looking down into the dark courtyard where there was some commotion of servants and guests arriving, voices of welcome and command lifting on the evening air. His figure was softened by the rich tapestries that clothed the wall on either side. Then he turned.

I inhaled, my heartbeat gradually slowing. I did not want him, but Lancaster had not punished me with a man I could not respect. He had simply allowed me to worry that he had negotiated my hand with some unwashed, illiterate lord who would bury me in his castle in a rural fastness, far from sight or sound of royal affairs. No such thing. I walked forward towards this man who was no stranger to me, since no one associated with the Royal Court would fail to recognise him. I had known him, albeit distantly, all my life; Lancaster could not have chosen better if I were amenable to remarriage, a willing bride.

Baron Thomas de Camoys, soldier, diplomat, administrator. King's friend. A man of considerable skill, a widower, older than I by almost two decades, I supposed. Dependable, loyal, with a reputation for sound judgement, he was the perfect gaoler to prevent my further involvement in Mortimer politics. Lancaster had made an exceptional choice for me, if I were willing to accept his goodwill in the disposing of my life.

I was not willing.

I laughed, a hard sound in the still room.

Of course. The perfect manner in which to keep my future loyalties under scrutiny and control. Marry me to a man who is your friend, your most loyal subject, a man who has the respect of every follower of Lancaster in the country, and many who are not, so that I am walled about by Lancaster supporters and goodwill.

It had been so carefully plotted, so thoroughly decided. Suddenly, unexpectedly, I could feel tears, bitter with regret, gathering in my throat.

I had been directed to meet with Baron de Camoys in one of the smaller rooms used when friends and family were entertained, which I supposed had the intention of encouraging intimacy, rather than a formal, vastly proportioned audience chamber, but I made no gesture of greeting or of grace. Rather I stood unmoving and unreceptive. The only blessing was that we were left to conduct this interview alone. I thought that I would have preferred the distancing of an audience chamber.

Baron de Camoys, cap in hand, taking no instruction from me, bowed with all the courtly manners that I had deliberately abandoned.

'My cousin says that I must wed you,' I announced when he had straightened again to his full and not unimpressive height. 'I presume you are in agreement with this proposed alliance. Did Lancaster have to pay you to take a wife who has shown herself to be not averse to treason? Lancaster denies the need, but my suspicions are rank. How much, my lord? Or was it a grant of land? A castle? An enhanced title, perhaps? I would be interested to know.'

'I know of your previous loyalties, my lady. Who does not? I think that I might understand why you took that dangerous path.'

His voice was low and well modulated. I sensed no criticism there, merely a sense of amenable negotiation, which I instinctively did not trust.

386

'I do not want your understanding, my lord.'

Slowly he walked towards me, to stand within an arm's length. He was, I acknowledged, closer to the Earl of Northumberland's age than to mine, not a comparison that I found comforting or appealing. The Earl was sly and deceitful, thoroughly selfish. Would this man prove to be the same when dealing with his own personal affairs? His reputation suggested a man of better qualities, but it still had to be seen. Many said that he was a man of great kindness. Tall and lean with the musculature of a soldier and a mass of silvered dark hair, he was a figure to take the eye.

'Very well,' he said, with no kindness at all, 'if you want straight speaking from me without the balm of compassion, this marriage is no more to my taste than I imagine it is to yours. You were unwise. You were badly counselled. As for this proposed alliance between us, no payment has either been mentioned or considered necessary. It was merely a suggestion made to me by the King. A royal wife with royal blessing.'

'For you to take me off his hands.'

'Something like that. If I was willing to shoulder the burden of a dangerous wife.'

'It is a bad bargain, so I warn you,' I said, undermined by emotion that I had thought had ebbed. Instead it came back with storm force to shatter against my utter loneliness. The rock on which I had based my life was broken; the comet that had blazed through my skies had foundered in the unforgiving depths of the sea. I wanted no husband. I did not want Thomas de Camoys. Nor would he want me with all my bitter thoughts of revenge and despair. He was a good man, I knew. He deserved better than me. But in that moment I despised him and all he stood for.

I looked up, dry-eyed, to see that he was watching me.

'What do we say now?' I asked, without grace.

'I have not yet told the King that I will accept this offer of your hand.' And when my brows rose in disbelief: 'You may not be to my liking. Indeed, you are not. I doubt there is any man in the country who would relish Elizabeth Percy as a wife. He would spend his life looking over his shoulder, expecting a dagger between the shoulder blades.'

It was like a blow, an unexpected blow from a gloved fist that had seemed as soft as the finest kid. Whereas I had expected gentle courtesy from this man whom Lancaster had chosen as one of those magnates to escort his new wife from Brittany to England, I had received a further battering of truth.

'I doubt that I will be to any man's liking,' I said, rallying fast. 'Unless my royal blood is sufficient to compensate for my disaffection. Obviously, in this case, it is not. I regret that you have been placed in this embarrassing position, my lord.'

'Forgive my plain speaking, my lady. I thought it was what you wanted. I too regret if I have given offence, but you are a hazardous choice as a wife.'

I turned away when I could find no immediate response, to take up a stance before an empty fireplace. 'I admire your good manners, Lord Thomas. I have none.'

'Good manners are ingrained from birth, whatever the enticement to lapse into crudity.'

Another unexpected blow. I looked over my shoulder in some degree of hurt. Seeing it, Lord Thomas withdrew from the attack.

'I expect yours are but hidden beneath your intransigence. I doubt you enjoyed the King's disposition of your future.'

It made me flush with mortification as he laid bare my lack.

'You are honest too,' I admitted. 'Honesty has been in short supply in my world of late.'

He marked his acknowledgement in a brisk nod. 'It would not be too late for you to be open with me before we leave this chill room where every action and every thought is laid bare in this glare of light.' Abruptly he quenched two of the candles at his side. 'I would be reluctant to accept your hand from the King if I thought you were not in agreement at some level. Tell me that you are not, and we will draw a line beneath the suggestion.'

'I am not in agreement.'

'Then there is no more to be said between us. There will be no compulsion from me. I will tell the King that we do not consider marriage between us acceptable.'

Which caught my interest in the likelihood of such defiance.

'You would not!'

'I am too old to desire a tempestuous wife.'

Which was no answer at all. Would it be so easy to thwart Lancaster, to simply refuse and risk the consequences of his regal temper? I considered this pre-eminent baron of Lancaster's court. His grave composure. His confidence. Even a layer of humour and, above all, of calm good sense.

'Do you not fear that it will bring Lancaster's anger down on your head?' I was curious, my thoughts dragged from my own worries.

'I am too old to fear that too. He may snap and snarl, but I am in no danger.'

'Perhaps Archbishop Scrope said exactly the same when he led an armed demonstration of citizens out of York, in support of Northumberland's signing the Tripartite Indenture,' I remarked. 'He paid for his misdeeds with his head.'

'I'll risk it. My lord the King has more trust in me than he had in Scrope who unwisely encouraged those who would rebel. The King and I have much history together, so much so that I think my head is safely attached to my shoulders. And yours too, I imagine. I don't fear Lancaster's retribution over a matter of a marriage that is not to our taste.'

'A fine way of describing my thorough detestation of the whole matter.' I found that I was smiling a little. 'Forgive me, Lord Thomas, I cannot marry you.'

'Why not? Have you given it sufficient thought?'

'No. No thought at all. I have a dislike of being manipulated, and being given no voice in the outcome.'

'Which is not flattering to your present suitor. Am I not offering you a voice?' Approaching, he surprised me by taking my hand, tightening his grip when I resisted, then leading me to a plain wooden settle set against the wall. I allowed it, and sat, as he sat beside me at a careful distance, much as two petitioners without knowledge of each other, waiting for an audience with the King. 'Think about it now,' he ordered, releasing me, 'and tell me why you cannot.'

I took a breath and obeyed.

'It would be ungracious of me to burden you with my affairs. I don't believe that you are in ignorance of them. You are expected to wed me to stop me from snapping at Lancaster's heels or taking a bite out of his calf as Constance Despenser did. You are expected to growl and ward off any further approaches by my brother Edmund Mortimer, to inveigle me into lending my weight in another uprising. You are intended, by whatever means you can, to deter me from plotting the release of my nephews. As for what the Earl of Northumberland is planning, in exile in Scotland with my son...' I shrugged a little. 'In short you are expected to play the guard dog.'

'You have a way with words, my lady. You can hardly

blame Lancaster for protecting his own back. There have been far too many would-be assassins dogging his steps.'

'I am not one of them, despite your fear that I might so attack you if you took me to wife.' I considered. 'I would not wish Lancaster's death. I think I am too weary for rebellion. But I doubt Lancaster will ever accept my loyalty, even if I were prepared to offer it.'

'Which would be almost impossible, knowing your past history.'

I lapsed into silence, unable to see the direction that we were taking, deciding to leave it in the hands of Baron de Camoys.

'Well, we have dealt with your own political inclinations,' he said. 'Now let us contemplate your present situation.' How calm he was, how drily appreciative. 'Would marriage to me be too unacceptable to you? If, as you seem to fear, it keeps you out of imprisonment, where your every action is restrained? I would not so restrain you. Surely marriage to me would offer you a better life than taking the veil?'

'I've no mind for a husband to keep a permanent eye on my movements.'

'I would promise to be very discreet.'

'I thought you said you did not want me.'

I looked at him, studying the lines of experience. Of a grief of his own.

'I am reassessing, as are you, and giving you the time and space to consider wisely, before casting yourself on the King's mercy. It is in my nature to be discreet. I would not demand to know your every thought. I would not chain you to the bed in one of my manors. I would accept your good sense, and a promise of loyalty to me even if you were not prepared to make one to my lord the King.' He thought for a moment, his gaze stern on my face. 'As long as I did not find Northumberland with an army at my gates, demanding admittance, demanding your participation in yet another hopeless uprising because of your Mortimer blood. England has had enough of upheavals to last a lifetime and so have I. Northumberland has a silken tongue when he chooses to use it, but is difficult to trust.'

Which made me laugh a little. There was a gleam in his eye. As if encouraged, he held out his hand again. I placed mine there, conscious that it was a soldier's hand, rough with rein and callous and swordplay, yet so different from Harry's. Square and broad-palmed, it had not the fine elegance of Harry's hand.

'Have you told me the worst, then?' Lord Thomas de Camoys asked.

'Is it not bad enough?'

'Perhaps, but it is not an impregnable barrier. It all depends on what you wish to do next. To live at peace or continue to stir the pot. Or the poisoned chalice may be a more apposite image.' Then: 'Is your heart given to another?' he asked, surprising me.

'Does it matter?'

'No.'

'My heart is dead and in pieces. Cut to pieces on a battle-field. I cannot love again, if that is what you mean.'

'Nor do you need to. People of our standing can marry for many different reasons. Love is the least valuable, I imagine. We can marry for affection if we are fortunate, for companion-ship. We might discover an ability to work together over the demands of estates and income. It might not be unpleasant.'

'Are you talking yourself into this marriage, or me, Lord Thomas?'

'Both of us, I think.'

I liked that he did not offer me compassion, merely an acceptance. 'What would it mean for you?' I asked.

'Do you wish for me to be truthful?'

'Since we are being so. Horrifyingly so.'

'The companionship of an intelligent woman as the years move on.'

'Even if her opinions do not march with yours? What an uncomfortable match if we could not share a single thought without argument.'

'And I would fear it, but it need not be so. You would find me often on campaign or with a need to visit my most widespread estates.' He smiled. 'We would not have to agree on everything, but perhaps you would have to learn discretion too.'

'Perhaps.' I no longer disliked the thought as much as I had. 'You have a son, I believe, and his children, if all you wish for is companionship to ward off loneliness in old age.'

'I do. Richard, who has grown into a fine man. But he and his new wife and family live their own lives, as they should.'

'Did you love your wife?' I asked, perhaps in response to the rather wistful comment from this brusque soldier.

'It was not a marriage of love, but we had an understanding. A close affection. She was called Elizabeth too.' He released my hand. I had forgotten that he had been holding it. 'I would not be a demanding husband.'

'Ah. Is your heart perhaps given elsewhere?'

He hesitated, just a moment. 'Yes.'

Now this I had not expected. 'Will she not wed you?'

'It is not possible.'

A moment of insight came to me. 'Does she know that you love her?'

'No. Nor will I tell her. She is not free to wed me nor would it be suitable. You would not need to feel threatened that a woman would undermine our marriage by her constant shadow. There will be no one there but the two of us, and your dead husband unless you choose to banish him. I hope that with the passage of time you might. Hotspur would make for an uncomfortable bedfellow.'

It took my breath, but before I could think of a response:

'Think about it, my lady. It would bring you much benefit and few problems. I will make life comfortable for you, make no unnecessary demands. I will respect your broken heart. It may be that we would find some pleasure in each other's company. If not, you will have security, and can depend on my absence in the King's service. I can at least offer you a home. It is better than any alternative offered by the King.'

Again unexpected emotion rose within me. He was indeed as kind as his reputation implied.

'You are considerate, my lord, more than I deserve. My heart is full of hatred and revenge.'

'I regret that. It will not lead to happiness.'

'I do not look for happiness.'

'Is it that you think you do not deserve it?'

How prescient he was, but I could not give my confidence, no matter how easy it suddenly seemed to be. 'That is not your concern, sir.'

'Then I will leave you to your complicated concerns, if you are unwilling to allow me to advise you on them. You must inform the King what it is you wish to do. I wish you well of your choice, my lady, for your own sake. But I would say that it is now approaching three years since your lord died. You have grieved. You have failed in an attempt to destroy the King and create a Mortimer dynasty. The past is dead and gone. A sensible woman could put an end to her grieving and look to the future.'

'I have no future. My future has been destroyed.'

Standing, he bowed and moved to open the door.

'Then that is what you must tell the King. And when you have decided, then you can tell me.'

I returned to the room where I had left Lancaster and his wife; I knocked softly to give them warning. There was no need. They sat apart, he staring into his wine cup as if it might provide the answer to some question, Joanna with a book on her lap but her attention not on the gilded and painted pages. The expression on her face as I entered, one of fear or perhaps a deep-seated anxiety, awakened an unexpected concern within me, but then she turned to me and smiled, stretching out her hand.

Slowly I walked forward although I was unable to return her greeting. Much of an age, it might once have been possible for a friendship to develop between us, an understanding based on shared interests. There was no friendship in my heart.

'Is it decided between you?' Lancaster asked.

'There has been no decision.' And when he rose to his feet, irritation paramount: 'Lord Thomas has allowed me time to consider.'

He put down his cup with a heavy hand so that the jewelled decoration flashed in the candlelight and the contents swirled dangerously to spatter onto the coffer lid.

'It was not to be a matter for your choice or your consideration!'

'Lord Thomas has been very courteous.'

Impatience etched deep lines across his brow. 'I don't have

time for Camoys's strange courtesies. I have a campaign to pursue. I want it settled, and if you won't settle it, I will. We have an altar and a priest. It would take no time at all. And I'm not in the mood to wait.'

I curtsied deeply. 'I will consider your wishes, my lord.'

'You will marry Camoys!'

'Allow me until tomorrow, if it please you.'

When my cousin turned away, shoulders braced, face hidden, Joanna, also standing, would have touched his arm yet was shaken off.

'Very well. Until tomorrow, Elizabeth. But I will not change my mind.'

When I left on that uncompromising note, I was surprised that Joanna chose to accompany me.

'It will not be too difficult,' she advised, her expression wiped clean of the fear I had earlier seen there.

'You think I will agree.' My reply was as bleak as my heart.

'Why not? I see the advantages to which you seem blind.'

'If you mean that marriage to Lord Thomas is better than embracing the life of a nun, then I cannot disagree. I know that you made a similar choice, in taking a second husband. But you were not threatened with a convent. And I think you loved the man you chose. It is not the same.'

'No, it was not the same, but the choice was still not an easy one.' We were pacing together through one darkened antechamber and then another. 'Faced with disapproval from the French court, I had to leave my sons behind in Brittany. I have had to win some acceptance from a hostile people who tend to despise all things Breton and resent even the dower that Henry gave to me. I have too much pride to do that easily or lightly, but I have done it and I would argue that marriage offers a woman so many possibilities that are closed to her as a spinster or a widow. Or a nun.' Her eyes were suddenly bright with laughter. 'You will not even consider walling yourself up as an anchorite. The advantages of marriage will be as familiar to you as they are to me.'

I walked in silence.

'I cannot think of a better man,' she pursued. 'Lord Thomas has been a friend for many years. He will be neither judgemental nor cold to your situation.'

'I would be a burden to him. He does not want me. He does it because your husband asks it of him.'

Joanna's grip on my arm drew me to a halt. 'Consider the virtues of marriage, Elizabeth. Living under duress at Windsor, even in comfort, or enclosing yourself in never-ending prayer and reparation, would be no life for an intelligent woman. If nothing else, that should persuade you. Lord Thomas owns a number of attractive manors.'

'I will not be persuaded against my will.'

She would have walked on, except that I now stopped her. I had seen the lines between her brows, the dark imprints of sleeplessness. And I had remembered Lancaster, his less than fluid movements, his rejection of her. For the first time I ventured a personal question, once again wishing that our relationship were closer.

'Joanna. Is Henry ill?'

She looked back at me, her brows rising as if she disliked the intrusion. 'No.'

'Or is it that he won't tell you? He is not the only one with too much pride.'

She grimaced a little. 'And you are not the only one in this palace with problems to solve.'

My cousin had allowed me the night in which to deploy my

thoughts and come to a decision over my future. In which to consider the advantages of his plan. And the disadvantages. And so, sitting in comfort in a damask robe before a fire, hair combed on my breast, a cup of wine to hand, that is what I did.

I considered the weight on Lancaster's shoulders, and Joanna's obvious anxiety, for I had not believed her brisk denial. The King was afflicted by some physical malaise.

I considered my Mortimer nephews returned to their life at Windsor after that briefest flirtation with freedom. And Lancaster's ambitions for them.

I considered what Northumberland might be doing, taking refuge in Scotland. Or no, by now, so court gossip informed me, he was seeking sanctuary with Glyn Dwr in Wales where the Welsh prince was trying to hold his insurrection together, still looking to France for an alliance and military support.

I considered my son, far removed from my influence; my daughter safe in the Clifford household.

I considered what life would hold for me, wed or unwed.

I considered the cause Harry and I had supported. The rights and wrongs of inheritance. The Lancaster crown that we had promoted. The Mortimer rights that had been denied.

I considered the state of my conscience and my soul. I considered the grief that had held me in thrall.

On the following morning, before Mass, I asked to see Lord Thomas de Camoys.

The same chamber but this time I was awaiting him. Dawn having broken, there were no candles, leaving the light in the room more kindly to its occupants. I had to admit to having taken some care with my appearance.

'My lady.'

'My lord.'

He bowed. I curtsied. He waited. I spoke.

'I have come to my decision.'

'I trust there has been no compulsion placed on you.'

'No compulsion?' I closed the book I had been holding with soft control. 'My cousin of Lancaster has made his wishes known without the mincing of any words. He needs to be on campaign and I am a problem that must be dealt with before he leaves. He threatened, as I understood it, to drag me to the altar in his private chapel here at Eltham.'

'But, as I made clear to you yesterday, I have no need of a wife who must be dragged. I have given you your freedom to accept or reject.'

'For which I am grateful. I am here because I owe you the courtesy that you showed to me.'

As before he took my hand, removing the book which he placed aside on a coffer, but not without a gruff laugh, as he led me to the settle against the wall, taking one end, a little distance away.

'What has amused you, my lord?'

'Your reading matter seems less than appropriate, my lady.'

I cast a glance at the book where he had placed it, recognising the gilded binding. I had not even considered what it might be, merely picking it up from those left for my entertainment in my bedchamber. I had merely wanted to give my hands something to do, for assuredly my mind would not be seduced by reading. No, the *Roman de la Rose* was not appropriate, with its delightful poetry of chivalry and courtly love.

'I was not reading it,' I said, conscious of the heat in my cheeks. 'It was an arbitrary choice.'

'I understand, my lady, even though the tale of the Lover

and his Quest – against the admonishments of Reason and the obstacles set by Jealousy and Resistance – to pluck the fair Rose in the Enchanted Garden would be a commendable choice.' And I thought that he did understand, which made me flush even more. So Lord Thomas was erudite too. 'So what is it you wish?'

'It is this. If you are willing, and I am not too distasteful to you, Lord Thomas, I will wed you.'

He paused for a moment before replying, then said: 'I am gratified that you will give yourself into my keeping.'

'So do you accept this bad bargain?'

His smile lit his face, deepening the lines of experience. 'I think it will be a better bargain than I had anticipated. It will mean that neither of us has to explain our wilful disobedience to my lord the King.'

I found that I was smiling in return.

But then my suitor became solemn.

'There are conditions. Yesterday I made light of them, but they are serious considerations. I have no wish to be put in the position of having to intercept treasonous correspondence from your brother, or from Constance Despenser. I have no wish to have any involvement with the ambitions of Northumberland or the Welsh prince Glyn Dwr. I know where your heart will always remain. I can tolerate your divided loyalties, as long as I know that you will be true to the vows that you make to me.'

I felt my cheeks burn with colour, but I replied in kind.

'I can tolerate your watchful eye, Lord Thomas, as long as I don't have a servant or an armed guard dogging my every footstep and lurking outside the door of my chamber. And if my chamber has a key to a lock, I wish to be in possession of it.'

'Of course, my lady. And I will buy you an enamelled chatelaine from which to hang it.'

We understood each other.

'Then I will be your wife.'

He took my hand and kissed my fingers. The bargain was made.

What choice did I have? Life under surveillance at the Lancaster court, powerless and ineffectual, my every action prescribed by Lancaster's servants, held no appeal for me. Here was marriage to a man who would give me a soft servitude with a promised degree of independence. In different circumstances I might have taken Thomas de Camoys as a friend.

Lancaster would be pleased.

I wondered what my brother and the Earl of Northumberland would say.

I had made a bargain with Lancaster. I would wed Lord Thomas if I could see my nephews again. I had not seen either of them since I had defied Harry and ridden south in fear of their safety. It seemed so long ago now.

'Let me see them and I will wed as you wish and without argument.'

'Which will be a miracle in itself. I have not had them murdered,' Lancaster had said, a wry twist to his lips, echoed in his voice.

'Will you arrange an escort to Windsor?'

'No need. Since you have agreed to become his wife, Lord Thomas will escort you. They are close to his own lands.'

Which rang a bell of alarm. Where had they been sent after the abortive plot? To some distant fortress where they would be forgotten? I remembered Richard being dispatched to Pontefract, never to be seen alive again.

'Where are they?' I demanded.

'Pevensey Castle.'

'Pevensey!' A castle far distant on the coast, its formidable walls and supreme defensive position looking over towards France.

Lancaster's smile was grim. 'Sir John Pelham, one of my most trusted counsellors, has been appointed as their governor. He will take good care of them, while you will be made most welcome.'

Would I? All the latent humour surprisingly awoken in me in Lord Thomas's company was flattened into nothingness.

'I am grateful,' I said. And then, before I could even frame the words in my mind, there they were, forcing themselves between my teeth.

'Will you ever allow my son to return to England?'

His reply was severe. 'Would you expect me to?'

In that moment it meant more to me than all the world.

'I beg of you, my lord...'

'It will all depend on Percy's willingness to come to terms with me.'

'But he will not. He will fear to set foot in England again.'

How bleak the future looked. Lancaster's pronouncement even bleaker, since he had robbed the Earl of his title. The Earldom of Northumberland was an empty vessel.

'He has made his peace once, he can do so again. I would regret losing a man of such skill in handling the northern March. But you have to accept my reasoning. Percy has become a danger to me. I have shown him mercy, when perhaps I should not. I gave him his life when many would have had his head for his insolence. Why would I reinstate the earldom for his grandson?' He must have seen the fear before I could hide it. 'If Percy returns to make restitution he will have to give me just cause to believe him. If he can do that, then I will consider allowing your son to return.'

'And inherit the Earldom?'

'At this moment, with the erstwhile holder of the Earldom plotting in France, inviting a French invasion to come to the aid of Glyn Dwr, I will not—'

'I had not known...' I interrupted.

'But it is true. His treason is twofold if he will make France a willing ally. Do you realise how dangerous the situation is, Elizabeth? I will not even consider the return of your son until matters between me and Henry Percy are settled.'

Before I left Eltham I was dragged back into the past, whether I wished it or no. I had not expected it, and for a moment, surrounded as we were by members of the household as we made our way to attend Mass, I was lost for words.

'Constance.'

I had not even realised that she was staying here. My last knowledge of her was that she was in semi-captivity at Lancaster's will in Kenilworth to keep her out of political mischief.

'Elizabeth. Now this I had not expected. So you too are to be kept under our King's suspicious eye.'

'You look in good health,' I replied, seeking for an innocuous conversation.

But I thought that she did not; rather a little tired, lines of strain on her fair features, although she was clothed with her usual flamboyance in heavy folds of an embroidered houppelande. The fur at neck and hem was particularly fine. So were the jewels in the net that encased her hair. Treachery had not, in the end, beggared Constance.

We turned to match our steps towards the chapel.

'Are you here to sue for mercy?' she asked, mistress as ever of bright malice.

'Yes. I was summoned. I am only here at Lancaster's command.'

'I too needed to make petition for what is rightfully mine. He took all my lands and goods from me. I have managed to persuade him to restore some of them, but he has kept my Welsh lands out of my reach.' She laughed softly. 'But I'll not give up.'

'I don't suppose you will.'

'He will reinstate them eventually, just to rid himself of my importuning.' She looked across at me. 'What is your penalty to be?'

'Marriage.'

'Who is the fortunate man?'

'Lord Thomas de Camoys.' I really did not wish to speak of it.

'It could be worse.'

'So Lancaster does not have an eye to a husband for you?'

'It would not be fitting.'

And Constance allowed, quite deliberately, the folds of the gown to fall, to outline the telltale swell of her body beneath them. There was no mistaking her condition, nor her lack of shame as her stare dared me to make comment.

'No, it would not be fitting,' I remarked, conscious of an unlikely compassion, for however complacent she might seem, this would be a humiliation for so proud a woman. 'Edmund Holland?' I thought it would be no other.

'Yes. My dear Edmund. My inestimable lover.' No, she was not complacent. There was ill-concealed fury in her clipped tones. 'He would have wed me, you know. He had been granted permission to marry whomsoever he pleased

404

within the King's remit. But then there was the plot and my fall from grace. I was no longer acceptable as a bride.' She shrugged, the fur silkily rippling on her shoulders. 'He is also in need of money, and I have none to entice him where my body obviously cannot.'

'Surely he has not rejected you and the child altogether.' The compassion grew in me for Constance who saw herself abandoned.

'No. He enquires after my health, much as you have just done. But he looks elsewhere for a spotless wife, rather than a notorious woman to warm his sheets. He is in negotiation with the family of Lucia Visconti. I expect he'll get her too. The Milanese woman is very rich. I suppose I must make the most of his attentions while I can.' For the first time in all the years I had known her, the slough of bitterness was a shock. 'At least Alianore is no longer with us to express her righteous disgust of my situation.'

'No.' On balance, I wished that she were.

Constance's sideways glance was pure challenge. 'I am grateful that you at least have not showered me with obnoxious pity. I don't deserve it, I assure you. This child will be well loved.'

And I realised that, for all her sins, Constance must have loved Edmund Holland. Perhaps she still did.

'The problem is,' she was continuing, lifting her skirts against her bosom to disguise her condition once more, 'if I get my Welsh lands back, the King might just order me to stay on them, to deter the rebels with a strong presence. I would rather stay at court.' At the door to the chapel she halted, her regard on the distant altar where the candles were lit to illuminate the crucifix in a soft glow. 'It was a good plan. I'm sorry we could not achieve it.'

For herself, or for the Earl of March? There was no reading her calm inscrutability, all bitterness and anger hidden. Moved by her plight against my will, I embraced her.

'So am I sorry,' I said.

As we knelt to pray, two widows together, I made petition for her, and for the unborn child who would be brought into this chancy world under such a cloud. I prayed for all of us. I hoped that I would not have to face Dunbar, another ghost from my past, before I left Eltham for good.

Chapter Twenty-One

I visited my nephews in Pevensey.

'Edmund.' I could even smile at what I saw.

He bowed with a well-tutored elegance, reminiscent of other, older Mortimers. This was Edmund Mortimer, Earl of March, my nephew, all but a man now at fifteen years. Beside him stood his brother Roger, a smaller version. They were obvious Mortimers, both of them, dark-haired, grey-eyed, features firming as they grew, so that memories of my brother Roger flooded back. There was even a touch of brother Edmund's flamboyance.

'And Roger too,' I said, revealing none of my emotion for what was past and buried. 'You have grown so tall. Would I recognise you in a crowd?'

It was six years since I had seen them. Grown tall, they were still youthfully angular, but now exhibited a nod to fashion and a confident demeanour as befitted the Earl of March and his brother. They bowed where once they might have run to me. I was not allowed the courtesy of speech alone, a cleric accompanying us, but he took himself to the far corner of the room, to study his missal. If his ears were trained on our conversation I could not tell, and I doubted that he would hear anything incriminating. Now that I was here, conversation escaped me. What to say to two young men who might never experience true freedom? To a young man who was old enough to wear a crown and take control of government in his own right.

'Madam Elizabeth.' They were impeccably mannered too under Lancaster's tutelage. 'We did not expect you.' Edmund took my hand and raised it formally to his lips.

'Are we to be released?' Roger asked, less circumspect.

'No.'

'We did not expect it,' Edmund said, as if he felt a need to offer me solace. 'Will you take a cup of wine?' Spurred into action by a mere glance from his brother, Roger poured and presented a cup to me and to Edmund.

'It is not within my power to have you released,' I said.

Edmund gulped the wine in a desultory fashion, then shook his head. 'I don't think it is in anyone's power to have us released.'

A statement of fact rather than any passion.

'We are to stay here at Sir John Pelham's will,' Roger added.

'But we have been made welcome,' Edmund confirmed.

'I am sorry that you are not at Windsor.' I sought for something that would break the glass between us, that would perhaps ignite the enthusiasm I recalled when they were young and exuberant. Anything but this dour acceptance of imprisonment. They were too young to be robbed of any hope.

'The hunting was better at Windsor. This is a bleak spot,' Edmund admitted.

And so it was on this windswept site overlooking the Channel, a gift to Sir John Pelham in return for his support when Lancaster had returned from his enforced banishment.

Its solid and encircling towers and high walls gave it all the appearance of a prison.

'I had to leave my hound at Windsor,' Roger admitted. 'Perhaps Sir John will give me another.'

'I presume Lancaster sent you here to punish you for the work of others,' I said, then regretted it. It was not well done of me to stir their hearts with my antagonisms.

'But it was not the King's doing, madam.' Edmund was quick to reply.

'Who told you that?'

'Sir John. It was the Royal Council. They decided we needed more secure custody, to prevent another escape. It was only then that the King sent us here to the hospitality of his loyal counsellor.' He must have seen the frown in my eye. 'We do not dislike Sir John. He allows us to ride out, with an escort, to hunt and hawk. We have books and music. We are allowed every comfort.'

'Then it seems that I must not blame your uncle of Lancaster. Although would he not have been able to persuade the Council differently, if he had wished to do so?'

'I do not know, madam.'

Seeing that I had troubled him, I turned the conversation into more comfortable areas. 'Are you allowed money of your own?'

'Yes. And we have a clerk to see to the spending of it.'

I lifted the long over-sleeve with its intricate stitching, which made him grin. 'Fine feathers.' I put down the cup, untasted. 'I can do nothing for you, Edmund.' Roger had wandered away to talk to the cleric. I could hear him laughing, which was some balm to my soul. 'I am here because my conscience troubled me, that you were alone with none of your own family to be concerned about you. We have not done well by you.'

'And we are grateful.' How solemn he was. 'We know that we have not been forgotten.' A little line appeared between his brows. 'We regret the death of our mother, without our seeing her again.'

'She suffered that you were not allowed to return to her, even for a short time.' And then, because I must speak of it: 'I am sorry for what happened.' Since Roger had returned, I caught a quick glance between the young men. 'You look as if you have been involved in mischief,' I said.

'It was exciting!' Roger was suddenly alight with all the exuberance of youth that he had earlier shed.

'It was dangerous,' I advised. 'Plots do not always have happy outcomes.'

But Edmund was stern in his judgement. 'It was dangerous, but far better to have risked it all and joined up with my uncle Mortimer and the Welsh lord.' Again he glanced at Roger, returning the grin. 'It was exciting.'

'Better than being here. Or Windsor.' Roger nodded in agreement.

And I was forced to acknowledge the tedium of long days with seemingly no purpose, their time planned for them, their actions curtailed. Edmund looked beyond me as if seeing that night when all hung in the balance. 'We rode as if the devil himself was behind us, like the wind. We knew the King's troops would follow us. We barely stopped to eat or drink, but rode on and on, Lady Constance encouraging us. We thought we had succeeded. Surely we would not be caught.'

There were the high spirits, lit by that frightful ride through the night. Only to be quenched in abject failure.

'And then the royal troops surrounded us,' Roger explained.

'And now we are back behind locked doors,' Edmund completed the tale.

My heart was wrung for them. 'Perhaps one day the King will show leniency. When he feels secure again.'

Edmund, older than his years, agreed. 'It may be so. We understand. Our blood is the problem for a Lancaster King. Perhaps we will never be completely released from surveillance of one sort or another.'

We had tried. Oh, we had tried, and we had failed them.

'Has Sir John talked to you about the future?' I asked as Edmund accompanied me to where Lord Camoys waited for our departure.

'I am to become part of Prince Henry's household. And Roger will come too.'

'Will you enjoy that?'

'Yes. I like him. I will like to go on campaign with him.' The light was back in his eye. 'And one day I will be allowed to marry. It is put into the hands of Queen Joanna. I can choose a bride on condition that I will marry only with the King's consent and the Royal Council's advice. And I hope one day to become a Knight of the Garter.' Then he added, taking me aback: 'If I was King, Prince Henry would not be so. He wishes it beyond anything.'

'Have you no wish for it?'

He thought for a long moment as he acknowledged Lord Thomas with another neat bow. 'Why wish for the impossible? I would rather be free than King. I would rather have my own life to direct as I choose than the crown of England. I wish I could live at Ludlow again.'

And Edmund bowed his farewell, unaware of the effect that those lightly uttered words had had on me. All we had striven for, so easily put aside. Harry's death, all for naught. The countless dead on the battlefield at Shrewsbury, dead on both sides, England weeping in streams of blood. *I would rather be free than King.* He had so cruelly rejected all that had been done in his name, not even realising the wound he had delivered against my heart.

A great well of tears lodged in my throat as Lord Thomas and I rode away from Pevensey, a vast space yawning in my breast.

'Are you satisfied?' he asked after graciously allowing me time to recover from so damning a blow.

'Yes, if you mean that they are well cared for and indulged to a degree.' I considered what I had learned. 'We were more ambitious than Edmund of March will ever be. He does not seek the crown. He never will.'

They were just young men, unaffected by great ambitions, merely straining to be free of the leash that Lancaster had placed on them. And then because honesty forced me:

'It was the Council that sent them here. It seems I have misjudged my cousin.'

'Many do. He is not an easy man to know.'

'But you are his friend.'

We turned our horses in the direction of Trotton, one of Lord Thomas's manors.

'We all need friends, Elizabeth.'

I thought it was the first time that he had used my given name. It made me feel more alone than ever. Who could I call friend? What a desperate meeting it had been, with no purpose, no achievement except for my continuing pain. Nothing but that I must accept the futility of it all; the failure for these young men; despair and desolation. I was relieved that Harry had not lived to see it. He would have found it impossible to accept that the hand of the Percy family could achieve so little.

Lord Thomas proceeded to drive the final nail into the coffin of my hopes.

'It might be politic for you to remember that Henry has four sons. As a dynasty they are secure. If Henry dies, he has able young men to step into his shoes. The Mortimer cause is dead.'

It was cruelly, brutally done and painfully accurate. All I could hope for was that one day my own son would come home and Lancaster would allow him to take up his own threatened inheritance. All would depend on the Earl of Northumberland making peace with the King who had placed the attainder on him.

All I could do was pray that he would.

Meanwhile in the little church of St George at Trotton, I made my vows and exchanged the wild Marches of the north and the west for the soft country of Sussex.

Queen of the North. Once that had been my ambition. Wife to the Earl of Northumberland when Harry came at last into his inheritance, aunt to the Mortimer King of England, a woman of influence within royal circles. Now I was Lady de Camoys, wife of a baron, a royal counsellor, with little status except for that borrowed from my husband. My royal blood held no power in the Camoys manors. I did not care. An empty hollow existed where my heart might have been.

Late in that year after I wed Lord Thomas de Camoys, on an occasion when Thomas was absent on royal business, a letter was written by my hand that I never thought to write.

To His Grace the Earl of Northumberland.

Even if he no longer had a right to that title, I would not demean him further.

I have sent this in hopes that it reaches you.

It was my understanding that he was returned from France and was in Wales again, seeking shelter once more with Glyn Dwr and Edmund.

It must be clear to you that all possibility of a successful uprising against the Lancaster King is at an end. You are under threat of attainder. Your title is no more, your lands under royal control, your castles in the hands of others. Your heir is disinherited.

I have spoken with my royal cousin. There is only one hope, if you wish your heir, Henry Percy, my son, to return from Scotland and take up his rightful place at Alnwick. Lancaster is willing to receive you and listen to you if you are prepared to make your peace with him. He was compassionate once before when you sank your pride and begged forgiveness. He will not be hard-hearted if you can find it in you to throw yourself on his mercy and come home. He has given me his word. We would both enjoy seeing a Percy in residence in Alnwick again.

You need not fear Lancaster's revenge. He will listen if you will accept your guilt and make restitution for the future. It may demand reparation with a heavy fine, but it will not be with your life.

For the sake of my son and Harry's I ask that you will return and make peace.

Your daughter by law
Elizabeth Percy
Now Elizabeth de Camoys

It was all I could do in a bid to have my son return home. I had married Thomas de Camoys to mend my reputation with Lancaster. The least the Earl could do was return and make redress.

Before I sent it on the long journey to discover the Earl, I sought out my husband on his return: 'You will wish to see this.'

I held it out to Thomas, barely giving him time to remove the sable pelts that lined his cloak in this bitter weather, giving no cognizance to his preoccupation. He took it but did not immediately read it. Instead, looking briefly at the superscription, he said: 'That you should write to Northumberland fills me with trepidation.'

'It should not. There is no treason here.'

'Are you asking my permission to send it?'

'No. As a good and trustworthy wife I am making clear my loyalties.'

He read it, with a growing frown.

'It will do no good, Elizabeth.'

'Why not?'

He made me sit, so I knew it was bad news. I also accepted how divorced from court affairs I had become since my marriage, that I was unaware of whatever hammered the groove between Thomas's brows. Once, after Harry's death, I had isolated myself; now it had been forced on me.

'Tell me what you know, that you have just discovered and of which I am ignorant,' I invited, a hard knot expending beneath my heart.

Thomas hitched a hip onto the edge of a substantial travelling chest that had arrived with him. 'The King will never pardon him now. Northumberland left Wales for France, to negotiate with the French King, making a bid for French support for Glyn Dwr's new offensive against England.'

'That I know…'

'But you will not know this. That to win over the French King, the Earl formally renounced his oath of fealty to King Henry. The result was a French expedition to Milford Haven, where it was greeted by Glyn Dwr who must have been delighted to see such a vast source of French power.'

'I have heard of no battle,' I said.

'There was no battle. Storms washed away King Henry's baggage train and persuaded the French knights that they had no wish to spend a winter in Wales.'

Which I realised was not the end of it. Lord Thomas had not mentioned Northumberland's involvement in Wales. 'And so?'

'And so – not in the best of moods, my lord the King arranged for Percy's trial *in absentia* by the Court of Chivalry, which was not inclined to be compassionate. London is awash with the news of a French landing as you can imagine. All that you feared has come to pass. Percy was attainted by the court. All his titles, honours, estates and chattels were declared forfeit. The southern properties now belong to the King's son, John. Northumberland House in Aldersgate Street is in the Queen's gift.'

It could not be worse. Thomas delivered the final blow against the Earl ever being reconciled with Henry of Lancaster. 'A man who negotiates successfully to bring a French army into the country cannot hope for royal restitution.'

'No. He won't return now,' I agreed.

'And the King will not forgive.'

All lay in pieces at my feet. I realised that Lord Thomas was holding out the letter to me.

416

'That's not all, Elizabeth. The death sentence for treason has been passed against him.'

'Then what use in my sending this?' I lifted the carefully constructed missive from his outstretched hand.

'None. None at all. Your only hope is that Percy retires from combat and allows my lord the King time to forget and for old wounds to heal. The King will never forgive him, but he may find it in his heart to be lenient to your son.'

I carried my letter to the fireplace, preparing to drop it into the flames, only to be brought to a halt by a fierce memory. The two letters from Alianore and Philippa when Henry of Lancaster had recently set foot in England. When we were still in doubt of the future and Harry had warned me of treason. *Burn them*, he had said, and so I had, with no real insight into where we would all be in the future.

For the moment it seemed that Harry stood beside me, but it was only a trick of imagination. I could do no more to bring about my son's restitution. I cast my letter into the flames, with a brief prayer that the erstwhile Earl of Northumberland would never again pick up his sword in battle against Henry of Lancaster. If he did, any chance of my son's return would be consumed into ash, along with my plea.

I slid into it as neatly, as smoothly as a hand into a kid glove that had been made for me. It was not difficult. I had been bred up to know what was expected of me. What was my life with Lord Thomas de Camoys in this manor of Trotton in the rolling hills of Sussex? It was gentle. It had a serenity. Lancaster had given me a punishment that was within my spirit to accept, and so I pretended a contentment, for my new husband's sake, but there was none in my mind or in my heart. All I had lost ate away at me, making me sharp with those over whom I now held sway. I could not envisage my future as Lady de Camoys with any tranquillity, so I merely tolerated what many would have said was good fortune indeed, while bitterness buried beneath my skin, giving birth to an icy resentment of all around me.

'Bitterness will harm no one but yourself. It will destroy you.'

I saw Lord Thomas's concern for me.

'I have no kindness in me.'

Yet I did my best because Thomas deserved a good wife. He was long-suffering and generous with his good humour when the demands on his time did not take him to court or to his other manors. I tried to be the wife and mistress of his household that he might hope for, but in truth, I saw myself living out my days, all my life behind me, my vision of the future rotten to the core.

Thomas and I had a son together in that first year, a quick, bright-eyed child. To my eye he had no Mortimer features, but Thomas declared he had a distinct connection with me, notably in his fierce stare. His hair was dark when he was born and his blue eyes soon became grey. We called him Roger, which was my choice and which Lord Thomas was gracious enough to allow. It was not a name favoured within his family but it meant much to me.

Sometimes, in a glancing sunbeam that lit the infant's face, he reminded me of Hal, now so far away from me. Reluctant as I was to allow my heart to be engaged, I grew to love him, but I missed Hal, and it grew no easier as the weeks and months passed. All I could do was hold fast to the belief that Bishop Henry Wardlaw was a good man who would raise him as I would wish, and that the Scottish court would see his value, even though his inheritance was compromised. Was

Hal happy? Such a facile thought, but one that troubled me. I must accept that his future was out of my hands.

'He'll be a man grown before I see him again,' I fretted on one of the few occasions when I spoke my anxieties out loud.

'So he will,' Thomas agreed. 'Probably with a northern burr to his words and an eye to an outspoken Scots lass with a sizeable inheritance as a bride.'

'I cannot be as hopeful as you.'

'No, of course you cannot. Because you are his mother. But you can be sensible and accept what cannot be changed. At this moment Hotspur's heir is probably enjoying beating the heir to the Scottish throne into the ground with a blunted sword, crying *Esperance!* as he does it.'

Which made me smile and accept, but still it worried me that I might not recognise him when we were finally reunited. If we were ever to be so.

Time passing, a respect, perhaps even an affection, developed between myself and Lord Thomas, who did spend much time travelling in the name of his King. I found it unnerving to live with so placid a man, yet one who could fight like the devil himself on the battlefield and who ruled his manors with painstaking exactitude. I had no experience of such placidity. Sometimes I missed the furious energy that could whip a household into a frenzy of activity.

Sometimes I missed Hotspur beyond bearing.

We never spoke of the old insurrections. Let sleeping dogs lie, Thomas would have said in his phlegmatic way. I did not speak of the messengers who came all the way to Trotton with word of Edmund, still in refuge behind Harlech's walls with his wife and son and three daughters, or of Glyn Dwr's intermittent campaigns, his followers no longer prepared to risk themselves in pitched battle, or even in minor ones against English forces. If Thomas knew of my informants, he made no attempt to hound them off his manor. He must have known as well as I that there was no room for scheming here. With the Earl of March still securely tucked away in Pevensey, there would be no further attempts to rescue him. The Welsh bid for independence under their own Prince of Wales was vanishing into the Welsh mist, like Glyn Dwr himself. What would Iolo Goch sing of now? Not of blazing stars and the glorious wings of dragons. Where were his Welsh heroes? All dead or fading from view. King Henry the Fourth was in the ascendant. The Earl of Northumberland might still dream of taking back his Percy lands, but what hope was there of that ever coming to fruition?

'And do I hold the keys to the household?' I asked, when I first saw my new home, thick-walled and high-windowed, with barns and mill telling of wealth and security, but which did not have the massive towers and curtain walls of my experience in the Percy strongholds.

'Is your loyalty to me embedded in your soul, my lady?' Lord Thomas enquired, imperturbable as ever.

'Did I not make the marriage vows, in all good faith?'

'I believe that you did. Then the keys are yours, Elizabeth.'

The keys were mine, and so was the chatelaine, a symbol of Thomas's trust in me, which I would not break. I grew to trust him too.

Chapter Twenty-Two

The Manor of Trotton in Sussex: Late February 1408

The Manor of Trotton in Sussex: Late February 1408

When I least expected it, the even tenor of my life was cast into disarray. Trust and loyalty between man and wife were abandoned. What Thomas did not know, he could not hinder.

On this day my Mortimer blood was stirred once more from its somnolence, alight with anger and defiance, with a resurrection of fear for the repercussions for my Percy son, brought to my attention by news of events in the north. I ordered up a horse and an escort. I would consider my excuses later, but now I must be in London, driven there by what could only be a desire for crude vengeance.

'By the Rood!'

I caught my breath.

The dark figure entering the door as I was leaving jolted me.

'Were you travelling, my lady?'

Lord Thomas, returned by some fell purpose, stooped to pick up my gloves.

'Yes.'

Since my horse was saddled and waiting for me, along with three de Camoys retainers and one reluctant waiting woman, denial would have been foolish. And why would I deny it?

Lord Thomas took my hand, led me forward and helped me to mount. His courtesy was unnerving, unsettling, and all without any question of what I was about to do. He would never deny me before the people of the de Camoys household.

'A long journey, I presume.' He cast an eye over the well-laden sumpter-horse as he helped me to mount.

'Yes.'

'Might I know why?'

'Not for any reprehensible reason.' My gaze held his, which was tolerant enough yet demanding of an answer from a possibly errant wife.

'Still I would know.'

'So that you might report my whereabouts to your lord the King?'

Still that unflattering resentment that occasionally caught me out.

'If it becomes necessary, then I will do it. You know I will, Elizabeth. I'll have no subversion in my household.'

I looked down at him from my higher vantage, and tilted my chin. I knew very well that he would not allow me to leave until I told him. He would brook no wifely insurrection.

'I am going to London. I am going to look at the head of the Earl of Northumberland which is, at this moment as I understand it, exhibited on the middle tower of London Bridge.'

Thomas's expressive brows climbed. 'Is it necessary for you to do this?'

'Yes. It is necessary.'

'Then I will go with you.'

Issuing orders to those awaiting his wishes, remounting his own horse, Thomas de Camoys set himself to ride beside me.

Was it necessary for me to be here? It was too complex, too shatteringly agonising, for me to explain, even to myself. It expressed the worst in me, and perhaps the best. I would stand for my family and those I loved until my last breath. This final, terrible event in the life of Henry Percy, first Earl of Northumberland, must not go unremarked by me.

It was so cold, this winter of the year of 1408. So cold that our steward could not write our records, the ink freezing before he could put pen to parchment. So cold that my breath became frost in the air as I, standing on the bridge, muffled in cloak and hood, my hands gloved and hidden within the wide sleeves of my houppelande, addressed the miserable remnant of once-great power.

'You ruined your son, the man I worshipped. You allowed him to die, and my heart to be broken. You sent my own son into perpetual banishment so that I will never see him. You launched a final worthless invasion, destined to failure, so that nothing can ever be made well again. I spit on your reputation, my lord of Northumberland.'

It was three years since I had last seen him, and there was no resemblance to the mighty Earl in the head above me, looking down with empty eye sockets. Blackened flesh had been attacked by weather and creatures of carrion. The vibrant red hair was no longer; instead a shock of white lifted lifeless in the wind. The years had not treated the Earl well, but there was no mercy in my accusation.

'What drove you against all good sense to challenge Lancaster's authority again? You have destroyed all hope of a Percy future.'

Not content with the disaster of the French expedition into Wales, the Earl had returned to Scotland, to plot and scheme the months away, only to be lured into crossing the Tweed into England to rouse once more the old Percy tenants from their northern firesides, to defy Lancaster's army that lay in wait for him.

'Was there any hope of his success?' I asked Thomas who stood at a little distance, silent and stalwart.

'None.'

'I thought not.'

I could not fault the Earl's bravery. I might even have pity for him, tricked as he was by an old retainer, Sir Thomas Rokeby, who invited the Earl into England before changing allegiance as he led the royal forces against him. Even John de Clifford, Bess's cautious husband, refused to answer the call of the old Percy–Clifford alliance. So all had gone awry. The Earl chose, when he had no choice at all, to fight to the last at Bramham Moor in the cruel winds and snow where he was cut down.

He lost his head on the battlefield that day.

My breath caught in my throat as I continued, without pity, to upbraid him.

'You were a traitor to your family. If you had only accepted your defeat when our cause was destroyed at Shrewsbury. If you had only been able to live at peace. Now all you have achieved is your death and the permanent banishment of my son. The great Earldom of Northumberland is no more. Why could you not make your peace with Lancaster? I have had to do so, why could not you? Was it pride? If so you are justly served, for you have no pride now!'

My face felt hard, as if frozen. I would never weep for him. All the old fury swept back over me, colder than the wind off the river that stirred the edge of my cloak, coating the fur in a sparkle of rime.

'Why did you betray your son? I swear you loved him well.'

'You do not need this, Elizabeth.'

Thomas had approached quietly, but he did not touch me.

'Yes, I do. If he had marched, as he promised he would, Harry would not have been slain at Shrewsbury.'

'You don't know that.' And then: 'Haven't you seen enough severed heads to last a lifetime?'

'Yes. Enough and more.' He must know that I had had to pass beneath Harry's on my journey into York. 'I have seen far too many, but I needed to see the end of the man who destroyed our family.'

I ignored any attempt at reasoned thought, as Thomas's stare kept away curious passers-by, no doubt attracted by a woman conversing with a severed head at this early hour in the morning.

'You made your peace with Lancaster. I accepted that, for the sake of your grandson's inheritance. But how could you lay all the blame at your son's feet?' I continued to denounce the man who had been a part of my life since childhood. 'By abandoning him, you doubled his treachery. You begged for mercy, by blackening the soul of your son.'

It was as if all the bitterness of the past years, all the disappointments, all the humiliations had fused into one tight ball of anger in my belly. My anger flowed out through my recriminations.

'In your lifetime you made the name of Percy one that was honoured and feared, in equal measure, by all who heard it. Kings of the North, we were. When Lancaster pardoned you, you could have salvaged so much of your past glory, for your grandson if not your son.'

I shook off Thomas's restraining hand, intolerant of its control.

'Then you destroyed all you had achieved through your

outrageous ambition. Could you not see that it was over? That Lancaster and his four sons now have this kingdom under their heel? You cannot kill them all. But no, you had to stir one last rebellion. Even Glyn Dwr has accepted the futility of it all. Even the French King had no wish to become involved. All you could see was one last battle that would sweep Lancaster away and lay the kingdom open to your own sword. Did you hope to take the whole kingdom for yourself? It was a hopeless cause, and you were so gullible, so driven with ambition, that you believed Rokeby's cunning invitation.'

I was breathless. Exhausted. But I must finish what I wished to say.

'And here you are. You have died, drenched in blood on a battlefield of your making. Attainted, disinherited, landless, penniless. There is nothing for your grandson to inherit. No land, no title. The proud Percy name is trampled on. It was your doing.'

'Elizabeth…'

I no longer felt the weight of his hand on my arm. I did not shake it off, but took a step nearer the terrible exhibit.

'I buried your son with honour when you fled for your life. I was forced to kneel before Henry of Lancaster to be allowed in his *pity* to do so. I will not bury you. Your soul may rot in hell as your body rots here for public degradation. I will not ask Lancaster for mercy for you, for I have none.'

I turned my back on him, on London Bridge.

'Where has Lancaster sent the rest of my once-noble Earl of Northumberland?' I demanded. 'To which gatehouse or bridge has he dispatched this foul warning of what will become of a traitor?'

Thomas answered without hesitation. 'To the four corners

of his northern kingdom, where it would have most effect. Where there might still be some who will resurrect the name of Percy and raise the standard once more in battle. The King will show no mercy.'

'The Earl does not deserve hallowed ground for what he has done.'

Thomas led me away without comment. If I had been able to see through the fury and grief that still shook me, I would have seen a stern visage. But I did not. Any fleeting peace I had achieved over the past months with the birth of my son had been torn asunder. I could not let the past rest. And there, lapping constantly in the recesses of my mind, were the wavelets of my own guilt.

Returned to the cold and cramped chamber at Westminster that Thomas used when in London about his King's business, I flung open the door, dropped my cloak, gloves and hood on a settle, refused wine and stood motionless in the centre of the room, my hands covering my face. I must accept that there would never be a Mortimer King, but to acknowledge that my son would never see his banner flying above Alnwick or Warkworth was a poison that swirled nauseously in my gut.

It might be that he would now be forced to live out his days at the Scottish court, but here was a new anxiety for me. Would he be as welcome there, without acceptable lineage, without a title or estates to inherit? The Scots might always have regarded him as a pawn, but now he was a useless one in any negotiation. My son was landless and thus dispensable.

I sat, but briefly, troubled by directionless energy, unable to put the past behind me, unable to embrace a future which held no comfort for me.

'I cannot bear it,' I said.

When Henry of Lancaster had returned to England I had had such hopes. Now all was Percy and Mortimer rubble beneath my feet; the existence of a new Camoys son, at home at Trotton, offering me no consolation in exchange. The existence of a husband who gave me more consideration than I deserved could not soothe my pain.

I walked the short width of the room and back, negotiating clumsily round a stool and a coffer, until Thomas, entering the room after me, stopped me by the simple expedient of setting his hands on my shoulders, tightening them when I would have pulled away.

'Release me.' The hard command in my voice surprised me.

'I will not. Not until you listen to me.'

I was not receptive to his command nor to the severity of it. 'Why? So that you can sing Lancaster's praises in bringing this kingdom to a peaceful settlement? I may despise the Earl but that does not, for me, put a gloss of admiration on your King's name. What can you say to me that will heal the wounds in my heart? Our Percy and Mortimer lands are forfeit to the crown. My dower is filling Lancaster's coffers. My son's inheritance is denied him.'

'You are so angry, Elizabeth.'

'Which you knew when you wed me. I have not changed.'

He shook me slightly. 'Then you must change. It is time that you listened to words of good sense.'

It was the voice of a commander of men. Still I resisted.

'Why must I? Why must I listen to you, friend of Lancaster as you are?'

'Because I am not involved. At least I can see the past years with some objectivity, which you never will. Unless you are beaten about the head with it.'

I looked up at him, at the shrewdness in the imprint of experience in his face. No, there was no distancing from the past in my mind. But what difference would Lord de Camoys's opinion make to my reading of events? All the affection that had developed in our marriage seemed to be no more than dust beneath my feet.

'Well?' he demanded.

'Then if I must, I will listen.'

His eyes held mine, relentless, remorseless.

'You blame the world for Hotspur's death at Shrewsbury. You blame Henry of Lancaster for taking a throne that was not his to take. You blame Sir Edmund for dragging you into Glyn Dwr's machinations that drew Hotspur into that battle at Shrewsbury.'

'No, I did not say that...'

Again he shook me, but gently. 'You blame Dunbar for betraying the Percy standard and siding with the King in a new and more lucrative allegiance. And, even at his death, you blame Northumberland for failing to come to his son's aid and undermining what could be salvaged.'

'Yes. And yes. All of those. Why should I not?'

I was defiant against his harsh tone.

'Do you ever blame Henry Percy, who will always be Hotspur in your heart?'

It was not a question I had expected.

'Blame him? No. For what should I blame him?'

'His impetuosity, for one.'

'I know that he was often so, but—'

'A battle plan that would not bring victory. It would not be the first time he had risked his health and his freedom by attacking without consideration.'

'No!'

'Yes. You are blind, Elizabeth. You see only his good qualities.'

'And you, of course, would have had a better plan at Shrewsbury.' The sneer shook me.

'I would never have taken to the field at Shrewsbury. But if I had I would not have launched into the attack as Henry Percy did.'

'What choice did he have, caught between the town and the river and Lancaster's army?'

'I'll tell you the choice he had: a viable position on a low hill, the approach to his forces difficult for the King in wet ground sown with crops. His Cheshire archers destroyed Henry's vanguard. Yes, his flank was under attack from Prince Henry, but what did Hotspur do? Exactly what you would expect him to do. Stake all on one last charge directly at the King, leading thirty of his knights in a final cataclysmic blow. Courageous, yes. Bold leadership, I agree. But it took him into the mass of the royal forces when the King drew back. Surrounded, they had to fight for their survival. He fell with his sword in his hand, fighting for his life. There was no need for it.'

Rejecting the hard words, I had no wish to discuss Harry's impetuosity or his death. Instead, taking a stance on grounds where I was sure of my argument:

'As you say, why was there need for such a battle? Lancaster refused to negotiate. Could he not have come to terms? Could he not have offered to parley, to prevent the bloodshed? The blood that soaked that battlefield was Lancaster's doing.'

'That is not so.'

'But it is.'

'I know what happened, Elizabeth. I was there, at the battle, and in the morning before the battle.'

I had not known it, but what would that matter?

'Henry moved heaven and earth to bring the rebellion to a peaceful conclusion.'

I frowned, shrugging off Thomas's hold, which he allowed, his hands falling to his sides, since I had long since stopped wishing to pace.

'There was no negotiation offered.'

'There was. Who was it who met with the King on that morning, to debate the offer made?'

I frowned. 'Worcester. Worcester was there. He said there was no value in what was offered.'

'Worcester lied.'

'But when I accused Lancaster of desiring Harry's death, he did not deny it. So what do you say happened, since you were there to see and hear?'

'They negotiated. The King did not want to fight. He did not seek all the death and had too much admiration for Hotspur to wilfully have him dead. I think he hoped to win his friendship again, to settle all the enmities. How would I forget it – the King spending the whole morning trying to hammer out a settlement? He sent the Abbots of Shrewsbury and Haughmond to Hotspur, offering safe conduct. Hotspur sent Worcester with the Percy response, a defence of their rebellion, listing all the reasons why they felt a need to challenge the King's authority. You know them all. They were promised peace and pardon if they would negotiate rather than fight, but what room was there for negotiation in such a list of the King's supposed crimes? Worcester refused to consider any grounds for a settlement. He said he did not trust the King. What more could King Henry do? He offered conciliation, but Worcester would have none of it.'

I could not believe it. It was not in Worcester's nature to refuse negotiation. Surely he would not.

'Worcester told Harry that Lancaster had refused to negotiate,' I said.

'Then, for whatever reason he had, Worcester lied. The King had done all he could. Battle was the only recourse, before the armies of Mortimer, Glyn Dwr and the Earl of Northumberland could join together to smash the royal forces to pieces.'

I thought about this, suspecting that Baron de Camoys would not lie to me.

'Do I believe you? How can I believe you?'

'I was there when they met. I was as baffled at Worcester's manner as the next man. I would not lie to you. What would be the value in my doing that?'

My thoughts unpicked what I had been told about the battle.

'Harry did not question his uncle's rejection of the negotiation.'

'No, Hotspur did not question Worcester's version of events. Hotspur wanted that battle. The battle fire was in his blood by then. You know what he was like.'

'Yes,' I whispered. 'Yes, I do.'

Thomas turned away from me, allowing me space to absorb these new facts.

'The battle was as much Hotspur's fault, and certainly Worcester's, as it was the King's. As for the Earl's absence, who knows? We never shall now. A diplomatic illness, as the rumours said? Perhaps. But we know that Westmorland and Sir Roger Waterton both had armies in the field, sent deliberately by the King with orders to keep Northumberland pinned down in the north, to stop him from marching west. Is that not so?'

'I did not know. The Earl would not give me the reason.'

'He had too much pride, Elizabeth. But if in truth he could not march, hemmed in by hostile forces as he was, then you must allow Hotspur to take some blame for the outcome.'

Anger flared again.

'So I am unreasonable. But you are too damned accepting of your King's motives and actions!'

Lord Thomas swung back towards me. 'My acceptance, as you put it, is growing less by the hour.' The dark brows had become a level line.

'Well? Of what other would you accuse me, as well as poor judgement?'

'You still don't see it, do you? In all the sorrow and death and loss of those miserable years, I don't think you have ever acknowledged your own culpability.'

Which effectively silenced me. When finally I spoke, my voice was little more than a harsh raven-croak.

'Explain to me, then, my blame in Hotspur's death.'

Thomas was without compassion. 'You do not need me to tell you. You are quite capable of working it out for yourself, if you will allow yourself to see the truth beneath all the dross. If you are willing to weigh and judge your own actions.'

I felt temper begin to rise, but Thomas was choosing his words with cold insight.

'You lived in a household of high-tempered, ambitious men. You lived there from a child. Did you learn nothing? Did you never consider being the voice of reason, of offering well-balanced advice? Of course you did not. The Percy support for Lancaster was crucial when he returned to claim his inheritance. The Earl and Hotspur made Lancaster's crown a reality. But you were not satisfied, were you…'

It was like clawing my way through a thicket, the thorns catching on my hem, my sleeves, my hair, at every step. 'Neither was Harry satisfied. He regretted trusting Lancaster to keep his oath…'

'But yours was the Mortimer blood. You were the one who desired above all else to see the Earl of March on England's throne. Did you see yourself in a position of power, as aunt to the Mortimer King?'

'No. Never…'

'I see the ambition in you.'

'Yes, for my nephew, for my son, not for me.'

But Lord de Camoys was intransigent.

'Did you never try to dissuade Hotspur from taking up arms against his King? Were you the one to sow the seeds of rebellion when Henry of Lancaster took the crown that was not his? You were the Mortimer voice in that tempestuous household. You were as keen to win recognition for your nephews as Harry was, if I know you as I think I do. Is that not true?'

He barely waited for me to answer, which I did not. I could not.

'When your brother clasped hands with Glyn Dwr, did you not see it as a miracle worked by God to aid your cause?'

'No…'

But Lord de Camoys, a man of such diplomatic skills, gave no quarter as any diplomacy was shredded into pieces, as smoothly as a knife slicing through fine silk.

'We all must carry the burden of blame in the horror of war within a country, subject against subject. It is a terrible thing. You must accept your part in it too, or the future will hold

434

nothing for you but dissatisfaction and bitterness that will grind you down. You will be angry and frustrated, gnawed at by ghosts from the past, until the day of your death. Is that what you want?'

I retreated to the old cry in my heart.

'I cannot forgive Northumberland.'

'Why not? Because he made his own peace with King Henry on the back of his son's desire for retribution?'

'He sent *my* son away.'

'Have you ever asked yourself why? Better the Percy heir with some element of freedom in Scotland than rubbing shoulders with the Mortimer heirs, locked in Pevensey Castle!'

I retaliated, but there was a hesitation before I spoke.

'Northumberland brought us all down.'

'Well, I can't argue against that, because he was a man of pride and ambition that had never been curtailed. He would never rest, until death forced him to do so. As it has now. He fought until hacked to death at Bramham Moor to restore Percy power in the north. Of course he was King of the North and fought for the right of your son to replace him. You would expect no less from a man of his demeanour.'

A little silence hung about us.

'I have no guilt,' I said.

'Then you are a fortunate woman. You can tell me that the dread signs and portents foretold the death of Hotspur. Maybe they did. A star racing across the heavens or the terrifying blotting out of the moon in blood red can be made to answer for any dire occurrence. I would question their role in the death of a man on a battlefield. I would look elsewhere for the driving force that sent a man of Hotspur's ambition to his death.'

'I cannot.'

'You must.'

His words were searing as if they cut into my flesh.

'What do I do?'

Different emotions had replaced the anger, but I would not weep on his breast.

'You search your own conscience, Elizabeth.'

'And then?'

'And then I will stand with you, whatever it is that you decide to do.'

Thomas's condemnation hung over me with the density of a funeral pall. What right had he to strip bare what he saw as my treacherous blindness to the truth? He had no right. What's more, he was wrong. I was not blind.

You search your own conscience, Elizabeth.

His words lashed at my thoughts again and again, while my heart was squeezed with hurt, not through the loss of shared love, which we did not have, but through the loss of that even platform of respect that I thought we had achieved. I had not been prepared for such an attack when my spirits had been at their lowest ebb, drained through damning the Earl's soul to everlasting torment and his body to destruction on the gates and bridges of the north. Through his unclouded vision, Thomas de Camoys had torn apart all my convictions.

The chamber was too constraining for me. Where I stood alone on the wall-walk, the breeze rippled across the river causing little wavelets in the metallic expanse. Gulls flying inland for the rich picking along the edges wheeled, their cries harsh. Small craft plied their trade this way and that. It was the world managing its own affairs with ease; when all within me was turmoil.

'Blessed Virgin! I did not deserve that! Why would he hurt me?'

My voice caused a soot-black crow to rise from the coping stones, cawing its disgust. I watched it rise and fall on the air, its mastery supreme, and as I did so, some measure of uneasy calm was restored to me so that I could think, rather than simply react with anger. Perhaps the Blessed Virgin had taken pity on me after all. My thoughts began to untangle themselves, to run more fluidly as the water lapped against the embankment.

I studied my hands, my knuckles white where they gripped the stone.

Thomas would not wound me out of malice. What he meant to do was open my eyes to what he saw as the truth in the violence and death of the past years. But was his truth more viable than mine? I had lived through the years of achievement and failure. I had known the heights of victory and the true depths of despair. What did Lord Camoys know of either?

I would banish his words if I could, to be washed away in the tide that was now turning, beginning its race towards the open sea. There they would be lost for ever, with the noisome debris from the city. But I could not banish them. They lingered, Thomas's words driving home in my mind.

'Do you ever blame Henry Percy?'

'For what should I blame him?'

'His impetuosity...'

What an image Thomas had painted of Harry's urgency when in the thick of the fray, of a man with no thought for his own safety or for the careful planning of the attack, only for the desire to charge at the enemy and lay them low. Was it true? I opened my mind to his feats in battle. His courage could not be questioned but his judgement could. Was it Harry's fiery temper, when he no longer saw with clarity, that had driven him to immoderate action?

I allowed the one image to form, blotting out the river scene, of Harry at his most flamboyant. Impossibly flamboyant, with all the recklessness that could fall upon him when his blood was up. Not that I had seen this clash of will for myself, nor any of his battle successes, but there were songs sung of it by our minstrels when supper had been eaten and much ale drunk. It made Harry flush with embarrassment at his youth and impetuosity as the rafters rang with this tale of an affair of lost honour. Of revenge for what he saw as his humiliation.

Deaf to the raucous calls of the herring gulls, it was as if I were there with him, at Newcastle in the days before Otterburn, the Scots Earl of Douglas well dug in around us for a long siege. After a day of skirmishes and a confused melee which achieved nothing, Harry was out of all patience.

'I'll fight you for this fortress,' he announced from the height of the barbican, looking down on his assailant. 'Single combat.'

'And I'll accept.' Douglas a man after Harry's own heart.

So they fought, lance against lance. Harry would risk death. He would risk well-nigh anything for the glory of action.

But Douglas, older and stronger, unhorsed Harry, snatching up the silken pennon from the tip of one of Harry's lances; to Harry's fury, dust-coated as he was, under that critical gaze of the whole garrison ranged along the walls. Douglas was joyous, waving the trophy with its gold stitching.

'I'll take this back to Scotland with me and set it on high

on my castle of Dalkeith. Everyone will see it for miles around and know of Hotspur's nose being ground in the mud.'

I could all but see Harry's rage, a shimmer of heat around him. 'By God! You'll never get my pennon out of Northumberland!'

Douglas's mocking reply was all the challenge Harry needed. 'Come and get your pennon back tonight. I'll plant it before my tent and we'll see if you have the courage to come and take it from me.'

Nothing would stop Harry from retrieving it. When Douglas's forces retreated north, burning and pillaging as they went, Harry was in hot pursuit.

I found myself smiling, as the image shattered into bright particles, my memories smashed into jagged-edged pieces by loss and distance. Perhaps one day I would lose the memories completely. I had been seventeen years old, and knew him not so well. Hotspur, the Scots had well named him. Never had an epithet been so well addressed, so assiduously sought. Harry was proud of it. He would always be Hotspur on the battlefield, and saw it as no detriment. For him to be Hotspur was the height of his fame and his achievement, a fiery star streaking across the battlefield, even more than the Percy lion unfurled above his head.

But it was a battle plan that would not bring victory, Thomas had said. How could I deny it? Harry's recklessness had driven him on so many occasions to feats of arms that were ill-considered, leaving me to live in fear. Otterburn, when Harry had ridden like the devil to retrieve his pennon, fighting a battle without formation or planning, conducted over the northern hills in the dangerous, masking shadows of moonlight. A battle which had ended in his being taken prisoner, kept in Scotland for well nigh a year until the ransom was raised.

Nor was that the only disaster. I knew about Homildon Hill, when Harry had wanted to lead a charge against the Scots, to obliterate once and for all the dishonour of that thrice-damned pennon. Only the Earl and Dunbar, who argued for the use of archers to destroy the Scottish forces, had prevented it. A frontal assault could have led to another disaster rather than a defeat for the Scots.

No, his strategy was often flawed; denial was not possible. Did Harry not see it? Yes, he did, but that would have been afterwards in cold blood, when there was no cold blood on a battlefield. This was the essence of Hotspur the mercurial hero, the glorious leader.

Hotspur the doomed.

You are blind, Elizabeth. You see only his good qualities.

There were so many exceptional qualities. He fought with honour, with respect for the enemy, conducting himself with chivalry, never brutality or crude violence.

And to me? There had been a marvellous depth of love.

But Thomas had damned him at Shrewsbury, for making that final, hopeless charge against the banner of Lancaster himself.

The battle was as much Hotspur's fault, and certainly Worcester's, as it was the King's.

I shivered, yet not with the cold, recalling the fear that had drenched me as the moon was hid from my sight.

'You still don't see it, do you? In all the sorrow and death and loss of those miserable years, I don't think you have ever acknowledged your own culpability.'

Was this true? Could I deny all Thomas's accusations? Mine was indeed the Mortimer blood, the Mortimer interest in that hot-blooded Percy household. I had been chosen as a child bride because of that blood, making an alliance between the ambitions of the Earl of Northumberland and the children of King Edward the Third. Had he seen the Mortimer link that I would bring? That one day the Earl of March would rule England and I would be his aunt, Harry his uncle by marriage? What power that would have given the King of the North. Controller of the King of the South too, if fortune smiled on him. The Percys would reign supreme.

But that was not my doing.

My mind snapped back to that other accusation. Would Harry have rebelled against Lancaster, and in Mortimer's name, without me? I thought that he would. I could not pretend that my influence with him was strong enough to put him on a battlefield, but without doubt I had stood at his shoulder and whispered in his ear. Shouted sometimes. I grimaced at a passing flock of pigeons as I remembered. No, I was not without blame. Nor was I slow in using Edmund's situation with Glyn Dwr to our advantage. I had gone readily to negotiate, sister to brother.

I cannot forgive Northumberland.

Still it rang loud and clear in my mind.

Forgive him for what? Perhaps it was true that Westmorland and Waterton both had armies in the field and orders to keep Northumberland from marching west. But I was unconvinced. Could the Earl not have sidestepped Westmorland's forces if he had truly wished to do so? And he sent my son away.

Think Elizabeth...

So I thought, striving to grasp the truth out of the morass of maternal emotions. Yes, he had sent Hal into perpetual banishment, but if my son had remained in England, what would have been his future in the debacle of our defeat?

Would I have wanted him to join the Mortimer boys under restraint? Lancaster would never have allowed him freedom, if Northumberland had made no gesture of Percy repentance. Waterton was sent to take him into custody once; it could happen again. Is that what I would have wished for him?

The Earl should have told me of his intent. He was my son.

Better the Percy heir with some element of freedom in Scotland than rubbing shoulders with the Mortimer heirs, locked in Pevensey!

And now, thrown into the mess of doubt and debate was this terrible accusation about Worcester's fatal role in the bloodbath that was the Battle of Shrewsbury. His refusal to accept terms. Any terms.

I could not believe it.

I must believe it.

Thomas might be partial in his loyalties but he would not lie to me.

So I laid all out before me on the glittering expanse of the Thames, as if I had cast a handful of petals to lie there. How hard it was to see and accept the world as Thomas de Camoys saw it. I had agreed with the raising of arms against Lancaster. I had wished Harry well. I had negotiated with Glyn Dwr and Edmund. I remembered the sense of completion when the agreement had been made to take up the Mortimer cause. I had sent Harry off to Shrewsbury with my blessing.

Now I felt like shouting my grief. Instead I closed my eyes, covering my mouth with my fingers. Until a noise, a disturbance in the air, attracted me as a magpie landed to my right, to strut along the stone coping, head tilted, eye bright as if it surveyed me. The sheen of its feathers in the sun was iridescent, yet it was a sign of ill omen. Magpies were malign birds, that demanded the onlooker ward off the evil eye. Instead I clapped my hands to send it into a swooping flight, to land again at a little distance. Omens and portents; were we not surrounded by them?

Who was to blame for Harry's death and the fall from grace of the Percy magnates? Was it indeed a supernatural power? How many of them spoke to us. The prophecy that Hotspur would die at Berwick. The fell shadowing of the moon. Was his death indeed some God-sent hand of destruction? If we believed the omens, then we had been forewarned but Harry had given it no credence. I doubted it would have kept him from a battle he wished to fight. He knew of Berwick's terrible power and the lost sword. Still he gave the order to advance against Lancaster.

The magpie continued to search and hop. Did we look at every omen, every flight of magpie or crow? Did omens dictate our future, or only reflect what man might do in his foolishness or his extremity to destroy his own life?

When I raised my hand, the bird opened its wings and took flight, leaving me empty and cold, shriven by my own condemnation, like the lance of a sharp knife against a boil, but it gave me no relief from pain.

'You are quite capable of working it out for yourself, if you will allow yourself to see the truth beneath all the dross. If you are willing to weigh and judge your own actions.'

Blessed Virgin forgive me.

Hands clasped on the coping stones, I lowered my forehead to rest there, imagining the demands in the Percy reply that had proved impossible for Lancaster to accept. That he had been false and perjured in his swearing on the Gospels, that he had allowed Richard to die when in his keeping, that he had refused to ransom Edmund from his imprisonment, and all the issues of money owing. A catalogue of Percy defiance. No, there would have been no room for manoeuvre there.

It had been a difficult hour. And because it was the obvious plea for me to make, I lifted my rosary in petition to the Blessed Virgin, letting the age-old comforting words of beseeching compassion in the *Salve Regina* touch my lips. My voice sounded strange in the open air against the bird songs and squawks, but I spoke them firmly, repentantly.

O Clement One, full of mercifulness
O Pious One, so full of rich compassion
O Sweet One, full of help in each distress
O Virgin, fairest way to our salvation
Mary the flower of sweetest meditation,
Hail…

The petition trailed into silence.

'Have mercy, Blessed Virgin.' I spoke again aloud.

Then I raised my head, opened my eyes, hearing Thomas in his wisdom.

'You must accept your part in it too, or the future will hold nothing for you but dissatisfaction and bitterness that will grind you down. You will be angry and frustrated, gnawed at by ghosts from the past, until the day of your death. Is that what you want?'

For here was my own culpability. How long could I blind myself to it? I had cast it off for so long, apportioning blame anywhere but on my own shoulders, barricading my mind from the hard words of blame. Mine was the Mortimer blood, mine the dreams, mine the blighted hopes for a Mortimer King. I too was accountable for sending Harry to his death and my son into exile. I had always known it, but had refused

444

to accept that I too had helped direct that final fatal blow that had stolen Harry's life. Thomas's words had wounded me to my heart because he had seen what I had shunned, but I could reject it no longer. This guilt that ate at me was my punishment. My purgatory. My living hell. To step beyond it I must make recompense.

My way forward was clear but it would be neither easy nor painless for me. Garbing myself in all the dignity I could summon, I turned my back on the sunlit water and the magpie and set out to accomplish it.

Because I would need his aid, I sought out Thomas, reluctantly, cautiously, for my mind could withstand no more belabouring, even if he had my best interest at heart. Moreover, he deserved an apology. With his habitual calm he showed no surprise, crushed into a corner of the small chamber, merely pushing back in his chair, abandoning the pen he had been applying to lists of figures on the lid of the coffer before him, much as a clerk might do. Behind him hung a tapestry, badly stitched by some long-dead Plantagenet lady, a lurid hunting scene complete with eviscerated stags. It seemed most apposite; I too had been hollowed out.

'What are you doing?' I asked the man who demanded some response from me. Confession was so difficult. I stood at his side. He looked up at me.

'Overlooking a muster of soldiers and sailors in the King's name.'

'It sounds dull.'

'It is dull. But necessary if we face a French invasion along the south coast.' He poked at another roll, with a grimace. 'And then there is the perennial matter of raising local taxes.'

445

'Money is always necessary.'

An image of Harry, railing against Lancaster for lack of funds, sprang fully formed into my mind. Money had always been an issue between them. But perhaps not the greatest. Not in the end. In the end it had been more personal, a betrayal of trust, a destruction of that once-bright friendship, forged on the tournament fields when they had exchanged blows and discussed their merits over a pot of ale afterwards. But they had been unable to mend that friendship when ownership of the crown had come between them. Yes, I had had my own role in that.

I could not afford to be distracted by painful memories. When I stood in silence, Thomas had picked up the pen again and begun to write, allowing me all the time I needed. I had never known a man of such acceptance.

Still I hesitated. Then: 'Thomas...'

He put down the pen once more, folding his hands one on the other before him. It had been a hard task that he had given me and I would not find the words easy as I slid the beads of my rosary at my girdle through my fingers, a gesture which he noted with a faint smile.

'You don't have to tell me what is between you and the Blessed Virgin, Elizabeth. I will never trample on your privacy. You may tell me if you wish, or not, as you see fit.'

His understanding drenched me with emotions I did not wish to have.

'I have accepted much of what you said,' I said rapidly, before I could lose my determination to bare my breast.

'I suspect that I was a hard taskmaster,' he replied.

'Yes.'

'I thought it needed saying.'

'And I resented it.' Still I had a tendency to bristle, hackles rising like a cornered cat. 'How would you know the truth, when you were not involved?'

Thomas remained unmoved. 'No, I was not involved. But you were, and are now chained to the past, blind to all but Hotspur's glamour. It's what love does to you.'

'What do you know about love?'

It was a cruel question, and one I had no right to ask.

'I know its power. I know its pain when not reciprocated. You were fortunate indeed.' He shook his head, as if regretting such translucence. 'But that is not why we are here. Guilt is a heavy burden, but better to admit it and share the weight with another who will help you bear it. I will help you if I can.' He stood and took my hands. 'What do you wish to do? I can see a struggle of decision-making in your eyes.'

Suddenly it seemed easier, since he would not condemn me again.

'I have a task. A duty to fulfil. I would wish you to come with me.'

'Then I will.' He leaned and kissed my cheek, with such gentleness it made my heart shiver. There had been so little gentleness within me of late. 'What is it?'

'First I need to see Lancaster.'

There was a glimmer of a smile. 'Do you wish me to come with you?'

'No. I have to do this alone.'

'Then I will escort you to his door.'

'In case my courage fails me?'

'It will not. I have every confidence in your courage,' he advised as we walked the corridors, my hand drawn through his arm, for fortunately Lancaster was in residence at Westminster, 'although not always in your choice of words. Will you take my advice?'

447

I sighed a little. 'I suppose that I must.'

'Try to find it in your soul to acknowledge Henry as King.'

'You do not know what you ask of me.'

'I do. As I know your ability to accept the inevitable. And one more thing for you to consider.'

I waited when he hesitated, braced against another stripping of my honour.

'The King is unwell. Gravely unwell. He'll make nothing of it, but allow him some compassion.'

He kissed my fingers and left me alone at the door to the royal apartments, allowing me the privilege of opening the door of my own volition.

But before he left:

'Thomas?'

'Well?'

'Do you despise me for my past sins?'

'No, I do not. I have enough faults of my own.'

'I know of none.'

'Then I will not burden you with them.' He was a little brusque, but managed a smile. 'Now go in and make your peace.'

Encouraged, at last I opened the door into the royal apartment with a sense of rightness warm about my heart.

I was directed by a servant into Lancaster's private chamber where he was seated, occupied with pen and rolls, much as Thomas had been before I interrupted him. He rose, his expression bleak and strained but not overly antagonistic.

'Elizabeth.'

How weary he was, how bowed his shoulders. Weight had leached from his face since I had last seen him, as had the vibrancy of his hair. Almost I felt compassion. 'I have not come to argue with you.'

'Which is a relief.' He was curt. 'We will sit.' He sank into the chair he had risen from, inviting me to take the one opposite, the busy table between us. 'Well, cousin?'

'I would ask one question.'

'I will do my best to answer it.'

How to ask it? But I must know.

'At Shrewsbury. I accused you of wanting Hotspur's death.' My mouth was dry. 'Did you offer terms to the Earl of Worcester?'

'Yes.'

'Did he refuse them?'

'Yes.'

'Why? Did you make them terms which were impossible to accept? I accused you of malice, but now I must ask you again. I think you were not honest with me, and so I thought the worst of you.'

'Not for the first time.'

I gave a brief nod in acknowledgement. And then, as if he were drained of all energy, the words were wrung from him.

'The challenge to my power was so widespread, so unequivocal, that it made mediation impossible. Yet still I would have offered a pardon. I did offer it, but it was Percy intent on proving my guilt through victory in the battle-field.' Leaning forward, forearms braced on the document-strewn surface, he studied the rolls, but his mind was not on their content. 'Why did Worcester turn his back on me? I don't know, but there was no meeting of minds on that day. I did not want to fight. I had too much respect for Hotspur, as friend and adversary, to see him dead on the field. I hoped to win his friendship and cooperation again, to settle all the enmities without waging war against my subjects. No King would willingly do that. Although many would think it ill-judged of me, I offered conciliation, yet Worcester would have none of it. He had served me all his life, and Richard before me, yet on that day there was no reasoning with him.'

'And what he told Harry Percy, we have no true notion,' I dropped into the little silence.

'No. Whatever it was, it did nothing to stop the Percy retainers launching an attack. We must presume it was not conciliatory.' He drew in a breath, looking up at me beneath his brows. 'I did not weep over Hotspur's body on the battle-field, but neither did I seek his death. I did all in my power, other than withdrawing from the battlefield, to stop it. But retreat was not a choice for me and my hold on this kingdom. My dealings with his body, which you consider reprehensible, were those demanded to make an example of any traitor. I would do the same again tomorrow. But I had no enjoyment in it. Believe it as you will, Elizabeth.'

I bowed my head, in a strange sense of relief to know the truth, even though the deliberate cruelty, the wish to humiliate and degrade, still wounded me.

'Whatever you believe or do not believe, Hotspur fought with great courage. He could not be faulted in that.'

Except in the execution of it. I now knew the truth.

'Thank you.' I looked up. 'I have a request, my lord.'

His smile was spare. 'You always have requests. Can I guess?'

'You might. I have a need to make recompense. And to so many people. I would bury the Earl of Northumberland beside his son, as is fitting.'

'As a site for pilgrimage for those who would still unseat

me? To worship at the remains of a rebel? We have had this conversation before.'

The driving will and harsh denunciation had returned.

'No. It will be unmarked. As is his son's.'

Leaning forward again, he thought, his elbows crushing the rolls, his fingers steepled. How spare and thin his hands had become, almost as if wielding a sword would not be an easy task.

'Then I will allow it. But not yet. This kingdom needs to see the penalty for waging war against its King. The remnants of the Earl will remain on display until I am satisfied that the lesson is learned. Then I will send the Earl's body to you.'

'My thanks,' taking heed that he still called him the Earl. How could Henry Percy not be Earl of Northumberland?

I stood, remembering Thomas's advice. Here was Henry of Lancaster, prepared to be generous in his victory. The Mortimer cause was dead. I knew it in my bones.

I made a deep curtsey.

'Thank you, my lord King.'

It was not so difficult after all.

As I turned away, I asked the question I had once asked before: 'Will you allow my son to return from Scotland?'

'No. Not yet. Perhaps one day. Perhaps my own son will have a strong enough hold to welcome back those who might once have undermined Lancaster's power. I cannot. But one day it might happen.'

There were limits to his generosity. But a little seed of comfort had been planted in my heart.

'And you should know,' he added as I opened the door, 'I will wage war against your brother Mortimer and Glyn Dwr until the final breath in my body. You should warn them. There will be no mercy.'

I curtsied again. 'Yes, my lord King. I will warn them.'

It was four months before a letter arrived at Trotton, the sun lighting the royal seals and the tabard of the royal herald into a glory of red and gold and blue.

It is done. I will leave the final arrangements for Henry Percy, Earl of Northumberland, in your hands, knowing that I can rely on your discretion.

It had taken four months before the King's political heart was satisfied, but at last it was done. I could make my way to York and lay more than the Earl of Northumberland's body to rest.

Chapter Twenty-Three

〰〰〰〰

York Minster: 2 July 1408

The voices of the monks rose and fell in the familiar responses, laying patterns on the still air, in the great church. It was Matins. How cold it was against my skin. Cold as forgiveness. Cold as a future without love, without compassion. But I had stepped beyond that. There was forgiveness and compassion after all, and there was an affection.

I stood once more in the chapel in the depths of the Minster church in the city of York. I would have come alone, and yet I thought that Thomas's unobtrusive presence but undoubted authority had smoothed my path.

Discretion, the King had demanded. Yes, I had been discreet. A simple coffin, a lack of retainers and mourners, an absence of heraldic achievements. Another unmarked grave. I had concurred with the King's demands and now I could end the whole tragic episode. The Earl had loved his son, whatever the rift between them at the end. I could acknowledge that love, and I must forgive him. They would lie together for eternity, unknown, unseen, unmarked, so that none would desecrate them further.

The coffin was lowered into the vault with prayers from the same cleric who had laid Harry to rest. I watched as the

453

stone was restored and made the sign of the cross on my breast.

All was finished. What now?

Nothing.

At the end, I knelt to touch the slab beneath which Hotspur lay, so cold against my palms. There was no sense of his vibrant spirit which had helped to carry him to his death and me to my despair, but I was suffused with a flash of burning, aching pity for these two proud men who had come to the end of their earthly days in such desperate circumstances.

'You led your life as the fates dictated,' I said. 'I would have had it no other way. You were Hotspur, and I loved you for it. Rest at ease. There are no more battles to fight. Your father is with you so that he too may rest. I will care for your son if I can, and your daughter's future is assured.'

And then:

'You will always remain in my heart as the brightest of memories. While I am alive, so will you be, because I will never forget what we were to each other.'

I stood, and walked to where Thomas awaited me, so that he could take my arm and lead me into the nave and then to the great west door that was open. We stepped from the chill into the warmth of a summer day.

I shivered.

'What persuaded you?' Thomas asked as we stood on the forecourt for a moment, absorbing the warmth, before walking towards our waiting escort. He had been deliberately forbearing, not questioning my change of heart.

'I took your advice.'

'Really? Which piece of advice was that?'

I enjoyed his deliberate levity as we waited to allow a

party of merchants to pass, self-important in their guild robes, badges and gold-fringed chaperons.

'You suggested that I had been as culpable as the rest. It was as you had said. I was not without sin. And I needed peace.' I sighed a little. 'Call it selfish if you will, but I would never have that until I had made my peace with the Earl.'

Still we stood.

'I was blind to Harry's faults, or if not blind, I was too willing to overlook them. To me they were not faults, only part of the essence of him as a man. And I had much to say about the rights of my nephews. It was a cause that we both embraced. No, I was not without blame in the disasters that followed.' I was aware of the sun warm on my face, a blessing. 'I knew I had been at fault, but I would not acknowledge it. I bore the pain of my guilt as my punishment. And now... well, I will say no more than that.'

It seemed to me that I had said quite enough.

'Nor do you have to. I will never deny the power of love between a man and a woman. Perhaps one day your son will regain the title and the inheritance, during this reign or more likely the next. There may be a proud Percy Earl of Northumberland yet to set his foot in the north.'

'Perhaps.'

I had not told him of the King's promise, if that was what it was, but there was hope. I could do nothing but leave his future in the King's hands.

It was becoming easier to think of him as King Henry.

'Is there less weight on your heart?'

'Yes.'

'What do you wish to do now?'

I looked at him, seeing the soldierly figure, the slight stoop when he was weary, the curl of his hair against his cheek where the frisky wind had blown it. I knew that his hands were gentle, and so were his lips. No, he would never compare with Hotspur, but he was a man of superb integrity, worthy of appreciation by a sensible woman.

I looked past him, seeing vistas that owned an importance only for me. Edmund still in Harlech. Glyn Dwr fighting for his survival, becoming more of a shadow by the day. Philippa dead. Alianore dead. The next generation living under restraint, except for Bess in the Clifford strongholds, with Dame Hawisia to keep her Percy memories alive with tales of Alnwick and her heroic father, if she would forget. What was there for me? What would my future hold? On that fair day in York I could not see it with any clarity.

'Well?'

There was one request that I did not wish to make, but then I did not have to.

'I know,' Thomas said when reserve kept me silent. 'I will escort you to Skipton and you can lavish your maternal affection on Bess. It is no distance.'

'Yes,' I said, unable to say more, for how well he had read me.

'And then?' he asked.

'Then let us go home.' That was also so easy to say in the end. I found that I was looking south rather than north. 'Do you have work for the King or can you come with me?'

'You used that title as if you had been using it all your life.' There was a gleam in his eye. 'I will come to Trotton. We have a son who will be forgetting what his parents look like.'

'Roger will have no thought of what we look like. He is less than one year old.'

'Then high time we were arranging a marriage for him.

Think of his value, with Plantagenet and Mortimer blood in his veins.'

I found myself smiling, the faintest sense of warmth wrapping round my heart. I would not yet call it happiness, but it was undoubtedly a contentment. 'I have missed my son. It will be good to return.'

Lord Thomas stooped, lacing his hands to help me to mount. Then as I arranged my skirts, he looked up at me.

'Do you know? You smiled at me for the first time in weeks. It is a good habit.'

I touched his hand, where it rested against my horse's neck, in thanks, enjoying the feel of his strength around my fingers as he turned his hand to enclose mine. Yes, I had made peace. With Harry. With the Earl. With King Henry. The past was behind us. We would look to the future, whatever it might hold.

'If you were in any doubt,' I said, 'I value your being here with me. I regret that I am not the woman whom you love.'

For did I not know that his heart was given elsewhere? It always had been, as he had told me. And that she, as Queen, had no notion of it. Nor would that love have been reciprocated, even if she had been aware. Her heart was securely in the King's grip.

'And I will never be a second Hotspur,' Thomas said after he had mounted and drawn his horse alongside mine. 'But we have a son and a life together. It may not be a passion fitting for a troubadour's song, but we can make of it what we will.'

I placed my hand in his and smiled again as he raised it with all formality to his lips. 'We will make of it what we will.' And then, freeing my hand, I sought in the thickness of the bodice of my gown, struggling with the catch. 'Will you wear this on your travels?'

My action, my words threatened to resurrect a terrible memory, but this was what I wanted, for what woman would not do everything in her power to keep so understanding a man safe from harm? In my palm rested a ring-brooch, an old gem with royal connections, the gold soft, the engraving blurred and the claws that held the gems uneven. A brooch whose words I knew by heart.

This which you have fastened on saves you either by sea or in battle.

Thomas took it from me, reading the inscription for himself.

'If you wish, although I foresee neither battle nor sea voyage between here and Trotton. But if it will give you peace of mind...'

Endlessly pragmatic, he had given me the answer I needed. It had not saved Harry, but then Harry had denied its power.

'I wish it.'

Baron de Camoys pressed the brooch to his lips, then pinned it to the folds of his chaperon in jaunty style before we set out to visit my daughter and withstand the caustic greeting of Dame Hawisia. I did not look back. There was no longer any need.

458

ACKNOWLEDGEMENTS

My tale of *Queen of the North* would not have come to fruition on its own. My grateful thanks, as ever, to:

My editor Sally Williamson at HarperCollins for her invaluable presence, not least a willing ear when I wished to discuss the joys and miseries of Elizabeth Mortimer and her troubled relationship with Sir Henry Percy. Sally's objectivity is beyond price, whereas after a year in their company I can be too closely involved to be objective. Thank you Sally for being a constant source of enthusiasm and encouragement.

My superb agent Jane Judd on whose clarity and honesty I know I can rely when my completed manuscript is sent out into the world and she is the first to read it. My thanks to Jane for her support and advice in bringing my historical characters to life.

And not least to the whole team at HQ and HarperCollins, for their ever-professional dedication to me and to *Queen of the North*.

What compelled me to write about Elizabeth Mortimer?

Some of my favourite scenes in Shakespeare are those in *Henry IV Part 1* between the magnificent Hotspur and Lady Kate. It is a relationship full of politics and power, one of conflict of personality and also of flirtation, of love and affection. As a couple they are very appealing and dominate the scenes in which they appear.

So who were they?

Hotspur, Sir Henry Percy and heir to the Earl of Northumberland, was such a dynamic, mercurial, glamorous figure in our history. The perfect hero. Brave and courageous, winning glory on the battlefield, he was also flawed, bringing his own downfall. He was more than tempting to write about. But what about Lady Kate? If I continued to follow my passion to write about medieval women, looking at history from a woman's viewpoint, who was she? Had she anything of importance to add to the medieval scene? Would she be a suitable heroine to give depth to a novel?

It was a surprise and a delight for me to discover exactly who she was.

Historically Lady Kate was not Kate at all, but was Elizabeth Mortimer, one of the powerful Mortimer family that ruled over the Welsh Marches where I now live. I am surrounded by Mortimer castles, so immediately Elizabeth was of interest to me.

Great-grand-daughter of King Edward III, Elizabeth inherited royal Plantagenet blood through her mother Philippa, daughter of Lionel Duke of Clarence, King Edward III's second son. This placed Elizabeth in the centre of the struggle for power from the Mortimer claimants to the throne after the death of Richard II and the usurpation of King Henry IV. All royal cousins, this would be another compelling family saga of power and treason, of betrayal and death. The Mortimer Earls of March had a strong claim to the throne even if it was through the female line.

Even better, Elizabeth's story with that of Hotspur would also draw in a whole panoply of characters. Henry Percy, Earl of Northumberland, cunning, ambitious and manipulating, determined to keep Percy hands on the reins of power in the north of England. Owain Glyn Dwr, the great Welsh Prince, driven in his struggle for Welsh hegemony. King Henry IV, the Lancaster king, fighting hard to stabilize a dangerously uneasy country after the death of Richard II. And then Thomas de Camoys, a most sympathetic character who played a large part in *The Queen's Choice*. What a marvellous set of characters to play with.

So why was I compelled to write about Elizabeth? Because of her Mortimer blood, she was a woman who deliberately took on the role of traitor to the crown in support of her nephew Edmund, Earl of March. She would know at first hand the resulting struggle between family loyalty and a desire to pursue what she saw as the rightful claim to the crown of England, despite all the pain it would bring her. She would also learn the constraints on her freedom, common to all medieval women. It is a story of loss and acceptance, of love and tragedy.

All is here to be enjoyed in *Queen of the North*.

And Afterwards...

—————————————

Elizabeth Mortimer lived as wife of Baron Thomas de Camoys until her death in April 1417 at the age of 46. The monumental brass on her tomb, just less than life-size in St George's Church at Trotton, shows her holding hands with Lord Thomas. She had a son with him, Sir Roger Camoys, who died without issue.

Thomas de Camoys outlived Elizabeth. He died in 1421 and was succeeded by his grandson Hugh de Camoys, issue from his first marriage. Thomas's history is dealt with in much greater detail, as is his connection with Queen Joanna, in *The Queen's Choice*.

Henry Percy, the Northumberland heir, was allowed to return to England and succeed to the earldom in 1416 in the reign of King Henry V, so becoming Earl of Northumberland and eventually recovering most of the estates. He married Eleanor Neville with whom he had children. He was killed, fighting on the side of King Henry VI, in the First Battle of St Albans and was buried in the Abbey of St Albans. We can presume that since Elizabeth did not die until 1417, she would have been reunited with her son on his return to

England in 1416. I hope that it was a time of great happiness for both of them.

Elizabeth Percy married firstly John Clifford, Baron Clifford who died at the Siege of Meaux in 1422 in Henry V's French campaigns. They had children together. She then married Ralph Neville, 2nd Earl of Westmorland by whom she had a son, Sir John Neville. Jane Seymour, third wife of Henry VIII, was descended from Elizabeth Percy and John Clifford, thus giving Jane a drop of royal Plantagenet blood.

Sir Edmund Mortimer came to a sad end, as did his family. Besieged in Harlech Castle, he died there in 1409, probably of the plague, when the castle was retaken by the English. Edmund's wife and daughters were taken into custody and kept in the City of London. Before the end of 1413 Lady Mortimer and her daughters were dead and buried within the church of St Swithin in London. A tragic story.

Edmund Mortimer, 5th Earl of March, remained in captivity during the reign of Henry IV but was released by Henry V and knighted on the occasion of Henry V's coronation. He was declared of age and allowed to inherit his estates. He participated in the Normandy campaigns of Henry V and was appointed a royal councillor for the child Henry VI. As King's Lieutenant in Ireland he died of plague in 1425 at his castle of Trim. His brother Roger had died at some point in 1409.

Owain Glyn Dwr's attempts to consolidate his power gradually fell into disorder and lack of support after 1406. His ultimate life and death are clouded in mystery, becoming part of legend, with Owain living in caves across Wales or taking refuge with his daughters who had married into Marcher families. The site of his grave is conjecture but many like to think he ended his days at Monnington Straddle in the Golden Valley where one of his daughters lived after her marriage.

Henry IV died at Westminster in 1413, after years of declining health, to be succeeded by his son Henry V.

Queen Joanna was accused of witchcraft and kept in confinement, mostly at Leeds Castle, for more than two years. Her property and dower funds were all confiscated. She was eventually released and was never brought to trial, nor were actual accusations brought against her. Joanna continued to live in England at Havering atte Bower until her death in 1437. Her story is told in *The Queen's Choice*.

Constance of York faded into obscurity after the attempt to rescue the Mortimer heirs. She was among the landowners ordered to remain on their Welsh estates in May 1409 to resist the Welsh rebels. She died in November 1416 and was buried before the high altar at Reading Abbey. Her child with Edmund Holland, Earl of Kent, was a daughter, Eleanor, who tried to claim her legitimacy but failed.

Archibald Douglas, 4th Earl of Douglas, after an eventful career in Scottish politics and diplomacy, fought in France for King Charles VII, and was created Duke of Touraine for his efforts. He was killed at the Battle of Verneuil in 1424 along with his second son and was buried in Tours Cathedral.

George Dunbar, Earl of Dunbar, continued to hold fast to his territory in the north and sought to gain more despite his advancing years, although he continued to suffer from lack of funds. His date of death is unknown, ranging between 1416 and 1423. He was buried in Dunbar Collegiate Church.

Tradition says that both the Earl of Northumberland and Sir Henry Percy were buried in York Minster in unmarked graves. The tradition still stands.

In the Steps Of ...

For those who would enjoy travelling in the footsteps of Elizabeth and Harry Percy, either in person or on an easy journey through internet browsing, here are the main historic sites where you might still, in a quiet moment, be able to sense their presence:

Alnwick Castle: the great Percy stronghold in Northumberland, the most important of all the Percy castles.

Warkworth Castle: the Percy fortress a mere ten miles from Alnwick, much enjoyed by the Percy family, being on a more intimate scale.

There are a number of northern strongholds to be visited, all with Percy connections: **Berwick Castle, Bamburgh Castle, Prudhoe Castle** as well as **Spofforth Castle** in Yorkshire. A week of Percy castle-visiting in Northumberland is obviously required.

And **Raby Castle,** home of the Neville Earl of Westmorland, rival for power in the north.

Ludlow Castle: by 1400 the main Mortimer stronghold in the Welsh Marches.

Wigmore Castle: once the centre of Mortimer power in the Welsh Marches but became less important as Ludlow was developed. Now much ruined but its position is superb.

Wigmore Priory, where many of the Mortimers were buried, is privately owned and is not open to the public. There are very few medieval remains there because of destruction in the Dissolution of the Monasteries.

There are many Mortimer castles worth visiting in the area – another holiday required. **Richard's Castle, Montgomery Castle, Clun Castle.**

York Minster: possible burial place of the Earl of Northumberland and Hotspur. The graves are unknown and unmarked but historical imagination can overcome this.

Shrewsbury Battlefield: scene of the fatal conflict between King Henry IV and Hotspur. Well worth a visit although there is no battlefield guide as such. A visit to the Battlefield Church of St Mary Magdalene, erected under the command of King Henry IV on the site of the grave pit, is particularly moving.

Shrewsbury Market Cross: where the Earl of Worcester was beheaded and Hotspur's body exhibited upright between two mill stones, to prove his death. The plaque is on the wall of the adjacent Barclay's Bank.

St George's Church, Trotton, Sussex: here is the splendid tomb with its ornamental brass of Elizabeth and Thomas de Camoys. However, genuine or not, it is the only evidence we have of Elizabeth's appearance.

Pevensey Castle, East Sussex: the fortress where Edmund, Earl of March and his brother Roger were incarcerated (as well as Queen Joanna for a short period when accused of witchcraft).

Westminster Hall: the only medieval remains of the Palace of Westminster destroyed by fire in the 19th century and subsequently rebuilt. The superb space of Westminster Hall was rebuilt by Richard II and is bound to impress. Elizabeth would have known it well.

ONE PLACE. MANY STORIES

Bold, innovative and
empowering publishing.

FOLLOW US ON:

@HQStories